CLOSE ENCOUNTER

Dominique backed into the corner, one arm and shoulder pressed against the door, watching Montville draw ever closer, the space between them narrowing bit by agonizing bit.

She felt his hands slide along her arms and settle on her shoulders, thumbs stroking the sensitive skin along her collarbone. She drew in a sharp breath. "What do you think you're doing?"

"Not thinking." His lashes lowered. Again, he studied her mouth.

Panic raced through Dominique. Or was that shocking tingle in her breasts caused by the way he was lightly running one fingertip just above the ribbon of her decolletage?

Ever so slowly, his hand moved to her nape. His touch was feather-light. She opened her mouth to speak, but discovered that she had lost her voice.

His fingers found a hairpin. She felt her chignon begin to tumble loose as he slowly pulled the tortoise shell pin free and buried his fingers in her hair, sending myriad streaks of fever rippling through her body, all merging on one unmentionable place.

"I think," he finally murmured, "that I'm about to kiss you."

THE HIDDEN JEWEL

VIOLET IVANESCU

LEISURE BOOKS   NEW YORK CITY

*I dedicate this book, with all my love and gratitude,
to Mamica and Taticu.
Without the two of you, this Jewel would have remained
forever hidden.*

A LEISURE BOOK®

August 1997

Published by

Dorchester Publishing Co., Inc.
276 Fifth Avenue
New York, NY 10001

Printed in the United States of America.

Chapter One

Chateau de Loches
Loches, France
March 1803

He looked nothing like a murderer.

Under the cover of darkness, Dominique Chantal sat on her heels in the corner, watching the man the guard had let into her cell.

She started. The movement caused the ropes around her wrists and ankles to bite into her flesh. She felt no pain, only bizarre prickly twinges that skittered up and down her legs, as if she were kneeling on burrs.

No pain. Her body was numb. Except her stomach, which tightened like a fist as she surveyed him.

For a moment, she wondered if the man was merely a figment of her imagination. It wasn't because of the lithe way he moved when he strode past her and headed for her cot, which stood against the wall opposite beneath a small, barred window. It wasn't because his midnight-blue coat and snug breeches fit his tall frame so well, they conjured images of

7

sorcerers wielding wands over his head. Exactly what it was, she couldn't say.

He shifted a little. His profile was worthy of a coin. Moonbeams filtered through the iron bars, shedding light upon the folds of his perfectly knotted cravat.

She tried to swallow, but her mouth was too dry. She focused on the neatly trimmed dark hair above the bit of white at his collar. Was he a prisoner? If so, that bronzed neck might be bared to take a noose tomorrow, perhaps even a well-honed kiss from Madame la Guillotine herself. So might her own. God, no. She couldn't bear to think of that.

His shoulders tensed. With a scrape of booted heels against rough stone, he turned. Swiftly, his gaze swept the recesses of the darkened cell. And stopped on her.

Another time, another place, she would have been overwhelmed. She couldn't clearly discern his features, nor could she tell the color of his eyes, but something indescribable sparked in them as they met her own. She felt it more than saw it. Something penetrating. Piercing. Dangerous. Another tremor rippled through her.

"Something I've said, perhaps?" he asked in a baritone voice, a voice that seemed to wrap around her like dusky silk on naked skin.

"Are you speaking to me?" Her voice sounded hoarse, but then, they hadn't given her any water since morning.

"As affable as the fellow looks," he softly replied, tipping his dark head almost imperceptibly toward the door, "I have a feeling he's hardly in the mood for conversation."

Dominique, too, stole a glance at the gaoler, who leered at her through the barred opening in the iron portal. A candle glowed in his raised hand, the flickering light lending his face an odd reddish hue. Thick brows, thin lips, hooked nose, a long, dark welt running along his right cheek. Positively demonic.

Out of the corner of her eye, she saw the tall man move out of the light. She almost gasped. "Don't come any closer!"

"He is no longer looking." He stopped a short arm's length away. "I've come to—"

Silence. She raised her chin, and though she couldn't see

his face, she felt his eyes upon her. Heat surged through her in a slow, descending spiral.

He came down on one knee beside her, leaning close. Her nostrils flared, sensing faint traces of sandalwood soap and rosemary. She thought she felt his fingertips brush the bindings at her wrists.

"Bon sang," he cursed under his breath. "Who bound you like this?"

He sounded outraged. Dominique stared at him in paralyzed stupefaction. And then her mind began to whirl.

Thank God, thank God, there was no pity in his voice. She couldn't bear it. Not from this man. Not after three days and nights of captivity in the dungeon of this old chateau. Or was it four?

She glanced at the door. If the gaoler caught them talking, the fiendish wretch might carry out his gruesome threats. But, mercy, how she had wished that there were someone here to talk to! Being deprived of food and water, being insulted, interrogated, even bound—none of it could compare to the torment of being alone with her own thoughts.

Thoughts of how she had failed to heed her brother's warnings. Thoughts of what they might do to her tomorrow. Thoughts of how much was at stake.

She ran her tongue over her lips, but still, they felt like parchment. "Demaitre." She motioned with her head, although it hurt her neck to do so. "The 'affable fellow' posted outside. He tied me up."

"What for?"

"I scratched him."

"A pity I didn't arrive in time."

What was he talking about? She stole a look at him through her lashes. Strong hands. A ring caught light and gleamed on one of his fingers.

Dominique's breathing quickened. He was no common thief, anyone could see that. If he was here for the same reason as she, then maybe, just maybe, through some sort of divine grace, he might know something of her brother. Unlikely, yes, but there was always hope.

"This morning they threatened to put a murderer in my cell," she ventured.

He was silent for a moment. "And for all you know, I just might be one, right?"

"Are you?"

He didn't answer. She sorely wished she could see his face more clearly. He came even closer, his shoulder brushing against hers, and suddenly his hands were upon her.

She jerked back. "What are you doing?"

"Shh. Hold still. I'm going to remove these cursed ropes."

She focused on his chin, a minute distance from her nose. "Thank you, monsieur, but that is not a good idea."

"Why not?" The barest hint of a smile played about his lips. "This cord would make an exceptionally effective weapon."

His smile widened into a full-fledged grin, and quite a dazzling one, at that. The criminal was mocking her! At least, she hoped he was. "I wouldn't know, Monsieur . . . ?"

"Montville. Andre Montville."

Pain seared her wrists, and Dominique realized that her hands were free.

He drew back a little. "You, I presume, are Dominique Chantal. I'm very pleased to meet you, mademoiselle."

It was all she could do to keep her mouth from dropping open.

He tossed the rope aside and calmly set about undoing the bindings around her ankles. "Pleased," he continued, "and more than relieved. The message I received read 'Dominic,' with a *c*, and I envisioned coming here to find a burly Spaniard." He shook his head. "Ridiculous, *n'est-ce pas?*"

Dared she believe he had come to take her out of this horrid place? Perhaps her chaperon had reached Colette, and her friend had sent this man to fetch her. Heart tripping, Dominique flexed her swollen fingers, burning to ask, afraid to speak for fear she was wrong.

Warm fingers lightly massaged her smarting ankles. Gradually, feeling returned to her limbs, and then the frigid dampness of the place began to overtake her, like icy water slowly sluicing down her back.

Her teeth chattered. The room dipped sickeningly before her eyes. She opened her mouth to ask him how he knew her name but changed her mind and took deep breaths of musty air instead. She couldn't seem to stop shaking.

"You're cold," he murmured.

She heard the whisper of cloth and felt the air stir as he shrugged out of his coat. Heavenly warmth enveloped her when he wrapped the garment around her shoulders, still carrying the heat and the clean, masculine scent of his body.

"Can you stand?" he asked gently.

She blinked and rubbed her aching wrists, willing her body to still and her head to stop spinning. "I—I think so."

"Here, let me—"

"Thank you." She pushed his hand away. "I'll try to manage by myself."

He hesitated, then gave a curt nod and stood. Pebbles cutting into her knees, the rough floor scraping her palms, Dominique rose slowly, on legs that felt like jelly. Her knees promptly buckled.

The next thing she knew, she was being hauled against his chest. She stirred, but he only tightened his hold.

"*Doucement.*" His chin brushed the top of her head. "Easy. Lean on me. I'm going to take you to the window for a breath of air."

She tried to draw away. "Monsieur, I don't think—"

"You needn't think. Just walk."

Truth be told, she didn't believe she could. She stood there, finding comfort in the strength of this stranger's arm about her waist, in the steady beat of his heart beneath her fingers, the softness of his clean shirt against her cheek. Lethargy gradually dissipated and, moments later, Dominique became vaguely aware of something hard and foreign pressing against her thighs.

Every sluggish nerve ending jerked to life. Gasping, she shoved away with all her strength. The coat slid off her shoulders and hit the floor with a soft thump. Before she could open her mouth to scream, she heard Montville's rich laughter ricochet off the walls of the dingy cell. "Not guilty," he said, lunging toward her.

11

She leaped back, only to slam into solid stone. Pain exploded in her head and shoulders, but somehow she found the strength to raise her hands, ready to defend herself if he attacked. "Touch me," she warned, "and I will make it twice as injurious for you, I swear it."

He looked at her as if he thought she'd lost her mind. His gaze held hers as he slowly bent down and retrieved his coat. Every movement deliberate, he straightened, brushed at a sleeve, reached into one pocket, and finally produced—

"An apple," he said flatly.

"I see it." Her fingers curled into fists.

He tossed the fruit in the air and deftly caught it in his other hand. "Who was it that so eloquently phrased it, mademoiselle?" He tilted his head to gaze thoughtfully at the ceiling. *" 'Honi soit qui mal y pense'?"*

Shamed be the one who presupposes lewd intentions, her mind repeated. For the first time in three days, Dominique was grateful for the lack of light. "King Edward III," she muttered. "Of England."

"Of course. An Englishman. I should have known. Calculating and austere, the English," he went on genially. "Feet firmly on the ground, ice in their veins. To them, an apple will always be exactly what it is: an apple. Unlike the French. We are just the opposite, *non?* Passionate, explosive, and imaginative. To us, an innocent fruit such as this apple can become"—his lips twitched—"quite a threatening thing." He snapped his fingers. "Just like that. With such opposing temperaments and mentalities, it's hardly surprising that we're on the brink of a bloody war."

Drowning in mortification, Dominique checked the impulse to press her hands to her burning cheeks. Determined to patch together whatever tattered shreds of dignity she still possessed, she raised her chin and looked him in the eye. "As I recall, you were the one who earlier mentioned weapons."

"And, naturally," he returned, "you saw me wearing navy blue and thought I carry around shot in my pockets."

She scowled at him.

He tipped his head. "No? Hot shot, perhaps?"

Dominique couldn't force her befuddled mind to seek a suitable rebuttal. And so she straightened, picked up her skirts and moved past him, noting that the man towered above her by a good head and more. Suddenly desperate for clean air, she made her way to the window.

An awkward silence ensued. His footsteps were light as he moved to stand directly behind her. Dominique willed herself to ignore him and to focus on the starlit sky, longing to be outdoors, away from this place and from this unknown man, whose overwhelming presence tugged relentlessly at her senses.

It was unnerving, really, the way he could affect her so, despite her plight and her miserable surroundings. What would her brother say if he knew?

Her brother. Oh, God. Paul.

Hot tears stung Dominique's eyes. Here she was, playing some indecent game with a stranger, while Paul rode somewhere in the night, a missive in his pocket, the fate of France, perhaps the future of the continent, weighing on his shoulders.

He would have reached La Baule by now. From there, if all went well and he managed to meet with the British agents and a man named Mehée de la Touche, he'd board a ship to England. Please, she prayed, let him succeed, and keep him safe. Don't let him end up like me.

She squeezed her eyelids shut and raised her chin, but one tear still slipped down her cheek. Furtively, she swiped at it, hoping that Montville hadn't noticed.

"Mademoiselle Chantal."

He'd noticed.

"Apple?" he asked gently.

"No, thank you."

"Afraid it might be poisoned?"

She gave him a sidelong look. "Should I be?"

Tense silence. "I think," he finally said, "I have offended you."

She didn't answer.

"It was a ribald joke. I shouldn't have made it."

She frowned and concentrated on a smoky cloud that drifted across the silver disk of the moon.

"I'm sorry," he said softly.

Dominique nodded. "Apology accepted." *Now, go away.*
He stepped closer.

Fine. She'd ignore him.

That proved impossible. He was so near that she could feel his breath upon her hair.

"Look at me," he murmured.

That voice. That deep, silky, seductive voice. Before her very eyes, the moon seemed to dissolve and liquefy into a shimmering pool of quicksilver.

She couldn't stop herself. Trembling a little, Dominique turned. And stopped breathing. Because Andre Montville was not good-looking. Far from it. The man was nothing less than beautiful.

Sorcerers. Images of sorcerers and dark angels drifted across her mind again. For an endless moment his eyes held hers, their pupils wide and dark, probing with such intensity that her already quickened pulse began to beat erratically.

She watched him raise the apple to his lips and listened to the crunch when he bit into it, her stomach clenching. Her mouth began to water. She gulped and watched him chew, feeling her entire body become one quivering mass of thirst and hunger.

Still munching, he turned the apple in his hand and held it out. She stared at the rivulet of juice that slowly trickled down the skin of the glossy red fruit. The air whooshed audibly out of her lungs.

"Please," he urged. "Take it. I remain very much alive, as you can plainly see." He raised the apple to her lips. "One bite?"

The aroma of it filled her nostrils, sweet, tart, and infinitely tempting. Before she knew it, she'd sunk her teeth into the fruit, not even bothering to first remove it from his hand. Closing her eyes, Dominique savored the tangy juice, allowing the precious moisture to linger on her tongue.

She felt him grasp her wrist and then the cool, wet flesh of the apple as he placed it into her palm. Immediately, her fingers closed around it.

When she opened her eyes, he was smiling. "You still haven't told me why you're here."

14

She shrugged. "I might ask the same of you."

"You might, but I asked first."

"You didn't."

"I just did."

She took another bite of apple. Her brother's fine-drawn features superimposed themselves on Montville's face, and cold washed over Dominique as wariness encased her like plates of armor. "Who are you?" she demanded. "Somehow, I doubt they've suddenly decided to make life merrier here by placing male and female prisoners together and letting them share apples in the cells."

He smiled in answer to her frown.

"Who are you?" she repeated.

"A friend."

She shook her head. "Acquaintances, monsieur, are people whom I know. And friends are those whom I can trust. You, I'm afraid, don't qualify as either."

Montville's smile faded. He slipped his hands into his pockets and turned to face the window, leaving her uncertain whether the wrenching in her chest was due to relief or disappointment.

Why should she care whether she had hurt his feelings? For all she knew, he could be another of Napoleon's many spies, sent here to try to coax information out of her, and Paul would be as good as dead if she uttered a single word about his mission.

Frowning, she focused on Montville's broad back. He stood there, unmoving, silver light gilding his hair. Smothering a sigh, Dominique swept a look around the cell, then lowered her eyes to the black floor. Although she'd fought it, the events of the past days had taken their toll, and she was not surprised to feel exhaustion grip her again.

Her feet dragged as she took the few steps to the cot. She finished every bit of her apple, tossed the core into a corner, then raised her hands to rub her throbbing temples.

"Desfieux is going to relish this," she heard him mutter under his breath.

Her hands were arrested in midair. To anyone else, the comment would have been inaudible; she didn't think he had intended to be heard. Paul often swore she must have been a cat in another life, what with her black hair, green eyes, and abnormally keen sense of hearing.

Her heart began to hammer. Desfieux—her brother's best friend. She'd heard his name as clearly as if Montville had shouted it. Perhaps Claude Desfieux had sent him?

She took a deep breath. "Monsieur Montville . . ." He didn't turn, but the slight movement of his head told her that she had his full attention. "I wish to thank you for untying me. And for the apple."

"You needn't thank me. I was simply following instructions."

Instructions? Her heart sank. *He's one of them.*

"I do not understand," she said, choking on bitter disappointment.

"All I can tell you is that I didn't happen by tonight." He closed the distance between them, shaking his head in answer to her raised eyebrows. "I don't know much, but based on the sorely wanting information I have been given, my guess is that you will be freed"—he pulled a watch out of his pocket and turned it toward the light—"within the hour."

He wasn't lying, she could tell.

He tucked away the watch. "Dare I hope you believe me?"

"Why didn't you say something before?"

"You would have believed a murderer?"

She had to smile at the mild accusation in his tone. "I don't believe you are a killer." She scrutinized his face. "Why are you here, Monsieur Montville?"

Footsteps sounded in the corridor. Dominique lurched to her feet and didn't miss the gloom that flitted across Montville's features when he looked over her head to the door.

"I believe, mademoiselle," he said, "that we are both about to find out."

Chapter Two

And none too soon, Montville thought, setting his jaw as the heavy door swung open and clanged against the wall. He watched the guard babble a greeting to a short, balding man. Behind the two loomed an imposing black-garbed figure, a candle in one huge hand, a heavy book under his arm.

Montville's spine went rigid. What the devil were they planning here?

The three newcomers filed into the cell. The bald man waddled forth, a crooked smile curving his fleshy lips, his black eyes flashing with malice as he thrust out one plump hand. "*Bonsoir,* Montville."

"Bavard." Swallowing his distaste, Andre briefly clasped the cold, stubby fingers.

"I trust you've had sufficient time to become acquainted with our beauteous Mademoiselle Chantal? She's quite a handful." Bavard's lecherous gaze was arrested just above the bodice of her rumpled yellow gown. "A truth to which Demaitre, here, can heartily attest."

"Is that right?" Andre was amazed that his tone betrayed no trace of the bile that rose in his throat.

17

"Look at this!" Demaitre pointed to the long welt crusted with blood that ran from his cheekbone down to his thin upper lip. "Tried to scratch my eyes out. Weren't for Monsieur Bavard's orders not to harm her, I would 'ave given her what she deserved."

Andre glanced at Mademoiselle Chantal, who was regarding the gaoler as if he were a dead roach she'd just squashed. "And you, of course, did nothing to provoke her."

Demaitre smirked. "I ain't a fool. I know that women sometimes hide things in their bosoms."

She clenched her fists. *"Sauvage,"* she said under her breath.

"Putain," Demaitre rasped, his eyebrows knitting into a single line. "Whore! I should 'ave—"

"Enough." Bavard spoke with chilling calm. Montville didn't have time to compose his features before the short man's gaze flicked to his face. "Your lips are twitching, my friend. I only hope your reaction will be similar when I reveal what your next assignment is to be."

Andre didn't like the self-satisfaction he detected in the older man's tone, nor the fact that things were being discussed in front of Mademoiselle Chantal. "I believe that is a matter we should speak of in private."

"On the contrary," Bavard returned. "I think Mademoiselle Chantal should hear this, since it concerns her." He rubbed his hands together and grinned to reveal large, yellow teeth.

Andre's eyes narrowed. Bavard never smiled so unless he was planning things he labeled "firm measures," which Andre believed amounted to unspeakable abuses of the power the man held as minister of general police. As one of many independent agents working with him, Andre had occasionally witnessed the ghastly results of these procedures. He looked down at the tiny young woman beside him, defiance stamped on her piquant face, and had to quell the urge to lunge at the old bastard and wrap his hands around his flabby neck.

"I suggest we go upstairs," Bavard said. "The library. There's food there. And drink. Nothing fancy, you understand, but we'll make do with what my secretary was able to procure on such short notice."

18

Andre searched the minister's face. Bavard never ate or drank while one of his victims was being "persuaded"; he claimed their screams interfered with his digestion.

What, then? Why the familiar, telltale grin? And, Andre thought, eyeing the stone-faced man who hovered in the doorway, why the colossus?

"How kind of you," Mademoiselle Chantal blurted out. "Am I to watch you eat while you interrogate me yet again?"

Andre couldn't believe his ears. Damn her, he thought, she's going to get herself flogged. A quick glance at Bavard confirmed his fears: the vein beneath the minister's left eye had begun to pulse.

"Food!" Andre smiled down at the shorter man's scalp with all the false charm he could muster. "That's just the word I hoped to hear, Bavard. I haven't had a decent meal in several days."

"They didn't feed you on your ship?" Bavard demanded.

This time, Andre didn't need to compose his features. "Seal food," he said with genuine loathing, the corners of his mouth turning down.

Bavard's brows rose. "I beg your pardon?"

Andre smiled. "Fish." The minister did not smile back, but his eye stilled, and that was more than satisfactory for Andre. "You summoned me from London as if I were an enlisted man being called to duty," he quickly went on. "The message reached me at dawn; there wasn't time to load provisions onto the *Eliote* before the tide turned. From Dieppe, I hastened here." He paused to give Bavard a sardonic look. "It's been a very pleasant trip, thank you for asking. The only stop I made was at an inn, to bathe and change, which is why you are yet able to recognize me. At this point, I'm willing to take in anything that appears edible. As for Mademoiselle Chantal," he finished in a light tone, "I have no doubt that she could use some nourishment herself."

"Mademoiselle's attitude belies her weakened state." Bavard's eyes were twin torches. "Perhaps I was mistaken in ordering that she not be violated in any way."

"I'm certain she appreciates that," Andre assured him. "Don't you, mademoiselle?"

Say yes, damn it! He concentrated the full force of his stare on the woman's profile. Slowly, she raised her chin. For an interminable moment, she contemplated him.

"Yes," she finally whispered hoarsely.

Andre almost shut his eyes, so great was his relief, but it was his throat that closed at the confusion he read in her glance. He wrenched his gaze away from hers, choosing instead to focus on her coiffure, noticing how several strands of black hair had escaped her chignon and now fell in soft waves to her shoulders.

Long hair. A vision of it, all of it, spread wild and wanton on a pillow, framing that delicate face of hers, flashed across Andre's mind. And in that fraction of a second, something inside him that he'd thought long dead and deeply buried roared to life. He closed his eyes for a moment, stunned at the direction his mind had taken. He hadn't had a thought like that since—

Since *her*. Two years. Two months. Six days.

The gold ring flashed on his left hand. Accusing him. He glowered at it.

Bavard's sharp bark of laughter made Andre's chin snap up. "Ever the diplomat, aren't you, Montville? Sometimes you almost have me convinced that your methods are more effective than my own. Almost, but not quite."

With that, Bavard turned and headed out, followed by the great hulk of a man. Demaitre remained where he was, fingering the gleaming bayonet on the end of his musket, his menacing gaze on Mademoiselle Chantal. "Move," he rasped.

She didn't. She stared transfixedly at Bavard's retreating back, her hands clenched in the folds of her skirts, looking, Andre thought, as if she might collapse. She swayed, an elusive, almost imperceptible motion, but he caught it.

He gripped her elbow. And felt it yet again, that thing tugging at his chest.

Foolish. No, insane.

She seemed to underline that last thought when she pulled her arm from his grasp. "A friend, are you, Monsieur?"

He couldn't answer. She picked up her skirts and moved past him, ignoring the musket-toting gaoler. Andre watched her go, his eyes taking in the elegance of her carriage, the slight sway of her hips. . . .

He looked away, then shook his head, as if to clear it.

She knew that she must keep her wits about her.

In the doorway of the study, Dominique blinked, her eyes stinging at the sudden assault of light from the many candles that burned brightly within.

Bavard stood in the middle of the room before a huge mahogany desk. Upon it, a loaf of crusty bread sat on a white cloth beside a platter of sliced beef, a small wheel of Livarot, a stack of plates, several forks, and a long knife. Next to the knife, a decanter of what appeared to be claret gleamed ruby red in the candlelight. The combined scents of malodorous cheese, candlewax, and stale cigars made Dominique's stomach lurch.

"Enter." Bavard made a sweeping gesture with his arm. "As you can see, there are no ropes in this part of the chateau."

Dominique hesitated, glancing at the ugly giant dressed in black already seated in a wing chair before the hearth. Above the mantel hung a huge canvas, depicting Bonaparte on a white horse, surrounded by smug-faced cavalrymen waving swords, while three dark-skinned men wearing nothing but white turbans lay bleeding, mere inches from the horse's hooves, their hands outstretched in one last plea.

Her eyes moved from the grisly painting to the giant's immobile features. A chill raced up her spine. She almost preferred that horrid cell to this. Behind her, swift, sure footsteps echoed in the hallway. Montville. Relief washed over her.

"Allez," she heard Demaitre growl. "Move!"

Before she could take a step, the gaoler shoved her from behind, and Dominique hit the floor with a force that snatched her breath away.

Wheezing, she drew herself up on all fours. Through her daze, she heard a crack and then a groan, followed by a muffled thud. She looked over her shoulder to see Demaitre's crumpled form sprawled in the doorway.

Fists clenched, face slightly flushed, Montville stood staring down at him, radiating wrath. Stepping over the unconscious gaoler, he bent and gently lifted Dominique to her feet. Against her will, she looked into his face.

His eyes were very blue. A most unusual, smoky shade, the color of a mountain lake at sunrise, when the first sunbeams delve into its depths.

He frowned. "Are you all right?"

She blinked. Wonder gave way to mortification as Dominique realized that she'd been gawking. She lowered her gaze and quickly stepped back, wincing as Bavard's burst of laughter grated on her ears.

"Most entertaining, Montville," he crowed, picking up the knife and touching it to his forehead in a mock salute. "An excellent commencement, although because of it, I'm left to slice this bread myself. Alas, no servants here at Loches."

The knife flashed in his hand. He peered from Montville to Dominique, then back to Montville again, and bared his awful yellow teeth. "Yes," he said in a pensive voice. "This arrangement could be the very weapon to blast the insurrectionists out of their viper hole and hack them to minute pieces."

From the strange look on Montville's face, Dominique gathered that Bavard's words puzzled him as much as they did her. There was tension in his stance, and wariness lurked in his gaze as he watched Bavard begin to zealously saw the loaf of bread into hunks.

Montville hadn't lied when he'd said that he couldn't tell her more, she realized. He didn't know what was going to happen. But had he lied about her release? Better ask now, before she lost her nerve. *"Monsieur le Ministre . . ."* She took a deep breath. "I understand I will be permitted to go home tonight."

Bavard's blade stopped in mid-slice. "Who told you such a thing?"

"I did," Montville admitted calmly.

The minister set down the knife. "Beware of divulging too much information to the wrong people, my friend." He turned and bent to retrieve something from behind the desk. "Now, seat yourselves."

Dominique moved woodenly to a nearby couch, aware of her feet sinking into the plush Aubusson carpet. Once seated, she nervously scanned the dusty wooden bookshelves that lined the walls.

The cushions gave as Montville settled himself beside her. He leaned back and crossed his legs, one ankle on the opposite knee. Dominique watched the tassel of one black Hessian boot swing back and forth, her fingers curling around the carved armrest.

A low groan drifted from the doorway.

"Wineglasses, Demaitre," Bavard said without turning around.

The gaoler grunted, groped for his musket, and staggered to his feet, gingerly probing the right side of his face. A lump had materialized at his jaw. He cast Montville an apprehensive glance, then hastened to do his employer's bidding.

"Now then, Mademoiselle Chantal." Bavard waddled across the room, then planted himself before her, folding his arms over his barrel chest. "Have you managed to remember anything since this morning?"

Dominique stared at his pockmarked nose and gripped the armrest more tightly. "No."

Bavard regarded her for a long moment, drumming his fingers on his upper arm. "I have reports concerning several persons suspected of trying to instigate yet another revolt in the Vendee."

She could not let him see her fear. "I don't know what you're talking about."

Bavard nodded. "So you've been insisting for the past three days." He looked at her with snakelike eyes. "My men say they arrested you on the road to Tours. What was your business there?"

Dear God, not again. Dominique had told the truth repeatedly; she'd had no ulterior motive for embarking on her journey, but the wretched man refused to believe her. "I was off to visit a sick friend," she said, hoping she sounded calmer than she felt.

"And the friend's name?"

"Mademoiselle Colette Desfieux."

"Try again, mademoiselle," Bavard said in a steely voice.

"I visited the girl this afternoon, and spoke with her for a good half hour."

Dominique thought she felt Montville tense beside her. "I'm pleased to hear she's feeling better," she said quietly.

The minister's mouth flattened. "Mademoiselle Desfieux was most distressed to hear of your unfortunate carriage accident." He gave a dour chuckle. "And quite upset to learn that your coachman did not survive it. In fact, she was beside herself, until I assured her that you are faring well and are, ah, quite secure in my chateau."

Dominique's spine stiffened. Nails scraping at the wooden armrest, she frowned down at the carpet, wanting to shriek at the top of her lungs, to call him a liar, a kidnapper. . . .

She swallowed hard. "The guard said that my coachman is imprisoned in the tower."

The minister smirked. "Correct. Until last night, the half-witted old fool maintained he didn't even know your name."

Panic threatened to seize her, and Dominique did her best to remain calm. "The coach was rented, sir. I hired—"

"Cease!" A vein throbbed beneath Bavard's left eye. "There are two things that I loathe most in this world. One of them is royalists." He drew near, stooping to stare directly into her face. "The other," he hissed, "is brazen women."

Dominique cringed inwardly but willed herself not to draw back. Nausea rose in her throat at the stench of his fetid breath.

"Do you know what strikes me as odd?" the minister snapped, sending another putrid blast her way.

She shook her head.

"That a young, unmarried woman such as yourself would be allowed to travel across half of France unchaperoned."

A tiny ray of hope warmed Dominique's breast. So, Madame Serin had somehow managed to avoid being captured. She must have gone on to Colette's and told her everything, which would explain why her friend had not insisted on coming here at once.

Demaitre entered with the glasses. As Bavard turned away, Dominique closed her eyes. *Grand Dieu,* how she wished she'd heeded Paul's warnings and stayed at home. She felt warm fingers close around hers and give a reassuring squeeze.

She started, but when her eyes flew open, Montville had already removed his hand and sat staring straight ahead.

The sound of liquid pouring made Dominique's mouth begin to water. She watched with eager eyes as Demaitre came to her with a glass filled to the brim. She didn't even care that wine sloshed onto her skirt when he thrust it at her.

"Small sips," she heard Montville whisper.

She took a gulp and promptly gasped, dissolving into a fit of shallow coughs.

Promptly, Montville swept the glass out of her hand and began to pound her back. "Bavard's special concoction," he explained when her chest finally stopped convulsing. "A third Bordeaux, a third Muscat."

"What is"—she covered her mouth and coughed again—"the rest?"

"*Zwetschgen-wasser,*" he whispered. "Madame Bavard's homemade plum brandy. She's from Strasbourg."

"His wife?" she asked.

Montville smiled. "No. His mother."

In spite of herself, she smiled back. Silently, he offered to return her drink. Dominique vigorously shook her head and widened her eyes in mock horror. He grinned, allowing her a glimpse of those perfect teeth before he took a sip himself, regarding her with dark blue eyes filled with interest.

Her smile froze when she realized that his hand lingered on the bare skin between her shoulder blades, his fingers lightly stroking back and forth.

"In a hurry, aren't you, Montville?" she heard Bavard sneer. "Keep your breeches on, my friend." He handed a full glass to the stone-faced, dark-garbed man seated before the fire. "You will have plenty of time to sample her, ah, womanly delights."

Dominique tensed.

Montville's smile vanished. He jerked his hand away. "What in hell are you alluding to, Bavard?"

A long, tense moment passed.

"I think," the minister finally remarked, "that your extreme fatigue impedes your judgment. So I will overlook your unceremonious attitude and answer your question." He took a

25

long draught of his tainted wine and smacked his lips. "We have established that a group of insurgents in the Vendee is planning a revolt against the government."

Fury exploded in Dominique. She leaped to her feet. "You have established nothing!"

Bavard's reptilian eyes narrowed to slits. "Sit, Mademoiselle Chantal. Before I send Demaitre for a whip."

Dominique's gaze snapped to the gaoler, who leaned against the doorframe, his thin lips compressed. She gritted her teeth but did as she was told.

Bavard sniffed and rubbed his pitted nose before resuming. "There are similar stirrings in Paris and in Provence. My agents have reported that French exiles in London are ready to make common cause with the traitors in an endeavor to overthrow Bonaparte. What we don't know, however, is who the conspirators are, and when they intend to strike. Mademoiselle Chantal either knows nothing"—he held her gaze, and Dominique did her best to keep her features neutral—"or, as I suspect, is unwilling to cooperate. But we shall remedy that minor problem."

Dominique stole a look at Montville, and saw fire smolder beneath the veneer of bored composure. His dark head was tipped to one side and his expression was bland, but his knuckles were white upon the stem of his glass. "You plan to watch her."

A wicked half-smile swept across Bavard's fleshy face. *"Oui."* He nodded emphatically. "Twenty-four hours a day, seven days a week. One of us will escort her home, remain by her side at all times, never let her out of his sight."

Either because of Bavard's words or from the strong liquor on a nearly empty stomach, Dominique saw the room swim before her eyes. *"His?"* she blurted. "But—but that's preposterous! That would mean—"

"You'll have to eat with him," Bavard cut in. "Bathe with him." He took another slurp of his drink. "And sleep with him."

Dominique stared at him, aghast.

"There are four men in this room who are able, and more than willing, to perform the task," he said, stressing the word

26

perform in a most lurid fashion. "Because I happen to be in high spirits this evening, I will magnanimously allow you the liberty of choosing one."

Dominique's jaw dropped in a silent scream.

"Your choice, mademoiselle," she heard Bavard decree with infinite satisfaction. "Which one of us will it be?"—he pointed to the large man in black—"Lepetit? The gaoler, Demaitre? Montville?" Lizard eyes aglitter, he placed a hand upon his chest and executed a dramatic little bow. "Or *moi?*"

Chapter Three

He needed another drink. Without a word, Montville surged to his feet and moved in swift steps to the desk. God help him, if he so much as glanced at Bavard now, he just might throttle him.

He couldn't do that. Not now. Not yet. Despite his efforts to compose himself, his hand shook slightly on the neck of the decanter as he lifted it. Yes, she was an innocent in all of this; but what was it about this particular young woman that triggered such an overwhelming need inside him to protect her?

"Well, mademoiselle?" he heard Bavard demand. "The hour grows late. Which one of us will it be?"

"I'll take 'er home," Demaitre volunteered, wriggling his hairy caterpillar brows. "An' take 'er, and take her, and take her."

An image of the gaoler bouncing away atop the woman served to make Andre feel ill. He set the carafe down with a clink and sipped the vile-tasting liquid, feeling it sear a path down to his churning gut.

He stared into his glass. The image wavered, and suddenly

28

he was fifteen again, watching the crimson blade flash in the sun, feeling warm droplets spatter his face, the iron smell flooding his nostrils, his ears filled with the sound of distorted laughter as the executioner's assistant again swept the gore off the scaffolding with a bunch of twigs . . . *Thunk.*

He shuddered. Saw the head swing, held up by the hair for all to see, and felt his heart and lungs collapse. Willing his hand steady as he brought the glass to his lips, Andre felt the old familiar sheet of ice envelop him, despite the fire of the alcohol he swallowed. The king, Louis XVI. His queen, Marie Antoinette. He'd witnessed both their deaths, and in his mind, he'd seen them die a thousand times more.

To be replaced by people like Bavard. Did Mademoiselle Chantal have any notion of how dangerous a game it was that she was playing? Perhaps she did, he thought, observing her over the rim of his glass, for at that moment the woman looked as if she faced the executioner himself.

Bavard moved to stand before her and grasped a loose strand of her glossy raven hair, allowing it to slide between his fingers. "Silky," he muttered, chuckling when she flinched. Slowly, he ran his hand along her neck and let it rest upon her shoulder.

Andre thought he heard her whimper. He saw the minister's dimpled hand snake downward toward her breast, and felt the blood roar in his ears.

"I'm famished," he declared, much louder than he had intended.

The minister swung around. Andre forced his lips into a semblance of a smile and looked pointedly at the food. "May I?"

He'd lost his appetite completely, but he'd gladly dine on his own jabot if it would keep Bavard from pawing her.

"By all means, my good friend, help yourself." Bavard sounded not a little annoyed.

Andre inclined his head. "Thank you. Mademoiselle?"

"Nothing for her," the minister snapped. "Not yet. I mean to get my answer first."

Watching her out of the corner of his eye, Andre picked up a plate and fork and jabbed at the cold beef, wishing it were

Bavard's thick hide instead. Well roasted. In a certain place beyond the river Styx, where cauldrons boiled and fires burned perpetually.

She clasped her hands and looked down at her lap. "I cannot—"

"Choose!" Bavard roared.

She jumped. "I choose Monsieur Montville." Her voice held a faint tremor.

"Mais, quelle surprise!" Bavard exclaimed. "Now, then, let us begin. My good friend Lepetit, here, being a notary, can stand in for a priest."

A priest? Andre smelled something foul, and it was not the Livarot cheese Bavard had served.

"A priest?" mademoiselle repeated.

"Of course," Bavard replied. "You didn't think I'd have you followed and arrested, then simply let you go without obtaining any information? Oh, no, my dear. I mean to use you well. You won't set foot outside of this chateau without first marrying my friend Montville."

The muscles in Andre's throat convulsed around the beef he was swallowing. Eyes watering, he gulped the mouthful down. "Marrying? As in, *espousing?* If that was intended as a joke, Bavard, may I assure you that I did not find it amusing."

Evidently, neither did the mademoiselle. Perched on the edge of her seat, she contemplated the minister as if he'd sprouted four more legs and insectile antennae.

Bavard chortled. "Hardly a joke. It is an order."

A few choice words sprang to Andre's lips. He bit them back. "I take no orders from the members of the Directory. Only from Bonaparte himself."

Bavard's mouth twisted. "Sometimes, Montville, I wonder where your loyalties truly lie."

Andre shrugged. "My record speaks for itself. I have no intention of marrying the mademoiselle."

Nor anyone else. Never again.

Bavard heaved an exaggerated sigh. "As you wish it, then, my friend. You leave me no alternative but to marry her myself. What say you, mademoiselle? Or would you rather have Demaitre?''

Qu'il aille au diable, *may he go to the devil, with all his cat-and-mouse games.* Andre stared at the minister through yellow spots that danced before his eyes, and heard the sound of steel jaws snapping shut.

Ironic, that he should twice become ensnared in his own traps. He hadn't any choice but to comply; he wasn't about to stand back and let them do this to her, let alone tear down what had taken him years to build, when victory was so close at hand that he could almost smell it.

He set down his plate. ''No need to sacrifice yourselves, monsieurs. I'll do it.''

''Excellent!'' The minister clapped once, then rubbed his hands together. ''Now then, shall we proceed?''

''No.''

It was more of a squeak than a word.

All eyes shifted to Dominique Chantal. There was a wild look in her eyes and heightened color on her cheeks that Andre hadn't seen until that moment. He watched her stand and draw herself to her full height. So very tiny, yet so courageous. He studied the shadows of fatigue beneath her wide green eyes, the flaming rope burns on her slender wrists. . . .

Damn. Andre's emotions collided in his soul, outrage battling with empathy and a disquieting trace of . . . what?

Frowning, he retrieved his wineglass. Whatever the feeling was, he refused to dwell on it.

''C'est odieux,'' she declared. ''I will not do it.''

''Am I to understand that you refuse?'' Bavard demanded.

Four more days, Dominique thought. If she could just endure for four more days, Paul would be safe. Uncle Guillaume had surely been alerted; he would come after her. Or maybe Claude Desfieux would come.

Stall them, she decided. That was what she had to do.

Bavard leaned closer. ''You will not do it?''

She set her jaw. ''I will not.''

Of their own volition, her eyes sought out Montville. She must have imagined it, the spark of admiration she glimpsed in his blue gaze. She dragged her eyes back to Bavard, and knew a surge of terror at the malice lurking in his stare.

"What of your chaperon's life?" he spat.

A thousand cold tendrils slithered up Dominique's spine and wrapped around her heart. "What are you talking about?"

"This." With a fiendish smile, Bavard reached into his pocket. His stubby fingers seemed to glitter as he pulled them out. She saw something small and round spill from his palm, then stop in mid-fall to dangle on a heavy chain.

The object flashed gold as he brought it to eye level, the single garnet in its center winking, red as a drop of blood. As if in a trance, Dominique watched the medallion swing back and forth, her eyes widening in horrified disbelief.

It couldn't be. Oh, no . . . A buzz filled her ears and grew louder, higher, until it was a deafening whine. Through a haze she saw a triumphant sneer sweep across Bavard's porcine features.

"That's right, Mademoiselle Chantal," she heard him hiss, as if from far away. "We do have your beloved Madame Serin."

Andre had no idea how he knew that she would fall. He simply did. His legs carried him forward before she even faltered, impelled by something he could not explain. He took the last step and opened his arms just before she crumpled to the floor. Easily, he swung her up. She seemed weightless. Or was it that his arms had suddenly gone numb?

Carefully, he laid her on the sofa. "Demaitre, open the window."

He glanced over his shoulder in time to see the gaoler cast Bavard an inquiring look.

Andre glared at him. "Now!"

Demaitre jumped. "*Oui,* monsieur. At once, monsieur."

Doing his best to contain his rage, Andre waited for the gaoler to draw back the curtains and throw open both heavy panes. "Good. Now, bring some water." His gaze settled on the large man in black, who sat there gawking. "Excuse me, Lepetit. I'd like a moment with Monsieur Bavard."

The wing chair creaked as Lepetit surged to his feet. Andre watched his retreating back as he lumbered out the door, followed by a sullen-faced Demaitre. Only then did he feel calm enough to trust himself to face Bavard. "So. You have her chaperon."

The minister nodded. "My men discovered her when they arrested mademoiselle." He snickered. "Squatting in the bushes, answering nature's call. They didn't even need to way-lay the coach; the stupid woman stopped it for them. Serin, indeed," he jeered. "The name quite suits her. She has a brain no larger than a canary's."

Serin. Excitement began to beat in Andre's veins. "That medallion," he said, careful to hide his avid interest in it. "Hers?"

"It is."

"May I see it?"

"Certainly."

Andre took one look at the sun-shaped trinket Bavard placed in his palm and wanted to whoop with triumph.

"You're welcome to keep it," the minister offered. "Can't be worth much. I have no use for such trifles."

Imbecile, Andre thought, pocketing it. If only you knew what you have just relinquished.

"Women." Bavard eyed the unconscious young woman with disgust. "Useless creatures. Look at her. With hips like that, she's probably not even fit to breed."

Andre looked, then wrenched his eyes away from what he thought were perfect hips. Suddenly feeling stifled, he rose and went to the open window. Bavard followed doggedly in his wake. Slipping his hands into his pockets, Andre fingered the medallion and gazed out into the distance at the black branches of the swaying trees.

He took a deep breath of fresh air. "I know you are anxious to unmask the conspirators," he told Bavard quietly, "but having me espouse the woman is extreme, to say the very least. You might have sent some agents to investigate."

The minister snorted. "Right. Eavesdropping in cafés has certainly brought us explosive results."

Andre knew exactly to what Bavard alluded; he hadn't for-gotten the horror of two years ago, when a bomb had exploded in central Paris, shattering the serenity of Christmas Eve. The lethal blast, intended for Bonaparte, had gravely injured several bystanders instead. And it had changed the course of Andre's life forever.

"Two years I have been stalking the cursed vipers." Bavard clenched his hands and began to pace the floor. "They're good at sniffing out informants, though. Last week, I had another corpse delivered to my doorstep, with both ears severed and the eyes gouged out. He was the third. I can't afford to lose another.

"You are the perfect man to do this. No one knows of your connection with Bonaparte, since all of France and England gave credence to your supposed disenchantment with our First Consul. As far as people are concerned, you are a former navy commander who has defected to the other side, a frustrated French exile who has been accepted in London's highest circles, given his noble birth." Bavard chortled. "Wouldn't the fools be shocked to learn that your blue blood is in reality very red, and that for two years you've been steadily supplying us with information?" He rubbed his hands. "For anyone who asks, you have returned to France because your dearest friend suddenly passed away, leaving his lovely daughter"—he pointed a stubby finger at Mademoiselle Chantal—"bereft. Since you promised many years ago to care for her should anything befall him . . ." He nodded. "Yes, the consummate cover. That's why I asked the First Consul to let me work with you. Besides, you are the best we have, Montville."

And conveniently expendable, aren't I, Andre thought angrily. "And did the Consul issue orders that I marry—"

"Not exactly." The minister halted. "The espousal was my idea. We suspect it is her brother who is heading the insurrectionists in the Vendee. I figured the arrangement might afford you some protection."

Or get me killed, thereby eliminating the threat I pose to your precious post. "I see."

"I knew you would." Bavard puffed out his chest. "It shouldn't be hard for you to prod her memory, if you'll pardon the pun. A few days in your bed and she'll be volunteering everything she knows."

Andre calmly closed the window. In measured steps, he returned to mademoiselle's side. The color that had stained her cheeks was gone, replaced by an alarming pallor. He sat on the edge of the couch, took her hands, and rubbed her wrists. "What is to stop her from unmasking me the moment I set foot in her hometown?" he asked, gazing at her still features.

"My hostages, of course," Bavard smugly replied. "One peep out of her, and I kill both of them."

Andre felt her arm muscles go rigid beneath his fingers. Either she'd feigned unconsciousness completely, or she had come awake at some point and given no sign of it. Whatever the case, she'd heard that last remark. He frowned. Exactly what else had she overheard?

Demaitre rushed in, a porcelain pitcher in his hand. "The water."

Andre swept a glance about the room. Finding nothing he could use to make a compress, he pulled off his cravat and passed it to the gaoler. "Here. Wet this."

He had to brush away a strand of mademoiselle's glossy black hair before placing the cool cloth on her forehead. She stirred and gave a little sigh, and Andre had to quell the impulse to snatch her up into his arms and run like hell.

"She's come about," Bavard observed. He bent to speak directly in her ear. "Get up."

She didn't move a muscle.

Bavard ground out a savage curse. "Demaitre," he said with chilling calm, "go tell the notary to leave. When you return, escort this little bitch downstairs."

Andre removed the wet cloth from her forehead. "You can stop this," he said to her under his breath. "Just say yes."

"Never," she returned, loudly enough for the minister to hear.

Andre shook his head, amazed. He had to admire her loyalty, but he was damned if he would let her sacrifice herself. He stood. "Give me ten minutes to speak with her, Bavard. Alone."

The minister pondered for a moment. "Very well, my friend. You have ten minutes to turn the full force of your diplomatic powers upon the mademoiselle." Snatching up some bread and cheese, he headed for the door. "Ten minutes," he said over his shoulder.

Dominique watched with wary eyes as the door closed with a click behind Bavard. *They have Madame Serin!* a voice screamed in her head. She rubbed her temples and sat up, forcing her foggy mind to concentrate.

The medallion . . . dear God. No one knew she was here except Colette, who thought that she was safe.

She felt Montville's fingers close around her wrist. His grip was painless, but implacable. *"Vite,"* he whispered. "Quickly. We must talk."

He helped her to her feet and headed for the corner farthest from the door. What to do? Dominique frantically thought, trying to keep up with his long strides.

He stopped and swung around so suddenly, she nearly collided with him. "You're playing with fire," he told her. "As evil goes, Bavard rivals the devil himself. I think you know that."

She did.

As if she had admitted it out loud, Montville nodded. "You also realize that he will not relent."

She couldn't answer.

Montville gave an impatient sigh. "Believe me, mademoiselle, I'm not your enemy."

That snapped her out of her state of speechlessness. "Indeed." She didn't bother to conceal her rancor. "You are an angel come to my rescue, disguised as the devil's helper."

Amusement briefly crossed his face. "Something like that." He took her hand, his features turning serious. "Marry me. I can protect you."

He sounded so sincere. Perplexed, Dominique lowered her gaze to the strong hand that held her own.

And then she saw it. She'd noticed that gold band in the dungeon but had been too dizzy to realize what it was. Hope soared within her. "You are married!"

There was the slightest hesitation before he answered. "She's dead." His voice was flat.

The tiny bit of optimism wavered, then crashed to the ground, shattering into a million fragments. "I am sorry."

He nodded. Stepped a little closer. She tried to back away but bumped into the windowsill behind her.

"I'm free to help you," he said softly. "And willing, if you will allow me."

The beauty of his face was striking. In fact, the man was quite indecently attractive, as dear Madame Serin would say. What would Madame have done in her situation?

A veil abruptly lifted in her befuddled mind. Of course! Why hadn't she thought of that before? She could allow him to take her away from here, and when she had the chance, she could escape. But then . . .

"If I agree to this, what of my chaperon and my coachman?"

His brow furrowed slightly. "That is a problem. Bavard is not one to renounce his trump card. He'll want to hold them hostage to ensure that you don't talk." He looked her in the eye. "Or run away."

Curse him. The man read minds. "Why should I marry you, then?"

A tiny smile. "Because you have no choice. Not if you hope to save yourself."

Dominique felt her arm drift upward. Her heart leaped when she realized that he meant to bring her hand to his lips. She yanked out of his grasp. "And who, pray tell, is going to save me from *you?* What could you possibly gain from this insane arrangement? What do you people want from me?"

He leaned so close that she could feel the heat of his body through the flimsy fabric of her gown. "You heard Bavard. He wants to plant a spy in the Vendee, one who will work from within."

His eyes . . . Her breath came faster. She wet her lips. "What on earth does that have to do with me?"

He cast a glance toward the door. His next words were barely a whisper, breathed warmly in her ear. "Your brother is the one suspected of leading the conspirators. His life is in grave danger, mademoiselle."

Chapter Four

Andre stepped even closer, his eyes trained on her stricken face. "Listen carefully," he whispered. "I know that even as we speak, your brother is on his way to London." He felt her bosom brush against him as she started, her fingers curling around the windowsill behind her.

Unwittingly, his gaze slid to the hollow between her rapidly rising and falling breasts. Not small, not large, he noted. Just the right size, breasts made to perfectly fit a man's palm. He tore his eyes away, feeling a twinge of self-disgust because his mind could stray in such a direction at a time like this.

Against his will, he answered the silent question he read in her glance. "A spy," he softly told her, "has several eyes, twice as many ears, and only one mouth, which he keeps closed." She gave him such a quizzical look that he had to smile. "The exception proves the rule, does it not?"

"Bavard—"

"Doesn't know." He sobered. "Marry me. You have my word that I won't tell him. You will be safe with me, I promise. Not even Bonaparte would dare to harm my wife."

She didn't believe that, he could tell. "It's true," he said. "I daresay he knows better than to do anything that would turn me against him."

"Why?"

"Because I am his right-hand man."

Her eyes widened. She tried to sidestep him, but Andre gripped her shoulders and refused to let her.

Her green eyes flashed. He tipped his head, unable to hold back a grin. "I didn't bring my pistol, mademoiselle. Will Monsieur Bavard's knife do instead? I'll let you carve out my tongue with it. The operation just might make me a better spy." Albeit most ineffective at kissing, he was tempted to add, but didn't.

She opened her mouth. He shook his head. "There isn't time." Andre again glanced at the door, trying to decide whether the idea forming in his brain was worth the risk. The braying sound of Demaitre's laughter, coming from the hallway, served to make up his mind. "I'll make you an offer: Promise me that you won't attempt to run away, and I promise in turn that I will not take you home. We'll go, ah, elsewhere for a while."

He watched her expression as hostility turned to puzzlement and finally to skepticism.

"I thought Bavard wanted you to spy on my family," she said.

Andre made an impatient gesture. "The devil fly with what he wants. Now, do we have an understanding, or don't we?"

She continued to look at him speculatively, and when she spoke, her tone was soft. "Why are you doing this?"

Sensing victory, Andre felt some of the stiffness leave his shoulders. "To save your lovely little derriere." He rubbed the taut muscles at the back of his neck. "Among other things."

He waited for a sharp retort, but none came. Instead, she frowned and searched his face. "What happens when Bavard finds out that you have defied him?"

For a brief moment, Andre envisioned the black hole of a pistol barrel before his eyes. He blinked away the image. "Perhaps he won't, or when he does, it will no longer matter.

39

He isn't a priority. I have important things to do."

"What could be more important than preventing a coup d'etat?"

Finding that sword, he thought. "Preventing a cursed war," he said aloud. "Does that suffice?"

Her brows furrowed. "What—"

"Is it too late to add a clause to our little verbal contract?" he interrupted, deciding that he had revealed more than enough. "A clause that specifies 'The wife shall ask no questions'?"

She shook her head. "Of course it's not too late. In fact, I wish to add one, too."

"Which is . . . ?" he prompted, though he could damn well guess what it was.

She swallowed. " 'The husband may not touch the wife.' "

He gave her a brash smile. "In bed? Or out of it?"

She colored slightly, but met his gaze directly. "Both."

Just as well. Abruptly, he let go of her shoulders. "Agreed. I promise not to touch you. Do we have an understanding?"

She shook her head. "Not yet."

What now? A blood vow? Andre teetered on the edge of exasperation.

"I won't agree to anything until I see my chaperon."

He hesitated. She raised her chin at a stubborn angle.

Andre suppressed a sigh. When God had handed out courage, He certainly had favored Dominique Chantal. "I believe she's being held in the Tour Ronde," he told her. "Come, I'll take you. I know of a hidden passage that leads outside."

A sinister place, the Tour Ronde.

Someone had placed candles in the many wall sconces along the narrow stairwell, but their faltering light did little to brighten the eerie place. A mounted suit of armor, complete with casque and sword, stood by the entryway. Menacing. Dominique half-expected the thing to come to life and charge her, blade gleaming in its invisible hand, cobwebs streaming from the helmet in wispy, transparent strands.

Climbing the narrow steps, she kept her eyes glued to her skirts, afraid to look around for fear she would see certain ghastly crawly things with many hairy legs. Or rats.

"Careful," Montville warned from behind her. "The steps are crumbling in several places."

She trod on a stone and almost yelped as the rock dug into her foot through the thin sole of her kid slipper. She made a hissing noise.

"Are you all right?" he asked.

"Fine," she replied with grim humor. "I just adore dank stairways in dark medieval castles."

His chuckle rumbled off the walls. The rich sound calmed her a bit. Quickly, she took the last few steps. Too late, she caught a glimpse of booted feet, and ran headfirst into an unyielding body. A pair of hands grabbed her just before she toppled backward.

"Excuse me, *ma belle*," a laughing voice said. "I wasn't watching where I was going."

Dominique looked up into a pleasant face, topped by a shock of bright red hair that shone like molten copper in the candlelight. The same guard who had brought her a small washbasin and soap this morning. The night of her arrest, he had materialized with a mug of steaming chicken soup. His uniform was immaculate, brass buttons gleaming. She gave him a faint smile.

"Rochefort," came Montville's deep voice, "do you intend to step aside, or shall I stand here in this drafty stairwell and smoke a cheroot while you ogle my fianceé?"

Rochefort's startled look mirrored Dominique's own, but he recovered quickly. "Your fianceé, is she?" He looked Dominique up and down, then smiled mischievously at Montville. "And all this time I was afraid that one of those willowy English blondes would reel you in and scoop you up into her net." His smile broadened. "I thought you forsook cheroots around the same time that you forswore fishing."

Fishing? Odd that a lowly guard should address Montville in such a jocular fashion. Even as she thought it, Rochefort released her and stepped back, his handsome features taking on the guilty expression of a chastised dog. A quick glance at Montville told her why. His face might have been chiseled in

41

marble, it was so hard and cold. Except his eyes, which studied her with hot intensity. Deep blue. Hot ice.

A thrill coursed through her middle. The man reeked with danger. Recklessly, she wondered if she could dodge him and make a run for the stairs. As if he'd read her thoughts, his mouth abruptly tightened. He clamped an arm around her shoulders and drew her firmly against him. "Unlock the door, Rochefort," he ordered in a frigid tone. "Mademoiselle wishes to see your prisoner."

Dominique eyed the weathered oaken door before her. How could she have considered fleeing when madame's life depended on her good behavior? She tried to ignore Montville's unyielding arm, which felt as if he'd donned that suit of armor she had seen downstairs.

"Before you go inside . . ." The guard paused, one palm braced on the door.

Dominique felt gooseflesh crawl up her arms. "What have you done to her?"

The man looked contrite. "Not I," he said defensively. "Demaitre."

Dominique felt Montville's arm tense. "Let me guess. He broke her legs."

Rochefort grimaced. "One of them. Yesterday morning, when we switched posts. It wasn't torture, though. The woman wailed for hours, feigning sickness. When he finally deemed to open the door, she slipped right past him and dashed toward the stairs. He grabbed her skirt, she fell . . ."

Dominique felt her legs go weak, and suddenly she was grateful to have Montville's arm support her.

Rochefort looked down at her, empathy gleaming in his hazel eyes. "I set the bone. Don't worry, I know the proper way to do it. You'll find her to be groggy, though." His beseeching gaze met Montville's. "I gave her laudanum for the pain."

Scarcely breathing, Dominique listened to the grating of the ancient lock while he turned the massive key. No sooner had he pushed the door open than the pungent scent of alcohol laced with opium assaulted her nostrils. Her chest convulsed as she stepped inside, her eyes arresting on a horrible contraption that looked like a giant iron birdcage, suspended from the ceiling. *"Bon Dieu,"* she uttered.

Oh, no. Had they placed Madame in *that?* A slit in the stone wall was the only source of light in the cramped cell. It took Dominique a few moments to spy the still form lying on a straw mattress in the corner.

"Madame!" She barely felt the candle Montville pressed into her hand. Her fingers tightened around the metal sconce, and somehow she managed to make her feet take the few steps to her chaperon.

She swallowed hard and knelt, alarm racing through her at the sight of Madame Serin's drawn face and misty brown eyes. The woman's dark hair framed her face in a riot of curls, accentuating the pallor of her cheeks.

"Madame," Dominique repeated. She set the candle on the floor and took up both her chaperon's hands, starting when she felt how cold they were. "Can you hear me?" She pressed the woman's limp hands to her cheek. "I never should have made this trip," she whispered, choking back a sob. "I never should have asked you to come with me. Madame, I am so sorry."

Madame Serin's eyes fluttered open. Dominique felt the slight pressure of slim fingers squeezing her own. "You mustn't blame yourself. Not . . . your fault, *chaton.*"

Chaton. Kitten. The endearment made tears sting Dominique's eyes. She blinked them back.

"It's not so bad," Madame assured her. "The medicine Rochefort gave me makes me feel positively drunk." A soft smile curved her lips. "And so does he. Handsome, is he not?"

Too much laudanum, Dominique promptly concluded. She watched her friend's gaze drift over her shoulder and focus on something behind her, then languorously travel up and down. "Oh, my," she heard Madame say in a voice that sounded very like a purring cat. "Who *is* that beautiful man?"

Just how much of the drug had she taken? Dominique's head snapped around in time to see Montville's lips twitch.

"Monsieur," she said, "may I have a moment with her, please? Alone?"

The guard opened his mouth, but Montville silenced him with a glacial look. Rochefort's mouth flattened. "Five minutes," he mumbled.

The door closed softly behind the men. "Your leg," Dominique whispered, reaching for Madame Serin's coarse woolen blanket.

"Hurts." Madame pushed her hand away. "Nothing more . . . that you can do. You're free to go?"

"Almost." Dominique felt a pang of guilt. "But they mean to keep you and Alphonse, I'm afraid. They're forcing me to marry one of their spies."

Trying unsuccessfully to hide the bitterness she felt, Dominique briefly explained the particulars of the arrangement. When she was finished, Madame was silent.

"Le beau," she finally murmured. "The gorgeous one. Him?"

Dominique's gaze fell to the candle that flickered on the dirty floor. She watched a clear drop ooze down the shaft and join the pool of hardened wax in the sconce. "Yes."

"That's wonderful, *chaton.*"

Dominique's head snapped up. "What?"

Her chaperon gave a wan smile. "Wonderful," she repeated. "You can . . . convey the signal."

Dominique's eyes grew round. "What do you mean? What signal? I thought we were off to see Colette."

Her chaperon moistened her lips. "No . . . the medallion . . ."

Why on earth would she care about that trinket at a time like this? "Madame, do try to remember!" Dominique pleaded. "Did Paul give you a message to deliver?"

Madame's eyes glazed over. A sheen of perspiration glistened on her upper lip. "No message."

She was delirious. Wildly, Dominique looked around for something, anything, that might help bring Madame to her senses. She spotted a bucket in the corner and moved to rise, but her chaperon gripped her arm. "Important. The medallion . . ."

Dominique shook her head. "Bavard took your medallion," she said gently. "He gave it to Montville."

"Oh, my God."

With great difficulty, Madame levered herself up on her elbows, her eyes frantic and suddenly almost lucid. She gripped Dominique's wrists. *"Chaton,"* she whispered urgently. "It's vital. You must get the medallion back and take it to the Grand-Duc. If you don't, our people will think Paul"—she sucked in air—"is a traitor. They'll kill him."

Icicles pricked Dominique's spine. "Which grand-duc? Which prince?"

"Not prince. Grand-duc, Eagle . . . Eagle Owl." Madame began to tremble. Her fingernails dug into Dominique's flesh. "Find Claude," she murmured. "Vizille. Provence. South of Grenoble. The medallion. Don't let anyone—"

Someone knocked on the door. Dominique started. Madame Serin released her and fell back, her face chalk white.

"Rochefort threatens to lock us in here if we don't leave at once," Montville said, striding in. He halted at the foot of the pallet and gave Madame an apologetic smile. "How is your leg, Madame?"

Madame's response was barely audible. "I hope to walk again."

Montville nodded. "I made certain that no further injury would be done to you or to the coachman." There was a trace of roughness in his deep voice.

Concern? Regret? Impossible. Dominique retrieved the candle and rose.

"Thank you." Madame's gaze wandered over the length of him, then settled on his face, now clearly illuminated by the flame Dominique held. Her brows furrowed slightly. "Have we . . . met before, monsieur?"

"I doubt it," he replied smoothly.

Dominique thought he sounded guarded.

Madame blinked a few times. "Paris? Perchance—"

"No. No chance at all. I haven't set foot on French soil in several years." He seemed composed, but Dominique knew better. His eyes were sapphire shards, and his smile seemed forced. "I'm sorry, we really must be going."

Intrigued, Dominique watched him step forward and take her chaperon's hand. Madame started. "You are—"

"Your very humble servant." He bent to graze her knuckles with his lips.

For a few seconds, the two stared at each other.

"Come here, *chaton.*" Madame Serin placed two fingers to her cheek. "Give me a kiss."

Heart pounding, Dominique leaned over Madame, hoping to find out who her chaperon thought he was. Her keen ears, however, only picked up two words: *le commandant.*

Of course. Madame's husband had died serving in the navy. Apparently, what Dominique had overheard while feigning unconsciousness in the library was true: everyone believed Montville was who he purported to be.

Though disappointed, Dominique gave a tiny smile. At least Madame would be content, believing that her charge would be protected.

Safe and sound. With Bonaparte's right-hand man.

"I, Andre, take you, Dominique, to be my lawful wedded wife."

Andre's voice sounded strained and foreign to his own ears. "... to have and to hold ..."

Hold? She'd made him promise not to touch her, for God's sake!

"... in sickness and in health ..."

He did feel sick. The words left an ashen taste in his mouth, and his stomach felt as if a knot was being pulled tight and yanked into his gullet.

"... till death do us part."

This couldn't be happening to him. Only a week ago, he had been prowling London drawing rooms, content with spying on the Brits, responsible only for himself. And now—

"I, Dominique Chantal . . .

Somberly, Andre stood beside his bride and listened to the sound of her voice as she nervously repeated the vows he had uttered, and more.

"... obedient in bed and at board ..."

Lies. God, how he hated them, yet his world gravitated

around them, and as of late his very life seemed nothing but one monstrous falsehood, spinning out of control.

The notary pronounced them man and wife. As in a dream, Andre nodded and stared straight ahead, suddenly awash in unwelcome images of another bride, another wedding; unwanted memories of indifference, guilt, and grief. Mimi. What a deception their marriage had been.

"Well?" Bavard's voice pierced his thoughts. "Need I remind you that it is customary for a new husband to congratulate his wife?"

For an insane split-second, Andre considered bolting. Reluctantly, he tipped his chin down to look into her upturned face. Her wide eyes mirrored his own shock at the enormity of what had just taken place between them, but there was something more there, too, a spark that seemed to leap forth and dive into the very core of his frozen soul.

He swallowed. His fingers laced through hers and gently tugged, turning her around to fully face him. To his amazement, she didn't resist. He felt as if he was falling headfirst from Mont Blanc, wind roaring in his ears, the ground beneath him spinning, rising to meet him and swallow him whole.

He bent his head. Vaguely, he heard the sound of her ragged breathing. His free hand glided over her hip and settled on her lower back, bringing her slight form fully against him. He felt the curve of her spine beneath his fingertips, her belly against his thighs, her firm breasts pressed to his abdomen.

A violent shudder racked his body. It had been so long. . . . He stared into her eyes, delving deeply, his heart slamming painfully against his ribs. He noticed flecks of gold around her pupils. He let his eyes rove over her delicate features, taking in every detail, the arch of her brows, the length of her lashes, the faint freckles across the bridge of her nose, the tiny cleft in her chin. . . .

His right hand released her fingers and drifted upward. He realized he was hardly breathing. He let his thumb caress her jaw, reveling in the softness of her skin. Perhaps, he thought, if I should tell her everything, then maybe . . .

He felt her fingers slide over his forearm to grasp his elbow.

47

Tightly. Her nails bit into his upper arm through the fabric of his shirt, digging into his flesh. Did she mean to hurt him?

He couldn't tell. Her eyes were fathomless and emerald green, just like the ocean before a raging storm. Bavard's derisive laugh resounded oddly in his ears. "What's wrong, Montville? Forgotten how to kiss a woman?"

Those green eyes silently dared him to try it. One kiss, his body screamed. Just one. He lowered his lips to hers . . . and grazed the corner of her mouth when she turned her head at the last moment.

His head stopped whirling as suddenly as it had started. Just what the devil had he expected? He let her go and straightened, composing his face into an impassive mask. His left arm stung where she had clawed his flesh. He wondered if she had actually drawn blood.

Bavard pulled open a drawer and slid a piece of paper across the glossy surface of the desk, then picked up a quill and proffered it with a derisive little bow. "Your marriage document," he announced, "is ready for your signatures."

Since she seemed rooted to the floor, Andre took the quill and slowly dipped it into the inkwell, scanning the contract before signing at the bottom, boldly crossing the *t* in Montville.

There. It was done.

Bavard rubbed his hands together. "Madame?"

His left hand still upon the paper, Andre swung around and extended her the pen. She plucked it from his fingers and quickly wrote her name beside his own, then dropped the quill as if it were some pernicious thing.

"Magnifique!" Bavard exclaimed. He snatched up the document, surveyed it with satisfaction, then retrieved the quill and scrawled below their signatures. Demaitre was next to sign, placing an *X* beneath the minister's ornate script.

"Lepetit, Demaitre," Bavard said. "Out." He waved his hand in dismissal.

The notary murmured his good-byes. The minister ignored him, looking to Andre, a lecherous grin spreading across his face. "Montville? Some more roast beef, my friend?"

What Andre wished to do was quit this place at once and never return as long as he lived.

"Desirous of something else, eh?" The minister cackled, his gaze moving over the woman's breasts. "You do not"—he gasped—"wish to pop the cork on a bottle of champagne?"

The marriage contract fluttered to the carpet. Andre's hands balled into fists. Measure for measure someday, he vowed, bending to pick up the document so that the minister couldn't see the murder in his face. "We leave at once," he gritted.

Rising, he saw a swirl of yellow skirts.

"One moment, madame," Bavard said sharply.

She halted, but didn't turn around.

"You are to be compliant, respectful, and obedient at all times." Bavard glared at her rigid back. "As is befitting of a female."

She nodded once.

"If anything happens to Montville, if so much as a hair upon his head is harmed"—Bavard's left eye half-closed, the other opened wide—"your friends will wish that they were dead, before I'm through with them. Is that quite clear?"

Another nod. Andre swept his coat off the chair and wrapped it around her. "You'll need this," he murmured. "You've seen how cold it is outside."

Bavard, however, wasn't finished. "You're entering perilous territory, Montville. See that you don't fall into some sort of trap."

"Compared to men I've dealt with of late," Andre dryly replied, "Paul Chantal will be a welcome change. I appreciate your concern, but I am perfectly capable of watching my own back."

Something unholy gleamed in the minister's eyes as he thrust out his hand. Andre clamped down on the sausagelike fingers, barely restraining himself from crushing the bones. Instead, he forced a smile. "Bavard, one certainly cannot cry ennui, working with you."

He followed his new wife to the door. Her gait was as stiff as a marionette's.

"Montville."

Trembling with impatience, Andre turned, his fingers tight on the cold handle. "Yes?"

"See that you don't lose your head between her legs, my friend."

Chapter Five

Dominique waited for Montville's driver to lower the coach steps, listening to the rustle of trees while blustery wind whipped her cheeks and neck. She'd get that medallion back, she vowed, even if she had to do away with Montville in order to retrieve it. She groaned at her thought. What was this? Was she really thinking of committing murder? Heavens, she'd been exposed to Bavard far too long. She shivered, and quickly crossed herself.

"Chilled?" Montville asked from behind her.

Dominique jumped. Shaking her head, she swiftly took the few steps to the coach and quickly climbed in before he could assist her. She sank back against the squabs and glanced around the spotless interior of the traveling chariot, her nose detecting the barest hint of his fresh-smelling rosemary fragrance over the predominant scent of new leather. She smoothed her skirts and turned toward the window. She heard Montville's laughter, rich and deep, then the seductive timbre of his voice as he spoke to his coachman.

It occurred to her that she had no idea where they were headed. She pricked her ears, but he spoke too softly for her to hear what he was saying. She leaned her throbbing temple against the glass. The coach lamps, she absently observed, cast golden light upon him, and shades of copper glinted in his chestnut hair, as if some pixie had dashed out of the nearby woods and sprinkled fairy dust over his head.

Dismay coursed through her at the poetic images the man evoked. She had no business thinking in that way about Andre Montville. He was a spy. He was her enemy. *He was her husband.*

She watched him climb the steps and duck inside, then felt his leg brush her knee as he moved to sit beside her.

"It smells like snow out there," he said.

It smells like you in here, she thought. Out of the corner of her eye, she saw his boots gleam blue-black as he leaned back and stretched his legs, crossing them at the ankles. A thrill dived somewhere in her belly.

The coach lurched into motion. The sounds of hoofbeats and jangling harnesses filled her ears, matching the rhythm of her drumming heart. The best way to proceed, she knew, was to pretend to go along with this charade until she could safely send a message to Claude. Some way, somehow, she had to earn Montville's trust.

Before she knew it, her gaze had slowly progressed along the length of his black Hessian boots. What long legs he had. Well-muscled, bespeaking boundless energy even in their comfortable pose, their power emphasized by the clinging beige moleskin cloth in which they were encased.

Dominique could feel his gaze upon her as keenly as she sensed his presence, tugging at her from less than an arm's length away. Her breath began to come in shallow pants. Her gaze insisted on staying with Montville, drifting upward, to the fine white linen straining across his chest. A memory of that chest up close, warm and alive beneath her cheek, hit Dominique with stunning clarity.

So did her situation.

Even if she should manage to seize the trinket tonight, it would be days before she could attempt an escape. She couldn't very well go traipsing across half of France alone, and she certainly couldn't leave Montville until she was certain that Claude had delivered Madame and Alphonse out of Bavard's clutches.

She knew nothing of this man, yet here she was, she frantically thought, trapped in his coach, with the appalling prospect of having to spend several days with him.

And nights.

Suddenly, she felt light-headed. He had treated her well thus far, but how honorable was he? What if he were to disregard his promise and demand his marital rights? Was that why he had helped her? What if he forced her to—

"I've seen you bestow far warmer looks upon Bavard." He shifted in his seat, his fingers sliding closer to hers when he moved.

She snatched her hand back. "Don't touch me."

Silence. Invisible sparks flew from Montville, and as he contemplated her, Dominique wanted to bite her tongue. This was hardly the way to stay in the man's good graces.

She tipped her head and gave him as affable a smile as she could manage. "You promised," she reminded him.

"So I did."

He sounded as tired as she felt. He let his chin drop to his chest, slumped a little lower in his seat, and closed his eyes. Long lashes, Dominique observed, black, spiky, and absurdly thick.

It occurred to her that the past few hours must have been hard on him, as well. She remembered his face when Bavard had revealed his scheme. To say that Montville wasn't pleased would be an understatement. Yet he had "saved her derriere," as he had phrased it. Why?

His life is in grave danger, mademoiselle. How had Montville known about Paul's trip to London? And if he knew, why didn't he simply issue orders for her brother's arrest? She buried her face in her hands, her head reeling, feeling too faint to make sense of anything.

"*Chaton,*" he said.

She tensed. Why would he call her that?

"Is there a story behind the nickname?"

Dominique relaxed a little. He only wanted to make small talk. "Madame and I used to play hide-and-seek when I was small. She was the bird—*serin*—and I was the cat.''

He smiled. "With sharp little claws, I'm sure." He raised his left arm, elbow up. She was abashed to see four brownish-red marks dotting his otherwise pristine white sleeve. Blood.

"I did that?"

"Yes." There was no accusation in his tone. He let his arm drop to his side, not bothering to open his eyes.

Dominique frowned. She hadn't meant to hurt him; the truth was, she'd felt like a trapped animal, and evidently she'd behaved like one. "I'm sorry."

"Why?"

Guilt immediately turned to frustration. She might have known he wouldn't let her off the hook with a simple apology. She shrugged. "It looks like an expensive shirt."

Another silence. Then, to her amazement, he began to chuckle. Shoulders shaking, chest rocking, Montville covered his face with his hands. What on earth did he find so humorous? Puzzled, she watched him slowly slide his fingers upward over his cheeks and grind the heels of his hands against his brow, massaging his scalp at the same time.

Nerves, she realized. He didn't look amused, he looked destroyed. Were it not for the rich peals filling the coach, Dominique might have believed the man was crying.

"You won't be laughing so heartily when your arm becomes poisoned with gangrene," she muttered, when his mirth had finally been spent.

He wiped his eyes. "Will you minister to it for me if that happens?"

Impossible! He couldn't possibly be aware of her extensive knowledge of physic. But then, Bavard might have informed him that most of the men in her family were doctors.

She wet her lips. "I might."

"Then it will have been worth it."

His gaze caressed her. She caught her breath, and for a moment she totally forgot her misgivings about him. She stared into his face, expecting some reply that matched the warmth reflected in his dark blue eyes, but all she got was a wistful smile before he turned his head and closed his eyes again.

Dominique seethed inside, furious with herself for having lowered her guard. She would do well to remember who this man was and why she was here, and never again allow him to draw her in like that.

Gradually, his breathing grew deep and even. She peeked at his relaxed profile and felt her stomach plummet. The intimacy of having him fall asleep beside her, as if it were the most natural thing in the world, was somehow worse than verbal fencing.

The chariot swerved sharply, hurling her against him. Her hand brushed the velvety fabric of his breeches. She gasped and hastily righted herself, grateful that he hadn't awakened. She glanced at him. His eyes were still closed, but he was smiling.

The tightness in Dominique's stomach increased to painful proportions. Her gaze darted around the interior of the coach and settled upon the silver door handle to her right. Before she could stop to reason, she'd reached out and grasped the smooth, cool metal.

"Bad idea," came Montville's slumberous voice.

Dominique jerked her hand away as if the handle had turned molten.

"Numerous scrapes and bruises, not to mention a fractured limb or two." He shook his head. "I strongly advise against it."

"Against what?"

"Jumping, of course," he replied matter-of-factly. "The thought did cross your mind, did it not?"

Whether she admitted or denied it, he would still laugh at her, and she refused to give him the satisfaction. "You are supposed to be asleep."

"And you," Montville returned, "are supposed to be behaving."

She willed herself to smile at him. "I'm not a child, Monsieur Montville."

His gaze moved to her breasts. In spite of Dominique's resolve to remain calm, her pulse began to hammer at her throat when he slowly raised intense blue eyes to capture hers. "*D'accord*, Madame Montville."

Dominique frowned. "Don't call me that."

For a long moment, he contemplated her without so much as blinking. " 'What's in a name?' " he finally quoted in a mocking tone. " 'That which we call a rose, by any other name would smell as sweet.' " He grinned. "Shakespeare. Romeo—"

"And Juliet," she interrupted. "I'm quite fond of that play, especially the ending."

It was true; she'd found it romantic that a man could love so much that he wouldn't want to go on living without his beloved. But that was not what she meant now, and Montville must have read it in her expression, for his grin faded. At length, he reached behind him, produced a small red and white tin, and flicked it open with his thumb. "Peppermint?"

Dominique didn't like the odd gleam in his eyes. She looked suspiciously at the white pastilles.

"For your malady," he patiently explained.

"Malady?"

"You have a stomachache, madame."

She wished he wouldn't call her that but didn't dare say so again. "How did you—"

"It is obvious. You are continually pressing a hand to it. You're doing it right now."

She looked down. Indeed, she was. "Thank you," she murmured, and selected a mint.

"De rien."

His eyes held hers as he took one for himself. She watched him snap it in half between his front teeth. Perfect teeth, white as the peppermints. She glimpsed the tip of his tongue when he drew the mint into his mouth, and felt hot flutters in her chest.

"Altoids," he pronounced. "The original celebrated curiously strong peppermints. From London."

His tone was mild; his expression was anything but. "Good?"

She nodded. "Mmm."

"They contain *mentha piperita*," he informed her. "It gives them that unique and icy bite."

The sheer seduction in his voice did alarming things to

Dominique's body. Never in her life had her insides felt like honey. Warm honey. And he wasn't even touching her.

"That's very interesting," she said nervously. She found herself staring transfixedly into his dark blue eyes, and as she struggled to continue breathing she realized that he was leaning toward her.

"Helps to settle a queasy stomach," he murmured. His gaze dropped to her lips. She bit down on the mint. It seemed to burn the roof of her mouth.

"Or so they say," Montville continued. "Myself, I always keep them handy in case I get a violent craving . . ."

She backed into the corner, one arm and shoulder pressed against the door, watching him draw ever closer, the space between them narrowing bit by agonizing bit.

". . . for a cheroot," he softly finished.

She felt his hands slide along her arms and settle on her shoulders, thumbs stroking the sensitive skin along her collarbone. She drew in a sharp breath. "What do you think you're doing?"

"Not thinking." His lashes lowered. Again, he studied her mouth.

Panic raced through Dominique. Or was that shocking tingle in her breasts caused by the way he was lightly running one fingertip just above the ribbon of her décolletage?

Ever so slowly, his hand moved to her nape. His touch was feather-light. She opened her mouth to speak but discovered that she had lost her voice.

His fingers found a hairpin. She felt her chignon begin to loosen as he slowly pulled the tortoiseshell pin free and buried his fingers in her hair, sending myriad streaks of fever rippling through her body, all merging in one unmentionable place.

"I think," he finally murmured, "that I'm about to kiss you."

She didn't know whether to laugh or scream. "You can't be serious."

"But I am."

He found another pin. Her hair fell in dark waves to her waist. Why was she incapable of moving? Through a haze,

Dominique searched his face for some clue as to what he was thinking.

Passion. She saw raw passion smolder there. But beyond the urgency, beyond the hunger, she glimpsed a naked vulnerability in his eyes that triggered a feeling akin to pain within her, something that made her want to reach for him and—

"Please," she whispered, "stop." His scent filled her head to near-intoxication. His lips were now a hairbreadth from her own. "You cannot do this."

"But I must." His voice was barely an undertone. She realized that his arms were trembling. His warm breath mingled with her own, sweet with the scent of peppermint. His left hand glided upward to cradle her chin, gently, reverently, as if he were touching priceless antique porcelain. She tried to turn her head.

"Don't," he whispered achingly. *"Pour l'amour du ciel,* don't turn away from me again."

His thumb moved back and forth over her lower lip, and Dominique felt the last of her defenses begin to crumble beneath the onslaught of sensation he provoked. Montville was going to kiss her, she realized, and this time, there would be no stopping him.

"But I don't want you to," she whispered.

The statement was a paradox, a truth and an untruth at the same time. He seemed to sense it, because his eyes searched hers intently, silently imploring.

"Please," he whispered thickly. "Just this—"

A loud rumbling rudely cut off what he was about to say. He started. His gaze dropped to her stomach. He drew back, blinking, as if he had just then realized where he was and what he was doing, and mortification overtook Dominique at the look of shock upon his face.

"Take your hands off me," she said, further embarrassed by the husky timbre of her own voice.

She heard his breathing, as ragged as her own, and felt the tremor in his hand, still at her nape. Good lord, how close she'd come to being seduced into his silken trap. She moved her head in an impatient gesture, and he obligingly released her.

For an endless moment, he continued to study her, and she was taken aback at the pained longing lurking in his eyes. She felt his hand on her elbow, but this time his touch was tentative, and held no demand. He reached into his pocket. "Your hairpins."

She looked down in confusion, then stared blindly at the two glossy pins before taking them from his open palm. "Thank you," she muttered.

"I—" He stopped and cleared his throat, seemingly annoyed that his voice had come out as a rasp. "Forgive me. It was wrong of me to force myself on you."

She watched him slide to the far side of the seat and shove his hands deep into his pockets. She quickly turned away, willing her heart to slow to a normal pace, rejecting the tempest he had unleashed within her with all the self-control she could summon.

They rode in silence for the remainder of the trip. By the time the coach came to a halt at the inn where he was staying, Andre sorely wanted to smash his fist through the window. That he should want this woman to the point of pain enraged him. That he was confined to such small quarters with the memory of what had almost occurred between them and her so near that he need only reach out to touch her, served to drive him to the brink of insanity.

Now, climbing the steps to his room with her asleep in his arms, he caught himself gazing at her mouth, barely suppressing the urge to stop and plunder those lips with his. He remembered the feel of her soft skin, the rapid rise and fall of her breasts when he had touched her, her warm breath on his face, and wished Bavard a million slow and painful deaths.

He misjudged the last step and lurched forward. Her eyes fluttered open, as green and shining as leaves after a summer rain. Something flickered in those eyes before she came fully awake, glanced at her surroundings, and gave him a questioning look.

"I couldn't wake you," he said apologetically. He hadn't

had the heart to do so, after the way she'd moaned in protest when he'd tried.

"Where are we?"

He started down the darkened hallway. "*L'Auberge Étalon*, the Stallion Inn. In Châtillon."

"Oh," was all she said.

He wondered if he should ask her whether she wished to be set down. She settled the matter for him by putting her arms around his neck. He raised his brows.

"I'm being"—she paused to smile at a well-dressed woman who approached from the opposite direction—"a compliant and obedient wife."

Abruptly, the lady stumbled, then caught her balance and halted, blocking his way. With clumsy fingers, she readjusted her hat. A black veil completely concealed her face.

Andre cleared his throat. "Excuse me."

The woman's veil fluttered. Without a word or so much as a nod, she sidestepped them and hurried toward the stairs, leaving a strong fragrance of roses in her wake.

He shifted Dominique's weight to fumble for his key. "I believe Bavard also mentioned the word *respectful* in his memorable tirade. Or have you already forgotten that one?"

"I haven't forgotten anything," she replied lightly. "Including who you are."

But you don't know who I am. He gave a frustrated sigh. Safer not to tell her anything. Not yet.

He finally managed the lock. He paused in the threshold, and she eyed the interior as if she expected demons to leap out of some corner. He followed her gaze, pleased to see that there was a good fire in the hearth, and three fat candles burning in the candelabrum on the rosewood table beside the bed.

It was the last that she was staring at, however.

He stepped inside and felt her stiffen, her wide eyes riveted to the four-poster. "The sheets are clean," he told her, feigning indifference as he surveyed the blue curtains and matching gold-trimmed canopy.

Her face reddened. "Put me down."

An image of her writhing beneath him in that bed sprang forth in Andre's mind, and he pushed it back, kicking the door shut harder than necessary before setting her gently before him.

"And where do you sleep?" she asked.

As exhausted as he was, the thought of having to share a bed with her seemed more than he could bear. Besides, after the brashness he had exhibited in the coach, he felt he owed it to her to keep his distance. "Wherever you want me to. I'll ask for an extra blanket and—"

"How did that get here?" she interrupted.

Andre's eyes fell upon the object of her surprise: her trunk, which rested against the opposite wall beside the armoire. "I arranged to have your things delivered here while you were visiting with your chaperon," he explained.

She tipped back her head. "Before I even agreed to marry you? You have amazing foresight, monsieur."

Someone knocked on the door. "The food Monsieur requested," a voice called.

"Excuse me," Andre mumbled, grateful for the interruption. He led the servant in and watched the man bustle to the far side of the room, carrying a silver tray laden with food. Fish, he noted with disgust. "There must be some mistake. I asked for—"

That was when Andre noticed the table in the corner. Upon it were one crystal glass and an unopened bottle of champagne. He hadn't ordered them. Bavard? he thought, then immediately rejected the idea as ridiculous. Perhaps this establishment coddled those customers who occupied the most expensive rooms.

"I am desolate to say that we haven't a drop of the Sancerre red the monsieur wanted," the servant said apologetically. "But we do have the magnificent rosé."

He kissed his fingertips, and Andre had to smile at the typically French gesture. "Sancerre rosé?"

"*Mais, oui.* I guarantee Madame will enjoy it," the man declared, bowing and grinning at her.

The genuine smile she gave the servant made Andre's throat constrict. "Rosé *and* champagne?" she asked. "Isn't that a bit much?"

The servant's attention had already returned to the bottle.

"May I?" He reached out and turned it, then eyed the elegant characters painted upon it and whistled through his teeth. "Monsieur has excellent taste," he said appreciatively, heaving an exaggerated sigh. "Ah, would the innkeeper keep such fine stock in his cellar." He leaned toward Andre. "Stingy old coot, you know," he said conspiratorially. "Afraid we'll plunder his provisions."

Andre studied the emerald-colored bottle. Moët & Chandon. Were he to live a hundred years, those letters would be forever emblazoned in his mind. He felt the blood drain from his face. And then the memories of that night flared in his head, in all their unspeakable horror.

Andre clenched his jaw. How had the cursed thing gotten here? He seized the bottle by the neck and thrust it into the servant's hands. "Bring the rosé, please. I do not want this."

The servant's mouth dropped open. "But, Monsieur—"

"Take it. It's yours."

The other man gaped at him. Andre fished in his pocket and handed him a bill. He had to say *"de rien"* several times before the elated servant stopped thanking him for his generosity and finally backed out of the room, clutching the champagne to his chest.

Still gritting his teeth, Andre stared at the door, fighting back sordid and macabre recollections that flashed relentlessly before his eyes. He drew his sleeve across his clammy brow and swung around.

His wife was sitting on the bed, skirts raised above her knees, taking off one yellow slipper. Her other foot was already bare.

He caught his breath. The dark memories trembled back, then faded away, replaced by the one now before him, of sunshine and blinding beauty. Her head was bent, her raven hair loose, grazing her thighs, a stark contrast against her daffodil-colored gown.

Entranced, he watched her slowly remove her garters and peel off both sheer silk stockings, taking her time with each, sliding her fingers along legs that were perfectly proportioned, long for a woman so petite, and shapely as hell.

Every muscle in Andre's body turned to iron. His mouth

felt as if he'd been stranded in the desert for a week. He felt the blood rush back to his face and roar in his ears but couldn't look away or move to save his life. Just when he thought he couldn't take anymore, she dropped her skirts.

He sought to meet her gaze, but she glanced up in surprise and then refused to look at him again, a blush slowly pinkening her cheeks.

Clenching his fists, Andre stood rooted to the spot, quivering as he struggled to control himself. Because suddenly, irrationally, he wanted to vault across the room, seize the woman by the shoulders, and shake her until her pretty little teeth rattled.

What's wrong with you, Montville? You've never so much as thought to harm a woman in your life.

Deep down, Andre knew what was wrong: he didn't need this. He didn't want that part of him awakened, didn't want to be brought out of his self-imposed passionless detachment. His gaze flicked to the cut-crystal champagne glass that caught the firelight and reflected it in glittering rainbow hues. He looked back to the woman on the bed. He lowered his eyes to the bloodstains on his left sleeve.

And then he knew exactly what he had to do. Swiftly, he began to cross the room, impatiently undoing the front of his shirt as he went. When the last stud wouldn't budge, he yanked the garment fully out of his breeches and tugged, sending the mother-of-pearl disk flying, to skip across the hearth and plunge into the flames.

He shrugged out of his shirt and heard a soft gasp from the direction of the bed. He draped the linen across a chair, then darted a glance her way, instantly wishing he'd kept his gaze averted. The woman sat there on his bed, her lips parted, looking positively thunderstruck. And she was staring at his chest.

In stunned silence, Dominique dug her nails into the coverlet as her eyes took in a vision that made her pulse throb madly at her throat. Looking like a feline predator stalking its quarry, Montville moved toward her, his eyes determined, as blue and cold as the pools they resembled. Icy. Frozen. Mountain lakes in winter. What was he going to do?

She licked her parched lips, unable to stop her gaze from

again traveling along his granite jaw, down his sinewy neck, over the broad expanse of his muscled chest, to the object that held her mesmerized. For there, nestled between fine black hairs, Dominique saw it.

The medallion. Montville *wore* the medallion.

"Not to worry," he said. "I've never been inclined to ravish a woman, even if she does happen to be my wife."

Dominique barely registered his words, or the mirthless chuckle that followed them. Her shoulders sagged with relief when he moved past her, halting before the armoire to throw open both polished oaken doors. She observed the play of toned back muscles beneath his smooth, tanned skin as he selected a clean shirt and shoved his arm into one sleeve. Just below his nape, the heavy chain flashed gold once, then disappeared, concealed by the white linen Montville drew over his broad shoulders.

Her spirit plummeted. *Grand Dieu,* not only did she have to retrieve the thing, she had to remove it from his person.

He tucked his shirttails into his breeches, reached inside the armoire again, produced a snowy cravat, and began tying it around his neck with swift precision. "You must be famished." He nodded pointedly toward the food.

Dominique rose. "And you?"

He raked a hand through his hair and eyed the platter of pike with beurre blanc. "I am not hungry."

She watched him stride to the table and pull out a chair, then silently invite her to sit with a polite gesture of his arm. Framed by the orange light of the fire, he looked even taller and more dangerous, glowing with a blatant virility that burned far hotter than the flames behind him. Pain knifed through Dominique's stomach. She pressed a hand to it, to no avail. Were she alone, she would have doubled over.

His features softened somewhat. "Please. Eat something."

Dominique nodded. Swallowing back a wave of nervousness, she took a step toward him, then jumped when she heard a knock at the door.

"Your wine, monsieur," the servant called.

The door opened slightly. Montville paled visibly. "Come in."

In silence, Andre watched the door swing open. Damn. He had forgotten to lock it. He couldn't remember the last time he had been so careless.

"*Mais,* you haven't even touched our *brochet rabellais-ienne,*" the servant scolded good-naturedly.

"I was preparing to." She seated herself. The man picked up a plate and filled it, then placed it before her with a little bow, obviously waiting for her to sample the dish. As she did so, the man grinned, and inexplicable fear gripped Andre, making the hairs at his nape bristle.

"Delicious," she pronounced.

The servant uncorked the bottle and poured peach-colored wine into the two glasses he had brought. "I'll tell the chef." Ordinary glass, not crystal, Andre noted, glancing at the exquisite goblet still sitting on the edge of the table.

"Does the madame wish anything else?"

She took a sip of wine and smiled. "A bath. If it isn't too much trouble."

"No trouble at all. Hot water takes about half an hour." He turned to Andre. "Monsieur?"

Fifteen minutes should be time enough to find out what he needed to know, Andre estimated. He wanted to be here when strangers entered the room. He shook his head. "Thank you, that will be all."

The servant headed out, and Andre moved to follow him.

"You're leaving?"

He halted. "I'm going downstairs for a while."

"What for?"

"I want to check on the horses."

"Isn't that the coachman's responsibility?"

"Usually."

"Then—"

"Am I to understand that you wish to forfeit?" he interrupted, irritated because she'd forced him to lie.

Her delicate brows furrowed slightly. "Forfeit?"

"Our bargain. You promised not to ask me any questions. I've answered three so far."

Her eyes widened. "You're keeping *count?*"

"That's four."

She swallowed hard. He looked into her eyes. How green, he thought. Forcing his gaze away from hers, he pivoted and headed out. He'd barely finished locking the door when he sensed movement behind him. Before he could even turn his head, something sharp pricked the back of his neck.

A knife.

Chapter Six

Andre froze.

"One sound and you're a dead man," a voice hissed in his ear.

His fingers tightened around the key he held. No way to double over and drive an elbow into his assailant's ribs; he'd only smash his head into the door. He darted a glance to the end of the darkened corridor. No one.

"Hands on your head, where I can see them. Do it." The voice now came from way above his head. A mammoth. Very carefully, Andre did as he was told, acutely aware of the blade searing his nape. Cold sweat tingled at the small of his back. He took quick, shallow breaths, nerves taut, heart slamming against his ribs, thinking of nothing but self-preservation and protecting the woman behind the door.

"You will take one step to the left. Misstep, and I ram this knife all the way in. Understood?"

Andre nodded, feeling the sharp tip cut into his flesh and warm blood trickle down his collar. He tried to place the voice but couldn't.

"Good. Now, move."

67

The next second his nose was nudged against the wall. Andre smelled fresh paint and his own blood.

"The key," the man behind him whispered.

The bastard. "You'll have to kill me first."

"Don't tempt me. Hand it over." The knife stabbed deeper, and Andre clenched his teeth to stifle a grunt. He gripped the key even tighter. The iron dug into his palm.

Behind him, the stairs creaked.

Andre sensed a tremor in the hand holding the knife. Seizing his chance, he braced his palms against the wall and kicked up and backward, slamming his booted heel into the other man's kneecap. With a yelp, his attacker went down. The dagger clattered to the parquet floor. In one fluid swoop, Andre retrieved it. The ruffian cursed between clenched teeth.

Andre whirled. Blood boiling, he kicked again, neatly clipping the villain's jaw. The man's head snapped back, sending the hat he wore flying. Andre thought he heard a gasp from the direction of the stairs before he crouched down, knife gleaming in his hand.

Booted feet clattered up the stairway.

"No!"

The newcomer's strangled plea barely penetrated Andre's senses. With grim determination, he yanked down the fallen man's black cravat and poised the blade against his exposed throat.

"Andre, in the name of God—"

A familiar voice. Andre looked up. Through a red haze, he saw a blur of blue cloth and gleaming brass buttons. Red hair. The stranger hovering over him looked like—"Rochefort?"

"Yes," Rochefort whispered urgently. "He's one of us. Don't kill him."

Andre's gaze flicked to the man who lay unconscious at his feet. "He tried to do the same to me."

Rochefort's mouth dropped open. "Why?"

He hadn't a clue. Slowly, Andre lowered the knife. Better to interrogate the man than give in to the impulse to slit his throat. He rolled his rigid shoulders, exhaled a hissing breath, and sat back on his heels. "Who is he? What are you doing here?"

"I—" Booming laughter drifted up the stairs. Rochefort clamped his mouth shut. "*Merde.* Someone's coming." He sprinted to the door beside Andre's room and shoved the key into the lock. "In here. My chamber," he whispered. "Quickly. Get his hat."

Andre grabbed the hat and tossed it to Rochefort. Tucking the weapon into the waistband of his breeches, he hooked his forearms beneath the unconscious man's armpits and began dragging the limp body. It was like trying to move the carcass of an elephant.

Rochefort threw the door open. "Good. There's light."

Feeling as if the veins in his neck would burst from the effort, Andre hauled the bandit inside. While Rochefort closed the door and locked it, Andre removed the large man's cravat, using it to bind his wrists.

He felt Rochefort's eyes upon him and glanced up. "Merely taking precautions, Etien. This diminutive friend of yours tried to kill me."

Rochefort's questioning expression turned to one of consternation. "He's not my friend." He reached into his coat pocket and tossed Andre a length of rope.

Andre wrapped the cord around the captive's ankles and fashioned the ends into an intricate halyard bend. "There," he muttered, pulling the knot tight. "Let's see you try to break this." He surged to his feet and turned to Rochefort. "You said you knew him."

"Did he cut you?"

Andre raised a hand to probe his nape. He brought his moist fingers around, examined the crimson-smudged pads, and felt his ire rise anew. Just grand; another ruined shirt. "Who the devil is this blackguard?"

Rochefort walked to the washstand in the corner and picked up a towel and the porcelain pitcher. "Fardeau. From Tours. Specializes in rescue operations." Returning, he wet the towel and held it out. "I've used his services once or twice myself."

"I've never heard of him." Andre accepted the cloth and dabbed at the gash. "What was he trying to do, rescue my neck from the misery of holding up my head?"

Rochefort grinned. "Let us find out."

With a flick of his wrist, he splashed the pitcher's entire contents over Fardeau's face. Immediately, the man jerked to his senses and began to cough, spluttering water and savage curses between hacks.

Andre flung the bloodstained towel aside, went down on one knee, and waited for the spell to pass. The moment it did, he placed the knife beneath his captive's chin. "Call out, and you won't see tomorrow." He lifted the blade, forcing Fardeau to meet his gaze. "Listen carefully. I have three questions, and I am only going to pose them once. Is that quite clear?"

The giant looked at him slantwise from beneath knitted brows so blond that they were almost white. He nodded slightly.

"Good." Andre pressed the blade against the vein that pulsed at Fardeau's throat. "Who sent you here, and for what purpose?"

Sweat beaded on Fardeau's brow, but he didn't flinch. He lay there, his chest heaving, and his blank stare did nothing to improve Andre's murderous mood. "Third question: Why were you so very eager to obtain the key to my room?"

Briefly, the man glanced at Rochefort. If he recognized him, he gave no sign of it; his gray eyes remained expressionless.

Andre's mouth curved into a glacial smile. "I admire your sense of loyalty, Monsieur Fardeau." At the mention of his name, the villain's eyes grew round. Deliberately, Andre trailed the tip of the knife downward along the man's chest, dispassionately watching the veins on Fardeau's neck stand out as he strained at his bindings. "Yes, loyalty is commendable," he went on. "It's only fair to let you know what it will cost you. When my patience wanes, you see"—he moved the blade to Fardeau's groin, deftly slicing the top button off his breeches—"your life is not the first thing I intend to cut short."

Andre lopped off another button, then another. Horror flickered in the man's colorless eyes, but he remained silent. Andre snatched up the towel. "One fastener left. Stuff this into his mouth, Rochefort."

"Wait." Blinking fast, Fardeau flicked his tongue over his lips. He swallowed hard, his eyes riveted to the dagger, still menacingly poised above his groin. "I came to rescue Mademoiselle Chantal."

Andre raised one eyebrow.

Behind him, Rochefort chuckled. "Really? Who hired you?"

"A man named Claude Desfieux."

Interesting. Andre's eyes narrowed. He'd thought Desfieux was still in London. He moved the dagger slightly. "Continue."

Fardeau cleared his throat. "He came to me last week. Seems a fellow showed up at his sister's doorstep claiming to have taken Mademoiselle Chantal to his chateau after her coach ran into his. She didn't believe his story and had him followed when he left her house."

It all made sense, except Desfieux's early arrival. Moreover, Claude could have taken matters into his own hands, yet had decided not to do so. Why?

Andre frowned. "And?"

"We stalked the grounds of Chateau Loches for days. Damned place is like a fortress, and those dogs . . ." Fardeau grimaced.

Rochefort laughed. "Got a taste of you, did they?"

Fardeau shook his head. "Mauled one of my men. Beasts nearly killed him. The other two refused to stay there after that. I couldn't stage a break-in, and had to follow your coach alone."

He paused. Andre gave him a level stare.

"I know nothing more," Fardeau said quietly.

He spoke the truth, Andre could tell. "This man who came to you for help—"

"Desfieux."

"Yes. What did he look like?"

"Average height. Brown eyes. Sandy hair. Large mole on his right cheek."

An accurate description. Andre turned the knife over in his hand. "Have you conveyed any information to Desfieux?"

"None. Said he was leaving town. We were to escort the mademoiselle to his sister's. I didn't mean to kill you, honest. I only meant to get the girl."

71

"And nothing else?"

"The 'girl,' that's all. I swear."

Andre's eyes bore into Fardeau's. "The 'girl,' " he gritted, "is a married woman, and hardly in need of rescue. I'm perfectly capable of protecting my own wife."

Fardeau stared at him in dismay. "Your wife? I thought—"

"Is something amiss with your hearing?" Rochefort interrupted cheerfully.

Slack-jawed, the man nodded once, then quickly shook his head.

Giving Fardeau one last warning look, Andre sliced through the bindings at his ankles. "Convey the following message to Mademoiselle Colette: her friend is well, and safe with me. Andre Montville."

"M—Montville?" The man's eyes threatened to pop out of their sockets.

"That's right." Andre held Fardeau's astonished gaze for a long moment, then calmly cut the man's wrists free.

"I didn't realize," the man choked out. "Mons—"

"You're free to go," Andre cut in, unwilling to listen to the string of apologies he sensed would follow. He stood, then carefully tucked away the knife.

The man lurched to his feet. Head ducked between his massive shoulders, he began limping toward the door. Rochefort hastened to open it, smiling and raising two fingers to his forehead in a mock salute. Without so much as a backward glance, Fardeau disappeared into the hallway, black coattails flapping behind him.

Rochefort motioned with his head toward the connecting door to the adjoining room, then looked to the brass hilt of the knife in Andre's waistband and grinned broadly. "Hardly your usual refined method of interrogation, but infinitely more amusing. Planning on doing some stabbing yourself tonight, old man?"

Andre's brows drew together. "I'm in no mood for crude jests, Etien."

Rochefort promptly sobered. "Sorry." He looked Andre up and down. "Are you all right?"

The wound had begun to sting like hell. Andre grunted.

"Only a scratch. Thank you for saving my hide."

Rochefort chuckled. "I think it's Fardeau's hide I saved, not yours. I have yet to repay my little debt to you, *Monsieur le commandant*."

Andre watched him try the door to ensure that it was locked and rubbed his throbbing temples, recalling that sweltering July day five years earlier when he'd first encountered Etien Rochefort.

It was in the Egyptian desert, some distance from where the French army was camped in El Rahmaniya. Andre was delivering a dispatch when he came across three Bedouins holding a Frenchman at swordpoint against a ruined hovel, jabbing him now and then with their scimitars while laughing and pointing to a body that lay facedown in the sand, evidently the soldier's companion, obviously dead.

Never in his life would Andre forget the look of disdain on the red-haired seventeen-year-old's face as he gazed down at his tormentors, oblivious of the blood oozing from several gashes in his arms and torso. Nor would he forget young Rochefort's lethal dexterity with the sword Andre tossed him. Or the silent tears Etien shed while they buried his dead brother when it was over.

That Andre was twenty-one and an officer hadn't mattered; the incident forged a bond between them that transcended rank and age. Upon their return home, Andre had discreetly used his contacts to obtain a position for his friend as one of Bavard's many assistants, knowing that, when the time came, Rochefort would help him further his plans. He hadn't been disillusioned.

"What are you doing here?" he asked.

Rochefort's hazel eyes danced. "Bavard sent me to follow you and inform him of your every move. Sagacious of him, was it not?"

"Very." Andre frowned. Was this a stroke of luck, or another of Bavard's notorious schemes? "Who's keeping watch over Madame Serin?"

"Bavard is moving both hostages to the Conciergerie." Rochefort's gaze met Andre's. "Don't worry, I've already sent word to the governor of the prison. He is a friend of mine."

He pointed to a chair. "Let me have a look at your so-called scratch."

Andre sat. Rochefort ground out an expletive. "You should have that tended to."

Andre shrugged. "I've suffered worse."

Rochefort lowered himself into the armchair across from Andre's, regarding him quizzically. "May I ask why you were out prowling the corridors tonight?"

Andre glowered at him. "You may."

He said no more. Rochefort grinned, then leaned back in his chair and crossed his arms, obviously enjoying himself immensely.

Andre's eyes narrowed. "Don't do this, Etien."

His friend regarded him with feigned innocence. "What am I doing?"

"Gloating."

"Damn right, I am." Rochefort nodded emphatically. "That woman is the answer to my prayers. I feared for your well-being, man."

"Lower your voice." Andre glanced warily toward the connecting door. "Better yet, keep quiet altogether."

Rochefort did no such thing. "That monklike regimen you imposed on yourself would have sent me straight to Charenton, with all the other lunatics." His disapproving gaze fell to Andre's left hand. "Still wearing that, I see."

Andre smiled bitterly. "I'm married."

This time, it was Rochefort who scowled. "That is another woman's wedding ring, Andre."

Andre's mouth twisted. "It serves its purpose."

"And what might that be? A constant reminder of your imagined culpability? For God's sake, it's been two years!"

Andre said nothing. Rochefort spread his arms in an exasperated gesture. "It wasn't your fault! There wasn't a damn thing you could have done to prevent what happened; I've told you that a thousand times."

Andre slumped forward, buried his face in his hands, and shook his head, suddenly feeling drained. "I don't want to discuss this, Etien."

Rochefort lapsed into silence, which proved to be, as usual, short-lived. "How is she?" he asked softly.

Andre rolled his eyes. The man never gave up. He rose and wandered to the fireplace, shoving his hands into his pockets. "She looks at me as if I'm Lucifer."

"I gather you don't mean Lucifer, the morning star. Is that why you were in the hallway?"

Andre stared blindly into the flames. Part of him sorely wished Rochefort didn't know so damned much. The other part welcomed the genuine concern. The man was as close to a brother as he would ever have. "That wasn't the only reason. I found—"

Someone scratched at the door. Andre shut his mouth so fast, his teeth clicked.

Rochefort winked. "That is Suzanne, bringing the Hennessy I asked for, I hope. You look as if you could use a drink."

"Only one?" One corner of Andre's mouth curved up wryly as he returned to his chair.

Rochefort leaped to his feet and bounded to the door. Presently, a buxom little maid followed him inside. She spied Andre across the room and giggled. Boldly giving him an appraising glance, she turned to Rochefort and murmured something that made him laugh softly and chuck her under the chin.

"Sorry to disappoint you, *chérie,*" he said. "Trust me, the monsieur would never consent to such a thing."

The maid batted her lashes, grinned to reveal too-small white teeth, and made a sound deep in her throat. "Mmm... Cognac gives one a voracious appetite," she cooed.

There was no doubt as to her meaning. Rochefort reached out and gave her rump a playful tweak. The maid squealed and slapped his hand away, but it was a halfhearted gesture. Suddenly feeling like an intruder, Andre surged to his feet.

"Don't go yet." Rochefort gestured with the bottle of Hennessy. "I have something for you."

Andre opened his mouth to protest, but Rochefort silenced him with a look that clearly said he didn't mean the cognac. Reluctantly, Andre sank back down into the cushions. Damn. Twenty minutes were almost up; too late to go downstairs and inquire about that champagne. Why hadn't he thought to ask the servant to find out who'd sent it? He'd been too shocked by the sight of it, that's why.

Rochefort uncorked the bottle, poured amber liquid into two glasses, and handed one to him. "What do you have to offer?" he asked the maid, his gaze trained on her ample bosom.

"Our chef fares from Auxerre," Suzanne purred. "He makes a very gratifying rabbit terrine."

Rochefort's eyes gleamed. "With pickles?"

Her answering throaty laugh assaulted Andre's ears, and he averted his gaze, swallowing a mouthful of cognac so that he wouldn't retch. He didn't understand what drove decent men like Rochefort to seek carnal pleasures with women such as this one. The mere thought of a meaningless animal coupling with a stranger had always repulsed Andre.

He eyed the maid over the rim of his glass, noting that her breasts sagged and her hands were red and large. An image flickered before him, of white hands gliding over slender legs, of high, firm breasts, of tiny feet with small, pink toes. He ground his teeth and willed himself to think of something else.

"Rabbit pâté sounds good," Rochefort was saying. He gripped Suzanne by the elbow and steered her toward the door. "And don't forget to bring up something for yourself, *ma belle.*"

The maid tittered, her eyes glittering as she lowered her gaze to brazenly regard Rochefort's groin. "Oh, that I will, monsieur, I promise."

When he had locked the door behind her, Rochefort rubbed his hands together. "And now, la pièce de résistance." He bent, reached into his boot, and produced a tightly rolled parchment. "I believe this is something you need," he said, passing it to Andre.

"What's this?"

"The map."

Andre's eyes widened. "*The* map?"

Rochefort nodded and flashed a triumphant grin. "The very one."

Andre stared at him in disbelief. "How—"

"You'd be surprised, the wealth of information one obtains

by sleeping with the mistresses of certain people." He shook his head in answer to Andre's raised brows. "I'm sworn to secrecy, so don't even ask."

Andre tossed back the rest of his drink and carefully unrolled the yellowed paper, which crackled and crumbled at the edges as he did so. He traced the faded lettering with his index finger. "I'll be damned." He stood and turned it toward the light, elation racing through his veins. "Why didn't you give it to me back at the chateau?"

Rochefort sipped his drink. "I didn't have it then. I picked it up on the way here, which is why I arrived late and came upon you and Fardeau in the corridor, thank God."

Andre cuffed his friend's shoulder. "Etien, do you realize what this means?"

"Mm-hmm. We've got the bastards by the *couilles*." Rochefort refilled Andre's glass and raised his own. "To the First Consul!"

"To everlasting peace, God willing," Andre added, swiping up his snifter and touching it to Rochefort's with a clink.

Rochefort's eyes twinkled. He raised his glass even higher. "To your new wife. May she fall madly in love with you and incessantly warm your—"

"Shut up and drink, Etien."

Dominique pressed her ear still closer to the connecting door, her mind reeling from all she'd overheard. Myriad questions spun in her head. She never forgot a voice, and she'd promptly identified the tenor pitch as Rochefort's. Obviously, Montville was good friends with the guard.

Curse Rochefort to perdition. Were it not for him, she would now be on her way to Colette's with this Fardeau, and in possession of the medallion, too. Something tightened in her chest. She'd heard the skirmish in the hallway. How badly was Montville hurt? She frowned. Why did she care? The man had said he hadn't meant to kill him. Was that why Montville hadn't killed Fardeau?

She strained to catch what the two men were saying, hoping to learn where they were headed and what they planned to do with this mysterious map they were so glad to have obtained.

But they only praised the cognac, and then their voices lowered to a murmur that even her keen ears couldn't discern. She thought she caught a few words about, of all things, swords.

Dominique rolled her eyes. Men. Trust them to discuss trivialities at a time like this. She concentrated on what she'd already heard and tried to make sense of what she had found out, only to end up with more questions. How did Montville know of Colette Desfieux? Dear Colette; she'd tried to send help, after all. A pity Fardeau's men had failed to rescue Madame.

The Conciergerie was a prison in Paris, she knew, the very one where Marie Antoinette had awaited her execution. It would be harder to ransom her from there, but as prisons went, that one was better than the horrible Tour Ronde. And Demaitre. And Bavard. Dominique shuddered.

As for Montville, the man was an enigma. Like a monk, Rochefort had said. What had impelled him to live that way? What was this guilt he'd harbored for two years? Two years. Dominique could not suppress a smile. No wonder the man had all but attacked her in the coach. If he'd been celibate for that long, it surely was of his own volition, and not from lack of attention from the opposite sex.

She'd have to be more careful. A man in his condition was like a gunpowder keg. One spark, and all would be ablaze. She knew enough about such things from overhearing Paul talk with his friends.

Booted feet stomped in the hallway. Immediately, light footsteps sounded in the adjoining room. Heart tripping, Dominique shoved herself away from the door and quickly tiptoed to the bed. Flinging herself upon it, she squeezed her eyes shut, feigning sleep.

She was quite desperate for a bath, but the idea of taking one with Montville present alarmed her, although there was a privacy screen in the corner. She must have been mad, requesting a tub. Unable to stand the filth a moment longer, she'd made good use of the washbasin and Montville's soap as soon as he'd closed the door behind him. She'd donned a clean chemise and dress, and that would have to do, for now.

She heard a soft knock on the door. Mad heartbeats later,

the key turned in the lock. Through her lashes, she caught a glimpse of Montville looming in the doorway, a blanket draped over his arm.

"My wife is asleep," she heard him murmur.

"What of the hot water, monsieur?"

A rustle of paper. "For your trouble." A pause. "Please tell the innkeeper she'll require a bath tomorrow morning."

The door closed softly. Again, she heard the grating of the lock. Her eyelids began to flutter, and she willed them to be still. It seemed like an eternity before he moved. She sensed him drawing nearer, though he trod lightly, his boot heels hardly clicking despite the parquet floor. Her fingers curled, the nails digging into the sheets. What if he should pounce on her?

He came to a halt beside the bed. For agonizing seconds, Dominique heard nothing but the sputter of candlewax and the crackle of the fire above the wild thud of her heart. She lay there, petrified, the intensity of his presence ravaging her nerves. Just when she thought she might snap, he sighed. She felt him draw the blanket over her and tuck it snugly about her shoulders.

Only when he snuffed out the candles and moved away did Dominique allow her knotted muscles to relax. Fatigue washed over her in a wave of dizziness. She thought she heard the sound of distant thunder. She drew air into her constricted lungs, breathing the scent of freshly laundered linen, feeling as if she were spiraling down into a bottomless pit.

The curtains. Montville had not drawn the bed curtains. She tried to summon strength to fight her exhaustion but found she could no longer ward off sleep. Some part of her mind perceived the rumbling again. And then the black void claimed her.

Careful to make as little noise as possible, Andre tossed his blanket down before the fireplace, stripped off his soiled cravat and shirt, and then ambled to the window and gazed out into the darkness. He fingered the map in his pocket and watched the night briefly become day, illuminated by a streak of lightning. Thunder boomed in the distance. The wind picked up and became a steady howl. A fitting end to this day, he thought, studying the violently swaying trees outside. And a fitting beginning to the most crucial mission of his life.

He heard a soft moan from the bed and forced himself to continue facing the window. If only he could go do this alone. If only he weren't responsible for her safety. He'd told Fardeau he could protect her. The truth was, he didn't know whether he could. God knew, he'd failed before. Whatever excuses Rochefort found, Mimi's death had been his fault, and no one could convince him otherwise.

Rain began to fall so hard that Andre could barely see through the heavy drops pelting the glass. He heard another whimper above the patter. He turned to see a huddled little form quivering under the covers. What was wrong with her? A nightmare?

Lightning streaked across the sky again, throwing a flash of silver light into the room. He'd taken two steps toward the bed when a deafening crack rattled the windows. Uttering a scream that made his blood thicken, the woman tore off her covers. In one flying leap she was on her feet, colliding with him with a force that knocked the wind out of his lungs. Instinctively, he grabbed her and crushed her to his body, barely managing to keep the both of them from falling over.

"Paul!" Her voice was hoarse.

His arms tightened around her. She shook so hard that her teeth chattered. His hand moved along her back and settled between her shoulder blades, stroking gently. She stood there in his embrace, her small hands propped upon his chest, her body racked with tremors, bringing such fierce protectiveness welling within him that Andre doubted he could loosen his hold on her if she asked him to. She didn't.

He cupped her head and gently pressed her cheek to his chest. "It's only a storm. Nothing to fear. The roof will hold, I think."

Another flash of lightning. Andre thought he felt her push at him. Immediately, he let his arms drop to his sides and took a small step back. She remained facing him, her hands tight fists, her eyes trained on the window. She looked, he thought, as if she were in shock.

80

He watched her drop to her knees, clap her hands over her ears, and curl into a ball, her forehead nearly touching the floor. Just before the thunder boomed, he threw himself down beside her. *"Petite,"* he murmured. "Little one. Let me hold you."

Light flooded the room again. He felt her hand grasp his, nails biting into his palm. And then she flung herself into his arms. For an instant Andre was so stunned, he couldn't move. Then his arms closed around her, gathering her close, and as he cradled her head against his heart and murmured mindless, soothing words into her hair above the rumbling thunderclaps, he realized that he was shaking just as violently as she was.

Her hands slid up around his neck, her fingers locking at his nape as if she never meant to let him go. "Make it stop," she said in an anguished little voice. "Oh, God, please make it—"

"I'm here, *petite,*" he whispered. "Nothing will harm you while I live and breathe." He brushed a kiss atop her head and rocked her slowly back and forth. "I won't let anything happen to you, I swear."

She relaxed a little, but still, she quivered. He buried his fingers in her silky hair, his thumb stroking the tender skin at her throat, feeling the rapid drumming of her pulse. Still holding her close, he shifted his weight to one hip and stretched out his legs, then drew her into his lap. She snuggled against him and buried her face into the hollow at his throat. Chest tight with emotions he fought to suppress, Andre rested his cheek against her hair, feeling wild heartbeats against his ribs. He couldn't say whether they were hers or his own.

With every lightning bolt, she winced and tightened her grip on him, and Andre soothed and caressed her as if she were a frightened child. After a while, there was only the patter of rain. When her constant shivering became an occasional shudder, he knew that it was time to let her go. He didn't want to. Not yet.

"Are you cold?"

She nodded, her cheek soft and warm against his naked chest.

"Do you want to return to bed?"

81

Her head snapped back. She squinted to discern his features in the weak light of the dying fire. He felt her go rigid and start to draw away.

"I'll put another log on the fire," he muttered, releasing her and rising.

Why did he suddenly feel uncomfortable, as if he'd been doing something wrong? He picked up the poker and stirred the flames, then tossed a piece of wood into the grate. From the corner of his eye, he saw her draw herself up and head for the washstand, her gait a bit unsteady.

In silence, he watched her splash water on her cheeks, then pick up a towel and bury her face in it, her shoulders slowly rising and falling as she took one deep breath. Andre replaced the poker. "I don't suppose you want to tell me the reason why you're so terrified of storms."

She lowered the cloth. "You're right. I don't." Her voice held a slight tremor.

"Then I won't ask."

She nodded. "Thank you."

His eyes took in her face, her long black hair, the high-waisted dress she wore, tinted orange by the firelight. A different dress. He wondered what color it really was. He wondered who she really was. When his eyes returned to hers, he realized that she was staring in dismay at his bare chest. His lips twitched. "I'll put on a shirt if you want me to."

He noticed an odd glitter in her eyes before she looked up, her hands restlessly pleating her skirts. "No need to trouble yourself."

Squaring her shoulders, she went back to the bed, grabbed a pillow, and tossed it his way. He caught it without looking, trying hard not to smile at the woman who, despite her visible struggle to regain her composure, still looked and sounded much like a terrified little girl.

"Good night, monsieur." She motioned with her chin toward the blanket at his feet. "I hope you sleep well on the floor."

He watched her climb back into the four-poster and yank the curtains shut. Frowning, he lay down and drew the blanket over himself, shifting uncomfortably on the hard parquet. He propped the pillow behind his head and stared at the ceiling. Much as he wanted to deny it, it had felt good to shelter her in his arms. And that admission alone was proof that he was losing self-control.

His ears detected a low groan. He jerked upright. Was she all right? Should he get up and—

Another moan. A muffled giggle. "Ah, yes, like *that*," a husky male voice urged. "Unh . . . My . . . oh, yes!"

Oh, no. Andre smothered a groan of his own and flopped back down, then rolled onto his side and glared at the connecting door, making a mental note to kill Rochefort, come morning.

"Good, hmm? Didn't Suzanne promise you paradise?"

"Don't stop, *chérie!* Dammit, why did you stop?"

Another giggle. "Patience, monsieur. Don't curse. We've only just begun. We have all night."

All night, Andre fumed.

"That's right." Rochefort groaned. "Wait . . . come here . . . I want to—"

From the direction of the bed, Andre heard a creak, then the rustle of bedclothes. A wicked smile curved his lips. So, Madame Montville could hear them, too. Good. He hoped she was enjoying this as much as he was.

Impassioned gasps and cries ensued, growing louder and more frenzied with each excruciating minute. Andre tossed and turned, trying in vain to find a comfortable position.

"Monsieur!" came Suzanne's shrill voice after a while. "Ahhh—aaa!"

More rustling. Andre glanced at the bed. The curtains fluttered. Squeezing his eyes shut, he snatched up his pillow and slammed it over his head.

Chapter Seven

It was the quickest bath she'd ever taken.

Dominique rubbed her head with a towel, then tossed the cloth over the edge of the brass tub and hurried to her trunk, running her fingers through her damp hair as she went.

Sunlight streamed through the windows, her just-scrubbed cheeks tingled, and the aroma of fresh eggs and buttery brioche teased her nostrils. She hadn't wanted to leave the blissful warmth of the hot water, and now she longed to stop and eat some of the luscious fare the servants had brought in with her bath, but she had no idea how long Montville would be gone, and time was of the essence.

Fingers clumsy because of her haste, she pinned up her hair, pulled on a pair of stockings, then wriggled into a clean chemise and snatched up the only other morning gown she'd packed, a square-necked white frock that buttoned in the back. It smelled of lavender and home. The scent served to strengthen her resolve to proceed with the plan that had dawned on her a half-hour earlier, when she'd awoken to the sounds of Montville's deep voice and servants shuffling around the room.

Once the room was quiet, she'd peeked between the curtains, only to see Montville half-nude again, shoving one arm into the sleeve of another pristine shirt. Her heart had stopped. Because Madame's medallion was no longer around his neck.

What had he done with it? The question raced through her mind as she struggled to push the slippery buttons through what seemed to be a hundred tiny eyelets. Her arms and shoulders ached from the strain. She managed to fasten most of them, but still, the portion at the middle of her back gaped open.

She grabbed a golden brioche and, sinking her teeth into it, eyed Montville's baggage, which he had packed before he'd left the room. Dared she go through with this? With her free hand, she pulled on the pair of white kid slippers she'd laid aside, her eyes trained on the trunk in question. A handsome trunk. Nary a scratch on the black leather. The brass latch gleamed as if it had just been polished.

Dominique swallowed the last of her brioche around the lump of panic growing in her throat. She was about to commit a grave violation of Montville's privacy, she knew. But if there was the slightest chance she'd find the medallion among his things . . . Taking a deep breath, she dusted the crumbs off her fingers and reached for the latch. She pulled on it.

Locked.

What to do? Gnawing at the inside of her cheek in frustration, Dominique mindlessly clutched at her chignon, which felt as if it was about to come undone. Her fingers closed around a hairpin. Of course! She'd once seen Paul unlock a door like this. How different could a trunk latch be?

She yanked the tortoiseshell pin free, snapped it in half, and tossed the shorter piece aside, not caring that her wet hair tumbled down and plastered to her neck like a cold compress. Frowning in concentration, she inserted the sharp end into the lock, then slowly worked it up, down, and around.

A click.

Feeling much like a thief, Dominique pulled out the pin and tried the latch again. This time, it flipped open easily. A quick surge of excitement made her breath catch in her throat.

She lifted the heavy lid. The smell of him, that scent she was beginning to know and like more than she cared to admit, rose to her nostrils.

Deep purple silk. She ran her fingers over the luxurious lining of the trunk lid, surveyed the white shirts resting within, and smiled. They were folded to the millimeter, as only a tailor or a valet could fold a gentleman's shirt. But Montville was no *valet de chambre*.

Apparently, he didn't need one, either, for all his other clothes were packed just as neatly. Doing her best not to disturb the tidy stacks, Dominique quickly inspected the contents of the trunk, her ears tuned for Montville's footsteps in the corridor.

Five cravats. Buff moleskin breeches. One coat, with silver buttons, just like the one he'd worn the other day. Gray kidskin gloves. An image of his strong hands flitted through Dominique's mind, and she resolutely pushed it away and dug deeper. A toilette set: razor, shaving soap . . . She picked up a small greenish bottle and glanced at the lettering. Hungary water. So this was the herbal fragrance he used.

Suppressing the urge to unplug the bottle and take a sniff, Dominique hastily replaced the kit and leaned closer, her cheek grazing the fine lawn of one shirt. Near the bottom of the trunk, her hand bumped into something hard, covered by rough cotton fabric. Some sort of sack. She tugged at the drawstring and encountered smooth leather.

His boots. Was the medallion inside one of them? Pushing back his clothes with one hand, she pulled out the sack and lifted one shiny black boot by its top. How huge it was! Yet, on his foot, the same boot looked quite normal.

She groped inside both pairs, but came upon nothing. Swiftly, she moved to put the satchel back where she had found it. Something sharp pricked her finger. Flinching, she jerked her hand away, raised her fist, and inspected the red droplet oozing from the pad of her right thumb.

Letting out a sigh of exasperation, Dominique brought her thumb to her mouth and sucked on it, then ran her uninjured hand along the inside of the trunk, seeking the object that had stuck her. In a concealed side pocket she had overlooked, she found it.

It was a medal. She knew it even without looking at the face. Large enough to fill her palm, the silvered, star-shaped decoration glimmered in her hand, defying the faded scrap of red, white, and blue ribbon to which it was attached. Engraved along the bottom border, beneath the pin, was the inscription: *"To Le Comte D'Arné, Defender of Liberty. With immeasurable gratitude. Gen. George Washington, Valley Forge, 1777."*

Why would Napoleon's best spy keep something belonging to a count? Brow furrowed in bafflement, Dominique studied the elegant script for a moment before shrugging and setting about searching for more. She came upon a sheaf of wrinkled papers, secured with a wide pink ribbon. The edges were worn, indicating that they'd been read often. Intrigued, she sat on her heels and skimmed the one on top, written in a graceful feminine hand.

My dearest Andre,
Once again, mon amour, *I feel compelled to write you, since our precious time together seems nonexistent of late. I wake each morning with the hope that this will be the joyous day when you return to me. . . .*

Dominique felt her face grow warm. She shouldn't be reading this. Unable to stop herself, she glanced at the signature.

I live for you, my love.
Your ever devoted wife, Mimi

A loud hammering made Dominique start and clutch the letters to her chest.

"Attention, Julien!" a male voice bellowed in the adjoining chamber. "You're going to bash somebody's skull with that accursed hammer! *Espèce d'idiot!* I told you—"

Dominique's shoulders sagged with relief. She cast a guilty look over her shoulder. It was high time she ceased this exploration.

The hammering resumed. She leaned headfirst into the trunk and was about to replace the letters when something round and shiny slipped from between them. Her heart skipped. The medallion! No. A finely crafted gold locket, encrusted with amethysts and emeralds arranged to resemble a cluster of violets. Tiny yellow topaz chips winked in the center of each flower. "How beautiful," she breathed.

Etched on the back was an intricate blazon. The locket must have belonged to Montville's wife.

In the next chamber, the rhythmic hammering stopped.

Silence fell. And then, behind her, the door slammed.

"Spying on a spy, madame?"

Good God. Montville.

Dominique's head came up so fast, she banged it on the edge of the trunk lid. Tears sprang to her eyes. Shoving the locket between her breasts, she swung upright and whirled to face him, the thud of the trunk lid falling shut a mocking testimony to her guilt.

Never in her life had Dominique seen such controlled rage. He stood there, dark blue eyes blazing, hands propped upon his hips. As she stared at him in paralyzed trepidation, she could have sworn she saw the air shimmer around the man. But then, her head still reeled and throbbed from the hard blow it had taken.

Unable to withstand the violence in his eyes, she let her own gaze drop to his feet. Tall, black boots. Snug charcoal breeches. Over his shirt, he wore a navy waistcoat, discreetly embroidered in silvered thread with what looked like snarling panthers. Tucked in a dove-gray sash wrapped twice around his narrow waist was . . .

A tingle shot up her spine. *Grand Dieu.* A pistol. Her gaze snapped back to his.

His eyes flashed. *"Eh, bien?"*

He took one menacing step toward her, then another.

She cleared her throat, resolving not to be afraid of him. "What do you want to know?" Somehow, she managed to make her legs move backward.

"Let us begin with how you gained access to my locked *coffre.*" His voice was taut. So was his body, which seemed to grow larger and more powerful with every swift stride he took toward her.

His gaze dropped to the floor. He spied a broken piece of tortoiseshell and flicked it aside in passing with the tip of one boot. His eyes glittered like twin blue glaciers when they returned to hers. "How very clever."

Her palms grew moist. She sought to move faster, but Montville quickly overtook her, because he took only one stride for every two of hers. To her dismay, her back suddenly met solid wall, and there was nowhere left to go.

"What were you looking for?"

He smelled of soap, clean air, and coffee. And he'd been consuming those peppermints of his. He planted himself before her, long legs braced apart, then leaned close and propped both hands on the wall on either side of her head.

For what seemed forever, he waited. He wasn't touching her, but if she moved a hairbreadth, her breasts would graze his middle. When he next spoke, his voice was a shade lower. "Let me rephrase that. Why were you looking?"

She drew her tongue across her lips. "You are my husband, and I know nothing of you."

Surprise flickered in his eyes. He nodded. "Granted."

His milder tone gave her assurance to go on. "I have been forced to place my life and, indirectly, the lives of those I love, in the hands of a man who is a mystery." Thoughts of Paul and Madame lent her more courage. "What would you have done, monsieur, were you in my position?"

She realized her mistake when she saw his jaw tense. "I am the injured party here. I'll ask the questions." He tipped his head. "For someone who holds another to his word, you certainly do go back on yours quite easily."

Her neck already ached from the awkward angle required to look up at him. The muscles there tightened further when he looked pointedly at the bed, then back at her. "What if I were to do the same?" he asked.

She swallowed. "I didn't ask you any questions."

"No. You sought answers on your own. Far worse, because I had no option regarding what I wished to unveil or conceal."

He was so close that she could feel his breath fanning her cheek. "What did you find?"

She quelled an overwhelming urge to squirm, and madly sought for some reply that would appease him.

His frown was ominous. "Dammit, woman! Do not attempt to feed me an untruth." He wasn't shouting. On the contrary, the suppressed anger in his voice made it lower. Deeper. "I'll tolerate anything, with the exception of a lie. Now, tell me, what—"

"You don't own any hats!"

Even as she blurted out the words, Dominique was stunned by them. And so was Montville, apparently, for he blinked once, then stared at her as if he thought her daft. "Hats?"

She swallowed. "Hats, *chapeaux-bras*. Like the one the First Consul wears."

A glint of amusement warmed the blue fire in his eyes. "Hats," he repeated.

She nodded. "I haven't seen you wear one. And there weren't any in your trunk." She wished she didn't sound so breathless.

Gradually, Montville's expression gentled. He made a muffled sound she hoped was smothered laughter. "I should hope not. The cursed things remind me of inverted chamber pots."

An image of Napoleon adorned in such an outrageous fashion caused a laugh to rise in Dominique's throat. Given her nervousness, it was impossible to keep it from escaping.

A corner of Montville's handsome mouth curved up in something just short of a smile. "Appeals to you, does it, that notion? When I next see him, I will inform him of your novel ideas regarding gentlemen's attire."

She hazarded a smile back at him. "And I won't hesitate to tell him my inspiration comes from you."

He studied her in silence. "Madame," he finally said softly, "I would relinquish whatever is left of my immortal soul to Satan in exchange for the privilege of inspiring you, just once."

She didn't know how to respond. Her gaze dropped to his throat, only partially visible because of his cravat. A sudden memory of burying her face in the curve of that strong neck made Dominique's cheeks grow warm. He'd been so tender . . . and later, when she'd climbed back into bed . . . *mon Dieu*. Her cheeks grew hotter at the recollection of the shocking noises and the thoughts she'd harbored.

He took a deep breath and expelled it, very slowly. "Your curiosity was justified, given the situation. It's partly my fault, I suppose. I'm sorry."

Dominique could hardly believe her ears. She looked into his face, intending to say that it was she who owed him an apology, only to have the words die on her lips when she saw that his lashes were lowered. Montville was studying her breasts. Intently.

She should have been mortified, yet the shudder that rippled through her was not exactly shame. What it was, she couldn't say. She only knew that she'd felt it the night before, in the coach, when he had tried to kiss her.

"What's that?" he asked.

"What?"

Dominique looked down. To her chagrin, she saw the end of a gold chain dangling from her bodice. The locket.

"I tried to put it back," she whispered. "It slipped out of . . ."

She closed her mouth. Methodical as he was, Montville surely knew exactly where he had put his late wife's locket. And now he also knew that she'd been reading Mimi's love letters.

His fingertips brushed the ribbon trim of her décolletage. Dominique closed her eyes, suddenly awash in contrition. He grasped the end of the chain and pulled. Her skin tingled as the locket slowly slid between her breasts. She felt a rush of cold air as he stepped back.

In the silence that ensued, all she could hear was the erratic pounding of her heart and the sound of Montville's breathing. Unable to withstand the tension any longer, she opened her eyes, bracing herself against the wrath she knew she'd find in Montville's stare. What she saw, however, made her heart contract. Dark head bent, Montville was contemplating the object that flashed in his hand, a faraway expression on his beautiful face.

He ran his thumb over the crest and then across the word engraved below it. "It was my mother's." He spoke so softly that she could hardly hear him. He turned the locket over in his palm and gazed at the green and violet jewels on the front before flicking it open, removing something from within, and snapping it shut.

"She wanted me to give this to my wife." Stepping forward, Montville took Dominique's left hand. "I never . . . no other woman has worn it before."

With that, he slipped a slender band around her ring finger. Dominique looked down at her hand. Four round-cut emeralds and three diamonds caught the light and sparkled as he released her fingers. "Monsieur," she whispered, "I cannot—"

"It was her wedding band," he interrupted. "Now, it is yours."

Dominique's throat constricted. "But I have nothing to give you in return," she said.

He shook his head. "Oh, but you do." Somberly, he slipped the locket over her head, then reached around to draw her hair from underneath the chain. "Give me your trust, madame, and I shall want for nothing more."

He bowed his head. She felt his warm breath on the bared skin of her bosom. Reverently, he raised the locket and touched it to his lips before letting it nestle in the hollow at the base of her throat. The metal was still warm from his touch.

When his head came up, Dominique thought that his eyes were misty, but she wasn't certain, because tears blurred her own vision. She felt unworthy. She also felt ashamed for having behaved so badly toward him, when all he had done was extricate her from Bavard's clutches and treat her well. "Monsieur . . . about our agreement . . ."

He looked at her, his blue eyes questioning. She held out both her hands. He hesitated, then reached out and clasped them firmly between his own.

"The hour grows late," he said. "Let us collect our things. The coach is waiting."

*   *   *

"Of all the inopportune times for one of my horses to require a new shoe," Montville muttered under his breath.

In spite of Montville's understandable aggravation, Dominique was secretly thankful for the delay; she had been loath to be confined again so soon, if only for a few hours, in his luxurious coach.

A gentle breeze stirred the ties of her bonnet. She turned her face toward the heavens, loving the clear blue skies and the rays of sun that warmed and caressed her cheeks, and greedily drank in the crisp morning air. But though the sounds of whickering horses and the scents of soil and damp hay were soothing in their familiarity, Dominique was as far from content as she was from home.

Strolling down the tree-lined path this way, her fingers resting on his arm, it would be easy to forget that Montville was her enemy, especially when what he'd done upstairs had raised more doubts in her mind about his motives and intentions. Had it merely been an act to gain her trust? If so, his performance had certainly been worthy of the Théâtre Français.

Two flocks of birds soared through the air, passed above her head, then slowly descended, circling, to finally rest upon the branches of a nearby tree. Immediately, the courtyard was filled with raucous chatter and the sound of flapping wings.

"*Sansonnets,*" Montville said. "Starlings."

She shielded her eyes with her palm and studied the glossy black birds. "How can you tell?"

"See the pointed bills, short tails, and iridescent plumage? Typical of the family *Sturnidae, genus Sturnus.* They're a gregarious sort. They're common in France, and throughout all of Europe, if I recall correctly."

"They're very lively."

"If by lively you mean brazen and belligerent, yes."

Dominique looked up at him. If possible, he was more handsome by the light of day. His chestnut hair shone in the sun, and she found herself wondering how it would feel to run her fingers through it. Her heart lurched at the thought. She looked into his eyes, which made the color of the sky seem dull by comparison, and suddenly felt the need to learn more about Andre Montville. "You seem to know much about birds."

"I studied them incessantly when I was young. My brother and I used to borrow my mother's lorgnette and wander through the woods for hours in search of new ones to add to our list." A smile tugged at the corners of his mouth, but Dominique could clearly see grief lurking in his eyes. "We'd drive poor *Maman* mad with worry. She was afraid we'd end up in some cave, at the mercy of hungry brown bears, and it was useless to insist that they'd be more interested in beehives and blackberry bushes than in two gaunt boys."

She raised her brows. "You have a brother?"

Beneath her hand, she felt his arm muscles contract. "Had. He died . . . some time ago."

A foggy recollection of her mother's body lying motionless in a coffin drifted through Dominique's mind. Her chest tightened. "An illness?"

He grimaced. "No. Victor was murdered."

The vivid image of her father's bloody corpse, compounded with the thought of Paul ending up the same way, struck Dominique like a kick to the stomach. She gripped Montville's arm more tightly, wishing there were something she could say to ease his pain, but well aware that such words did not exist. "I'm sorry," she managed to whisper.

He nodded curtly, then turned his head and took a deep breath. When he looked down at her again, his features were impassive. "As I said, it happened long ago."

His tone was as dispassionate as his expression. Dominique took this as an indication that the subject was closed and fell silent, listening to the crunch of gravel beneath her slippers and Montville's boots.

"Let us see whether the farrier has finished." Montville led her in the direction of the stables. He glanced over his shoulder, and Dominique felt uneasiness emanating from him as if it were a tangible thing. "It's high time we departed," he said. "Our destination is quite a ways from here, and I want to cover as much ground as possible before nightfall."

"Where are we going?"

He frowned. "I cannot—"

"I shouldn't have asked," she interrupted quickly. "Our agreement—"

"Is quite absurd, if we insist on following it to the letter." He halted, then turned to face her and caught both her hands. "We are about to spend a great deal of time together. If we are going to get along, we must communicate. Impossible, if we are constantly worried about touching one another and asking questions." His gaze fell to the ring upon her finger. "You've made a concession. It is my turn to do the same. I'll answer as many questions as I can, save for the ones that would endanger lives." He swept a glance over the length of her, a frown creasing his brow again. "What I can tell you is that we're headed for colder climes. I don't suppose you've packed anything suitable for freezing temperatures."

She looked down at the dark green velvet coat she wore. "Only this."

He shook his head. "Not warm enough. We must stop somewhere along the way and acquire some proper clothing. I believe I—"

He stopped abruptly. His gaze flicked to the left, eyes widening as he focused on the trunk of an oak across the path, his expression swiftly changing from concern to disbelief to horror. Dominique turned her head, barely catching a glimpse of a brown-clad figure holding something that glinted in the sun before Montville grabbed her by the shoulders and shoved her down.

She crashed to her knees. Pain knifed through her thighs and lower back, so intense that she gave a strangled cry. Time seemed to slow to a crawl, and she dug her nails into the gravel, overcome by an eerie sensation of unreality as Montville followed her down. Something whooshed overhead, and when he finally hit the ground beside her, Dominique heard a thwack above the sound of air rushing out of his lungs.

A second later he was up again, balancing on one knee as he whipped out his pistol.

A click. He aimed. Too late. The figure whirled and disappeared behind the oak.

"Villain diable," he gritted through his teeth.

Out of the corner of her eye, she saw someone burst out of the trees and tear across the path in pursuit of the archer, dust and gravel flying beneath his boots. Halfway, the man looked back at them and his hat toppled, revealing tousled hair that looked like a flaming torch. Rochefort, Dominique recognized.

Lunging sideways, Montville clamped an arm around her waist and hauled her against him. "Are you hurt?"

Dominique tore her gaze away from Rochefort's retreating back and stared into Montville's blue eyes, the hairs at the back of her neck bristling when she read the terror in them. She shook her head.

He expelled a harsh breath.

She moistened her dry lips. "What happened?"

"An arrow."

He motioned with his chin. She followed his gaze to the oak before which she'd been standing and saw the feathered end of a wooden stake protruding from its trunk.

Every muscle in her body turned to ice. Her heart squeezed painfully, sending blood rushing through her chest and limbs. She wanted to jump up and run, but to her horror, she found she couldn't move.

Angry voices drifted from somewhere beyond the trees. Montville thrust the pistol back into his sash and surged to his feet, taking her with him.

The pop of pistol fire. The cacophony of chattering birds and beating wings. Dominique clutched the lapels of Montville's coat and choked back a scream, her knees threatening to buckle.

Another shot. An ear-splitting screech. Dominique felt Montville's arms tighten around her in a death grip. He cast one last quick look about, then swept her up into his arms and dashed toward the stables.

Chapter Eight

In contrast to the bright sunlight outside, the stables seemed as dismal as the dungeon at Chateau Loches. Her head still spinning, Dominique clung to Montville, barely aware of her new surroundings. All she could see in her mind's eye was the faceless figure holding a taut bow, the metal arrow tip flashing, pointed directly at her head. Or at Montville's heart. A chill snaked up her spine.

Montville leaned against the wooden planks and exhaled sharply, still gripping her so tightly, it almost hurt. His greatcoat had parted, and through the layers of his clothing, she could detect the rapid thud of his heart. The brown-clad image filling her mind dissipated, replaced by a vision of Montville lying motionless in the grass, his blue eyes wide and sightless, a crimson stain slowly spreading around an arrow piercing his white shirt.

Dominique's pulse increased to a frenzied throb at her throat. How close he'd come to being killed.

He reached up and gently unclasped her stiff fingers from around his neck. The smell of leather, dried grass, and manure filled her nostrils, and when he set her down, her knees threatened to buckle. He caught her easily, drawing her firmly against him, then lunged sideways to peer out into the courtyard. She held her breath and listened but heard nothing except the soft nicker of a horse over the drumming in her ears.

After a moment, she felt some of the tension leave Montville's body. "No one," he murmured.

"But if we've been pursued—"

"I think not." He swung around to face her. "For now, we're safe."

She pressed her face into his chest and drew a ragged breath, reveling in the scratchy feel of his wool coat and its faint rosemary scent. "How can you be certain?"

"Instinct." His arm tightened around her waist. "Are you all right?"

Dominique nodded. Her knees still ached and her palms stung from being scraped raw by the gravel. He stroked her lower back. Instinctively, she closed her eyes and nuzzled his chest, soothed by the warmth of his body and the strength of his arms around her, not caring, for the moment, whom Montville really was or what he represented. She only knew that for the first time in many years, she felt protected.

He shuddered. "It almost happened again."

What was he talking about? Dominique glanced up and found him staring straight ahead, a haunted look on his beautiful face.

"This . . . this has happened to you before?" she asked.

Slowly, he tipped down his chin. His eyes were wide, almost glassy, the blue irises barely visible around dilated pupils.

"Who do you suppose tried to . . . ?" She gulped, unable to make her lips form the words.

"I haven't a clue." A muscle flexed at his jaw. "But I'll be damned if I will place your life in further jeopardy."

"*My* life? Do you think the attempt was directed at me?"

He didn't respond, only continued to scrutinize her face as if he meant to commit every freckle upon her nose to memory. Beneath her palms, she could feel his chest rapidly rising and falling with every labored breath he took. Unwittingly, she slipped her hands inside his waistcoat, plaiting fine lawn between her fingers, feeling the heat of his flesh through the smooth fabric. . . .

That was when she saw red smears on his white shirt. "You're hurt!" she cried.

He shook his head. "It's not—"

"But there is blood—"

"Blood?" He followed her gaze to his shirtfront and studied it for a moment. Frowning, he caught one of her hands and examined her fingertips.

Her eyes widened at the sight of blood beneath her nails. "What—" she began, then stopped, recalling last night's skirmish in the hallway. "Oh," she breathed, and reached up to touch the nape of his neck.

She came upon the oozing lesion there and gasped. He didn't so much as flinch, but the slight twitch at the corners of his mouth told her she'd caused him pain.

"I must have reopened it," Dominique whispered around constricted muscles in her throat. She brushed his jaw with the backs of her fingers. "I am so sorry."

For an interminable moment, he didn't move, nor blink, nor breathe. "Are you?" he finally asked in an odd voice.

She started to remove her hand, but he quickly covered it with his and kept it pressed against his cheek, and Dominique shuddered, suddenly awed and a little frightened by the hungry intensity with which he regarded her.

The next moment, he crushed her to him with a strength that stole her breath away, and as his thighs collided with her hips another rush surged through her. This time the hot, fluttering sensations spreading from her belly to her knees had more to do with the feel of him against her than with fear.

His gaze moved to the locket at her throat. Something akin to desperation glinted in his eyes, and with a heartfelt groan, he pressed a kiss into her palm before he let go of her hand, cupped the back of her head, and drew her upturned face to his in one swift movement.

Nothing could have prepared Dominique for the gentleness with which his mouth closed over hers. He paused for a heartbeat, as if to give her a chance to draw away, and when she didn't he angled his head and pressed onward, his warm lips sliding over hers, slowly, deliberately, as if he had all the time in the world and he intended to spend each moment doing this.

Senses reeling, lips tingling, she let her head fall back and propped her hands upon his chest, feeling as light and dizzy as if she were teetering on the edge of a cliff. She clung to his broad shoulders for support.

He raised his head a little. *"Embrasse-moi,"* he whispered against her mouth. "Kiss me. Kiss me back."

His rich voice had the effect of cognac on her already befuddled brain. "I—"

He silenced her with another kiss. She made a sound between a moan and a whimper and rose on tiptoe, letting her fingers twine in his hair, glorying in its silky texture, drawing him closer, wanting, needing. . . . His palms came around to caress her face, sending shivers along her neck that traveled to her breasts and made them tingle. She fitted herself even closer to his taut frame, heedless of the pistol digging between her breasts, while her lips parted and sipped at his, as if she could draw life and breath from him. She felt his belly lurch beneath her bosom and ceased to reason, abandoning herself completely to sensation, forgetting everything but the feel and taste of his mouth on hers. Moist. Soft. Sweet, with the faintest trace of peppermint.

Peppermint?

Dominique went rigid. My God! What was she doing, and with whom? "Mmnh—" She tore her mouth from his and wrenched out of his embrace, leaving him to stare down at her in evident confusion, his lips parted, his arms still open.

Dominique stepped back, suppressing the urge to bring a hand to her still-tingling lips. She watched him let his arms drop to his sides and briefly clench his fists.

What sort of madness had possessed her, allowing him to kiss her thus? Bavard's hideous yellow grin drifted across her mind, and Dominique felt her already flushed face turn scarlet. A thousand times a fool, that's what she was.

Her entire body still trembled. She waited for Montville to say something, but he only cleared his throat and lowered his gaze, and the shock and disappointment upon his face said more than any words he could have uttered.

Something twisted painfully in her breast. Why did she feel an insane compulsion to fling herself back into his arms, she, Dominique Chantal, whom everyone had always said was levelheaded?

A horse's whinny reverberated in her ears. Before Dominique could gather her wits about her, Montville had grabbed her by the waist, thrust her behind him, drawn out his flintlock, and whirled, his movements like those of a panther preparing to spring.

Dominique fought to regain her balance on legs that seemed to have turned liquid. She heard swift footsteps crunching on gravel. Her breath caught. Montville flattened himself against the wall, pistol muzzle pointing upward, and raised a finger to his lips. The next moment, he leaped forth, hooked an arm around the newcomer's throat, and dragged him inside, thrusting the weapon into his ribs.

"Andre . . . Wha—" The word ended on a choking sound.

Montville froze, his blue eyes manifesting shock. Abruptly, he released his red-haired victim, who staggered forward, wheezing, and brought a shaking hand to tug at his rumpled cravat.

"Etien." Montville's brow furrowed. "I didn't—"

"Didn't what?" Rochefort croaked, turning to glare at him. He coughed and gasped for air. "Didn't think I'd mind your amicable attempt to snap my neck?"

His gaze fell upon Montville's pistol, now lowered, but still aimed in the direction of his groin. His hazel eyes widened. "For God's sake, man, replace that wretched thing!"

Montville looked down at the weapon. "Sorry." He tucked the gun back into the gray sash at his waist. "Did you catch the knave who tried to skewer us?"

Rochefort shook his head and gave him a guilty look. "She fled."

Montville's brows shot upward. *"She?"*

"Oui." Rochefort withdrew something from his coat pocket and passed it to Montville, and Dominique's mouth nearly

dropped open when she viewed the delicate black kid slipper, so small it might have belonged to a child.

Montville, too, seemed perplexed. "Are you certain—"

"Positive. I saw the slipper come off her foot. She stumbled over a fallen oak when I shot her." He bowed his head and swore under his breath. "She drew a pistol and sent a round my way, then ran faster than the cursed mistral in December."

"Have you searched the grounds?"

"Yes." Rochefort cast a wary glance toward the door. "But inasmuch as the woman got away—"

"It isn't safe to venture out," Montville interrupted. "Not yet."

"What do you intend to do?"

"Remain here."

"In the stables?"

Montville made an impatient gesture. "The hayloft. Until nightfall."

Rochefort snorted, the glimmer of a smile curving his lips. Casting a sly glance toward Dominique, he opened his mouth to say something, but Montville gave him a look that could have pulverized granite. "Find the maid who, ah, ministered to you last night, and tell her that you wish to offer her employment."

"What—"

"Do it," Montville gritted.

Rochefort's boyish features twisted in evident disapproval. "I gather you still intend to go after—"

"Do as I ask, please, Etien," Montville repeated sharply.

What was he planning? Dominique hoped Rochefort would ask him to elaborate, but the man merely lowered his head and shuffled from one booted foot to the other, pale brows drawn together, gaze fixed on the floor. "I'll see what I can do," he muttered. "I only hope to God you realize the risk you're undertaking."

Montville smiled wryly. "No need to pray for us. We'll be just fine." He turned toward Dominique and motioned toward the rickety ladder leading to the hayloft.

She gathered her skirts. "And you?"

"I must have a word with Etien. I'll join you shortly."

The Hidden Jewel

* * *

"Have you any idea who that woman was?" Dominique dabbed at her lips with a napkin and shifted on the straw, which stuck her even through the horse blanket Montville had spread for her.

"No." His features impassive, Montville selected a slice of ham and bread from the basket Rochefort had brought after the stablehands had gone for their midday meal. "God knows, I have enough enemies."

Dominique tensed at the coldness emanating from him. He had been taciturn and distant ever since he'd returned from his brief discussion with Rochefort. Her gaze fell upon his left hand, which rested on his thigh. The wedding band gleamed on his third finger, a small but blatant reminder of his loyalty to a woman who had adored him. And who was dead. Had his foes murdered her?

With difficulty, Dominique swallowed her food. "But you said earlier that you thought the attempt could have been directed at me," she said, careful to keep her voice matter-of-fact.

The wedding ring disappeared from view as his fingers curled into fists. "Your brother has enemies, as well."

"My brother doesn't—"

"Tell me it isn't true," he challenged.

She couldn't. To deny it would be to lie, and by now she knew he'd see straight through her. Besides, if she was to gain any information about their itinerary, she'd have to remain in his good graces. She took another bite and looked away, aware of his piercing gaze upon her.

"I'll promise you this, however," Montville went on. "I'm going to make certain that this does not happen again."

Dominique brushed the crumbs off her lap. "How?"

"We're going to take a different route. If everything works out as I have planned, no one except Rochefort will know where we are"—he reached to tug at his cravat—"or what we are doing."

Her heart sank as she realized what he meant. "You intend to go into hiding."

"Exactly."

Dominique frowned. "For how long?"

"For as long as is required."

Oh, no. How was she going to accomplish her mission if she was headed for some remote area, with no possibility of contacting Desfieux? Her hand shook slightly as she reached into the basket and withdrew one of two dusty bottles.

"No glasses," she muttered. For some reason, the thought of sharing a bottle with Montville brought that kiss to mind, and Dominique nervously picked at the cork, feeling heat creep up her cheeks.

"We'll make do," he said, avoiding her gaze. If he had noticed her discomfiture, he gave no sign of it.

What was he thinking? Looking at his impassive profile, it was impossible to believe this was the same man who had kissed her with such tenderness a short while ago. Her stomach plummeted at the memory, and she quickly took a sip of wine.

Out of the corner of her eye, she watched him loosen the strip of white cloth at his throat and carefully pull it off. She drew her tongue over her suddenly burning lips, tore her gaze from his Adam's apple, and took several more draughts of claret.

The sight of dried blood on his neckcloth made her nearly choke on the bittersweet liquid. He tossed away the cravat and bowed his head, then closed his eyes and reached up to probe the back of his neck.

"It hurts, doesn't it?" she asked gently.

She expected him to deny it, as men were wont to do, but Montville nodded once, not bothering to raise his head. The motion made his chestnut hair spill across his brow, and something pierced her heart like a sharp needle.

"I could tend to it," she offered. Strange that her own voice should sound so far away. Her vision blurred, returned to crystal clarity, then blurred again. Her mouth and throat seemed to be on fire.

His chin came up. Briefly, he looked her in the eye, and Dominique saw something flicker in those unusual deep blue irises before his lashes lowered. "That won't be necessary."

"If that wound isn't cleaned, it will become infected."

His jaw hardened. Plucking the napkin off his lap, he took

the bottle out of her hand, sloshed a good amount of wine onto the cloth, then scrubbed at his neck with it, so vigorously that Dominique cringed.

"Will that suffice?" he asked coolly when he had set the reddened cloth aside.

Curse him. Were it not for the medallion, she would have dumped the contents of that bottle over his head and left him with the barn swallows and pigeons for company. Suppressing a laugh at the thought of Montville's dark hair plastered to his head and dripping with red wine, she smiled and said, "It might improve your disposition if you drank some."

He passed the bottle back to her and moved to withdraw a smaller one from the basket. "Thank you, but I prefer cognac."

She blinked against a sudden onslaught of dizziness and stared dumbly at the bottle in her hand. Her vision grew fuzzy again. Her eyelids felt heavy. Before she knew it, her wrist went slack and the wine tipped over, gurgling onto her skirt. She barely felt the moisture in her lap, nor heard what Montville said as he snatched the bottle from her numb fingers and gripped her shoulders. No longer able to keep her eyes open, Dominique slumped forward and let her head rest on his chest.

Andre lay motionless, peering out through a small hole in the wood. Thank God for rotting planks missing knots; even in the faint light of the setting sun he could clearly see the courtyard below, where a black-haired woman wearing a dark green velvet coat with white lapels stepped into his traveling chariot, aided by an immaculately dressed fellow sporting buff moleskin breeches, a navy coat, and tall black Hessians. Upon his head was a *chapeau-bras,* which, thankfully, concealed his telltale hair.

Abruptly, the man pivoted and ostentatiously scratched his left ear before leaping into the coach and slamming the door behind him.

Recognizing Rochefort's signal denoting that everything had gone as planned, Andre felt some of the tension leave his rigid shoulders. He watched the coach lurch into motion and followed its progress for as long as it remained within his

105

range of vision, then rolled onto his back and exhaled the breath he'd been holding, giving a silent prayer that his friend be shielded from any other lethal weapons meant for his own head.

He stared up at the beamed ceiling. The charade just might prove successful; except for that ridiculous hat, Rochefort might have been his twin. Even the chambermaid looked convincing, with that coat concealing her figure.

He breathed in the earthy scent of hay mingled with lavender. The latter fragrance brought an unwelcome awareness of the woman sleeping soundly on the straw pallet beside his. Against his will, he turned his head, and immediately wished he hadn't.

She lay on her back, her lustrous hair splayed in unruly strands around a face that looked as pure and guileless as a child's. One delicate hand lay curled against her cheek. Sweet Lord, how small and frail she looked. Flushed, too.

Every muscle in Andre's body tightened. Just how much of that sleeping powder had Etien put into her wine? He forced himself to look away. God, how he'd hated having to drug her. When she had tipped her head back and raised the bottle, it had taken all of his self-control to keep from snatching it out of her hands and hurling it to the sawdust-covered floor below. But she was too observant, not to mention given to asking questions, and the less she knew, the better. At least, for now.

Besides, the circles under her eyes betrayed her need for rest, and Andre knew she'd never fall asleep with him so near, certainly not after his feral behavior toward her after the attack. What in hell had possessed him, kissing her like that, when he knew damned well she felt nothing for him save mistrust?

Andre rolled off the pallet. The powder could wear off at any moment; best go meet with the innkeeper and see about finalizing the arrangements for the journey.

The only way out of the hayloft was to crawl over her. In passing, Andre's knee bumped her hip, and a tiny sound escaped her lips. His gaze flew to her face, and the remembered warm sweetness of that mouth beneath his own hit Andre like a boulder to the head.

She stirred and turned. Her fingers encountered his knee and slid upward, advancing dangerously toward . . . Andre groaned. With one last muttered oath, he brushed away her hand and vaulted over her, so fast he nearly toppled over the edge of the loft.

She dreamed that someone was caressing her hand. Dominique rolled onto her side and tried to move her legs, which felt as heavy as tree trunks, and every bit as limber. *Grand Dieu*, her mouth was dry, and her head throbbed.

Where was she? Again, she felt silky softness brush her fingers, then move along her arm and rub beneath her chin. This was no dream. She jerked her head aside, her eyelids flying open.

Darkness. The heavy scent of dried clover and the prickle of hay. And fur.

Fur? Cold tingles raced up Dominique's spine. She'd fallen asleep in the hayloft, and now something was burrowing beneath her chin. A rodent! She opened her mouth to scream, but all her parched throat managed was a rasp.

She promptly heard a weak mew, then felt the chill of a moist nose nuzzling her neck. Her muscles went slack with relief, and a smile curved her lips. *"Chaton,"* she whispered.

Another mew, this time louder and more demanding. A velvety ear brushed across Dominique's jaw as the kitten cuddled closer.

"So soft." She ran her fingers through fur as sleek as a rabbit's. "What color are you?" She gently picked up the animal and squinted, but all she could see in the blackness was the outline of a furry head with tiny pointed ears.

"Ma pauvre petite," Dominique crooned. "Where is your maman?"

As if in answer to the question, a second, deeper meow sounded from somewhere behind her. The kitten began to squirm, and Dominique regretfully set it free. The pad of tiny feet upon straw. A low purr-growl. And then she was alone.

Or was she? She groped at the cover tucked snugly around

her. Montville's greatcoat. Propping herself up on one elbow, Dominique glanced around, and though she could see nothing but contours, the stillness told her that there was no other human presence in the loft.

Heavens, it must be late. Perhaps Montville had tired of waiting for her to awaken and gone for something to eat. She hoped so; her belly ached, and her head felt as if it were about to split in two.

She eased back down and pressed two fingers to the bridge of her nose. Strange, hunger usually caused stomach cramps, never such dizziness. Could it be the ham she'd eaten had been spoiled? That had been all she'd . . .

Her eyes widened. The wine! She remembered Montville's stony face during *déjeuner*, the way he'd avoided meeting her gaze, his strange expression as he watched her drink the claret. He had partaken only of the cognac, while she . . . Her lips tightened. No wonder she felt so groggy; the blackguard had drugged her.

She tore off his coat and flung it aside. Where was her own cloak? Wretched, deceitful . . . Dominique hiked up her skirts, gripped the first rung of the ladder, and descended as quickly as her unsteady legs would allow. The stables were strangely quiet, and Montville wasn't anywhere to be found. Moonlight beamed through the yawning door, and chilly night air enveloped her. Dominique wrapped her bare arms around herself and hastened past the stalls.

And then she realized what was different. Save for one horse that blew softly as she passed, the stables were empty. No trace of Montville's team of grays. She shook off the feeling of foreboding that made her scalp tingle and headed resolutely for the door. His traveling chariot must be outside, waiting. It had to be.

Yet when she stepped out, nothing greeted Dominique save the deserted courtyard. She stood unmoving for a moment, her gaze fixed on the blurred disk of the moon visible behind the clouds. Impossible. He couldn't have left. And if he had?

No need to pray for us, he'd told Rochefort with a wry smile. What if the killer had found him while she slept? She shuddered. Perhaps she could steal the one remaining horse, and . . . and what? Go where?

No, the sensible thing to do was go to the carriage house and look for his traveling chariot. Hands clenched in the folds of her skirts, she swiftly moved toward the brick structure beside the stables, casting wary glances over her shoulder as she went.

Her ears detected rustling noises coming from just around the building. Montville? Dominique peered around the corner and caught sight of a corpulent peasant crouching beside the wheel of a wagon, examining intently something on the ground.

Intrigued, Dominique leaned a little farther and craned her neck, and as she did so the man sat on his heels and pushed back the wide-brimmed hat he wore, allowing her a glimpse of a dagger flashing in his hand.

Dominique's gaze flicked from the knife he tucked at his waist to the figure lying motionless at his feet. A sack covered the head. Upon the twisted torso, silver thread glimmered in the moonlight. A jolt coursed through her body, jarring her from head to toe. There was only one other place she'd seen that silvery pattern.

On Montville's waistcoat.

Chapter Nine

Dominique brought her fist to her mouth and swallowed back a scream, refusing to equate that lifeless form with the images flickering relentlessly in her mind.

Montville striding into her cell, looking for all the world like a phantasm. Montville tossing an apple into the air. Montville comforting her during the storm . . . slipping his mother's locket around her neck . . . pushing her out of the path of a deadly arrow . . . kissing her . . .

"No," she whispered. Oh, please, no. He couldn't be dead. He couldn't be.

As if sensing he was being watched, the peasant turned his head, and Dominique ducked behind the building and pressed her fingers to the rough brick, feeling her palms grow moist.

She held her breath and listened.

Footsteps. Lord, he was headed toward her! She glanced toward the stables. Not enough time to reach them without being spotted. Heart threatening to leap from her chest, she gathered her skirts, then sprinted to the carriage house door and yanked it open.

She'd barely ducked behind it when her outstretched hands

bumped something. She groped for the object blocking her path. Her fingers grasped a wooden handle just as she heard the muted tread of boots behind her. Dominique whirled, raised the newly found weapon high above her head, and swung. She heard a smack as wood connected with flesh and bone.

"Merde!"

The peasant's voice rang vaguely familiar, but Dominique paused only for a heartbeat before raising the rod again. The next moment splinters pricked her fingers as the stranger yanked the shaft out of her hands.

The farming tool clattered to the floor. A pair of hands gripped her shoulders and jerked her against a portly body, so hard that air whooshed through her parted lips. She took a breath and screamed, but he promptly smothered her shriek with his palm. She started to sink her teeth into it.

"Don't."

That sonorous voice. This time, Dominique took notice and stopped in mid-bite, her head snapping back so abruptly that pain knifed down her neck. It was too dark to see clearly, but like his rich timbre, that firm jawline could have belonged to none other.

"You," she breathed.

"In the flesh. Battered flesh, that is."

She swallowed hard, her pulse still pounding in her ears. It took her several seconds to acknowledge that Montville indeed stood before her, emanating vitality though he didn't move a muscle.

"Oh, God." She slumped against him and expelled a shuddering breath.

He loosened his grip a little but didn't let her go. His warm breath stirred the fine hairs at her nape. The coarse homespun of his shirtfront scraped her cheek, but Dominique didn't care. She let her hands rest on his hips and leaned a little closer into him, needing the support.

Montville flinched. Throat tightening as she recalled how hard she'd hit him, Dominique drew back. "Your arm—"

"I have a spare," he said dryly.

She didn't smile. "Here. Let me see."

Before he could protest, she caught his left elbow and gently began probing his forearm. "Does this hurt?"

He grimaced. "Not really."

That served to convince her that it must ache a great deal. She came upon a lump, but nothing seemed broken, and Dominique gave a silent prayer of thanks that she hadn't done more damage. "The bone is intact," she pronounced, releasing him. "Is there a well nearby? A cold compress would reduce the swelling."

Montville made an impatient gesture. "There isn't time for that." He clapped the tattered hat atop his head. Her eyes now adjusted to the meager light, she watched him rearrange his rotund belly and realized it consisted of padding positioned beneath his too-large peasant garb.

His legs and thighs were swathed in similar fashion. The overall effect was realistic, indeed, and Dominique rationalized that given his ensemble, she couldn't possibly have recognized him. "You certainly scared me witless," she said. "I saw you holding—"

"What?" he demanded harshly.

Her gaze flicked to his hands, arrested just above his stomach, stiff fingertips digging into the padding. "I didn't recognize you in those peasant clothes," she admitted cautiously.

"That was the general idea. What did you see?"

What has upset you so? She fingered the ring on her left hand, almost unable to believe he'd been the very one who'd given it to her. "I saw you kneeling with that knife."

"And?"

She looked into his shadowed face and swallowed. "And your waistcoat. On the ground."

Silence. A muscle worked at Montville's jaw, and Dominique had the distinct impression that he'd anticipated a different response. He searched her face, eyes gleaming like onyx in the darkness, before he abruptly turned away.

On impulse, she caught his sleeve. "May I ask what you were doing?"

His lips thinned. "Packing."

"In the courtyard?"

He shrugged, extricating himself from her grasp at the same

112

time. "A foolish thing to do. Almost as foolish as letting you out of my sight, if only for a spell."

She suddenly recalled how he had rendered her unconscious and felt her stomach clench. "Apparently, you deemed it safe to leave me in the stables by myself all afternoon." Eyes narrowing, she scrutinized his features, but they might as well have been chiseled in ice for all the emotion they betrayed. "Why did you taint my wine?" she demanded.

It must have been the play of moonlight that made her think she glimpsed guilt on his face. "For your protection," he muttered.

"When mixed with alcohol in the wrong proportions, monsieur, sleeping powders can prove fatal."

He cleared his throat, dark hair spilling over his brow. "I'm sorry," he muttered.

Though patently grudging, his apology softened Dominique a bit. She gave him a half-smile. "From now on, I won't put anything into my mouth unless you taste it first."

His shoulders visibly relaxed. "Fair enough." Giving his belly a final pat, he took her hand, tucked it in the crook of his elbow, and guided her outside. "We're going to travel in disguise. Rochefort is already headed west, toward the Vendee, dressed in my clothes, accompanied by a maid posing as you."

He led her to the waiting cart and withdrew two bundles from the back, one of which he passed to her. It most assuredly was wool, because it prickled her bare arms. Atop the cloth lay a shoddy pair of mud-smeared shoes.

She squinted at the fabric she held, which, in the light of the moon, looked black. "What's this?"

"Your clothing."

She almost snorted. "You are joking."

He shook his head. "Rochefort took your trunk with him. If that maid is to pass as the grand lady, she will need proper attire."

Dominique almost dropped her bundle. She'd packed some of her best clothes in that trunk, not to mention a pair of ruby earrings she'd meant to return to Colette and a valuable medical manual she'd borrowed from her uncle's library without permission. Thinking of Uncle Guillaume inevitably led to thoughts of Madame. How was she faring in the Conciergerie? Or had Bavard changed his mind and kept her in that horrid tower at Loches?

A lump rose in Dominique's throat. Eyes burning, she pressed her quivering lips together and stole a glance at Montville, but he appeared to be too intent on scanning the surrounding shrubbery to have noticed.

"No need to fret," came his deep voice.

Did the man have eyes on the sides of his head?

He raised the satchel he held. "Your indispensables are in here."

Dominique halted. "My . . . indispensables?"

He nodded. "I packed everything I thought you'd need." A ghost of a teasing smile curved his lips, making him look far more appealing than she cared to admit. "I hope you don't mind my having taken the liberty to go through your belongings."

What could she possibly reply to *that,* given what she'd done that very morning?

"No, not at all." Dominique resumed walking, pressing the woolen garments to her chest.

"Oh, that reminds me." Out of the corner of her eye, she saw him hold up something white. "I wasn't certain what to make of these."

She glanced at the men's drawers dangling from his fingers, then looked up to see the corners of his mouth begin to twitch.

"Good quality," he remarked with exaggerated appreciation, rubbing the flannel between his fingers. "The fellow who owns them truly is a connoisseur of fine gentlemen's undergarments. Not to mention short and quite emaciated."

Emaciated, indeed! It was all she could do to keep from snatching the garment out of his hand. Dominique turned toward the stables, making haste lest her tongue get the better of her and she blurt out something she'd later regret.

"Where are you going?" he asked from behind her, his tone betraying barely contained laughter.

"To don these . . . these *things.* In one of the stalls."

"Wait."

She quickened her step. He grabbed a handful of her skirt. Dominique stumbled. She swung around, intending to wrench out of his grasp, but turned the wrong way and ended up wrapped in her dress. And pressed firmly against him.

A jolt ran from her navel to her heels. His fingertips tightened on her hip for just an instant before he tore his hand away and jerked back, as if he'd touched a burning stake.

He took another backward step, his hands clenched, his gaze fixed somewhere above her head. "Stay close to me. I must make certain no one awaits inside."

She nodded stiffly, confounded at the wrenching sense of loss he'd caused by simply moving away. Alarming, what the mere brush of his fingertips could do to her.

Dominique stood rooted to the spot for a moment, her eyes riveted to his broad back. She'd been convinced it was his face and that immaculate attire of his that affected her so, but now . . . now, she knew better. The padding and ill-tailored garb took nothing away from his allure. God help her. The man could destroy all that she loved in one fell swoop. How would she manage to remain with him long enough to retrieve that medallion, and keep from falling hopelessly under his spell?

She wished it were only the prickly woolen fabric of her dress that made her feel as if thousands of ants were creeping along her skin. Dominique discreetly raked her thumb over a particularly itchy spot below her breast, her gaze roving over the barren black trees and shabby cottages along the winding country road.

Exactly where was Montville going? She looked up at the clear night sky. From the position of the three-quarter moon and stars, she gathered they were headed east. That suited her just fine, but at this pace, he'd soon take her so deep into the wilderness that escape would be impossible.

It occurred to her that if he'd sent her luggage with Rochefort, his own trunk must be right along with hers. What if he'd put the medallion there? She had to think of some way to find out without arousing suspicion.

She filled her lungs with chill night air, tinged with the

smoky scent of burning wood. Above the drumming hoofbeats of the horse, she could discern the howls and screeches of nocturnal creatures. Never in her life had Dominique experienced such an eerie feeling while passing through a village, but then, she'd never before traveled in an open cart, nor in the dead of night.

Whatever you do, don't think of highwaymen or wolves.

The cart ran over a bump, and Dominique lurched on the hard wooden box, undoubtedly adding more color to what she suspected must already be an elaborate black-and-blue pattern on her derriere.

She brought a hand to her aching lower back and rubbed. "Are we stopping anytime soon?"

"Probably not."

Dominique suppressed a sigh. Save for crunching noises while he consumed one peppermint after another, Montville hadn't made a sound during the entire trip. Time and again she thought she felt his gaze upon her, but when she turned her head she always found his attention focused on the road.

Whooo!

Montville tensed, his head jerking toward the source of the sound. *"Grand-duc,"* he murmured.

Dominique gulped. *"Grand-duc?"*

He cocked his head. Another ghostly hoot resounded from somewhere in the trees. He nodded solemnly. "The eagle owl."

Chaton. It's vital. You must get the medallion back and take it to the Grand-Duc. If you don't, our people will think Paul . . . they'll kill him.

Dominique's scalp began to crawl in earnest. She tried to scoot away from Montville, fearing he'd sense the sudden tremors racking her body, but there was no room left to move within the cramped box.

He glanced at her. "You're chilled."

Transferring the whip and reins to his left hand, he drew the blanket from beneath him and held it out.

She willed her fingers steady and reached for the proffered coverlet. "Thank you."

"De rien."

116

Her fingertips brushed his, and again, Dominique felt that odd rush of excitement course through her body at his touch. She hastily threw the blanket around her shoulders and snuggled into it, still shuddering even as its warmth enveloped her.

She closed her eyes. The warmth of Montville's body. The torrid urgency of his lips . . .

How could she even contemplate such things a moment after having been reminded of Paul's peril? She frowned. Bavard had said Montville had spent time in England, posing as an exiled nobleman. As good a subject as any with which to start to gain some information, she supposed.

"What is London like?" she asked.

"London?" His brows arched, but his gaze remained between the horse's ears.

"I've never been there."

"A dreary place. You didn't miss much." A shadow passed over his face, darkening his features for an instant before he continued. "There's fog. It rains a lot. One cannot step outside without an umbrella, even on a sunny day. And it's perpetually cold. I've always thought the climate perfectly matched the people."

Interesting. Paul had incessantly spewed accolades about the city. "You cannot possibly judge a population by the attitude of the few acquaintances you've made over . . . ?"

"Two years," he provided.

"That long?"

He inclined his head in acknowledgment.

"Have you not come home to visit during that time?"

He shrugged. "I had nothing to come back to."

She noticed the grim set of his mouth, and felt her heart contract. "No family?"

He shook his head.

Dominique touched the locket at her throat. He'd told her that his brother had been murdered. How had his mother died? What of his father?

"Friends?" she asked gently.

"A spy cannot afford the luxury of having friends. Too dangerous."

She clearly registered the strain in Montville's voice, in

117

spite of his ostensible nonchalance. "But quite lonely for you, I'm sure," she said.

A gust of wind ruffled his hair. He shoved a dark strand out of his eyes. "Being alone suited me just fine."

She stared at his serene profile. "I don't believe you."

He smiled bitterly. "And what, may I ask, do you believe?"

As always when she thought she glimpsed vulnerability beneath his carefully controlled demeanor, Dominique felt compassion surge in her breast. "I know it's difficult to bear at times. And I think you do, too."

"What are you talking about?"

"Solitude. Loneliness."

That made him finally turn his head. "Solitude," he said through his teeth, "is not synonymous with loneliness." He briefly looked up at the coal-colored sky. "I'm afraid we cannot set up camp just yet. We should have passed that landmark over an hour ago."

Obviously, he wished to change the subject. Better not probe too deeply. "What landmark?"

He pointed with his whip, and she caught sight of a structure looming a short distance away, just beyond a bridge that stretched over a rushing creek.

Dominique surveyed the dilapidated little building, and thought of a one-eyed pirate with a pockmarked face. Upon the steepled roof was a lopsided stone chimney. The door and trim, which once must have been white, were flaked with peeling paint. Large chunks of plaster were gouged from the facade, and on one side a blackened board sealed the opening where a window should have been.

"That gatehouse is all that remains of what once was a sizable estate," Montville said. "The chateau burned to the ground in all of one night."

Something in his hushed tone troubled Dominique profoundly. "How do you know?"

"I knew the owners." He paused. "Actually, my parents did. In what seems like another lifetime."

"Before the Revolution?"

He snapped the reins. "What do you know of the accursed Revolution? You must have been, how old? Two? Three?"

118

Dominique raised her chin. "Eight."

"Eight." He snorted. "Happily playing with dolls, no doubt."

"Gathering herbs," she countered. "And, yes, I had a wonderful time of it. I had an even better time a few years later, helping my uncle gouge balls out of good people your valiant Napoleon's troops shot full of lead."

Montville sat up straighter and gave her a long, hard look. "Your uncle allowed a female child to assist him?"

A typical reaction. She hadn't really expected him to take the bait regarding Bonaparte, either. She shrugged. "My father was off tending the wounded on the battlefield. Paul always fainted at the sight of blood, and so—"

He chuckled. "Your brother *fainted* at the sight of blood?"

She bristled. "I've never met a man without at least one weakness, monsieur."

"True," he acknowledged. "What of your mother?"

Her fingers toyed with the edge of the blanket. "My mother passed away when I was six."

His gaze fell to the locket at her throat. His jaw clenched. "How?"

"She was six months with child, and had a mis—" She broke off, uncertain that she should relate such details to a man. The sympathy on Montville's face, however, impelled her to continue. "The infant was stillborn. After the birth, she began hemorrhaging, and . . ."

"Grand Dieu," he murmured.

"Father tried everything to stop the bleeding. He even sent for a specialist from Nantes. But even he—" She swallowed back the lump threatening to close her throat. "They couldn't save her," she finished softly.

After that horrible winter night, her father had never been the same. Awash in memories she seldom allowed to surface, Dominique fixed her gaze on the wagon's flickering lantern, hanging from the dashboard.

After a moment, she felt Montville's hand slide over hers. His touch was hesitant, barely a graze of fingertips, but when Dominique turned up her palm, he laced his fingers through hers and squeezed firmly.

"I am sorry."

119

"Thank you." She made no move to remove her hand from his reassuring grasp. She stole a glance at him and recognized the grim look of someone who had known similar loss.

"What happened to your mother?" she questioned.

He briefly closed his eyes, then flinched, as if the recollection caused him physical pain. He gripped her hand a little harder. "You do not want to know."

She did. Very badly. "Tell me."

He took an audible breath, then exhaled slowly. "It was during the September—"

The flutter of wings. Dominique felt a sudden rush of air overhead as Montville stopped in midsentence and looked up, wrenching his hand away. The next instant, a shrill neigh pierced her eardrums, sending a thousand needles down her neck and spine.

As if in a nightmare, she saw the horse toss its head, then rear, front hooves flailing, nose pointed toward the sky. Instinctively, she braced her soles against the footboard before the cart rumbled forth, jouncing in the frantic animal's wake.

"Hold tight!" Montville bellowed.

Dominique barely heard him above the din of hooves, wheels, and harnesses. She grabbed hold of the side of the cart as it gathered speed and pressed her lips together, knowing that if she screamed, she'd further spook the horse.

The world became a blur. Frigid air stung her eyes and cheeks. Montville leaned forward and pulled hard on the reins, but the animal stretched its neck and clattered onward like a rabid steed from Hades.

Hail Mary, full of grace . . . A twig scraped her forehead and snagged her hair, but Dominique hardly noticed. *The Lord is with thee* . . . she quelled the absurd urge to snatch the reins from Montville and attempt to halt the runaway animal herself.

Blessed art thou among women . . .

Something snapped. The left side of the cart collapsed, sending her slamming into Montville. He half-turned and made a wild grab for her, managing to hook his arm around her middle a second before they toppled out of the cart.

Dominique screamed.

Montville's back hit the ground.

"Ooph!"

Rustling leaves. Snapping twigs. She barely felt the impact, and dimly registered that he'd cushioned her fall with his body. She pressed her face into the side of his neck and clung to the fabric of his shirt, exhaling a sigh of relief. It turned into a gasp when she realized they were sliding downward.

They'd landed on the slope that led toward the creek.

Montville ground out a curse. Burying his fingers in her chignon, he pressed her cheek to his chest and clamped his other arm around her waist as they began to roll.

The hillside seemed to tilt, then whirl around her. Earth, sky, earth, sky . . . Branches and thistles scratched her calves and ankles through her woolen stockings. A jagged rock struck her derriere. Searing pain ripped through her thigh. She heard the sound of rending fabric, and suddenly Dominique lurched to a halt.

With a hoarse cry that made her blood congeal, Montville catapulted out of her arms. Sobbing for breath, Dominique lay helplessly on her side, her fingers digging into the muddy earth, watching in horror as he went hurtling headfirst toward the water.

Chapter Ten

"Montville!" Dominique cried. The only answer was a splash. She sucked in a panicked breath. *"Grands Dieux!"*

Pain seared her leg as she shoved to her knees, and green specks swirled before her eyes. Gritting her teeth, she began clawing at her tattered skirt, caught on the stump of a broken sapling. The mud-covered fabric slid between her fingers.

She wiped her palms on her blouse and raked the tangled hair out of her eyes. Hooking her thumbs into the cloth on either side of the stump, she gave a mighty yank and was rewarded with the muted sound of tearing wool.

She drew her sleeve across her clammy brow and staggered to her feet. "Montville!"

Again, no answer. She stared into the shadows, heart thumping, the blood roaring in her ears. She gathered the remnants of her skirts in one fist and hobbled downhill, grabbing at branches and dried shrubs with her free hand, tripping over stones and roots as she descended. Thank God no clouds obstructed the full moon tonight.

It didn't take her very long to reach the bottom. She heard the gurgle of rushing water. Dead leaves rustling beneath her feet, Dominique limped toward a row of tall weeds silhouetted in the moonlight, her chest constricting when she spotted the opening he'd obviously made.

She stepped through it. A strangled cry tore from her throat. Montville lay facedown in the shallow water, his long legs straight, his arms spread wide apart. "My God," she whispered hoarsely.

Energy shot through her body. Shoving her skirts between her knees, she waded into the creek, sucking air through her teeth as icy liquid seeped into her shoes. The water served to partially numb her aching leg. She grasped Montville's shirt near the shoulder and at his waist and pulled, stumbling backward, fighting to maintain her footing on the slippery rocks while struggling with his considerable weight.

With a supreme effort, she rolled him onto his back. His head lolled to one side. Dominique caught his wrists. Grunting and gasping for breath, she somehow managed to drag him to dry ground, then fell to her knees at his side. Breathing hard, she leaned over him and lightly ran her knuckles along his jaw.

She smoothed the drenched hair off his brow and wiped a mud smear off his cheek. "Montville?"

Silence.

"Montville!" She gently slapped his face. "Speak to me, please!"

He didn't respond. Gooseflesh rose on her skin as an ominous feeling swept through her. She'd found him half-immersed in water. If it had failed to rouse him, then . . . Swiftly, she bent and put her ear to his nose and mouth. No respiration. She touched his throat. No pulse.

Dead. The syllable echoed like a knell in Dominique's head. "No!" she screamed.

Oh, no. No. This couldn't be happening. She couldn't accept this. Wouldn't. She'd already believed him lost once tonight. Twice was simply more than she could bear.

Her self-control snapped like a frayed thread. Dominique seized Montville's shirtfront and began to shake him, unleashing all her desperation on his lifeless form. "No! You cannot die! You can't!"

It was like jostling a sack of coal, and every bit as effective. No longer realizing what she was doing, Dominique balled her hands and began hammering at his chest with all her strength, as if she could beat the life back into him.

"No!" Again, she brought her fists down on his rib cage. "I will not let you go! I won't! Do you hear me?"

She pummeled him until she lost sensation in her hands. Feeling as if she'd aged a hundred years within the past few moments, she let her smarting palms rest on his abdomen and slowly bowed her head. Defeated. A wrenching feeling gripped her chest and throat. Had she not distracted him while he was driving, this wouldn't have happened.

A diamond on her slim wedding band caught a moonbeam, and Dominique's vision blurred with tears. "Oh, Lord," she murmured, "Creator and Redeemer of all the faithful . . ." She choked on the words, and found that the rest of the age-old prayer for the departed had escaped her. "Please, God," she blurted, "take care of him."

Beneath her palms, she thought she felt his belly muscles spasm. Her gaze flew to his face. Impossible. Her mind was surely playing tricks on her.

He started. Then he coughed. Water gushed out of his mouth. He coughed again. More water. Dominique stared at him, not daring to let herself believe what she was witnessing. The next moment, he opened his mouth wide, emitting a frightful wheezing noise as he struggled to draw in air.

To Dominique, the sound was more melodious than any symphony or choir she'd ever heard. He was alive. She wanted to shout, to leap up and dance, to laugh and cry at the same time, but she couldn't seem to move or take her eyes off him.

He drew another shaky breath, then glanced around, his eyes meeting hers in a blank stare. Dashing her tears away, she crawled a little closer and eased his head into her lap. "It's all right. Breathe slowly. Relax a bit, and you'll be fine."

If only she truly felt as certain as she sounded. She had to consider the multitude of injuries he might have sustained during that dreadful fall.

For what seemed a very long time, she guided him through one labored inhalation after another, making small sounds of encouragement, stroking his wet hair. When his chest finally stopped convulsing, his teeth began to chatter. He raised his chin and looked at her as if he'd never seen her before. "Wha—" He clenched his jaw in an obvious effort to still the rattling. "What . . . h—happened?"

"We took a nasty spill."

Tremors racked his body. "A spill."

Dominique cast an anxious glance over her shoulder. She had to get him warm, and quickly; never mind that her own feet had grown numb long ago and that her thigh felt as if someone had thrust a knife into her flesh and twisted. She took one of his hands and rubbed it briskly between her palms. "How do you feel?"

"Mm. Cold."

She knew it wasn't only the moonlight that made his face look as colorless as plaster. "Does anything hurt very badly?"

He grimaced. "Everything."

"I meant excruciating pain. As one would feel with broken bones." She ran her hands along his ribs, probing gently. "How about here?"

He gave no sign of pain. Breathing a sigh of relief, she vigorously rubbed his upper arms. "If you lie here much longer in those wet clothes, you'll catch pneumonia. And this"—she drew the shirt out of his breeches, exposing the flannel around his middle—"this must come off."

She started to remove it, then sat back on her heels. There was too much of it to unwrap without lifting him. Gnawing on her lower lip in frustration, she cast a look around, then suddenly remembered his knife.

She fumbled with the leather sheath strapped to his hips, shuddering when she viewed the gleaming steel that seemed to take forever to emerge. Well-honed. It could have dropped out of its holder and plunged into his belly as he fell. Chasing away the morbid thought, she placed the sharp tip beneath the padding, sawed it in two, and pulled it out from underneath him. It felt like lead. She tossed it aside.

"Do you think you can stand if I assist you?"

He braced himself on one elbow, then groaned and passed a hand over his forehead. "Why . . . wet?"

"I found you lying facedown in the water."

He stared at her in confusion.

She hastily tucked in his shirt. "Don't you remember landing in the creek?"

He frowned. *"Quelle crique?"*

A terrible suspicion gripped her. She looked him in the eye. "What is your name?"

"Philippe Laurence . . ."

What? Dominique's mouth dropped open, but his huddled body began to quake alarmingly, so she bit back her question and caught his wrist. "We must seek shelter," she said softly. "I'll try to help you up."

Grimacing, she braced most of her weight on her good leg, then stood and held out her hands. He grasped them both in one of his and, tottering, got to his feet. His knees buckled. She grabbed his waist, somehow managing to keep from crumpling with him to the rocky ground.

"All right?" she asked after a moment.

He nodded once, his broad chest rapidly rising and falling. Draping his arm around her shoulders, she took hold of his middle and motioned with her chin toward the incline. "Slowly. Lean on me."

Sharp pangs coursed down her leg, but Dominique squared her shoulders and pressed on, supporting him with every bit of strength she had. Where could she take him? There wasn't anywhere else to go except the grotesque-looking gatehouse she'd seen before the accident. If only she had her satchel of medicines. How could she tend Montville with nary a bottle of liniment at hand?

And why on earth had he said his name was Philippe Laurence?

He felt as if round shot had exploded into a million jagged fragments in his head. He focused on the tips of his boots, biting the inside of his cheek to keep his tenuous grip on consciousness from slipping.

One, two. Right, left. Don't pass out. Dangerous.

"At last," she murmured. He caught a glimpse of a road

126

through the shrubs just ahead. He let his arm slide off her shoulders and straightened.

Too fast. His center shattered. He stumbled on something, clutched at a thick branch barring his way, then wrapped his arm around it and leaned his forehead against the rough bark while the world revolved around him in a blur of gray and black.

"What's wrong?"

Her voice reached him through the loud hum filling his ears. His mouth watered profusely. He thought he might vomit. He gulped, forced himself to breathe, and gradually the dizziness subsided. Slowly, he raised his head, and found her staring up at him, a look of panic on her face.

Who was she?

"Are you all right?" she asked.

Nausea hovered at the back of his throat. He swallowed. "Never better." Lord, now there were two of them. He blinked the double image away. "I'll live," he muttered. He eased away from the tree, tensing his muscles against a new onslaught of shivers as a gust of wind turned his clothes into a mantle of ice.

"You're trembling again." He felt her tug slightly on his sleeve. "Do try and keep moving," she urged.

Clenching his jaw, he staggered forward, ignoring the voice in his throbbing head that told him to simply let himself drop to the ground and sleep.

One, two . . .

He didn't know when they crossed the road, nor how he ended up indoors, but suddenly he was being leaned against something solid and a pair of gentle hands settled on his shoulders, pushing him downward.

Hard wall. Cold floor. Darkness. Ghostly shapes. His stomach lurched again, and he buried his face in his hands and groaned. His head drummed with the patter of running feet. A moment later, gold beams streamed through his fingers. He spread them, and sighted a tiny form scurrying to and fro in a swirl of inky skirts. Lighting candles. Another, then another. Flickering.

Dark hair. Strands of black silk. That hair . . . he recognized

... He held out his hand. "Dominique," he whispered.

She turned, then smiled and floated toward him in a disk of diffused light, uttering words he couldn't comprehend. The orb clouded around the edges, growing smaller and smaller as she drew near. The sweet, intoxicating scent of lavender and woman. His head fell forward. His hand dropped limply to his lap, and he sank sideways to the floor.

"Andre!"

He moistened his parched lips and tried to answer. Couldn't. The disk became a tarnished coin. A dot. Then, nothing.

The burning candle tilted in Dominique's hand, spilling hot wax across her knuckles. With a startled cry, she righted the sconce, then crouched and slammed it on the floor.

She grabbed his arm. "Andre," she repeated hoarsely.

He shifted, made a muffled sound, and Dominique felt his body go limp. She braced her forehead on his shoulder, breathing deeply, then raised her face and pressed her mouth and nose against his raspy cheek. His skin was cool, but his breath was even.

"Mercy, but you frightened me," she whispered.

Tentatively, she placed the backs of her fingers beneath his jaw, and felt his pulse beat steadily against her knuckles. She glanced at the fire she'd hastily kindled, now burning strong and steady in the hearth. Despite its warmth, Montville still shivered.

What could she use to cover him? Scanning the little room, she spotted a dented bucket in one corner. Beside it, several large paint brushes lay on a folded piece of whitewash-splattered canvas.

That would do. Ignoring the throbbing in her leg, she went to fetch the cloth. Unfolding it, she found that despite its stiffness, it was dry, intact, and large enough to accommodate the two of them. She draped it across her shoulder and hobbled back to Montville's side.

Her brow furrowed. How pale he was. Though not exactly blue, his lips were far from normal coloration. *"Mon pauvre,"* she said softly, brushing one fingertip across his beautifully shaped mouth. "Why did you ever offer to protect me?"

She wished it was she who lay there, hurt and helpless. She wished there were some incantation she could utter to magically heal him. Most of all, she wished to see him open those startling blue eyes of his and smile at her again.

"I'll make you well, I promise. The first thing we must do is get you warm."

She started to undo his shirt, only to find that it was fastened with crude ties instead of buttons. Sighing in frustration, she set to working the woolen cords, picking at the tight knots with her fingernails. When the last one came undone, she tugged the shirt out of his breeches, smoothed it apart, and began rubbing his bare shoulders.

Whatever he'd been doing over the past few years, she doubted he'd spent much time idling in London's fashionable parlors. Or boudoirs. The thought of Montville visiting a lady's private chamber made her insides twinge, and her fingers tightened reflexively on his upper arms.

"Unh."

His soft moan snapped her to her senses. She halted, frowning, as she noticed the red crescents her nails had left upon his skin. What was she doing? Moreover, what was she thinking? She couldn't possibly have come to care for a man who—

Who risked life and limb repeatedly to protect you. Who treated you with kindness and respect. Who married you, defied Bavard's instructions to take you home to spy on your family, then went under disguise to ensure your safety.

"Why?" she whispered tenderly. "Why did you do all that for me?"

A tiny smile dawned on his face, as if he had a secret he would never tell. Her heart skipped a beat. Good Lord, how beautiful he was. The man could easily pass for a prince, only no inbred royal could ever hope to look like that.

Stop it.

The bindings had left marks on his skin. Dominique gently traced the reddened welts, wistfully thinking of the salve in her medical kit that could have soothed them. Her gaze lingered on his muscled torso as she raised his arms and pulled the soggy shirt off him. Tossing it aside, she covered him with the tarp. Eyeing his muddy boots, she moved to grasp one by the heel and ankle, wincing as agony shot along her injured thigh.

The right boot slipped off easily. The left, however, refused to budge. It took her three attempts to finally yank it free, and when she did, a long cylinder flew out of it, slipping between his legs and hitting the floor with a muted thump.

What was this? Letting the boot slide from her fingers, Dominique stared at the object.

Dared she? She had to. Her heart leaping to her throat, she held out her hand, darting a glance at Montville's peaceful face as her fingers closed around the tightly wrapped tube. Feeling as guilty as she had when she'd searched his trunk, she peeled back the oilcloth in which it was encased.

Some sort of ancient document. Intrigued, Dominique turned toward the fire and unrolled the yellowed parchment, and as she did so her eyes grew round. It was a map of the mountains of Cordes, near Arles, in the Provence.

This had to be their destination.

Vizille. Provence. Close to Grenoble.

Provence. Exactly where Madame had told her she must go. A rush of excitement suddenly made her giddy. She tensed her shoulder muscles and pressed her lips together, suppressing a triumphant shriek.

Rustling noises coming from behind her made her start. She glanced up to see Montville shivering again, chest laboring, head turning restlessly from side to side. His fingers groped at the makeshift cover. Oh, no . . . Was he developing a fever?

Dominique hastily replaced the map where she had found it, then caught one of his hands and gently tugged the cloth from his clenched fingers. He gave a muffled cry.

"Hush," she whispered, placing a hand against his forehead. To her relief, he didn't feel abnormally hot. She brushed a dark strand of hair off his brow.

A log fell in the grate, sending sparks flying. He winced. His eyelids fluttered.

"Sleep," she murmured, running her fingers through his damp hair. "I will take care of you."

As if he'd heard her, he gave a shuddering sigh and relaxed. She tucked the cover snugly at his sides, but when she moved to do the same around his legs her fingers brushed against his breeches. Positively sodden. He'd never get warm as long as he still wore them.

What to do? He spread his legs, as if in invitation, and Dominique's cheeks flamed. In all the years she'd helped Uncle Guillaume, he'd never even allowed her in the same room with an unclothed male patient. Then again, she couldn't let Montville freeze. Taking one fortifying breath, she placed her hand below his waistband, seeking buttons.

She found more knotted ties and groaned. "Not very easy to get into your breeches, is it?"

What was she saying? Unable to hold back a nervous laugh, she plucked the lacings loose as quickly as she could, now and again darting a glance at Montville's face. *Please, please don't let him awaken and find me doing this.*

At last, she eased the garment past his hips. Fine drawers, whiter than sugar cubes. Silk. In spite of her nervousness, Dominique smiled. She should have guessed he wasn't one to wear flannel.

She pulled his breeches down over his calves, then cut the padding off his legs. Unwittingly, her gaze wandered to where the damp, sheer fabric strained at the juncture of his thighs. Outlining everything. No, emphasizing it.

Grand Dieu. Feeling the blood surge to her head, she looked away and yanked the canvas down, covering him from chin to toe. A moment later, he began shaking more violently than ever.

There was but one thing left to do for him. Dominique kicked off her shoes, then stripped her scratchy dress and peeled away the remnants of her stockings. Another stab of pain made her twist around to finally examine the back of her right thigh. Only a bruise, albeit an ugly red one, the size of an apple. Dismissing it, she lifted the canvas and slipped underneath, pressing her body to Montville's, giving him her warmth.

No sooner had she touched him than he went rigid. Swiftly, he turned and grabbed her by the shoulders, his fingers digging into her flesh. She cried out, more with surprise than pain. He only tightened his hold.

"Bastards," he hissed. "Stole . . . everything."

With that, he shook her once, then shoved her so hard that her back hit the wall with a thud. In a daze, Dominique fought for breath, only to have it catch in her throat at his next words, spoken as distinctly as if he were fully conscious.

"Take me instead. Curse you. Heaven . . . hell . . . it doesn't matter." His voice broke. "Nothing matters anymore."

In shocked silence, Dominique pressed to the wall and watched him thrash about, her gaze fixed on his face, transformed beyond recognition. Deep furrows creased his brow. His mouth contorted. His nostrils flared, perspiration beaded on his brow and upper lip, and even his teeth gleamed predatorily.

"Take me," he rasped. "My life . . . is nothing."

What sort of private hell was he reliving? Even the best imagination couldn't possibly conjure such violent nightmares out of thin air. He writhed on the stone floor, arms flailing, legs kicking, uttering half-syllables between groans. His foot caught the edge of the metal bucket containing fireplace utensils, sending the irons crashing against the bricks.

The deafening clatter didn't rouse him. Wide-eyed, Dominique dodged a hurtling broom and pressed her fists to her mouth. She could no longer understand what he was saying, and every jerky move he made brought him closer to the blazing hearth. The fire . . .

Without a second thought, she shoved away from the wall and launched herself at him, clamping her knees around his thighs, using all her strength to keep his lower body still while grappling to catch his flailing arms.

She pinned his wrists to the floor and squeezed harder with her legs, fully expecting him to buck and fight her.

Instead, he immediately went limp. "That's right. Take me. Take me now."

Were it not for those words, spoken so softly she could barely hear them, she might have thought that he'd blacked out again.

She loosened her grip a little. "Where? Where should I take you?"

A long pause. "Courtyard."

132

"Why?"

With bated breath, she waited for an answer. None came.

"Andre." She let go of his wrists to cradle his face between her palms. "What's in the courtyard? Tell me."

He shook his head. His lower lip began to quiver. He pressed his lips together, and tears spilled from the corners of his closed eyes and trickled down his temples.

"Oh!" She brushed the moisture away with her thumbs, feeling her chest contract. "Oh, don't."

Leaning forward, she buried her fingers in the damp hair at his temples, then brushed her lips across his cheek. She felt his chest lurch beneath her, felt fresh tears slip between her fingers and run warm over her knuckles, and her heart turned over.

She kissed his brow. "Oh, no. *Mon coeur.* Oh, please don't cry."

Suddenly, he clamped an arm around her waist and rolled onto his side, taking her with him. His unshaven chin scraped her forehead. He pressed her cheek to his bare chest.

She tried to turn her head, only to feel his arm tighten inexorably about her ribs.

"No," he growled.

She stayed in his crushing embrace and did her best to remain still. Only when she heard the sound of his even breathing did she relax. It was a long, long time before she slept.

Chapter Eleven

His mouth and throat felt as if he'd eaten sand. Andre wet his parched lips and tried to open his eyes, only to be stunned by a shaft of sunlight that seemed to pierce the very center of his brain. He squeezed his eyelids shut and groaned. His body felt like one colossal bruise, and his head . . .

What the devil had happened to him? He tried his damnedest to recall, and found it even hurt to think.

Darkness. Cold. Dizziness and agonizing pain. And through it all, a vision with gentle hands and a soothing voice, caring for him, telling him that he would be all right.

Everything came to him then. The accident. The petrifying moment when he'd lost his grip on her and gone flying, then rolled and rolled before he'd banged his head on a boulder. . . . He flinched and opened his eyes again, and as his pupils adjusted to the light he realized that he lay on the stone floor of a dusty little room. Alone.

Where was he? Moreover, where was *she?* Glancing about, Andre pushed aside the grimy cloth covering him, then stared down at himself in disbelief. Save for his drawers, he didn't have on a stitch of clothing.

134

She had undressed him? He scanned the room, but aside from several fireplace tools scattered before the hearth and a few burned-out candles, he found nothing.

Where were his shirt and breeches? His boots—good God! Andre sat up so fast, his vision blurred. His boots! If he had lost them, the map would surely be gone, as well. He'd never be able to locate the sword, and everything he'd spent half his life building would be in ruins.

He spotted them in a corner and felt his muscles go slack with relief. He stared at the muddy footwear, then dragged his hands over his face and rubbed his throbbing forehead.

"Merde."

This damned crusade was one disaster after another. He should have been halfway to Arles by now; instead, he lounged here half-naked, like some useless—

The map. She'd most assuredly seen it. *"Merde,"* he repeated.

Gritting his teeth, Andre hoisted himself up, bracing one palm against the wall behind him for support. An onslaught of nausea nearly made him double over. Spotting an open window, he staggered to it and took deep gulps of fresh air, noting that the sun was bright and high in the sky.

Past noon. And Dominique was nowhere to be seen. Gone. She'd fled, taken his clothing with her, and God only knew how far she'd managed to walk by now. Perhaps she'd even found the horse, in which case going after her was futile.

He didn't want to go after her. Hell. He did. Taking one last lungful of air, he pushed away from the windowsill and slowly made his way across the room. What had she done with his shirt and breeches?

His gaze was arrested on the ash-filled hearth. *Nom de Dieu!* She hadn't *taken* his clothes, she'd *burned* them! Cursing again, he thrust one foot into a boot and yanked the map out of the other, then tapped the cylinder against his palm.

Just as well. Deep down, he'd known that all she wanted was a chance to get away. Imbecile, that's what he was, for imagining that she might stay with him. Now more than ever, he didn't need anyone slowing him down, nor did he need the constant upheaval Dominique's little body provoked.

Dominique. He frowned. When had he begun thinking of her by her first name?

He carefully replaced the map and swept another glance about the room, which he now recognized as the Lucrece gatehouse. Suddenly feeling stifled, Andre sought the door, moving as quickly as his stiff legs would allow. Not even bothering to look for his knife, he grabbed the poker from the pile of tools before he staggered out.

In the entryway, he paused for a moment, blinking. The sky was so clear and blue, it hurt to look at it. The breeze felt good on his face and bare chest. He thought he detected the faint blow of a horse, but when he stopped to listen, he realized he'd only heard the rustle of trees.

Hell. He was far better off alone. Despite that thought, he caught himself searching the premises for any sign of her as he wended his way to a cluster of poplars. No sooner had he relieved himself and hiked up his underclothing than he sensed someone's eyes boring into him from behind. Snatching up the iron, Andre pivoted, teetering a bit before catching his balance.

He almost lost it the next second. Standing there holding a bulging satchel in one hand, a bucket of water in the other, was none other than Dominique.

His heart began to pound as he took in the indescribable expression on her face. The odd glint in her eyes, combined with her red cheeks and that hair of hers in disarray, made her look as if she'd just left a lover's bed.

He had a sudden urge to seize her. Shove his fingers into those unruly black tresses. Kiss her until she begged for mercy.

He lowered the instrument to the ground and pushed its tip into the dirt. Half-turning, he leaned the poker against the poplar again and finished fastening his drawers, feigning nonchalance even as his fingers shook. "I thought that was my specialty," he said over his shoulder.

"Pardon?"

The mere sound of her voice caused heat to spread within him. So much for trying to convince himself that he was better off without her. He turned to face her. "Sneaking up on people. You do it well."

To his surprise, her full lips actually curved upward. "You obviously weren't watching your back, and so I thought I'd do it for you."

That floored him even more than the bright smile she continued to bestow on him. He wondered if she, too, had hit her head.

She set her burdens down and swiftly closed the distance between them. "You shouldn't be up and about. Not yet."

He gave a wan smile. "I seem to have misplaced my chamber pot."

She made a noise that might have been a muffled laugh.

"Not to mention my clothes," he went on. "And you. Where have you been?"

"Looking for the horse."

"And did you find him?"

"I followed the tracks. He was headed back toward the inn."

She motioned with her chin. At first, Andre saw only the scarred side of the building, but then a shiny black rump and burr-knotted tail came briefly into view.

"The cart, I'm afraid, is beyond repair." Dominique slapped the dust off her skirts, which, Andre noted, were in tatters. "I discovered it in splinters between two trees."

So many things could have happened to her while she'd been out and about with no one to watch over her. Andre took a step back and braced himself against the tree trunk. "Did you encounter anyone?"

She shook her head. "I found our things strewn over the incline. I'm afraid most of the food was rendered inedible, but there's enough left to tide us over for a day or two."

Immediately, his stomach turned. "Ugh."

Her smile turned sympathetic. "I know you are not hungry now, but you will be. How does your head feel?"

"Like a church bell at high noon."

"A rhythmic throbbing?"

"Mm."

"I brought something that will make you feel better in no

time.'' She started to turn away. ''It will only take a few minutes to boil—''

''One moment.'' Andre caught her elbow. This drastic change of attitude required an explanation. ''Why are you doing this?''

''What do you mean?''

''You had the perfect chance to flee and didn't take it.''

Her brow furrowed, but she said nothing. He gripped her arm a little tighter, trying his damnedest to look stern. ''Why?''

She hesitated. ''I couldn't.''

''Couldn't what?''

''Couldn't leave you, after you . . .'' Her gaze dropped to his hand on her elbow, making him wonder if he was hurting her.

He loosened his grip, but not by much. ''After I . . . ?''

She drew her tongue across her lips. ''I found you facedown in the creek after the accident. Your heart had stopped, and you weren't breathing.''

''You're telling me I came back from the dead?''

''I'm telling you what happened.''

''Why bring me here? Why not simply put me out of my misery?''

She gaped at him. ''Why do you say a thing like that?''

Such compassion in her eyes. And fear. Not *of,* but *for* him. He couldn't recall the last time anyone cared whether he lived or died, himself included.

He looked away. ''What else happened last night?''

''Are you certain you wish to know?''

He hesitated. ''Yes.''

''You fell asleep and . . . you seemed to be waging a battle of some sort in your dreams.''

''A battle?''

She nodded.

''As in war?''

She looked him in the eye. ''As in whatever horror took place in a certain courtyard, Monsieur Philippe Laurence.''

He felt the blood drain from his face. *Bon sang,* what had he babbled in her presence?

138

He let go of her arm. "What more did I reveal last night?"

Her gaze flicked downward, pausing somewhere below his navel, before she raised serious eyes to his and replied, "A great deal, I would say."

For a moment, he could do nothing but gawk at her. "Would you care to elaborate?"

"No. Not really."

His energy was sapping with every passing second. He clenched his teeth. "But I insist."

A tiny smile. "And what will happen if I don't tell?"

His head was now reeling in earnest. He needed to sit down. "Do not play games with me," he grumbled, swallowing hard. "Lives are at stake, and well you know it."

Her smile faded. Delicate brows drawing together, she took his hand and tugged. "Sit. Better still, lie down. You're as white as a sheet."

He let himself sink to the grass, taking her with him, closing his eyes against the whirling colors of the landscape. Before he realized what he was doing, he caught a handful of her skirts and moved to bury his face in them.

"Don't."

He stiffened and started to roll away, but her hands upon his shoulders stopped him.

"It's filthy," she said quickly. "My dress, I mean. I only need to . . ."

Yanking the skirt above her knees, she took his face between her hands and gently but firmly pressed his head to her lap. "Don't get up. Please."

Those small hands. The feel of them on his person seemed exactly what he needed. Stifling a sigh, Andre lay down, closed his eyes, and let himself relax, breathing in the lavender scent of her, rubbing his cheek against the soft flannel of her—

He opened one eye. "Men's drawers?"

"You found them in my trunk last night, remember? I am the short, emaciated connoisseur of fine gentlemen's undergarments who owns them."

Andre groaned, noting the way the flannel clung to her shapely calves. "Shoe leather."

"I beg your pardon?"

"Shoe leather," he repeated, letting his eyes drift closed. "That odd taste in my mouth."

She laughed, a throaty sound that seemed to seep into him, infusing warmth. Presently, he felt her fingers in his hair, stroking.

It felt good. Very good.

After a while he sensed her gaze, and he opened his eyes to find her regarding him as if he were a puzzle she sought to solve. He spotted a small scratch on her chin and raised a hand to brush his thumb across it.

"Did I do that?" he asked.

She shook her head. "A branch. During the accident."

"I didn't . . . did I hurt you last night?"

Her fingers paused before resuming their gentle stroking. "No. Not really."

She was underplaying it, he knew; he'd terrorized poor Mimi with his night fits more times than he could recall. "I should have warned you that I occasionally thrash about in my sleep. What did I do? Tell me."

"You were shaking. I thought you were cold and tried to warm you, but you pushed me away."

Andre grimaced. "To put it mildly, I'm sure."

She shrugged. "I didn't break."

"No," he quietly replied. "No, you didn't."

Dominique. How well the name suited her. Soft and strong at the same time. It reminded him of a song he had loved in his childhood, when nights were peaceful and red wine didn't remind him of blood.

He looked into her eyes. "I am so sorry."

"No need to be. You didn't do it deliberately."

The words struck a tender spot deep inside him. She'd saved his life. Cared for him. And now, instead of calling him a maniac, she was finding excuses for his crazed behavior.

At the very least, he owed her some sort of explanation. His mother's locket gleaming at her throat seemed to emphasize the thought.

Where to begin? He'd never told a soul about that day. Never allowed himself to even think of it. Andre took a deep gulp of fresh air and expelled it, feeling the old familiar garrote tighten about his throat even before he commenced speaking. "*Maman* was from Salzburg," he said, so softly that he could barely hear his own voice.

Her eyes widened. "You are part Austrian?"

"Yes." He raised his eyes toward the heavens and watched a rounded cloud slowly elongate. "Just before the horse went wild, you asked me how she died. Remember?"

Dominique nodded. "You said I did not want to know."

He sighed. "But I suppose you should, if you are to continue to endure my night spells."

She said nothing, but he could feel tension building in the subtle shift of her legs beneath his head.

"I lost my entire family in one day. Sometimes I see it happening again. In nightmares."

She gasped. "Your *family?* You mean—"

"All of them. My mother, my father"—he gulped to relieve the tightness in his throat—"and Victor."

"Your brother."

"Yes."

"How?"

"All three were seized . . . and slain."

"The guillotine?" she whispered.

"No. The guillotine would have been a quick caress compared to what they went through."

"Then . . . ?"

"They were butchered. Knives and swords." Andre clenched his fists, seeing their petrified expressions, hearing their stifled screams, sounds he knew they'd struggled to control. A violent shudder racked his body. "I saw it. Watched every damned grisly detail, and to this day I can't explain why I didn't cover my eyes or look away."

A long pause. "My God. When did this occur?"

"It will be eleven years in September. I was fifteen."

He heard her breath come out in a soft hiss. "How is it that you survived?"

I didn't. "Our driver hid me. Sometimes I wish to God he hadn't. Or that I'd been man enough to show myself and let them hack me to pieces, too."

He felt her thighs grow rigid. "You don't mean that."

141

Andre started to say he did, but before he could utter a word she put her hand over his mouth. "Foolish man. Don't you see? Part of them lives on through you. If you had shared their fate, that wouldn't be possible, would it?"

Her eyes implored him to agree. He recalled what she had told him about her own mother, and realized that she wanted him to reinforce a conviction that had allowed her to endure enormous losses. But Andre couldn't do it. How could he tell her that most of him had died that day, that whatever spirit left in him had later perished and been buried with Mimi?

Slowly, Dominique removed her hand from across his lips, her intense gaze roving over his features, as if by sheer will she could somehow force him to reply. When he continued to be silent, a frown creased her brow. "You do not see it that way, do you?"

"No," he admitted quietly.

Her chest rose and fell in a silent sigh. "Then how were you able to carry on?"

The look of utter sorrow on her face made his heart turn over. Obviously, she was no stranger to pain. Neither was he, but unlike her, he'd never allowed himself to take the time to feel it. Now, looking into the depths of her green eyes, not only was he experiencing the agony of his old wounds being ripped open, but of hers, as well.

Tentatively, she placed the backs of her fingers beneath his jaw. "Tell me," she said softly.

Andre could only stare up into her eyes, afraid that if he began to speak, he wouldn't cease until he'd revealed far, far too much. For her protection, he couldn't do that.

He shook his head. "I can't."

"I understand." She pressed her fingertips against his throat, then moved her hand a little lower and stroked his Adam's apple with her thumb, making his pulse immediately increase.

Back and forth. Her explorations made him feel like dry logs touched by flaming kindling, and Andre thought of ancient healing ceremonies, of priestesses of old whose hands possessed mystical, life-giving powers. He raised his chin, allowing her better access, amazed that such slight contact could provoke so powerful a response in him.

He prayed she wouldn't stop. His prayers were answered in the next moment, for she ran one fingertip along his collarbone, then splayed her fingers wide and moved her hand even lower, smoothing her palm over his bare chest, rendering his flesh hot and his throat bone-dry. It was becoming harder to keep from sitting up and taking her in his arms, but Andre willed himself to remain still, afraid that she would stop if he moved so much as a muscle.

"Andre . . ."

Had she actually whispered his name, or was he experiencing hallucinations?

Her gaze dropped to his lips, and suddenly nothing mattered, not that he'd vowed never to tie himself to anyone, not that their union was a sham, not even that she seemed to have embarked on some crusade to rouse his emotions from the dead.

The only thing that mattered was that she was touching him of her own free will, looking at him as if he were someone to be cherished.

No longer able to keep his hands to himself, Andre took her hand and guided it slightly to the left, pressing her palm to the spot above his pounding heart. Her eyes darkened. As if in a trance, Dominique slowly leaned forward, closer, closer, until he could feel her breath upon his face.

He felt her silky hair spill across his throat and shoulders. She grasped his chin and tipped back his head slightly. Hesitated. He held his breath.

It seemed like ages before her mouth finally brushed the corner of his. Fine tremors shook his body, the blood roared in his ears, and he could have sworn that every last drop of it rushed downward, making him rigid. Again, she grazed his lips with hers, then moved her head from side to side, until he thought madness was a certainty if he didn't have more.

Cautiously, he opened his mouth under hers, capturing her lower lip to savor its warmth and fullness. Still, it was not enough; the desire to taste her was now a raging need. Cupping the back of her head, Andre let his tongue slide between her lips. She started, made a small sound of surprise, her nails digging into his skin.

The slight sting gave him pause, but to his bewilderment, instead of pushing him away, she cradled his chin in her palm and, hesitantly, touched the tip of her tongue to his.

He couldn't breathe. Didn't need to. He'd never known . . . ah, he'd never known that kissing a woman could feel as if she was taking away his very soul. And God help him, at that moment, he would have willingly ripped out the remnants of his heart and given them to her.

Half-rising, he slid one arm around her shoulders and increased the pressure against her mouth, bit by bit easing her onto her back, knowing he shouldn't be doing this, yet unable to stop himself from covering her body with his. He wanted to feel . . . he wanted . . .

She curved one hand around his neck, then buried her fingers in his hair, tugging gently, and Andre felt another violent upsurge where her hips met his. He groaned, letting his tongue slip farther into the recesses of her mouth, chasing hers in a fervent rhythm. She strained against him, her soft breasts pressing to his bare chest, and it took everything he'd ever learned about chivalry to keep from shoving his hand inside the bodice of her woolen dress.

Instinctively, he ground his hips against her. Dominique's body jerked. She countered his movement and gave a guttural sound that made him harden even more, though he hadn't thought it possible.

Oh, God.

He had to cease. Had to, before he lost all restraint and succumbed to the overwhelming urge to make her his, right then and there, with the sun and the open sky as witnesses. She deserved better. Better than this. Better than him.

He started to draw away. She didn't let him. Helpless to refuse what she was offering, Andre let her draw him in again, let her take control, let her kiss him until he thought he'd surely lose his mind or break apart.

Or both.

At last, with a superhuman effort, Andre closed his mouth and pulled back. She raised her chin and regarded him drowsily, her reddened lips parted slightly, her beautiful green eyes questioning. Her fingers were still tangled in his hair, and it was all he could do to keep from bending his head and taking her sweet lips once more.

But Andre forced himself to sit up and move away, although his eyes refused to leave her face, taking in the way her lashes lowered and her cheeks flushed even more under his gaze.

His head began to pound anew. He put the heels of his palms to his temples and pressed. "You"—he cleared his throat—"mentioned that you'd brought back something that would relieve my headache?"

The words sounded strained even to him. She stared at him for a moment, then lowered her gaze and began to rearrange her clothing. "Yes. Willow bark."

She tugged her skirts into place and smoothed her hair, then went about retrieving her satchel, leaving him to stare at her back. Andre closed his eyes and rubbed his temples, wondering what in hell he was going to do with her. And what he was going to do without her, when all of this was over and she left him.

Andre awoke to scraping noises and a smell so foul, he thought he'd died and gone to hell. With great difficulty, he opened his eyes and propped himself up on one elbow. Sitting beside him in the shade of the massive tree he'd been dozing under, Dominique was bent upon cleaning a silver abhorrence she held by the gills.

He swallowed back a sudden surge of nausea. "Dare I ask what that is?"

A brief glance over flying scales. "Our supper."

He grimaced. "Yours, perhaps."

She paused, scale-covered knife gleaming in her hand, and though she frowned at him, he sensed that she was holding back a smile. "I went though a great deal of trouble to catch this trout without a proper rod, monsieur."

"You really shouldn't have, madame." He meant it.

She tilted her head to one side. "You're serious, aren't you?"

"Dead."

"Then go back to sleep. I'll wake you when I finish cooking this, and then you can tell me you won't eat it."

"Agreed."

He eased back down. It wasn't long before he drifted off, only to dream that he was once again in the bowels of a navy brigantine, staring into yet another steaming bowl of grayish, lumpy bouillabaisse.

Too soon, he was being shaken awake. "Andre."

"Mm."

"It's ready."

He squeezed his eyes shut tighter. "I'm not."

"You must eat something. Now, sit up."

Scowling, he did as he was told. He glanced around, bracing himself for the sight of the dreaded denizen of the deep—or, rather, of the shallow—but all he saw was a circle of round water rocks beside a mound of glowing embers. He watched with growing interest as Dominique swept them aside with a stick, revealing a small, smoldering hole.

Andre crossed his arms and smirked. "How fitting. You buried it."

Without regard to his remark, she picked up a second, forked twig, slipped both into the opening, and carefully withdrew the fish. At least, he thought that's what the charred thing was.

He pressed his lips together. "I'd rather partake of another mug of that bitter brew you gave me earlier. At least it made me sleep."

"Have you not heard of the amazing properties of fish?"

"No."

"For one, it remains in the stomach longer than any other sort of meat. And it's delicious."

With a deft hand, she placed the fish on the makeshift plate she'd fashioned from the rocks, then utilized the twigs to halve it.

He gave her his best skeptical look, watching as she speared a small piece of moist white flesh. "What's on it?"

"Sage, rosemary, and mustard seed. Among other good things." She raised the morsel to his lips. His teeth clenched. Her expression reminded him of a mother about to scold her child. "You haven't had a thing to eat since yesterday."

Somehow, he managed to resist the strong urge to turn his head, but opening his mouth proved impossible.

A stomach-turning moment later, she shrugged. "Fine. Suit yourself."

Using her twig for a fork, Dominique began to eat. With manners suited for a formal dinner party, he noted with an inner smile. He swallowed. Fish. Damned if she wasn't enjoying it. And damned if his stomach wasn't rumbling.

He wet his lips. "Uh . . . Dominique?"

She paused, her fishy stick arrested in midair, and the smile she gave him whetted a completely different sort of appetite. Without comment, she leaned forth and slipped the chunk into his mouth.

With caution, Andre sampled it. And to his utter amazement, he found it to be . . . well, edible.

"Who taught you how to prepare fish this way?" he asked.

"I have a friend who is a gypsy."

Andre's brows lifted. Most people would not even think of associating with gypsies. Then again, he was rapidly coming to realize that Dominique was unlike anyone he'd ever met.

And what is that supposed to mean?

Forcing his attention to what Dominique was saying about her friend, he helped himself to more fish. And spent the rest of the meal trying to keep his mind from wandering along some very unsafe paths.

Chapter Twelve

Dominique tightened her grip on the coarse black mane, trying her best to ignore the feel of Andre's solid body repeatedly pushing against her from behind. His thighs clamped hers, his fingers clutched her waist, and his breath came in short bursts, growing more labored with every passing moment.

A glance over her shoulder confirmed her fears: judging by the sweat on his brow and the pallor of his face, the man was on the verge of collapsing. Frowning, she turned her gaze westward, where the last rays of the sun tinted the gray horizon. "Do you intend for us to ride all night?"

"I wish that were possible," he quietly replied.

"The horse needs rest, and so do you."

"I know that."

"Yet you're not stopping."

He pulled on the reins and leaned back, bringing the animal to a brisk walk. "No."

Dominique gave an exasperated sigh. He wasn't well enough to travel in a coach, let alone ride across fields and pastures from sunrise to sunset, yet on the third morning after the accident she had no longer been able to hold him back.

The horse stumbled, and Dominique felt Andre's fingers briefly brush the side of her breast. A tingle coursed through her. Today was the closest she'd been to him since that kiss, the kiss she hadn't been able to forget, the kiss that had made her pulse race and her knees grow weak every time her gaze encountered his. She knew that he was thinking of it, too. His behavior over the past few days was proof. He'd drunk all the infusions she'd prepared for him, politely thanked her for her ministrations, but when he hadn't been dozing—or pretending to sleep—he'd avoided her as much as possible, given the close living quarters.

Pressing her palms to her burning thighs, Dominique gazed with longing at a well-tended cottage in the distance, where a boy herded cattle into a pen. She wasn't used to riding without a saddle, and the blanket Andre had thrown over the horse's back didn't afford much protection against incessant pounding and friction. She shifted, trying in vain to find a position that wouldn't further cramp her aching legs.

Behind her, she felt Andre flinch. "Stop that." He sounded irritated. She moved again, and felt him give her waist a squeeze. "Don't fidget so. Two riders are hell on a horse's kidneys. The last thing this one needs is a burden that squirms."

Prevaricator. Dominique could not contain a knowing grin. Numerous candid talks with Madame had taught her certain things regarding men, and even if she were ignorant, instinct would have quickly enlightened her. All day her derriere had come into intimate contact with Andre's front, and his state was hard, if not impossible, to overlook.

A sudden spur of devilment made her wiggle her bottom again. "I cannot help it. I'm quite uncomfortable."

He muttered something indistinct under his breath and dug his heels into the animal's flanks. The horse bolted, and Dominique caught hold of the mane again, swallowing back a burst of laughter.

"Is it necessary to keep this frenzied pace?" she asked after a while.

"I told you. There's something I must find."

She turned to look at him. "Other than our untimely demise?"

His jaw hardened. "It will not only be our demise, but that of many others, if I fail to unearth—" He clamped his mouth shut, and the dismay upon his face gave her the distinct impression that he'd nearly blurted out a crucial piece of information.

Unearth. Did he mean that literally? Figuratively? Was he referring to the conspiracy to overthrow Bonaparte? Dominique faced forward again. Over the past few days, she'd actually come close to believing he was not her enemy. In fact, the morning after the accident, she'd scoured the incline for the medallion, half-hoping that she wouldn't come upon it.

What was happening to her? Where was her sense of loyalty? For the first time in quite a while, Dominique knew an overwhelming urge to run, to head for the distant hills and keep going. She checked the ridiculous impulse and took one fortifying breath. "What is it you must unearth?" she ventured.

He tugged on the right rein, veering the horse toward a chestnut tree. "I cannot tell you that, I'm sorry. But it is something of paramount importance."

"To whom?"

"Many." With that, Andre pulled back on the reins, and when the animal halted he cocked his head. "I think I hear the sounds of flowing water. The Arnon should be somewhere near." Dismounting, he held up his arms. "Come. We're going to set up camp."

Dominique simply sat there, staring down at him.

He opened his arms a little wider. "Trust me."

"Would you trust someone who never told you anything of import?"

"Maybe. Maybe not." A hint of a smile curved his lips. "But I do promise not to drop you."

She wanted to scream, she really did. He reached for her, but Dominique quickly faced the opposite side and slid down by herself. Pain stabbed up her calves when her heels hit the ground. She squeezed her eyes shut and grabbed hold of the bridle.

"Dominique."

Her eyes flew open. Other than when he'd been half-dead, it was the first time Andre had called her by her given name. She'd never cared for it, but now, spoken in his rich voice, it sounded rather nice. In fact, it sounded wonderful.

He tethered the horse, then came around and gently took her face between his hands. "Look at me."

She did, knowing full well that she should not, because those eyes of his never failed to unnerve her. This time was no different. She stood there, struck by their dark intensity, feeling herself begin to come undone as he grazed her earlobe with the tip of his finger.

"What do you see?" he asked.

A man more beautiful than any human has a right to be. A man of character, whom under other circumstances I would have held in high esteem. Unable to avert her gaze, Dominique held her tongue, hoping he couldn't read her thoughts or hear the hammering in her chest.

He waited. Waited. His gaze dropped to her mouth. Her heart dropped to her knees. At last, he took a deep breath, expelled it in a broken sigh, then bent and lightly kissed her cheek. "If you can't bring yourself to trust me, then trust your instincts."

How could she, when at that moment her every instinct clamored to draw that handsome face to hers and see if kissing him again was as soul-stirring as she remembered? Best listen to her judgment instead, to concentrate on whom this man was and the consequences of letting herself succumb to his allure.

She nodded curtly, sidestepped him, and turned her attention to the satchels strapped to the black's back, all the while feeling Andre's gaze upon her. "I'm famished," she announced. "How about you?"

A cake of soap tumbled out of one sack, and Andre bent to pick it up. "You go ahead and eat." He patted the horse's neck and caught the reins beneath the animal's chin. "I'm going to find that stream. He needs a drink."

She nodded, fished inside the second satchel, and withdrew an empty flask. He took it without a word. Watching him lead the horse beyond the trees, a lump rose in Dominique's throat.

151

God help her, she was beginning to resent her wretched duty to erect walls between them.

He awoke to darkness and the impression that something was amiss. Andre sat up, then glanced around to find Dominique kneeling before a fire she'd built, absently stoking the dying embers with a twig. "What time is it?" he asked.

She started and gave him a blank look, as if he'd roused her from a trance. "Past midnight, I believe." She tossed some sticks into the flames.

"Why are you still awake?"

She shrugged. "I couldn't sleep."

He yawned and rubbed his eyes.

"Besides, I wanted to bathe," she added.

Alarm raced through him. "You ventured to the stream alone?"

"Mmm."

He wanted to admonish her, but didn't. She looked so desolate. What was she thinking? He let his gaze linger on her bowed head, loving the way the fire gilded the tresses escaping her chignon. Her profile brought to mind a cameo, and even wearing shapeless peasant garb she was the picture of gentility, like the fairy-tale maiden forced by her wicked stepmother to dress in rags. Andre smiled. He hadn't thought of that story in decades. *"Cendrillon,"* he said under his breath.

She thrust the stick halfway into the fire and sent him a sardonic look above the sparks. "And you, I presume, are my dashing prince."

His mouth nearly dropped open. How could she possibly have heard him? He glanced down in disgust at his rumpled homespun shirt and brown wool pantaloons, the cuffs of which concealed the tops of his purposely muddied boots. "Who else could I be, attired so splendidly?"

Was it a trick of the firelight, or did he see amusement glimmer in her eyes? He hazarded a grin. "You have uncommonly keen hearing, madame."

She nodded, the corners of her mouth curving up slightly. "Remember that next time you're tempted to voice unflattering associations."

As always, that smile of hers tugged at him with a force he

was unable to resist. Hoisting himself up, Andre took his blanket and moved closer to her fire, feeling more like the proverbial moth with every step.

"Unflattering?" He spread the blanket on the ground beside her and sat down. "Oh, but *Cendrillon* was exquisite, besides hard-working and unselfish. Why else would the prince have confronted all those demons and eight-headed dragons along his quest to find her?"

Her brow furrowed slightly. "I don't recall there being demons or dragons in that story."

"Of course there were." He patted the spot next to him. "And other creatures," he continued, when she had seated herself. "Trolls. Sorcerers. Giant insects. Long serpents with several flicking tongues."

He smiled in answer to her raised eyebrows. "My father had a wild imagination."

She looked incredulous. "Your father told you stories?"

"But of course. Didn't yours?"

A faraway look entered her eyes. She lowered her gaze to the stick she held and peeled away a strip of bark before she answered. "He was far too involved with his patients to spend much time with us."

"Not even after your mother—" He saw her snap the twig in half and wanted to kick himself. "I didn't mean to—"

"It's all right," she interrupted quietly. "I don't mind talking about my parents."

He didn't believe her. In fact, he sensed she rarely, if ever, spoke of them.

She tossed the bits of wood into the fire and watched them ignite before resuming. "After *Maman* died, my father withdrew from us completely. It was as if she took his spirit with her."

Andre sought to displace the terrible need to take her in his arms and chase away her sadness. "Your father must have been an excellent physician. He certainly taught you well."

A nearly inaudible sigh. "I commenced learning when I was five. If I wanted to see Father, I had to assist him. He didn't believe in idling."

"And your mother approved of his putting you to work?"

"It wasn't strenuous work. *Maman* never . . . she loved him far too much to challenge his beliefs. He was already bitter about Paul's refusal to have anything to do with medicine, so she was quite happy when I showed interest."

"But all you wanted was his attention."

"At first, yes. Before I knew it, though, I became fascinated with what he could do. He planned to send me to study at Montpellier; I would grow to be the first female physician in France. Then my mother passed away, and . . ."

"And?"

"He . . . he began to avoid me. It was difficult for him, you see. I looked so very much like her. He rarely came home anymore, except to eat and sleep, and even then he never left his study. Sometimes, late at night, I'd hear him crying. When the revolts broke out, he insisted he was needed behind the barricades, and nothing any of us said could stop him. He had the strangest air about him when he left . . . I'd never seen him so euphoric. I didn't understand why until some peasants brought home his body in a wagon."

Sometimes I wish I'd been man enough to show myself and let them hack me to pieces, too. Andre's own words rang in his head, and suddenly he understood Dominique's extreme reaction to them. He tensed, recalling another damn fool thing he'd said to her: *What do you know of the accursed Revolution?*

He covered her hand with his, selfishly tempted to ask her forgiveness, but found he wanted to give, not take. Gazing at her somber profile, Andre realized why she'd touched him like none other: she had more stoicism than he'd seen in any woman. Come to think of it, more than he'd seen in anyone.

She looked down at his hand, then slowly turned to search his face. Whatever it was she saw there seemed to satisfy her, for she leaned into him, snuggling close when he finally allowed himself to hold her. He felt her softness in his arms and closed his eyes, inhaling her sweet lavender scent, resting his cheek atop her silky head. "What did you do after that?" he murmured.

"I carried on as best I could. While Papa was at war, his

brother Guillaume had come from Nantes to tend the practice. He never went home. I agreed to assist him.''

And Paul? he almost asked. But that was the last place he wanted to take this conversation. ''And Montpellier?'' he inquired instead.

''That became . . . I decided against it.''

Some sixth sense prevented him from asking why, but he could not refrain from posing another question he'd been withholding. ''How old are you, Dominique?''

''Twenty-two.''

''Why is it that you're not . . . ?'' He hesitated, struck by the notion that she might think him rude.

''Married?'' she offered, a bit sarcastically. ''But I am.''

As if to prove it, she raised her left hand, making the wedding band he'd placed there sparkle.

''I think you know to what I am referring.''

She tipped her head back, gazing at the stars. ''My parents married for love. I wished to do the same.''

Her barely audible reply fell upon Andre's ears like a thundering accusation, and it was all he could do not to wince. ''That is uncommon,'' he managed.

''Is it?''

''Most people marry for . . . more practical reasons.''

''Such as?''

He fingered his own wedding band, which suddenly felt heavy and too damned tight. ''Money. Power. Social advancement.''

''It sounds as if you speak from experience. Which of those admirable motives was yours?''

''For my first marriage? None,'' he muttered, grateful her back was to him, and that she couldn't see the guilt upon his face.

''You loved her, then?''

He stared into the flames, now feeling like the slithering creature that had yet to *become* the proverbial moth. ''I married Mimi for political reasons.''

''I'm sure she was aware of that.''

Lower than a larva, he decided. The accursed thing at least

possessed the ability to fashion itself a cocoon. "I tried my best to keep her happy."

Bon sang, why was he justifying himself? He willed away an unwanted remembrance of Mimi, her bare legs wrapped around his waist, murmuring endless avowals as she matched his every thrust. The image faded, replaced by another sordid episode, then another. Nausea rose in Andre's throat. How many nights had he spent using his body in methodical attempts to sate her need for a love he couldn't give? How many days had he spent trying to convince himself that deception was essential to his ultimate success?

"Andre."

Andre, mon amour, *I'm carrying your baby. He's going to be beautiful, just like you.*

He closed his eyes, only to be assaulted by an even clearer image, of green shards from a smashed champagne bottle beside a toppled night table. Once more, he smelled the acrid odor of stale wine, felt the crunch of broken glass beneath the thin soles of his boots. . . .

The muscles of his arms convulsed and hardened, squeezing, as if he could crush the memories until they were pulverized to dust and blew away.

The bed. Blood. Blood on the floor. So much of it, God, so much of it.

"Andre, please!"

Please, please don't let it all be hers.

A shriek pierced his ears, snapping him to awareness.

"You're hurting me!"

A living, breathing woman was floundering in his arms. Dominique! He let his arms go slack, and she pitched forward, gasping, on all fours. His heart lodged in his throat. "What have I done? Are you all right?"

She sat back on her heels, then turned to fix him with a wild-eyed stare, her chest rapidly rising and falling. "My"—she fought for air—"my ribs are still intact, I think."

How could he have let himself harm her? Regret scorched Andre's throat like acid. He shoved himself to his knees and held out a shaking hand, then let it drop to his side, not trusting himself to touch her again.

She studied him in silence. "You look as if you've seen the netherworld."

"I'm sorry. I've no idea what possessed me."

A poor excuse for nearly cracking her bones; he fully expected her to let him know he was a savage, then turn away. Instead, she crawled back to him, green eyes delving deeply into his. He tried to close his mind, but he could tell she saw through every barrier.

She laid a gentle hand upon his cheek. "Another ghost, perhaps?"

His eyes suddenly stung, as if smoke had blown into them. He blinked and swallowed hard.

"Andre . . ."

So much tenderness in her quiet voice. He set his jaw and lowered his gaze. "For God's sake, don't."

"Don't what?"

"Don't be so good to me."

Her thumb grazed his cheekbone as she drew the tip across his lashes. "Why?"

If only you knew. "I don't deserve it."

Ever so gently, Dominique ran her fingertips over his clenched jaw. "What you don't deserve," she whispered, "is all this pain."

He shook his head. "You are—"

His words ended in a rush of breath as she shoved her fingers into his hair and tugged, yanking him forward. He caught his balance, looked up, and glimpsed vehemence in her stare.

And then her mouth crushed his.

He couldn't believe it. For a few seconds Andre went still, his arms out at his sides, nearly stunned senseless as her tongue slid between his lips and urged them apart. Heat flashed through him with staggering intensity. Before he knew it he was rolling with her, propping himself up onto his side, wrapping his free arm around her, and wedging a knee between her thighs.

He opened his mouth a little wider and rocked against her, unable to suppress a groan when she slid one leg along his thigh and arched into him in response, imprisoning his face between her hands, drawing so hard on his tongue, it almost hurt.

She sought to devour him. Specks whirled behind his closed eyelids, from lack of air, or maybe from the violence of the desire she'd given rise to, he didn't know. He didn't care. Didn't care if she continued kissing him like this until she robbed him of his final breath.

He moved his hand over her upper back, gathering fabric in his fist, struggling to regain some fragment of control. But she relinquished nothing, holding his head firmly in place while she plundered his mouth, taking him to the edge of endurance, until his mind clouded and his memories crumbled, until he knew nothing but this moment and his need.

Need. For her. He ached with it. He unclenched his fist and ran his open palm over the coarse wool of her dress. His fingertips encountered softness. He moved his hand a fraction, feeling his last thread of restraint stretch taut.

A ragged sound vibrated in his throat. And then he let his fingers close around her breast. She started. He felt the pull of her gasp against his mouth as she jerked back her head to stare at him, breathing hard, still cupping his face.

Dizziness gripped him. He couldn't seem to suck sufficient air into his lungs. He felt her heart race under his palm, felt her shudder as her fingertips pressed into his jaw, and tried in vain to judge her expression through the fog clouding his vision.

Lunacy, that's what this was. The very moment he'd laid eyes on her he'd known it lurked nearby, ready to claim him if he surrendered to the urges she could provoke with just one smile. Three days ago, when she had kissed him, he'd felt it start to overtake him, and he had reaffirmed his vow to keep his distance. And now . . .

He bent his head. She tensed. He stopped and searched her face, noting the way she shook her head almost imperceptibly and drew her bottom lip between her teeth. Abruptly, she released him, but Andre seized her hands and held them to his chest, unwilling to let her go just yet. Her lashes lowered, then slowly lifted to reveal the emerald windows to her soul.

The next instant, Andre felt as if a bayonet had speared his heart. For what he saw glint briefly in her eyes before she looked away surpassed all of Mimi's adoring words and gazes put together.

Chapter Thirteen

By noon the following day, Andre's reticence had nearly unnerved Dominique. Not to mention the weather, which matched his chilly disposition, and the way he rode, as if driven by Satan himself.

She wiggled her numb toes and did her best to keep her seat on the horse, unwilling to risk sparing a hand to wipe away the tears caused by the wind whipping her face. Good thing he sat behind her; the last thing she needed was for him to see her tears and draw the wrong conclusion.

An hour later, dull pain cramped her lower belly. She pressed her lips together, longing for another dose of the valerian and dandelion root tea she'd prepared that morning, cursing, as she did every month, the cross of being female. Just when she thought she might double over, Andre steered the horse behind a thicket and pulled back on the reins. The sudden change from motion to repose made her light-headed, and when he leaped to the ground she made no move to follow.

"Make haste this time," he said over his shoulder. "We only have four hours until nightfall."

She concentrated on simply inhaling and exhaling, not bothering to reply. He took another step, then swung around, obviously annoyed. She must have looked ghastly, for his expression immediately softened. "What is amiss?"

Dominique shook her head. "Nothing. You go ahead. I'll wait here."

His lips thinned. "*Sacrebleu!* Why didn't you tell me you were ill?"

"I'm not," she protested, watching him storm back toward her.

He took hold of the reins and stared up at her in stony silence. Frowning, he guided the horse to a fallen tree, then stepped onto the trunk and mounted in one graceful vault. The black blew vigorously, prancing under their weight. She felt Andre's arms enfold her and pull her close, and wished she dared take his strong hands and press them to the spot where it hurt the most.

"Lean on me," he told her in the mildest tone she'd heard from him in days.

He'd said the same thing in the dungeon at Loches, when he'd unbound her. It seemed so long ago, but as she relaxed against him, Dominique felt that same warm sense of security. She closed her eyes. For several moments, he merely sat behind her, letting the gelding stomp in place. Why the delay? She glanced over her shoulder to see him staring fixedly in the direction from which they'd come. She felt a subtle tightening of his body. And then he wheeled the gelding around.

Dominique lifted her brows. "What are you doing?"

"Exactly what it looks like," he replied in the lower-than-normal pitch that always betrayed his uneasiness. "Heading back."

"*Regarde.*" Andre pointed. "Just ahead."

Dominique looked, and saw civilization in the form of a modest stone farm house with white shutters and a red clay-shingled roof. Beyond it loomed a barn and a much larger building, undoubtedly the main house where the landlords lived. "*Dieu merci,*" she muttered as yet another spasm gripped her. "Where are we?"

161

"The summer home of an acquaintance."

"Oh."

This time, she didn't think to protest when he held up his arms to help her dismount. Once on the ground, her wobbly legs refused to sustain her, and Dominique clutched Andre's shirtfront, unable to keep from briefly resting her head on his broad chest. She felt his muscles stiffen and tried to move away from him. He placed a hand on her upper back, then caught her chin and tilted her face to meet his assessing gaze. "How do you feel?"

"Fine."

He nodded gravely. "Lying, madame, is definitely not your forte."

Was that a trace of a smile in his blue eyes? Before she could decide, he swung her up into his arms and headed for the house in swift strides. "Where does it hurt?" he demanded.

Dominique leaned her head against his raspy cheek. "Nowhere," she murmured, "and everywhere."

He shifted her weight to rap on the door. "Meaning?"

She was spared the mortification of having to reply when brisk footfalls and an irritated voice came from inside. "Jacques, you lazy good-for-nothing! I send you to fetch some eggs, and it takes—"

The door burst open and a plump, red-cheeked woman appeared in the entryway, brandishing a rolling pin coated with flour. The matron's eyes widened, and whatever words she'd meant to utter became a slack-jawed wheeze. For a good few seconds silence reigned, broken only by the squawk of chickens from the nearby barn.

Dominique felt Andre's arms tighten around her, and when he spoke, his voice was strained. "Hello, Edelle."

The rolling pin clattered to the floor. "Merciful heavens! Monsieur! Is it really you?"

"May we come in?"

Still in a stupor, the woman reached out to lay a hand on Andre's arm, as if needing physical proof that he was real. "What brings you here?" Edelle's gaze moved to Dominique, making her feel thoroughly appraised with only a sweep of those alert gray eyes. "And who is this you're carrying?"

Not an artful bone in her body, Dominique thought, giving Edelle a smile, which the older woman returned, albeit somewhat distractedly.

Andre cleared his throat. "This is—"

"*Mais,* where's my head, keeping you standing there like that?" Edelle interrupted. "Enter, enter!" She stepped aside, wringing her hands, and ushered them into a sparsely furnished room that smelled faintly of baked apples and cinnamon. "Where is your carriage?"

"Horse," Andre corrected. "I left him at the bottom of the hill."

"Him? One horse? Is he alive?" Edelle demanded breathlessly. "Mercy! I'll go tell Jacques to tend to him. You find a place to rest your weary bones." With that, she rushed out in a swirl of light gray skirts and slammed the door behind her.

Dominique blinked, momentarily forgetting her discomfort. "Who was *that?*"

Andre gave her a half smile. "Officially, Edelle is the cook here. But she's considered part of the family."

Whose family? Andre evidently knew his way around this place, for he crossed the room and headed straight for an adjacent door, which led to an enormous rustic kitchen. He lowered Dominique onto a wooden bench beside a sunny window. "Better?"

He looked quite pale himself. She gazed into his worried dark blue eyes, wanting to run a fingertip along his unshaven jaw. "Yes, thank you."

He nodded curtly, then swung around to retrieve a bucket of clean water from several sitting in a corner. No sooner had they washed their hands with the chunk of lye soap Andre found than Edelle bustled in. "You both look as if you could use something to eat. And good, strong coffee, *oui?*"

The mention of food made Dominique's mouth water. "Thank you, I'd like that."

"Don't worry about your horse," Edelle said, snatching two plates and a half-full platter from a cupboard. "He'll be fine. I convinced Jacques to feed the poor thing some of the good hay he hoards. Wanted to run straight here and see you for himself, the lazy good-for-nothing. Would I lie about something like the monsieur dropping in out of the blue?''

Andre pulled up a green chair and straddled it, not even attempting to reply. Not that he could have gotten a syllable in edgewise, Dominique thought.

"This is all I have," Edelle went on apologetically, plunking down the platter, upon which sat three-quarters of a golden apple tart. "I was just fixing to make cheese pies, but I used every last egg for the tart crust this morning, and—'' She clasped her hands together, her eyes suddenly misting as she beamed down at Andre.

He gave her a fond smile. "It's good to see you, too, Edelle.''

"Oh, monsieur . . .'' Edelle dashed her tears away, leaving a trace of flour on one round cheek. "I'm overjoyed to see you sitting in that chair again, but I can't help thinking you wouldn't be here unless you were in some sort of trouble.''

Andre folded his arms over the chair back, saying nothing.

Edelle sighed. "You and your secrets.'' She whirled, snatched up a knife, and began cutting the pastry, casting a curious glance at Dominique. "Don't tell me anything. And I don't think I want to know about those rags you're wearing, either. Just promise me you'll let me burn them, as soon as you change your clothes.'' She slid a generous wedge of tart onto a plate and pressed it into Dominique's hands. "You do mean to stay for dinner?''

He nodded. "And overnight, if it isn't too much trouble.''

Edelle rolled her eyes. "Trouble, he says.'' She handed him his plate. "Eat your tart, young man, and stop talking nonsense.''

Andre's lips twitched as he took up his fork. "Yes, ma'am.''

The older woman watched them each take a bite, then set to making coffee. Dominique marveled at the flavor and texture of what was truly the best pastry she'd ever tasted, and tried not to eat too fast, only half-listening to Edelle's chatter. It was more interesting to watch Andre, who, despite his evident familiarity with his surroundings, seemed tense and kept glancing out the window.

Presently, Edelle brought Dominique a cup of fragrant coffee. "Monsieur doesn't take sugar, but I thought you'd like it sweet."

"You guessed correctly," Dominique assured her, smiling. She took a sip and drew her tongue over her lips, wondering what other things this woman knew about Andre.

Edelle rounded on him. "We worried and worried about you." She clucked her tongue. "Working yourself to death, living in that rainy foreign place and spending all your time with snooty folks, without a soul to keep you warm at—"

"Edelle!" He'd almost shouted it. Poor Edelle jumped, looking thunderstruck, and Dominique regarded him with raised eyebrows, noting the redness of his ears.

He set down his fork. "You haven't given me the chance to introduce my wife, Dominique."

Edelle's expression didn't change. "Your *wife*, monsieur? Your wife? Are my ears failing me?"

He shook his head. "Not in the least. We were married this past week."

Edelle's round eyes sought confirmation from Dominique. She nodded, and was rewarded with a grin that could have turned stone into rock candy.

"Oh! *C'est sensationnel!*" She caught one of Dominique's hands and squeezed. "*Ma chère petite.* May God bless you with joy, every day." She clapped her hands. "What a surprise for Mademoiselle!"

Dominique didn't miss the way Andre's cup paused briefly en route to his lips. "The mademoiselle . . . is here?"

As if on cue, the kitchen door swung open. A tall blond woman paused in the entry, fingers still gripping the handle, and when her distressed black eyes arrested on Andre she pressed her free hand to her throat. "Andre," she said in a choked voice.

Venus incarnate, Dominique thought, taking in the newcomer's flawlessly coiffed blond hair, doll face, and slender figure. Slender, save for her chest, which threatened to rend the satin-edged bodice of her high-waisted pink dress. Dominique surreptitiously glanced down at herself, suddenly feeling flat as a crepe without the filling, and every bit as dull.

The scrape of wood on stone grated on her ears. Andre surged to his feet. "Yvette," he said in the deepest baritone she'd ever heard from him. "I wouldn't have come here if—" His voice broke.

Yvette shoved herself away from the door, leaving it to bang against the wall as she ran to him and launched herself into his arms. "Jacques told me you were here. I didn't believe him. Oh, God, it's been so very long—"

"I know." Andre clasped her to his tall frame and briefly squeezed his eyes shut, as if stricken by physical pain.

Who was this woman? Dominique watched Andre's face take on an expression that, for some reason, made her scalp tingle. After a moment, she realized why: it was the same haunted look he'd had the night he'd told her about his family's slaying.

"You're looking well," he said.

Yvette wrenched out of his embrace, caught both his hands, and looked him up and down. "And you, *mon cher,* look positively frightful."

A humorless smile. *"Merci bien."*

"Why are you dressed like that? What mischance has befallen you?"

"A carriage accident. We acquired these clothes—"

"We?"

Andre nodded, casting a glance at Dominique over Yvette's blond head. Yvette turned and followed his gaze. Her eyes widened. "You dragged a *lady* across the countryside upon one horse?" She shot him an accusing glare. "Andre, how could you?"

"And not just any lady, mademoiselle," Edelle piped up. "She is the monsieur's wife."

"His wife?" Yvette breathed. She took Dominique's hand and crouched before her, pink skirts rustling. "Please, do forgive my rudeness. Welcome to Manoir de Châtaigne. I am Thérèse Duval, but everyone calls me by my middle name, Yvette."

"I'm pleased to make your acquaintance. My name is Dominique."

"Dominique Montville." An emotion Dominique could not describe briefly glittered in Yvette's eyes. "How melodious. Enchants the ear, like lovely poetry. You met in London, yes?"

"That's right," Andre interjected before Dominique could even open her mouth.

A warm smile curved Yvette's lips, but Dominique saw tears brim in her dark eyes. "I never thought I'd come to hear such news. I wish you every happiness."

"Thank you." *Who are you?*

"*Je m'excuse.* I am a sentimental goose." Rising, Yvette blinked and shook her head, as if to clear it. "You must be utterly exhausted. How does a hot bath sound?"

Dominique smiled. "Like heaven."

"Good. You shall have it at once. I've come upon some marvelous bath oils, guaranteed to soak away any and every ache." She turned to give Andre a hopeful look. "You do intend to stay at least for a few days?"

He shook his head. "We must depart first thing tomorrow morning."

"I don't suppose there's anything I can say to change your mind?"

"I'm afraid not."

Yvette seemed crestfallen. "Very well. I'll have Claire prepare your chamber." She smiled at Dominique. "But I will personally see to your bath. Let us go to the main house, shall we?"

Dominique rose.

"We don't want to impose," Andre protested. "Edelle's spare room would suit us just fine."

Yvette arched one delicate brow. "Impose? What utter foolishness. I haven't seen your face in ages, and Dominique and I must get acquainted." She took Dominique's hand and tucked it firmly in the crook of her elbow, her warm black eyes expectant. *"N'est-ce pas?"*

Dominique smiled, suddenly realizing how much she'd missed feminine companionship. *"Oui."*

Yvette nodded. "It's settled, then." She breezed toward the door with Dominique in tow, leaving Andre no choice but to follow.

They'd barely stepped outside when Yvette halted. "Oh, and Edelle"—she cast Andre a sidelong glance—"about that trout for tonight's dinner . . ."

Andre's lips parted, his blue eyes manifesting such horror that Dominique could not contain a burst of laughter.

Yvette laughed, too, as did Edelle.

"No need to fret, monsieur," the cook said cheerfully. "I'll take that fish and feed it to the cats."

"Such gorgeous hair. I would have given anything for mine to be that color."

Dominique turned away from the cheval glass to smile at Yvette, who had just let herself into her chamber with something green and silky draped over one arm. "My best friend always tells me I resemble a gypsy." She dragged the brush through her hair one final time, her scalp smarting from all the snarls she'd had to disentangle.

"Your best friend is undoubtedly as envious as I am," Yvette replied good-naturedly. "And I have never seen a gypsy with green eyes."

"I have."

"Have it your way, then. I'm afraid I have no bangles, bells, nor tambourines to give you. So"—she took up the apple-green garment she'd brought and shook it out—"you'll have to settle for a pleated skirt."

Dominique surveyed the high-waisted satin dress Yvette held by its puffed sleeves. The skirt was, indeed, creased in the latest fashion, and discreet gold embroidery edged the hemline and heart-shaped décolleté.

"I've worn it only long enough to try it on." Yvette spread the gown on the bed with care and smoothed her hand along the bodice. "Do you like it?"

Like it? She'd never even dared to dream of wearing such costly things. Dominique glanced down at the heavily embroidered ivory chemise she'd donned a moment earlier, which the chambermaid had boasted belonged to the mademoiselle herself. And now, this dress. It was too much.

"It's exquisite," Dominique began, "but I don't—"

"Do," Yvette countered. "Please. I had one of the maids alter the bust while you were bathing, so it no longer fits me. Besides, you wouldn't want to see what light green does to my complexion."

"Then why did you have it made?"

"It was a gift. I pass it on to you."

Dominique tipped her head. "Well . . . *si vous insistez. . . .*"

A flash of perfect teeth. "Absolutely. May I help you put it on?"

Smiling, Dominique set down the hairbrush. "Very well."

Moments later, she stared in awe at her own reflection in the looking glass, holding her hair aside as Yvette fastened the lacings in the back. The dress might as well have been tailor-made for her, and her alone.

"Your maid is a very talented seamstress," she said. "A perfect fit, and no one even took my measurements."

"I must confess to cheating a little. I took the liberty of giving Marie your chemise." Yvette stepped back, looked Dominique up and down, then moved to adjust one sleeve. "There. Now all we need is for Marie to tend to your coiffure, and you'll look positively stunning for Andre."

The mention of his name brought a flush to Dominique's cheeks. She'd been so preoccupied with ridding herself of days of road dust, tending to her intimate needs, and then with playing dress-up, that she hadn't considered having to face him at dinner. And later, when it was time for bed.

"Where is Andre?"

"Out at the stables, to see about a proper mare for you to ride tomorrow." Yvette shook her head. "One horse, indeed! How long have you two been journeying through the countryside in that barbaric fashion?"

"Not long. A week or so."

"One week! *Mon Dieu!*" Yvette placed a hand on Dominique's arm and lowered her voice conspiratorially. "He told me of that frightful incident at the inn, and of your accident. You are very courageous, Dominique. I couldn't have endured half of what you've been through and still be standing, let alone look so well.''

Dominique tried not to show her surprise. Whoever this woman was, Andre considered her a confidante. She recalled the fierce way he'd embraced her, and felt a twinge in her chest. Exactly how close a friend was she?

"What is his hurry, anyway?" Yvette inquired.

Evidently, he doesn't trust her any more than he does me.

Dominique tensed. "Your supposition is as good as mine."

Yvette rolled her eyes. "Men. They'd do well to remember we haven't the constitution to keep up with them." She nodded pointedly toward the neatly folded stack of white linen cloths upon the dressing table. "And you in that predicament. If you feel as awful as I always do that time of the month—"

"Probably worse," Dominique admitted, glad for the change of subject. She didn't bother telling Yvette that all she suffered from was cramps, and it would be at least another week until she'd need to use the cloths.

"La pauvre." Yvette patted her shoulder. "And what an inconvenience, to have this come about during your honeymoon. How do you feel?"

Dominique relaxed a bit. At least Andre hadn't told her about the highly irregular particulars of their marriage. She forced a smile. "A hot bath always helps."

Yvette's black eyes crinkled at the corners. "And dinner will restore your strength, I promise. I know for a fact that Edelle has something special planned. In all the years she's worked for us, she's never disappointed." She picked up her skirts. "Which reminds me, I'd better send Marie to do your hair or you'll be late for dinner."

Dominique opened her mouth to protest, but Yvette stopped her with a wave of one manicured hand. "I won't even hear of it. A special dress requires a special coiffure."

"Thank you. You have been more than kind."

"De rien. Actually, it is I who should express my gratitude. Were it not for you, I wouldn't have known the joy of seeing my brother again."

Brother? It was all Dominique could do to keep her mouth from dropping open.

Yvette's brow furrowed. "Oh, dear. I fear I have committed a faux-pas. He didn't tell you, did he?"

Dominique shook her head. "He spoke of a brother, but not of a sister, I'm afraid."

"Um . . ." Yvette lowered her gaze in evident chagrin. "In truth, Andre is my brother only by marriage." Her next words were spoken so softly, Dominique had to strain to hear them. "You see, your husband's first wife was my younger sister."

Chapter Fourteen

The first thing Andre saw when he strode into the dining room that evening was a provocative rear view of Dominique's figure, clad in a flimsy light green gown that clung to every curve. The second thing he noticed was what she was staring up at.

The painting. Oh, no. His throat closed. Mimi's favorite portrait of the two of them sitting in her father's prized rose garden on their wedding day, the very canvas that once graced the mantel of his own house in Paris.

Sweet, sentimental Yvette. Apparently, the clothes he now wore weren't the only things she hadn't had the heart to sell at auction. His gaze shifted from Mimi's radiant face and his own post-adolescent countenance to Dominique's artistically braided chignon, and Andre seriously considered heading for the open patio doors to seek refuge in the blackness of the night.

"Andre." Skirts swishing, Dominique turned to face him. He tensed, expecting to encounter censure in her glance. Instead, he found quiet compassion and . . . and something else that, of late, sparked in her eyes whenever she so much as looked his way. He wanted neither, yet some abysmal part of him reached for both with a ferocity that left him tongue-tied.

"I couldn't help but pause to admire it," she said self-consciously.

He managed a nod. She slid an arm around his waist. He didn't draw away, but put his arm about her shoulders and drew her to his side, needing the feel of her, warm and alive, against his suddenly chilled body.

"She was extremely beautiful," Dominique said softly. "She might have been Yvette's twin, except . . ."

Except for her brown eyes, and that air of naïveté about her, Andre completed silently.

Two harried-looking menservants marched in, arms full of covered dishes, followed by a stone-faced elderly butler who watched with an eagle eye as each placed his burdens on the already laden table. "Dinner is served," he intoned.

Andre guided Dominique toward a seat where her back was to the painting. "Where is Mademoiselle Yvette?" he asked the butler.

"Here I am."

Andre turned, doing his best to give his former sister-in-law a smile. Always solicitous, never complaining. After Mimi's death, she'd been invaluable to him, insisting on taking on numerous responsibilities that ought to have been his. Such as making funeral arrangements and finding a buyer for his house.

Yvette returned his smile and looked him up and down approvingly. "My, what a transformation! Amazing, how well those old clothes fit." A teasing gleam entered her eye. "Take your rightful place at the head of the table, monsieur."

He hesitated, but the butler ceremoniously pulled out the chair in question, giving Andre no option but to take it. As he sat down, his knee inadvertently brushed Dominique's. Unconsciously, he glanced up at the painting. From her permanent place upon the wall, Mimi seemed to stare straight at him, and guilt coiled in his belly like a poisonous snake.

"Do you still favor Sancerre red?" Yvette inquired.

Andre tore his gaze from the canvas, longing for cognac. "Yes." He spread his serviette on his lap and listened to

Yvette instruct her servants before she took her place, knowing a twinge for having forsaken her along with the rest of his past when he'd debarked at Portsmouth that rainy winter morning. Good God. How could two years of his life have passed so quickly?

"You haven't lived," Yvette said, "until you've tasted Edelle's marvelous coq au vin. Isn't that right, Andre?"

"Yes." Andre discovered he had no appetite but feigned interest in the plump brown bird, garnished with croutons and surrounded by steaming mushrooms and potatoes.

A servant filled his glass with ruby liquid, which Andre immediately downed. For the next half-hour, he shoveled forkful after forkful of food into his mouth, listened to Yvette relate numerous tales of Paris for Dominique's benefit, and lost count of the times his wineglass was refilled.

The more he drank, the harder it became to avoid looking across the table at Dominique. She was beautiful in that green dress. His gaze kept straying to the gold ribbon along her décolleté, his hands shook at the remembered softness of her flesh when he had cupped her breast, and he questioned again the wisdom of having brought her here. In fact, he wouldn't have, had he known that this year Yvette had retreated from Paris to Les Châtaignes a full two-and-a-half months early.

He willed himself to focus on Dominique's face, only to see her pop a good-sized mushroom into her mouth. His fork arrested in midair and wavered, a steaming chunk of potato plopping back onto his plate.

"You've yet to tell me how the two of you came to meet and marry," Yvette said during a lull in the conversation.

"I was arrested the first time I saw Andre," Dominique replied without so much as blinking.

Andre nearly pierced his tongue with the tines of his fork.

She gave him a brilliant smile. "He actually swept me off my feet."

Beneath the table, Andre sought Dominique's foot and tapped it with the tip of his boot. She looked at him through her lashes, then raised a morsel of chicken to her lips, discreetly licking off some dripping sauce before sucking the meat into her mouth. He shifted in his chair. Compared to this, purgatory would surely prove more pleasant than a spa vacation at Aix-les-Bains.

"A whirlwind courtship." Yvette inclined her head and beamed. "How romantic."

"Quite." Andre took a gulp of his Sancerre. "And what of you, Yvette? As I recall, at every ball you had innumerable gallants by your side, and several others groveling at your feet. How is it that your father hasn't yet forced your hand to wed?"

Yvette flushed. "You exaggerate. And, yes, Father is becoming more impatient with every passing season." She leaned forward and lowered her voice. "I'll tell you a secret not even Father knows. I've set my sights on someone, but the gentleman in question doesn't know it." Her eyes twinkled. "Perhaps he will, in the near future."

Andre raised his wineglass. "Here's to the fortunate man, whoever he may be."

Yvette, too, swept up her drink. "To marriage, and to many healthy children."

Andre looked up in time to see Dominique's glass tip slightly in her hand. Lips parted, she stared at him above the rim, two spots of color staining her cheeks.

Andre, mon amour, *I'm carrying our baby.*

His stomach squeezed into a painful knot. Forcing a smile, he wrenched away his gaze and tossed back all of his wine in one quick swallow. By the time dessert arrived, he'd lost all hope that alcohol would grant him impassivity.

". . . the Treaty of Amiens," Yvette was saying. "It remains to be seen whether England will evacuate Malta if Napoleon withdraws from Holland and . . . what other territories, Andre?"

"Switzerland," he mumbled, watching Dominique pick up her napkin to dab at her lips, now reddened from all the hearty eating she had done.

They'd looked the same after he'd kissed her. He turned away so fast, his vision blurred. And ended up viewing the accursed portrait.

"That's right, *la Suisse.* But there are other—"

Merde. Andre shoved himself away from the table, barely

noticing the servant who rushed forth to grab the back of his chair before it could hit the carpet. Through a haze, he saw both women start and turn to stare at him.

"Is something amiss?" Yvette questioned.

Everything. "Not a thing." He patted his breast pocket and withdrew one of the thin cigars he'd found earlier in his chamber. "I do not wish to foul the air with this, that's all. Enjoy your torte."

Doing his best to keep from faltering, he made his way toward the *porte-fenêtre* leading to the garden, the butler following in his wake.

"But it is raining," he heard Dominique protest.

He quickened his step and yanked open the door before the butler could even reach for the handle. The glass panes rattled and a gust of rain-swept wind rushed in, wetting his boots and the curtains that fluttered around him. Behind him, he heard Dominique utter words he failed to distinguish, and wished he were too drunk to discern the worry in her tone. "Fear not, madame," he said over his shoulder. "I will not melt."

He stepped outside and tipped back his head, welcoming the sting of cold droplets pelting his face and hair.

Dominique lurched to her feet, but Yvette's restraining hand on her arm stopped her. "I must go to him," she said, wincing as the other woman's nails pressed into her flesh.

Yvette shook her head. "Trust me. Going after him right now would be a bad idea."

Dominique's gaze remained fastened on the doors through which Andre had disappeared into the night.

"Believe me," Yvette persisted, "he's not good company when he has had so much to drink. Would you care to take dessert in my sitting room, where we can speak in private?"

Dominique hesitated.

"You're looking rather pale," Yvette said softly. "How are you feeling?"

The truth be told, the dull ache at the base of Dominique's spine had increased throughout the course of dinner. "Far from well," she admitted.

"In which case a promenade in the freezing rain will do you nothing but harm." She rose, her hand still clutching

Dominique's wrist. "I had Edelle brew a pot of very special Indian tea. Wouldn't you like some?"

Dominique shook her head. "Thank you, but I'd like to retire, if you don't mind."

"Very well. I'll escort you to your room."

"No need to trouble yourself. I know the way."

"No trouble at all." Yvette murmured something to the butler, then looped her arm through Dominique's and gently but resolutely guided her out into the hallway. As they ascended the stairs, the patter of rain upon the roof grew louder, and Dominique glanced at the ceiling, thankful there was no thunder.

Yvette patted her hand. "Don't worry. In all the years I've known Andre, he's never so much as suffered a cold."

"There is a first time for everything," Dominique muttered.

Hours later, Dominique descended the stairs on tiptoe, a red silk robe concealing her nightdress, a lighted candle flickering in her hand. Sleep hadn't come, and neither had Andre, and the rain still hadn't ceased. The last step creaked under her slippered feet, and Dominique hurried to a window and pushed aside the heavy shutters, but she could see nothing for the condensation fogging the glass.

She eased the blinds back into place. What had disturbed Andre so? The painting? Her play on words regarding her arrest? Heart heavy with concern for him, she started down the darkened hallway. Every hearth in this part of the house had been extinguished, and save for the rhythmic tick-tock of a clock, all was quiet.

She shivered, wishing she'd accepted Yvette's offer to lend her a book from the extensive library she'd spoken of with pride. Prowling about the manor like a thief wasn't seemly for a guest, but Dominique was certain she'd go mad if she had to spend another moment tossing and turning in bed.

She passed the door she knew led to the dining room and paused in an open entryway. Elegant furnishings, a plush Aubusson carpet. No books.

None in the next room, either. Pulling her collar tighter about her throat, she made her way to the third door, which was closed. Carefully, she pressed down on the handle and eased it open, gritting her teeth when the ancient hinges squeaked despite her efforts to refrain from making noise.

A musty odor filled her nostrils. This had to be the library. Dominique slipped inside, and as she did so she realized that what she'd sensed was not the smell of books, but that of aged canvas and oil paint. She raised the candle higher. Paintings. They occupied every bit of wall space. And each depicted Andre.

Dominique's mouth fell open. She ventured farther inside, candle and sconce wavering in her hand, an eerie feeling gripping her as her gaze shifted from one likeness of him to another, and another. Andre impeccably dressed in a French navy uniform, standing beside an elderly and obviously high-ranking officer. Andre sitting on a blanket overlooking a lake, a picnic basket at his feet. Unmoving on the bow of a tall ship, his blue eyes bleak, his chestnut hair ruffled by the sea breeze.

Andre smiling. Laughing. Scowling. Musing. Every possible mood and pose was represented in vibrant detail, so masterfully that Dominique could almost sense his chest rising and falling as he breathed.

"A marvelous subject, was he not?"

Dominique nearly jumped out of her skin. She whirled to find Yvette, one shoulder propped against the door jamb, three candles burning in the silver candelabrum she carried. "I didn't mean to startle you," she said.

Dominique pressed a hand to her pulsing throat and exhaled a lengthy breath. "I didn't hear a thing. I was too taken with . . ." She gave Yvette an apologetic look. "Forgive my intrusion. I sought—"

"You are welcome to explore every corner of this house, if you so desire. I only came down to see if you needed anything."

"Did I wake you?"

Yvette shook her head. "Lately, I haven't been able to fall asleep until two or three. My physician has yet to prescribe an effective sleeping elixir."

"Still, I must apologize. I meant to find the library and ended up here instead."

Yvette nodded distractedly and came to stand at Dominique's side, treading lightly, as if she were entering a sanctum. "It's been a while since I last ventured in here," she said in a soft voice, her gaze skimming the walls. "I had forgotten how very..." Her dark eyes turned expectant. "What do you think of them?"

"They're splendid. Whoever painted these possessed a wealth of talent."

Yvette beamed. "I am so pleased you think so."

Dominique's eyes widened. "You painted them?"

A strained laugh. "Heavens, no. I can barely fashion a decent embroidery pattern. Mimi, on the other hand..." She sighed. "My sister was an artist. These are her so-called failed attempts to capture Andre's spirit."

It dawned on Dominique that the canvas she'd admired before dinner had been done using an identical technique. "The painting in the dining room—"

"Her favorite," Yvette confirmed with a nod. "The only one she considered worthy of display. She called it a self-portrait, because she thought of Andre as part of herself." A long pause. "She loved him very much, you know."

Dominique shifted, not knowing what to say.

Yvette's lashes lowered. "I'll never forget the evening when ... when they first met. My father had returned from Egypt, and had invited some friends and a few officers to a dinner party at our home in Paris. Even the First Consul was there."

Dominique raised her brows. "Bonaparte?"

"Mais, oui." She pointed to the portrait of Andre with the heavily decorated officer. "My father was an admiral."

Dominique scrutinized the older man's features and noted smiling brown eyes identical to Mimi's. "I see."

So, that was the political reason for Andre's first marriage. Unquestionably, the alliance to an admiral had helped further his career. Dominique's candle sputtered, and a drop of hot wax singed her wrist. She flinched.

Yvette promptly took the sconce from her, set it on the mantel along with her massive candelabrum, and stood staring fixedly at the dancing flames. "Mimi had long since set her sights on someone. A young architect . . . I believe he hailed from Nantes. She talked about him constantly, although she'd only spoken to him briefly once or twice. He was a guest that night. I thought I'd help, and arranged a midnight rendezvous for them in the garden." Yvette's mouth thinned into a twisted line. "Had I known what that would lead to, I would never have done such a thing."

Dominique could not suspend her curiosity. "What *did* it lead to?"

The flickering candles cast dark shadows on Yvette's pale face. "I didn't realize that the scoundrel thought he was meeting me. When it became clear it was not I, but poor Mimi, who'd sought his company, he laughed. Told her he'd never be seen with a cripple, no matter how comely her visage might be. And then he made her an indecent proposal."

Yvette began to pace, her blond head bowed, her hands clenched in the skirts of the long nightgown that swept the bare wood floor. "You see, a . . . a frightful accident had left Mimi with a limp when she was barely six. There were times when she relied upon a walking stick because of the pain." Her chin came up, her eyes flashing. "And that—that bastard treated her like so much baggage." She halted before the largest of the paintings and contemplated it for a few moments. "Andre happened to be outside smoking one of his cigars," she went on in a softer tone. "Mimi said he appeared out of nowhere, looking like wrath itself dressed in a navy uniform. He felled the architect with one blow to the jaw, then picked him up by the cravat and tossed him into the rosebushes." A tiny smile. "There wasn't one guest who failed to hear him bellow when his derriere connected with the thorns. I heard it said the insolent wretch was ever after known as 'Porc-épic'."

Dominique's lips twitched. "Porcupine?"

Yvette's smile widened. "That's right. Although Mimi maintained the first four letters alone would have suited him better." She moved closer to the portrait and ran her fingertips lightly along the gilded frame. "After that, she believed the sun rose and set with Andre. He always treated her as if she weren't a cripple." She shook her head. "Can you imagine? That same night, he insisted that she accompany him to a

coveted ball taking place the following week. She told him
she couldn't dance, but he would have none of it.''

It sounded like the sort of thing Andre would say. Dominique smiled. ''How chivalrous of him.''

Yvette nodded. ''I thought the world of him for that. So did
my father. He'd nearly given up on finding her a husband, and
then Andre asked him for her hand . . . so soon. Such a surprise. Andre was . . . he could have had . . . anyone. So many
women wanted him, even though he had no money, and everyone knew . . .''

Dominique strained to comprehend Yvette's words, now
spoken so rapidly and tonelessly, the woman might as well
have been talking to herself.

''Anything my sister wanted, Andre gave her. He always
seemed to find the funds somehow . . . so good to her . . . kept
her satisfied. At least, he did when he was home.''

''I gather he was away often?'' Dominique asked.

''Constantly. His work . . . Forgive me for—for rambling,
but . . .'' Yvette's chin began to tremble. ''We've been so very
worried about him. For two years, he has been living alone,
hasn't even . . .'' She bit her lip and lowered her gaze. ''I do
so want Andre to put the past behind him.''

*That monklike regimen you imposed on yourself would have
sent me straight to Charenton, with all the other lunatics.*
Rochefort's words, the ones she hadn't understood when she'd
been eavesdropping that first night, struck Dominique with
crystal clarity.

Yvette raised tearful eyes to hers. ''He blames himself for
what happened to Mimi,'' she said in a hoarse voice.

Dominique's throat tightened. ''What makes you think
that?''

Yvette sniffed. ''One day when he returned from one of his
missions, he . . .'' She paused to take a shuddering breath,
tears rolling down her cheeks, and Dominique's heart froze at
the wild gleam in her eyes. ''He found her . . . at the foot of
the bed . . . and she was . . . she was . . .''

*Wedding ring . . . constant reminder of your imagined cul-
pability.* Dominique squeezed her eyelids shut in horrified understanding. ''Oh, my God.''

"How I wish he hadn't been the one to find her . . . like that," Yvette blubbered, wringing her hands. "But he did, and it destroyed him. The day after the funeral, he boarded a ship for London and never looked back once. The only news we ever learned of him was through letters from Edelle's cousin Pierre, who was his valet and insisted on following him to England. And what Pierre wrote was never encouraging." She wiped her wet cheeks with her sleeve, struggling visibly to compose herself.

Dominique placed a steadying palm on the woman's arm. "Why have you told me all this, Yvette?"

A wan smile trembled on Yvette's lips. "You must be an exceptional woman, to finally draw him out of his isolation. I've seen the way he looks at you. You don't know what it means to me, to see him once again regard a woman that way." She clamped her hand over Dominique's, her fingers tightening in a grip that was almost painful. "It's time for him to lay Mimi to rest. And I believe you are the one to help him do it."

I've seen the way he looks at you.

Oh, if only Yvette knew the truth. Dominique threw the coverlet aside and swung her legs over the edge of the bed, feeling positively heartsick. She wished she'd never ventured out of the bedchamber, never seen those paintings, never learned how Mimi had worshipped Andre. She wished she'd never found out that he had, indeed, loved his first wife. And most of all, she wished the knowledge didn't bother her so much.

Again, she went to the window and parted the shutters to squint into the blackness. Again, she saw the same barren rose bushes and chestnut trees, and not much else. Again, she heard a dog howl in the distance. Or was it a wolf?

Shivering, she turned away from the glass, pressing both hands to her aching lower belly. At least, the rain had finally stopped.

Where was he?

First wife. Dominique shook her head. Had she actually begun to consider herself his *second* wife? Moreover, had she been hoping he would come to . . . she swallowed hard, recalling the way she'd thrown herself at him, not once, but twice. The way he had responded . . .

Oh, Lord. She crossed her arms over her suddenly tingling breasts, mortified by her immediate and intense reaction to the mere memory of his hand upon her. Foolish. Unutterably foolish, that's what she was, for provoking a man who'd been alone for so very long. He was only human; of course he would respond that way. Had he been anyone else, he would have surely pressed his advantage.

Would she have let him? She shut her eyes, refusing to ponder the answer.

Somewhere in the house, a clock chimed. Nine times. Ten. Eleven.

Silence. Footsteps. In the corridor. His.

Her heart lurched as the rhythmic sounds came nearer, and she snatched up the red robe she'd earlier discarded, barely managing to thrust an arm through one sleeve before Andre paused at the door. She fumbled with the second sleeve. And then, to her utter disbelief, his strides resumed. She tipped her head and stared at the opposite wall, as if by doing so she could somehow see his progress. A door creaked open, then closed with a soft click.

He'd entered the adjoining chamber. She dropped her hands to her sides, letting the robe slip off her shoulder. Of course he hadn't come. He needed to change out of his wet clothing first.

Dominique swept up the wrap and started to don it again, then changed her mind and tossed it on a chair. She glanced at her reflection in the looking glass. The long-sleeved cotton nightdress covered her modestly from neck to toe. Her loose hair, however, was a tangled mess. She raked her fingers through it, then ceased, struck by the realization of what she was doing.

A sneeze resounded from his room. She heard a muted thump, and then another. His boots, most probably. She crawled back into bed and pulled the covers to her chin, listening to the squeak of the floorboards as he moved about. An image of the way he'd looked that first night, when he'd all but torn off his shirt, flashed before her eyes. She squeezed them shut, but Andre's muscular chest persisted, in such stark detail that her breathing quickened and her pulse began to race.

The clatter of fireplace utensils. Light footfalls. Utter stillness. It stretched on and on, until she finally realized that he'd gone to bed in the other room. He wasn't coming.

Dominique rolled onto her stomach. Evidently, he didn't wish to insult Mimi's memory by sharing a bed with another woman in this very house. She wouldn't have to sleep beside him, after all.

She should be relieved. Why, then, the sudden tightness in her chest? Why the painful lump clogging her throat? No reason, she thought, then buried her face in her pillow and cried herself to sleep.

Chapter Fifteen

"More coffee?"

"Please."

Andre murmured his thanks to Yvette and brought the steaming cup to his lips, hoping against hope that the strong brew would chase away the ache that seemed to expand his brain. He wished to hell he hadn't made a visit to the wine cellar last night. The cognac he'd found hadn't helped him to sleep, and this morning he felt as if all of it was sloshing about inside his skull.

"You've hardly eaten anything," Yvette observed.

He glanced at the ormolu mantel clock. Twenty past nine. And Dominique had yet to make her appearance.

"Andre?"

"Hmm?" He looked down at the omelet before him, swimming in melted butter, and had to take another gulp of coffee to keep his stomach from rebelling.

"You haven't fallen ill, have you?"

He set down his cup down, meeting Yvette's worried gaze with a half-smile. "Don't tell me. I look positively frightful."

She tipped her head, her black eyes gleaming. "That was

yesterday, *mon cher*. Today, you look absolutely hideous.''

Andre studied her. There was no pretense in her teasing smile, no censure in her glance. Had anyone told him she would take his presence here so well, he would have refused to believe it. He wished he could say the same about himself. Smothering a sigh, he reached for a croissant, knowing his doting sister-in-law would not relent until he ate at least one. ''Thank you,'' he told her.

She raised her brows. ''Whatever for?''

''I truly appreciate everything you've done.''

''I have done nothing.''

He shrugged. ''Call it whatever you wish. I'm grateful.''

She rolled her eyes. ''You are family, Andre. And if you try and thank me one more time, I'll throw you out.''

He smiled. ''No need. I intend to leave as soon as—''

Her spoon clinked as she let it drop onto her saucer. ''But you can't!''

It was his turn to raise his brows. She only waved her hand and continued in the same vehement tone. ''I will not hear of it. The roads are muck; no one in their right mind would even attempt travel after such rain.'' Yvette frowned over the rim of her cup, then took a sip of coffee. ''Like it or not, you will remain at least another day.''

''Impossible.''

''There's no such thing.''

Andre shook his head. Her temperament never failed to surprise him. Because she looked so much like Mimi, he half-expected Yvette to act like her, as well. Mild. Acquiescent. If anything, Yvette was just the opposite.

''How is Dominique?'' she asked.

''Asleep,'' he muttered, feeling guilt tug at his chest.

He'd managed to stay away from Dominique all night, but at dawn's first light he'd lost the battle with his will and stolen into her chamber. He'd found her slumbering restlessly, sighing in her sleep, her black hair fanned on the pillow, and it had taken much determination not to pull her into his arms and kiss her awake. In this very house.

He took a bite of his croissant and gazed across the table at the woman who looked so much like his first wife. He'd always considered her a beauty, a more sophisticated version of Mimi, but now he found himself thinking that her eyes were too dark, her hair too light, her brows and lashes colorless . . .

"Have I changed that much?"

The question snapped him out of his musing. "Hmm?"

Yvette smiled, smoothing her fingertips over her temple. "You were staring as if you'd spotted a wrinkle or two."

"No." He gripped the croissant so tightly, it flattened to greasy crumbs between his fingers. "No wrinkles."

She studied him for a moment, her pale brows drawing together. "You used to be able to tell when one was teasing."

He looked away.

"What happened to you, Andre?"

He couldn't bring himself to meet her gaze. "You, of all people, should know what happened."

"Three years have passed since then."

"Two. Only two."

"Do you think she would have wanted you to go on suffering this way?"

He set his jaw.

"Andre—"

He tossed the mangled croissant onto his plate. "I'd rather not discuss this now."

"Good heavens! If not now, when?"

He didn't reply. Exhaling a harsh breath, Yvette pushed back her chair and rounded the table, moving so close that he could smell her perfume. Rose—the very scent Mimi always wore. The pressure in his head increased until he thought his skull would split.

"I wasn't going to say anything," she began.

"Then don't."

"But I must, since I doubt anyone else has had the nerve to tell you." He gave her his most challenging look, but she went on, undaunted. "She was my only sister, but she's gone, and no amount of anguish will bring her back."

The misery must have shown on his face because her voice softened, as did her features. "The customary mourning period is one year. You've more than exceeded it."

He needed to get away from that nauseating fragrance, not

187

to mention her remarks, which fell upon his ears like daggers. Without a word, Andre rose and went to open the window. Yvette followed. He felt her sharp gaze pierce him as he clasped his hands behind him and took his fill of crisp spring air.

Such purity and light outside. He longed to capture just a fraction of that brightness for his soul. The notion immediately led to thoughts of Dominique, and suddenly Andre wished it was she, and not Yvette, standing beside him. Why wasn't she awake yet?

"What of Dominique?" he heard Yvette demand.

Andre tensed. She couldn't possibly have read his thoughts. "What of her?"

"Do you love her?"

He cast Yvette a glance over his shoulder, unable to believe his ears. "What sort of question is that?"

She shrugged. "A pointless one, I guess. You married the girl."

"That's right."

She took an audible breath. "Then again, I cannot help but wonder . . . your marriage was so sudden . . ."

He swung around to face her. "Who told you that?"

Yvette pressed a hand to her throat and took a small step back, making him regret having practically snarled at her. "Why . . . no one. I merely deduced . . . Pierre never mentioned your courting anyone. Quite the contrary."

"Pierre."

A nod. "He wrote to Edelle quite often."

Andre gritted his teeth and turned back to the window, making a mental note to wring his valet's neck when he next saw him.

"Which is more than I can say for you," Yvette admonished gently. "Before you left, you promised to send a missive now and then. Remember?"

Oh, he remembered that lie, all right. He nodded curtly and forced himself to focus on the barren rosebushes below. The last time he'd been here, they had been laden with glossy leaves and blooms big as his fist.

A heavy silence settled between them. It was Yvette who

finally broke it. "I will not ask what sort of crisis brought you to France after all this time. But tell me this: Would you have come to Les Châtaignes were it not for Dominique's, um, predicament?"

What did the woman want of him? He bowed his head and pressed two fingers to the bridge of his nose.

He felt her hand on his shoulder. "Are you all right?" Yvette gave him a shake, leaving him no choice but to look at her. "Would you have stopped to see me?" she repeated.

He tried to swallow. Couldn't. "No."

She nodded, seemingly not surprised at his answer, but hurt showed plainly in her dark eyes. Her mouth twisted almost imperceptibly. Enough to make a familiar crease appear at one corner. Enough to make her look exactly like . . .

He suddenly found breathing impossible. Mimi. Mimi. She'd stared at him that way a thousand times. The pain in his head snaked to his neck, his shoulders, coiling around his heart so tightly, he wanted to scream.

Pain. He hadn't felt it so acutely since the funeral. A windy day. He remembered Yvette's black veil whipping about her face as she stared at him throughout the eulogy, silently deeming him responsible—"I'm sorry," he blurted out before he could stop himself.

She stepped a little closer and took hold of his hand, clutching it tightly. "What for?"

He turned up his palm, his fingers tightening around Yvette's. "I might have stopped them. I should have . . . God, had I but come home earlier that night—"

"No." Her voice shook. "You couldn't have prevented what happened."

He thought he might choke on her loathsome floral scent. It took a conscious effort to keep drawing air into his lungs. "I could have—"

She grabbed hold of his other hand. "Listen to me. You had no fault in what occurred."

She sounded so convinced. He searched her face for something that countered her words and found nothing but sorrow and sincerity. He cleared his throat. "Are you trying to say . . . you have forgiven me?"

Tears brimmed in Yvette's eyes. "Dearest," she whispered, "you have done nothing wrong. I've nothing to forgive."

Andre stared at her, stunned beyond words.

"But if you're ever going to be happy"—she drew a shuddering breath—"you must forgive yourself."

And all this time, he'd been convinced she'd thought him guilty. His throat constricted as he watched Yvette struggle to smile at him through her tears. Tears he had caused. God only knew how many more she'd shed.

"I know how very much you miss her," he said.

She sniffled, swaying slightly. He caught her before she could collapse, wrapping one arm around her waist. He bent his head. "Yvette . . ."

Out of the corner of his eye, he saw a blur of white. He halted. Glanced to the side. And spotted Dominique standing in the entryway. Staring. To say she had a shocked look on her face would have been an understatement. The next moment, Yvette saw her, too. With a gasp, she tried to pull out of his embrace, but Andre held her fast, knowing that manifesting guilt would only make matters worse.

And so he finished what he'd started, placing a brotherly kiss on Yvette's wet cheek. Only then did he release her and turn to greet his wife. "Good morning."

"Indeed, it is." Dominique swept inside, her lips curving upward, but he could tell the smile was false.

"Perhaps you'd like some breakfast," he suggested, hastening toward her. "There's—"

"But I've eaten. I meant to find Yvette and thank her for the wonderful tray she sent up."

Andre stopped in his tracks and turned to look questioningly at Yvette, but she avoided his gaze. "I'm glad you enjoyed it," she said politely. Though she returned Dominique's smile, it was more than obvious that she was perturbed.

Suddenly, the cool air from the open window was not enough for Andre. As soon as Dominique moved within his reach, he took her hand and tucked it firmly in the crook of his elbow. "Will you excuse us?" he asked Yvette, who leaned against the windowsill, her hands clenched in the folds of her skirts.

"Certainly."

Dominique looked up at him. "Where are we going?"

He clenched his teeth at the resignation he read in her eyes and escorted her toward the doorway. "Out."

Andre rounded the house with Dominique in tow and headed straight for the copse near the lake. Only when he was certain they were completely hidden from prying eyes from the manor did he stop and let her go.

For a while, he simply stared at the ripples the gentle breeze created on the sunlit water, taking even breaths, trying his damnedest to put what had just occurred out of his mind. Dominique stood by his side, saying nothing, as if she sensed his need for quiet and some time to compose himself.

The crisp air did wonders for his raging headache. A few quiescent moments passed, and somehow, it did not surprise him that he felt entirely at ease sharing the silence with her. He picked up a smooth round pebble and skipped it across the surface of the water. She did the same, only with more speed, sending it a greater distance than he had. He raised his brows.

She shrugged, her gaze fixed on the horizon. "Paul taught me."

"Oh."

It was immeasurably gratifying to merely look at her. The white morning dress she wore emphasized her ebony hair to perfection. She'd arranged it herself this morning, and he discovered the familiar simple chignon suited her far better than the elaborate coiffure she'd worn the previous night.

"I like your hair this way," he said, reaching out to tuck a stray lock behind her ear.

She took a sideways step, but Andre caught her hand, squeezing her delicate fingers as if they were his last hope for survival. Her gaze remained averted, her small hand limp in his grasp. "What's wrong?" he asked.

Again, she shrugged. "It's not important."

"It is to me, if something bothers you."

No reply. Andre frowned. He knew exactly what was wrong but hadn't a clue why he needed to hear her admit it.

"How did you sleep last night?" she inquired tightly.

191

He gave a humorless smile. "Like hell."

With his free hand, he cupped her chin, attempting to tilt her face to his. All he obtained was a brief glance before she obstinately lowered her lashes, but he did notice that her eyes were rimmed with red. He squeezed her hand. "It doesn't look as if you fared any better."

Dominique made no response to his less-than-complimentary remark. Indeed, she stared right through him, with such a bleak expression that his heart grew heavy. That wayward tendril of hair blew across her lips. It struck him that she was the most desirable woman he had ever set eyes on. Even with red eyes and dark circles. Even with her hair ruffled by the wind.

Especially with that hair of hers ruffled by the wind. He bent his head enough to cleanse his rose-overcome senses with her fresh lavender scent. "Perhaps you'd like to stay and rest another day?"

She yanked her hand from his and raised her chin. "Would *you?*"

The question sounded almost like an accusation, which, for some reason, warmed his heart. "That would depend," he said.

"On what?"

He tried, and failed, to keep his lips from twitching. "On what's for dinner."

She gave him a strange look, and shivered.

"Are you cold?"

"No."

The toneless monosyllable served to thrust him beyond the limits of his patience. "But I am," he said, and with one swift move, Andre pulled her against him in an embrace so fierce, she gasped. He buried his face in the fragrant hair atop her head, inhaling deeply. "In fact, I think I'm freezing."

She stood passively in his hold, making him wish that she would try to push away. Or better yet, respond. Where was the woman who only the other day had kissed him until he thought he'd go stark, raving mad? "Where is she?" he whispered.

She stirred a little. "Who?"

192

He loosened his grasp a bit and brushed his lips against her temple. *"Cendrillon."*

A lengthy pause. "Lugging her pumpkin back home, of course."

Just what the devil was that supposed to mean?

His head began to pound anew, the pain far worse than before. The past twenty-four hours had been utter pandemonium, and now he felt as if he was on the verge of losing something priceless.

Hell. So be it.

Abruptly, he released her and turned on his heel, almost ramming into a wooden bench as he staggered off, one hand pressed to his throbbing forehead. This was exactly what he'd been avoiding for the past two years.

Women.

"Andre!"

Nothing but trouble.

"Andre, wait!"

He heard her running to catch up with him, every footfall a mallet striking his skull. He would have quickened his step, but he couldn't find the strength.

She grabbed his sleeve. "I'm sorry."

He halted. "For what?"

"I'm sorry that . . . that you had to come here because of me. I know how difficult it is for you."

What? "What do you know? What do you know of anything?"

"I do know. I learned everything. Yvette—"

"Yvette." He almost snorted. "I might have known. In her blind eyes, I'm an accursed saint."

"And in yours?"

He gave her a sardonic look. "If I'd wished to unburden my conscience, madame, I would have sought the services of a priest."

She shook her head. "It wasn't your fault."

"Wasn't it?"

"No."

Confound it. First Yvette, now Dominique. But then, how could either of them know the ugly truth, when he had hidden it so deep inside that only he and God could see it?

He rounded on her, fists clenched. "Did Yvette tell you I married her sister because her father happened to be one of Napoleon's closest friends?" She didn't seem surprised, so he continued. "That I took any and every assignment away from home because I couldn't stomach the endless lies I had to feed her?"

Still, no reaction. He grabbed her shoulders, leaning so close that he could see the gold flecks in her irises. "That in return for her love, I used her like a whore? Hmm? Did she tell you all of that?"

At last, he saw something glint in her widening eyes. "No," she said in a faltering voice.

He nodded curtly. "No. Then perhaps she told you how I decided to stop shunning Mimi only when I learned my false devotion had gotten her with child."

She gaped at him. "You . . . had a child?"

"I fathered one. She never had the chance to give birth to it."

A strangled sound escaped her. He'd finally managed to shock her. Good.

He let go of her rigid shoulders and shoved his hands into his pockets. "That's right. Mimi was pregnant when she was murdered. Shot in the middle of the night by people who were after me, and I wasn't there to do a cursed thing to stop it, or take the lead ball that was meant for my own worthless skull."

There. The truth was finally out. For years, he'd kept it within, a thorn imbedded in his heart; he'd grown accustomed to the ache, and sometimes even managed to forget it.

Until the day he had encountered Dominique. One look at her, and what he'd thought were hardened scars had burst open, smarting far worse than when the wounds were fresh. Because she made him yearn for something he did not deserve. It was high time she recognized him for the vile bastard he really was.

"I was in Paris," he began. "I had returned that very evening."

In time for Christmas, as Mimi had begged him to do, when he had needed to reflect on the staggering news that his efforts

194

to feign love had taken seed. He'd lied to her, saying he'd been called away on assignment, then dashed to Orléans to confide in Rochefort and seek solace in male companionship and cognac.

Rochefort had helped him come to terms with the reality that he'd created a new life. A week later, Andre was prepared to embrace it. Ready to be a good father, if not a good husband. And then . . .

He felt a gentle hand upon his arm. "What happened?"

It nearly killed him to recall, but, for the first time since that night, he felt impelled to talk about it. "We'd barely begun eating dinner when a messenger arrived. The missive said Napoleon's coach had nearly been blown to bits."

"You worked for him. Of course you would assume he'd need you in a crisis."

Why was she finding excuses for the inexcusable? "She needed me more!" he bellowed. "That deranged Corsican runt could well have waited!"

Dimly, he registered her staggered expression at his irreverence toward Bonaparte. Some fraction of his mind warned him that he'd gone too far, said too much, but he could no sooner stop the torrent of words than he could cease the uncontrollable tremors that overtook him. "I left, and didn't venture home until after midnight. I found her . . . lying there . . . cold . . . blood . . . shattered glass . . . everything strewn all over. They'd searched the house . . . even slashed the chair cushions. While I was busy mollifying our First Consul and his precious Josephine, Mimi was shot. In the face."

Dominique pressed her fist to her mouth, her horrified gaze fastened to his.

Andre's vision blurred. He took a backward step and braced himself against a tree. "Ironic, isn't it? She wanted me to stay at home because she feared something would happen to me."

"Oh, God."

He blinked and swallowed hard, tasting bitterness and salt. "I used her. And I got her killed."

Dominique stroked his arm. "That isn't so."

"Damn it! Don't try to tell me—"

"How can you possibly believe you used her?" she demanded. "If you didn't care for her at all, then why do you feel such torment? Why do you still wear her ring after all this time?"

He bowed his head and buried his face in his hands.

"Why, Andre?"

The deep breath he sucked in did nothing to ease the spasm racking his chest. He felt as if he were slowly crumbling inside. "You're wrong. I didn't love her. Couldn't."

Not after what happened to his parents and his brother. The day he'd seen them slaughtered, his heart had all but ossified.

"I think she knew," he whispered. "She knew . . . and loved me anyway."

"Mon coeur," Dominique murmured, "she couldn't have known. Because I'm sure you showed her nothing but affection."

His body lurched with the effort to contain himself. Just when he thought he could no longer withstand it, he felt her arms encircle his waist, her soft cheek warm against his chest, her body a vivid reality against him. "I know," she whispered. "I know how very much it hurts."

He drew a ragged breath and held it, wanting to retain her sweetness. "Don't waste your sorrow on me. I am not worth—"

"Hush." She tightened her hold, let her head fall back, and Andre stared into her eyes, marveling at the tenderness shining in their beautiful green depths. "Don't waste your breath, Montville," she said, "I ascertained your worth some time ago."

He exhaled sharply, feeling his heart contract as the pieces of his past begin to crumble and fall away, one by one, like fragments of an ancient mosaic. Then he was clasping her to him, leaning his chin atop her head, not caring who happened to see or come upon them.

He held her for a very long time, rocking her slowly, marveling that such a tiny woman could infuse so much strength, even as he selfishly absorbed every bit of it. He remembered how his father used to say that everything happened for a reason. Was there a reason fate had brought him here?

He turned his gaze toward the heavens. Sunlight filtered

through the dense boughs overhead, and for the first time Andre noticed burgeoning buds and light green leaves upon the branches. Spring. Green growth and new beginnings.

He cast a glance around, suddenly feeling confined despite the fact that he was surrounded by acres of land and trees, the sky his only ceiling. Muddy roads or not, he wanted to get away from this place with its ghosts that refused to leave him be, away from everything and everyone.

Everyone but Dominique. The tiny sorceress who had the power to penetrate the depths of his lost soul.

He brushed a kiss atop her head. "Do you think you're well enough for travel?"

An emphatic nod. "I'm fine. Strong as a bull."

"An ox," he corrected absently.

"Is there a difference?"

"Yes."

Dominique looked up at him, delicate brow furrowed.

"Huge," he added pointedly, smiling in spite of himself.

As understanding dawned on her face, a lovely blush colored her cheeks, and Andre felt his spirits rise and soar. Keeping one arm about her shoulders, he pushed away from the tree and guided her toward the mansion.

"We haven't far to go," he said. "Two hours, at the most. And at a reasonable pace, I promise."

She mumbled something under her breath.

He inclined his head. "Pardon?"

"I said, I'd rather we rode hard and fast."

Andre gave her shoulders a squeeze. "Me, too. And I know just the horse to accommodate you."

Dominique shifted her weight from one foot to the other, waiting for the groom to finish tightening the cinches on Andre's chestnut gelding. Beside her, Yvette stood twisting a handkerchief in her hands, looking pallid despite the rouge on her high cheekbones.

"Are you certain you cannot remain for dinner?" she asked Andre in a strained voice.

"After that copious lunch you fed us, I doubt we'll want to even look at food until tomorrow." When she continued to regard him with concern, he took her hand and pressed it to his lips. "Don't worry. The roads aren't nearly as bad as you think."

Dominique couldn't help but contemplate the two. Aphrodite and Apollo. Yvette's carefully coiffed blond tresses complemented Andre's dark hair perfectly, and unlike herself, the woman was tall enough to look into his face without having to strain her neck. Stomach knotting, Dominique watched as they embraced, noting that when Andre attempted to pull back, Yvette clung to him for a moment longer.

Dominique's spine grew rigid. Though Yvette had been nothing but proper throughout the meal at noon, Dominique hadn't forgotten the not-so-sisterly expression she'd seen in those black eyes when she'd happened upon the two of them that morning.

"Good-bye, Dominique."

Dominique faced her with her best smile and extended a hand, but Yvette caught her shoulders to kiss her on both cheeks instead. "Take care," she whispered. "Remember what I told you."

Meeting Yvette's conspiratorial gaze, Dominique couldn't find a trace of artifice or venom. An uncomfortable guilty feeling settled over her. Perhaps she was mistaken. Perhaps Yvette truly did look upon Andre only as a brother.

The farmhouse door burst open and Edelle bustled out, round cheeks flushed, clutching something to her ample bosom. Her pale eyes watered as she rushed forward to press a small satchel into Andre's hands. "For you, monsieur. Your favorite. I found this way in the back of the larder." She wiped her eyes with one corner of her snowy apron, then turned to Dominique. "God be with you, madame. God be with you both."

The groom finished outfitting Andre's horse, then disappeared into the stables and returned with a second, smaller mount, a pretty black mare with a striking white blaze between her huge brown eyes.

"She's beautiful," Dominique breathed.

"Her name is Étiole," Andre said, patting the mare's withers. "I promised Yvette you'd take good care of her."

Dominique's discomfort increased tenfold. Not only had Yvette just given her a practically new blue velvet riding habit, now she was lending her this magnificent animal, as well.

"I am indebted," she said to her as Andre lifted her into the sidesaddle.

"Indeed," Yvette returned, regarding her prized mare with pride. "Be forewarned, I do intend to collect."

Dominique's gaze snapped to Yvette's face. Again, she could discern nothing hidden behind the merry gleam in the woman's dark eyes. She gripped the reins. The mare pranced, chomping at the bit, and Dominique took up the slack, deciding it was only the brisk afternoon breeze that raised the fine hairs along the back of her neck.

Chapter Sixteen

Andre leaned forward in the saddle and stared straight ahead, suppressing the urge to turn and scan the narrow path behind them. Although he'd done that often during the past half-hour, he'd seen and heard nothing unusual. If someone was following them, he knew how to do it well. Or else the strain of the past couple of days had muddled his instincts.

Dominique looked at him over her shoulder. "This is what you call a reasonable pace?" she called over the sound of pounding hooves.

"I want to arrive there before dark," he said. "As I recall, you were the one who wanted to ride hard and fast."

She smiled, and he grinned back. She seemed to be enjoying testing Étoile's capabilities. No sense in worrying Dominique unnecessarily.

Two hours later, they brought their horses to a halt in front of a provincial house, so well hidden in the woods that no one traveling the main road would have suspected its existence. Though obviously old, the dwelling, with its brick exterior, neatly trimmed hedges, and a candle in every window, looked very inviting.

A short, muscular man appeared out of the darkness, a lantern glowing in his hand. His face brightened when he spotted Andre. "Monsieur Montville! At last! Welcome, sir, welcome!" He took hold of the chestnut's reins and bowed to Dominique. "Madame."

"Georges." Andre nodded, his gaze searching the second-story windows as he dismounted. "Monsieur Rochefort waits inside?"

Dominique's brows rose. Rochefort was to meet them here?

Georges shook his head. "No, sir." He reached into his breast pocket and withdrew a wrinkled letter. "He sent this for you, though. The messenger brought it late last night."

Dominique stroked Étoile's coarse mane and looked on as Andre anxiously took the parchment. The moment he unfolded it, his expression tightened.

"Bad news?" she asked gently.

He grasped her waist and lowered her to the ground, the note still in his hand. "I don't know."

He held it up, and even in the dim light of the lantern Dominique could see that the ink had run, and all but a few words were smeared beyond recognition. "Oh, no," she said.

Georges looked aghast. "Damned fool. He let it get wet in the rain."

Andre gave him a level stare.

"I swear, monsieur," Georges said defensively, slapping his barrel chest, "I put it right in here as soon as it arrived."

Andre stared at him a moment longer, then crumpled the note and stuffed it in his pocket. "Let's hope he was only writing to inform me of the delay."

The other man's shoulders sagged visibly. "I'll tend to your horses," he mumbled, then caught Étoile's reins and began guiding both mounts toward the stables.

Dominique found the interior of the house every bit as homelike as its facade. A fire blazed in the hearth, numerous candelabra held lighted candles, and the wine-colored velvet furnishings, though worn, looked clean and bespoke of comfort.

She contemplated a lovely antique tapestry adorning an entire wall. "Whose house is this?"

Andre smoothed his hand along the lacquered top of a mahogany secretaire. "Everyone's and no one's. Given its isolation, it is used as a safe haven."

"By whom?"

"People in need of one. Such as we are."

Ambiguous, as usual. He probably saw the frustration on her face, because he pulled her into his arms, and before she could react he'd placed a kiss on her nose.

"Did I say you could do that?" She tried to frown at him, but the effect was ruined by a smile she couldn't contain.

"No," he replied, "but *I* did."

She met his gaze, and Dominique's heart was arrested when she recognized the Andre she'd first met, the one who teased her and looked at her with hunger in his intense blue eyes. She swallowed. "Oh. I didn't hear you."

His lashes lowered. "I need to practice my delivery."

Slowly, he bent his head, warm fingers curving around the nape of her neck in a grasp that was gentle, yet unmistakably possessive. Her knees grew weak the moment his lips brushed the corner of her eye. She let her hands slide up his chest, parting his coat, glorying in the feel of the familiar rigid contours beneath her palms.

God, how she'd missed him. She fitted herself to his powerful frame, felt him shudder as he kissed her temple, cheek, the corner of her mouth. . . . The sound of a gate slamming shut penetrated her senses, and Dominique's fingers tightened on Andre's shoulders as she remembered that they weren't alone.

"Wait," she murmured against his mouth. "Georges—"

"Is outside, guarding us. And that is where he'll stay."

Guarding them? Against what?

His lips sought hers, and all questions spun out of her mind. Her hands glided upward, linking behind his neck while his mouth slid back and forth across her parted lips, softly, gently, like a first greeting. He kissed her with such care that Dominique felt tears burn her closed eyelids, and when he angled his head to deepen the kiss she arched against him, feeding on his urgency.

A horse's neigh. A man's harsh cry. Another, louder whicker, followed by a string of curses. It took Dominique a moment to register the commotion, and as she did Andre tore his mouth from hers.

Then he was wrenching out of her embrace and dashing to the window. Dominique followed on legs that felt like pudding. Her already pounding heart threatened to leap from her chest when she saw him take one look outside and turn away from the glass, his face devoid of color.

"Merde." He rushed to the secretaire, yanked open a drawer, and pulled out the longest pistol Dominique had ever seen.

Her eyes widened. "What is it?"

"Trouble. I want you to latch the door and go upstairs. The bedroom. Don't let anyone in except Georges or myself."

She gaped at him. "What—"

He made an impatient gesture. "I think someone has followed us here. Do as I say, I beg you. There's no time to explain." Then he was gone, leaving her to stare as the door slammed shut behind him.

He'd caught a glimpse of a white horse disappearing between the trees, of that Andre was certain. He bounded down the front steps, his grip tight on the pistol. "Georges!"

"Monsieur!"

The stables. Andre ran to the back of the house and found Georges standing in the entry to the ramshackle structure, looking annoyed but apparently unharmed.

"Are you all right?"

Georges glowered at Étoile. "Uh-huh."

"What happened?"

"Damned mare went wild. I went to unbuckle her cinches and she nearly kicked the living . . ."

Andre hastened into the chestnut's stall and took hold of his reins. Thank God the gelding was still saddled. "Never mind that. Go inside. We have a visitor."

"Has Monsieur Rochefort arrived?"

"I wish."

Georges cursed.

"My sentiments exactly." Andre grabbed the chestnut's mane and vaulted onto the saddle. "Whoever it is lurks in the woods. I'm going to find out what he wants."

George frowned. "Let me go after him instead."

"No."

"Then I'll go with you."

Andre shook his head. "The knave followed me here. He's obviously after me."

Georges looked dismayed. "Monsieur, I've orders to protect you—"

"Damn it, Heroux! *I'm* ordering you to guard my wife!"

Georges gulped and took a small step back. "Yes, sir."

Still, he seemed unconvinced, and Andre gave him his hardest look. "Stay with her, no matter what happens. If anything harms her, I'll have your head."

With that, he dug his heels into the gelding's flanks and charged into the night.

Nerve-shredding stillness. Her panic escalating with every passing second, Dominique braced her palms against the enormous picture window, squinting into the darkness in hopes of spotting Andre. She hadn't seen or heard a thing since he'd gone tearing away at full gallop, so fast that she'd instinctively crossed herself. It couldn't have been more than five minutes, but it seemed like all of five hours. She'd actually considered going after him, only to realize she had no idea which direction he'd taken.

She pushed away from the glass, paced the small bedchamber, then went to the window again. Who could have followed them here? Why hadn't she thought to demand that Georges search for the pursuer instead of letting Andre place himself in danger? She knew he was well armed, but still, her sick fear grew, congealing in her chest until she could hardly breathe.

Andre. If anything happened to him . . . No. No. She wouldn't think of that.

Just when she thought she might go mad with worry, she heard the unmistakable grating of a key in the downstairs lock. Knees nearly buckling with relief, Dominique picked up her skirts and rushed down the hallway toward the stairs. On the landing, she paused, her heart thumping. Andre?

The front door squeaked on its hinges. Dominique tipped back her head, both hands clenching the rail as she listened to the creak grow softer.

Silence. The door slammed shut.

She jumped. If not Andre, then Georges, she hoped. Despite the urge to call out, Dominique kept quiet. Did someone have a key other than the two men? Rochefort, perhaps? She descended one more step, but something kept her from venturing any farther.

The next second Dominique gasped, gripped by such terror that all her muscles seemed to turn to ice. At the foot of the stairs, a figure came into view, gliding like a ghost as it advanced, arms motionless at its sides.

That brown monk's habit. That cowl concealing the face. She'd seen this nightmare apparition once before. But this time, instead of a bow and arrow, it held a glinting dagger in each hand.

The animal seemed to know precisely where to go. After several vain attempts to steer him toward the place he'd sighted the white horse, Andre gave up and gave the gelding free rein. Perhaps his mount sensed something he could not.

He blinked hard. His eyes hurt from the cold air and the strain of trying to see in near blackness. Just his luck, to have to ride by a mere sliver of a moon. Without warning, the horse stretched its neck and turned sharply to the right, veering onto a side path Andre had failed to distinguish. He slackened the reins and tightened his knees, tired legs burning with the effort to keep a grip on the chestnut's sweaty flanks.

In the distance, a blur of white crested a hill, then disappeared down the incline. Andre's eyes narrowed. Apparently, the villain fancied a game of chase. So be it. He'd gladly pursue the bastard down to the pits of hell, if that was what it took to keep him away from Dominique.

Gritting his teeth, he urged his mount onward. A moment later, Andre clearly saw the galloping white's rump and almost cried out in surprise. A long rope was tied to its girth, and something indistinct bumped and dragged behind, no doubt alarming the poor horse.

But there was no one in the saddle.

A raspy cry tore from Dominique's throat. Whirling, she scrambled up the stairs. Footfalls pounded behind her. Just as she reached the landing, something whooshed past her right ear, hit the wall in front of her, and clattered to the floor.

A dagger. The knave had thrown it at her. Dominique kicked it away, sending it skittering toward the bedroom. Tripping on her skirts, she rushed through the open chamber doorway, then swooped down, grabbed the knife, and slammed the door behind her.

No key in the lock. Clutching the knife, she looked around for something with which to block the entry. She'd barely gripped the back of a chair when the door burst open and crashed against the wall, making the windows rattle.

Stay calm. You have one of his daggers. Dominique's fingers tightened around the metal handle concealed in the folds of her skirts. The next second, the villain sprang forth in a flurry of brown cloth, and Dominique hurled the chair at him with all her might. He dodged it, and as the scroll feet splintered against the door jamb he lunged at her, knife held high above his cowl-covered head.

Her back hit the floor so hard, her vision dimmed. A clammy hand closed around her throat and squeezed. She kicked and struggled in vain to break free. Her consciousness began to fade. From the corner of her eye, she saw the flash of the descending knife. Instinctively, her hand came up to block it.

And met resistance. The blade Dominique held ripped through cloth, then plunged to the hilt into yielding flesh. A screech pierced her eardrums. Something warm splattered her face as the attacker's hand went slack and his dagger slid from his gloved fingers. Pain seared her shoulder, and then she heard the clunk of metal hitting the carpet.

With one mighty heave, Dominique shoved his body off her, coughing and gasping as she grappled for his fallen knife. Her shoulder throbbed. Through green specks swirling before her eyes, she saw the villain hoist himself up, her knife protruding grotesquely from his arm.

The cowl had slipped to his shoulders, revealing a black hood that concealed his head and throat. No mouth, no nose. Only diabolic dark eyes glittering from two slits cut into the cloth. "Whore," he hissed.

Breathe. Run.

Somehow, she staggered to her feet. Sobbing for air, she hiked up her skirts and went careening toward the doorway. She'd nearly reached it when she felt fingers dig into her chignon, yanking so viciously that tears sprang to her eyes.

The room seemed to tilt around her as she swung one way, then the other, struggling in vain to twist out of his savage grip. Repeatedly, she tried to stab his thigh, but this time her blade only slashed the thick folds of his habit. Eyes watering, scalp burning, she was inexorably dragged across the room.

Dear God. She was going to die.

An image of Andre's face fleeted through her mind. With the last bit of strength she had, Dominique launched herself backward in a desperate attempt to ram the killer's back into the wall.

He lurched rearward, hauling her with him. Breaking glass. Shards everywhere. Oh, no. The window.

Her feet flew out from under her. She made a frantic grab for the curtains. Missed. And then she saw the star-studded black sky, and she was flying through thin air.

Andre leaned low over the galloping horse's neck, wind wailing in his ears as he rounded the last bend toward the house. She had to be safe with Georges. She had to be. Even as he tried to convince himself of that, a terrible feeling of foreboding made his blood run cold.

He'd ridden halfway up the path when a crash shattered the stillness of the night. He looked up in time to see something explode through the second-story window in a hail of broken glass.

Shrill screams. Flailing arms and legs. Great God, it wasn't something, but *someone*.

Please, Lord, not her. Not her, not her. Andre's hammering

heart seemed to rend as he watched the body plummet, skirts fluttering, to plunge into the shrubbery below. Abruptly, the screaming died.

"Dominique!"

His cry was lost in the din of hoofbeats. Andre yanked on the reins, leaped off the horse's back before the animal came to a full halt, and went tearing around the corner of the house.

As in a dream, his legs moved, but he didn't seem to gain ground. By the time he reached the spot where he'd seen the body drop, he was irrationally praying that this was, indeed, another of his nightmares. Except that none of them had ever been as horrible as this.

His breath came in burning rasps. As he neared the shoulder-high yew bushes, he heard branches snapping, and then a groan that didn't quite sound human. His vision blackened around the edges. "Dominique!"

"Andre!"

The sound of her voice nearly brought Andre to his knees. He didn't know how, but suddenly she was in his arms, clinging to the lapels of his greatcoat, her tiny body quaking with tremors.

"You're hurt!" he choked out.

"No. No." She buried her face in his chest. "I fell on top of—"

"What happened?"

That terrible moan again. The bushes behind him rustled. Wrapping an arm tightly about Dominique's shoulders, he swung around and cautiously moved to take a look. By the light coming through a nearby window, he could see someone sprawled among the branches.

"He tried to kill me," Dominique said in a strangled voice.

Bile rose in Andre's throat. His gaze flicked from the gloved fingers, slowly clenching and unclenching, to the face, devoid of features and black as pitch. His free hand went to his pistol, but stopped when the assassin suddenly convulsed, emitting an odd gurgling sound.

"Punctured lung," Dominique murmured.

Another gurgle. "Help . . . me."

Andre's lips curled. "You're headed straight to hell, with

or without my help.'' Holding Dominique securely against him, he reached for the killer's mask. "But first—''

He buried his fingers in the cloth. And then, with one swift tug, he yanked it off the bastard's head.

Chapter Seventeen

"Yvette!"

Impossible. But then again . . . Blood oozed from several gashes marring her face, staining her disheveled blond hair. All Andre could do was stare at her, this woman whom he'd regarded and cared for as a sister.

Impossible, his mind repeated. *There's no such thing,* Yvette's cynical voice echoed in his head. Feeling as if someone had kicked him in the gut, Andre sought Dominique's gaze, unable to accept what he clearly saw with his own eyes. "Tell me it isn't her," he murmured.

Dominique's eyes mirrored his shock, and magnified it tenfold. "I wish I could."

Agony sliced through him. Dominique slipped her hand into his, and Andre clasped it tightly, linking his stiff fingers with hers.

"Andre—ahh." Yvette stirred, branches snapping beneath her. Her mouth gaped open, her chin quivering as she fought for breath. "Forgive . . . me."

"Forgive you?" He felt the blood rush to his head. "Who did you mean to kill, Yvette? My wife? Me? Both of us? Why didn't you do us in at Les Châtaignes? You had the perfect opportunity.''

''An . . . my . . .''

Her body convulsed. Andre's gaze skimmed over the bizarre loose cloak she wore. He'd seen that garb before. But where? His eyes widened. ''The courtyard at the inn—the bow and arrow—that was you, wasn't it?''

She babbled something he couldn't comprehend.

''Wasn't it?'' he demanded harshly.

Her hands clenched. ''. . . es.''

He swallowed back his disgust, fought to control the escalating rage that made him want to shove his humanity aside and seize a dying woman by the throat. ''How did you learn I was in France?''

''Pierre.''

No wonder his valet had been elated when Bavard had summoned him to Loches. Andre remembered how Pierre had insisted he should lodge at that particular inn. ''Since when has Pierre been spying on me for you?''

''England.''

''Why?''

''You . . . always . . . you.''

Andre frowned. ''I do not understand.''

Yvette exhaled, her chest laboring as she drew another whistling breath. ''You . . . never . . . did.''

Exactly what was that supposed to mean? ''Why did you try to kill us?''

''No—''

''Why, Yvette?''

''Not you . . . only . . .'' Her gaze slid to Dominique, and Andre's jaw grew rigid at the malice glinting in her eyes. ''Mimi,'' she rasped.

Damn. Her thoughts were jumbled; she was confusing Dominique with Mimi.

''Mimi,'' Yvette repeated with conviction.

Grand Dieu, what was she trying to tell him?

She fought for air. Andre waited, nerves stretched so taut, he felt that they might snap. ''What of Mimi?''

Yvette moistened her pale lips. ''Shot. Your bed . . .''

Why was she ranting about Mimi, and where they'd found her? "Yes," he said hoarsely.

"Your bed," she repeated. She coughed. "Your ba—by . . ."

Dominique clamped down on his fingers. Andre squeezed back, feeling as if her tiny hand was his sole grip on warmth and sanity. "You knew about the child? She told you?"

Yvette nodded almost imperceptibly. A chill coursed through him, stiffening his spine as an unthinkable notion struck him. "What else do you want to confess, Yvette?"

She looked at him imploringly.

"Tell me. Who shot Mimi?"

Her wild gaze fastened on his face. "I . . . did."

A ragged sound escaped his throat. "Why? For the love of God, why?"

Her body tensed in a spasm. "Not . . . God," she sputtered. "You." Blood trickled from the corner of her mouth. Then she went limp.

Andre stood there, unable to move, incapable of looking away from those dark eyes he knew so well, now glazed in a blank stare. The one person in the world he'd trusted. A murderess.

"A woman?" Georges gawked at Yvette's body, one beefy hand pressed to the back of his head. "Well, I'll be blasted! Is she dead?"

Dominique shuddered. Even a dozen paces away, with her back turned and Andre's strong hand enveloping hers, she still felt Yvette's sightless eyes chilling her every bone.

Georges whistled through his teeth. "One helluva blow she dealt me with that manure shovel. Thought I was done for." He turned to Andre, his eyes bulging. "I know you said you'd have my head, sir, but I didn't hear her coming, I swear. I was at the front door, fishin' in my pocket for the key, and—"

"Spare me." Andre's deep voice shook slightly but brooked no protest.

Georges nodded. "*Oui,* monsieur."

"You will harness the black mare to the barouche, and take the body to—"

"Tonight? Can't it wait till morning?"

Heart aching, Dominique watched the lines of strain deepen around her husband's mouth as he shook his head, then quietly gave the man directions to Les Châtaignes. "Return here at once, and wait for Rochefort," he finished. "Tell him what happened, and that I'll meet him the day after tomorrow. Understood?"

"Where should I say you'll be?"

"He will know."

Georges nodded and went to do Andre's bidding, grumbling under his breath and rubbing the back of his head. Only when he had rounded the house with Yvette's body in his arms did Andre turn to Dominique.

"Are you all right?"

She nodded.

He took her hand and held it to his raspy cheek. "I don't know what I would have done if—" His beautiful mouth twisted. Before she knew it, he'd pulled her to him in a fierce embrace, sending pain ripping through her wounded shoulder. Dominique winced but held him just as tightly. She needed to be strong. For him.

He drew back, searching her face intently. "Did she hurt you?"

His eyes were unusually bright, shining with tears he was too stalwart to succumb to. Dominique slid her fingers up his chest to clutch his broad shoulders, feeling her own eyelids begin to sting.

"Did she?" he demanded raggedly.

She swallowed. "No."

He exhaled sharply, a rush of warm air caressing her brow. *"Dieu merci."* He caught a handful of her hair. *"My Cendrillon."*

And then his lips crushed hers.

A shudder racked Dominique's body as his tongue invaded her mouth. Fingers gripping her scalp, Andre deepened the kiss, his lips quivering, and suddenly his desperation became hers. Yearning. To make him lose himself, make him forget, to give him back all fate had taken from him. Anything.

213

Everything. She wanted to absorb him, to make him part of her. She wanted . . .

He groaned. The sound reverberated in her throat. Dominique rose on tiptoe and kissed him back, feeding his hunger with all the pent-up longing in her heart and soul.

After a long, long time, he raised his head. "I know I promised you a short trip and a good night's rest, but—"

"No." Still breathing hard, she reached up and gently ran a fingertip along his moistened lips. "What I need is for you to take me away from here."

A bit of spirit lit Andre's haunted eyes. Nevertheless, he seemed reluctant. "You've ridden at night before?"

"Once." She cast a glance toward the house and shivered, wondering how she'd ever considered the gruesome place inviting. "Don't ask me to go back in there. Please."

He pressed a kiss into her palm. "I'll go tell Georges to saddle his horse for you. And God help any highwayman who dares to cross our path."

"You will be staying overnight?"

"Perhaps." Andre surveyed the modest room. With its low beamed ceiling, bare stone floor, and wooden crates stashed in one corner, it looked more like a storage closet than a bedchamber. It did, however, have a bed and a lighted fireplace, and, according to the gaunt old woman who was now jangling a ring of keys between her bony fingers, this was the only large house with a room to let in the village.

"Monsieur," the proprietress snapped, "if you don't decide very soon, I think your wife will faint."

He glanced down at the top of Dominique's bowed head. Indeed, she leaned back heavily against him, as if no longer capable of supporting her own weight, and Andre wanted to kick himself for having bypassed the first village they'd encountered.

"We'll take the room," he told the woman. "Please see that our horses are attended to, and—"

"You want the good feed?" she interrupted, squinting up at him with weasel-like eyes. "That'll be extra."

"Fine."

"Breakfast is at seven. Not seven-ten, not seven-thirty. Seven. I got chores to do, and with no one to help me with 'em . . ." Her gaze shifted to Dominique. "Lookin' at the bathtub, are you? That's extra, too, you know."

The "tub," Andre realized, was the sawed-off remnant of a barrel sitting in front of the stacked crates. "We will require hot water," he said, "but not in that. I trust you have a clean washbasin somewhere. It looks as if we'll need more firewood, as well."

Had the ill-tempered hag still possessed eyebrows, they would have disappeared into her hairline. "More wood? That's—"

"Extra," Andre finished for her. Reaching into his pocket, he fingered and discarded two coins before he found the Marianne he sought. He held it up, then passed it before the woman's nose. "I trust this will suffice."

Eyes glittering, the proprietress snatched the shiny piece from his extended fingers. "Maybe."

Regarding him suspiciously, she slipped the coin between her teeth and bit down. Her subsequent brown-toothed grin might have shattered a cheval glass. "Does monsieur desire anything else tonight? A bed warmer? Food? Drink?"

"Some bread and cheese will do. And a bottle of wine."

He guided Dominique inside and started to shut the door behind him, but the old woman stopped it with her foot. "Red or white?" she asked.

Andre shrugged impatiently. "Surprise us."

No sooner had he slammed the door than Dominique leaned into him again. Feeling his own exhaustion threaten to overtake him, Andre propped his back against the jamb and cradled her head against his chest. "You must be cold." He nuzzled her hair. "Let's go sit by the fire."

The only move she made was to slide her arms around his waist.

"Dominique?"

"Mmm."

Struck by the feeling that something was terribly wrong, he placed his hands on her shoulders, intending to hold her away

215

from him so he could see her face. She flinched, sucking air through her teeth in a hiss.

Andre jerked back. "What is it?"

"Nothing."

"Nothing?" He studied her closely, and then Andre saw red. Literally. "*Grand Dieu!* You're bleeding!"

Because of her cloak's dark color, he hadn't noticed the stain on her shoulder, which was about the size of his palm.

"Not any longer." Gingerly, she touched the spot. "It's dry. The fabric has adhered to it."

"Adhered to . . . let me see!"

With trembling hands, he partially undid the garment and eased it apart, revealing a cut marring her smooth shoulder. Though not deep, the gash ran all the way to her armpit. He felt his stomach tighten. "This happened when you fell through the window?"

Dominique shook her head.

"Then, how?"

"Yvette," she replied quietly.

A curse escaped Andre's clenched teeth as all his suppressed outrage engulfed him in one violent surge. "Why didn't you say something? How could you let me ride on for hours—"

"I was the one who asked you to, remember?"

Carefully, he covered the wound again. "Where in hell is that old woman? This wound needs to be cleansed and bandaged. Damn. It's probably going to leave a scar."

"No matter. Scars are a consequence of living."

"*Sacrebleu!* You are supposed to be the weaker sex! Don't you ever whine and complain? Do you even know how?"

Slowly, Dominique raised her head. Her lovely face was pale, so very drawn that her eyes appeared enormous, and at that moment she seemed as small and fragile as a newly blossomed snowdrop.

Why in God's name was he shouting at her? Disgusted with himself, he took her hand and pressed it to his lips. "Forgive me."

She held his gaze for a long moment, silently assuring him that she understood. As always when she looked into him that way, he felt completely open and exposed to her, but this time, oddly, he didn't feel entrapped.

"Come." He linked his fingers through her cold ones and drew her toward one of the chairs facing the hearth. "We need to get you warm."

Once she was seated, he quickly shrugged out of his great-coat and tucked it about her. Watching her snuggle into it with a little sigh, protectiveness stabbed through him, along with an overwhelming sense of guilt. A fine protector he'd turned out to be, rescuing her from Bavard only to place her in constant mortal danger. Then again, he'd never figured that the demons chasing him were real. Nor that they'd end up hurting someone other than himself.

Snatching up a poker that leaned against the stone hearth, Andre crouched down and thrust the iron repeatedly into the flames, unleashing his frustration on the sparking logs. God help him, he could not understand it. Yvette, who always had an encouraging word and a shoulder for everyone to lean on, who seemed so fiercely protective of her family, especially her sister. Sweet, sensitive Yvette. What could have driven her to commit—

A scratch on the door. "Monsieur, your food and water!"

"Finally." Andre replaced the iron and hastened to let in the proprietress. When the old woman had gone he found Dominique watching him, a troubled expression in her eyes.

"Are you all right?" she asked softly.

He filled a small basin and dipped a serviette in the warm water. "You are the wounded one."

"And you are not?"

Andre wrung out the cloth, squeezing until his knuckles whitened. Part of him wanted to push Yvette and her unspeakable crimes out of his mind and carry on. As he had always done. Moved forward, looking straight ahead, never once turning back. Another part of him wanted answers to the questions Yvette's confession had raised. The same hollow, wretched part that had grown tired of running.

"Strange, isn't it?" he heard Dominique say. "Just when you think nothing and no one else can surprise you . . ."

He swung around to face her. How right she was. There she

217

sat, cold, bleeding, and exhausted, yet offering to lend a sympathetic ear to a man who, for all she knew, was working to destroy all she held dear. Did she still think of him that way?

"I've learned to expect the worst," he said, retrieving her saddlebag to rummage for her satchel of medicines. "That way, I'm never disappointed. Is there a certain salve you use for cuts?"

She nodded. "Comfrey ointment. The small green tin with a dark pink flower on the lid."

He quickly found it, then knelt before her. "Let me see that cut."

Her lashes lowered. All of a sudden she seemed self-conscious, and something in the way she slipped one finger beneath the velvet and slid the fabric down her shoulder made Andre's mind depart from Yvette and the task at hand. Such flawless skin. He wanted to taste the curve of her neck, to feel her pulse beating against his lips and tongue.

His body came to swift awareness. But then the gash came into view, and fear drove like an icicle into his chest. Save for the grace of God, he might be contemplating Dominique's broken body instead of a superficial wound. A violent shudder shook him. Again, he saw Yvette's contorted face, the hatred in her eyes as she regarded Dominique.

"Damn her." As gently as he could, he began dabbing at the dried blood, wishing it were his own flesh instead of Dominique's. "Damn her to hell eternal."

"You couldn't have known. She hid her madness very well."

Madness. Indeed, that was the only plausible explanation. "How could I not have guessed, or even glimpsed it? I never thought of her as anything but sensible and selfless, like . . ."

"Like Mimi?"

No. Like you.

He shook his head. "Mimi was . . . uncommonly fragile, even for a woman. Childlike in many ways." He folded the serviette and used the unstained side to finish cleansing the wound, which had begun to seep again.

The sight of fresh blood triggered pain. And a distant memory. "When I told Rochefort of our impending nuptials, he predicted she would cling to me so tightly, she'd slowly squeeze the lifeblood out of me."

A pity he hadn't listened; his friend had proven correct. "Come to think of it, her father was the only one who approved of the marriage."

"Yvette disapproved?"

"Entirely." He cast aside the cloth and began applying the ointment with a gentle hand. "In fact, she tried to talk me out of it."

Dominique started.

He looked up. "Did I hurt you?"

"No. Tell me, why did Yvette object?"

Andre gave a sarcastic smile. "Would you believe she said she didn't trust me to take proper care of her sister?" He set the tin aside and reached for a dry cloth. "When I think how Yvette took care of everything, never breathing one word of complaint—"

"Took care of everything?"

Andre withdrew his knife from the sheath at his waist. "She ran our household."

"She lived with you?"

"Mm-hmm." He cut the edging of the clean serviette, then tore it into strips. "Mimi seemed lost without her, so a few weeks after the wedding I invited Yvette to stay with us a while."

"And she forgot to leave."

He wasn't certain what to make of Dominique's unusually derisive tone. "Mimi was incapable of giving orders," he explained. "Hesitated to bother the servants for a simple cup of tea. As for me, I didn't give a damn who dealt with the staff, as long as a hot meal and clean sheets awaited when I went home."

And it had been oh, so convenient to stay away and let Yvette provide for all of Mimi's needs, companionship included. At least, most of her needs, he thought with self-loathing. "As I said, not once did she complain. She appeared content with the arrangement, and utterly devoted to her sister."

"And to you."

He nodded absently and began wrapping the makeshift bandage around Dominique's upper arm. "Remember that painting you admired at Les Châtaignes? It was her wedding gift to us. She slaved over that canvas night and day to finish it in time."

Her muscles tensed beneath his fingers. "Yvette? *She* was the one . . . ?"

"Indeed." Taking care not to make the dressing too tight, he passed the last of the strip around her shoulder and began to tie the ends. "She could breathe life into the most banal of inanimate objects with only a few strokes of her paintbrush."

"All those portraits . . ." she said in a hushed tone.

"No, the portraits of ancestors you saw hanging in that corridor were done by other artists. Yvette liked to paint still life. Peaches and cucumbers in porcelain bowls and such."

How could this same woman have murdered her own sister in cold blood? How? And why? He shook his head. "It makes no sense. No sense at all."

Dominique said something under her breath, and Andre sat back on his heels, surveying the bandage with an assessing eye. Satisfied that the cloth wouldn't unravel, he sought her approval, only to find her staring at him strangely.

"What is it? Does it bind?"

"Not in the least. You did a fine job. Thank you."

"Then . . . ?"

She tipped her head. "You have no idea, have you?"

He looked at her in confusion.

"She was in love with you, Andre."

It took him a moment to make sense of her softly spoken statement. "In love with me? Yvette? That is absurd."

"*Au contraire.* She renounced her own home and social life in order to assume her sister's burdens, not to mention yours. Why would a beautiful, unwed, and sought-after young lady do such a thing?"

He shrugged. "I've no idea. Tell me."

"I suspect she hoped you'd tire of Mimi's weaknesses and realize you'd chosen the wrong sister."

His brain recognized reason in her words. His heart, however, denied them with a vehemence that threatened to make him ill. "I never would've—"

"Of course you wouldn't have." Though Dominique spoke very softly, he could perceive the tremor in her voice. "Not you. You are . . . you aren't the sort of man who would forsake his wife and baby."

Baby. His flesh and blood. The one last tiny chance to recapture some meaning in his empty life. He swallowed hard. "I didn't know Mimi had told her of the child."

"The knowledge must have pushed Yvette to desperation." *Murder.*

"She must have been convinced you'd turn to her. Instead, you left the country."

"Turn to her? Why in God's name—"

"For comfort."

"Comfort? There wasn't a cursed thing *left* in me to comfort! She stole every last—"

"That isn't true. There are some things no one can take from you."

"Such as?"

"Your heart. Your soul."

He waved his hand. "Black, both of them." He clenched his jaw. "I never should have fled to England."

"It was your only option at the time."

"I should have stayed and tried to find out—"

"You would have overturned every stone in Paris and never thought to search your own courtyard. You never noticed her feelings for you. She was too crafty to betray anything that might have led you to suspect her of . . . of doing . . . what she did."

But he should have. Might have, had he not been so utterly self-absorbed.

Images and memories began to crowd his mind. The time he'd come home unannounced to find Yvette, red-faced and tight-lipped, hovering over a sobbing, miserable Mimi. After a moment of stunned silence, Yvette had patted Mimi's shoulder, then rushed forth to greet him with her usual placid smile. "Thank God you've finally arrived. The pain in her leg has been excruciating for the past few days. She missed you something awful, *la pauvre.*"

And then there was the time he'd questioned Mimi about her infirmity.

"How did you break your leg so badly?"

"We fell," Yvette had jumped in quickly.

"We?"

Mimi had scrupulously avoided her sister's gaze. "Yvette and I were running down the stairs. She was behind me and tripped, I broke her fall . . . she managed to seize the banister, but I tumbled to the bottom of the staircase."

Yvette had smiled and gestured with her thumb and forefinger. "I came this close to being an only child again."

Andre's stomach turned. Sweet Lord, had Yvette actually pushed her? He squeezed his eyes shut, only to visualize that bottle of Möet and Chandon, the champagne Mimi always drank with dinner. Waiting for him in his chamber at the Stallion Inn.

He saw himself carrying Dominique upstairs and suddenly recalled the elegant lady who'd stopped in her tracks to stare at them in the darkened hallway. His eyes flew open. "Good God. That was her."

"Who?"

"In the corridor, at the inn. The woman we encountered en route to our room. She wore a veil, remember?"

"No."

"She must have sought to meet me there . . . brought the champagne . . ." Only to see him retire to his chamber with a woman in his arms. His head began to spin as the scrambled pieces of the puzzle fell into place to form one atrocious picture.

Such evil. He'd been oblivious to it all, and his indifference had cost Mimi her life. "She kept insisting I couldn't have prevented what happened to Mimi," he whispered.

A soft sigh. "And you didn't let yourself believe it."

He braced himself against the grief, waited for the old familiar guilt to coil and burn within his gut. It didn't come. He was dazed. Like a prisoner whose gaoler had suddenly cut his chains and shoved him toward the open doorway, he wavered on the threshold of his private dungeon, blinded by the sunlight.

All he seemed capable of feeling was relief. Relief that he'd finally solved the enigma that had incessantly plagued his days and nights. Relief that Dominique was here, safe and alive, her mere presence casting warm light into the darkest corners of his soul.

His sweet, courageous little *Cendrillon.* She was a flower in his winter, a bloom whose vibrant tenderness had awakened in him sentiments he'd believed forever trapped in ice. Watching as she let her eyes drift closed and rested her chin upon her chest, Andre's heart ached. She looked exhausted, and not only physically. Heaven, how he hated having brought her to this.

It suddenly occurred to him that it had been a while since her last meal. "There's bread and brie. Would you like some?"

She shook her head. "I don't think I could eat right now."

That wasn't a good sign. Frowning, he caught one of her booted feet. "Are you still chilled?"

"Not any longer."

He began undoing her shoelaces and felt her hand settle on his head, her fingers threading through his hair.

"You needn't do that," she murmured.

"I want to."

When he had set both boots aside, he propped one small stockinged foot on his thigh and ran his thumbs along the arch. Out of the corner of his eye, he saw her tense, then go completely limp.

Her moan of pleasure brought a smile to his lips. "Feels good, *oui?*"

"Oh, yes."

His hands stilled. Two innocent syllables, but the breathy way she'd uttered them was enough to send excitement shooting along Andre's every nerve. His gaze snapped to her face. His senses were further heightened when she let her head fall back, drew her tongue over her lips, and swallowed.

Oh, God. Only her injury kept him from yanking her to his chest and claiming her with his hands and mouth until he'd thrust aside every last barrier between them. Until he'd buried himself so deep inside her, he could feel all of her warmth encircle every part of him.

"Please," she breathed, "don't stop."

Breathing erratically, Andre resumed, trying his hardest to concentrate on massaging her feet, and only her feet. As he carefully slid her sheer stockings off, he could clearly see how perfectly formed they were. Before long, his mind rushed ahead of his resolve, conjuring images of his palms sliding along her calves, over her knees and up her thighs. And beyond.

He gulped. It was becoming increasingly hard to maintain his control. Harder and harder, with each stroke of his fingertips along her soft, round heel.

He stifled a groan. His hardness to her softness. He fantasized letting his hands explore her every curve as she writhed beneath him and called his name, of looking into her eyes and finding them dark with passion. For him. He saw himself using his teeth to slowly part that velvet bodice and reveal her breasts, and he could almost feel her heartbeat against his questing tongue.

God help him, he wanted her, wanted to join his life with hers as badly as he'd ever wanted air to breathe or water to quench his thirst. As he had never wanted another woman before.

Did she have any idea what she meant to him? Taking a deep breath, he hazarded to look and see. Only to find her slumped in the chair, her dark head to one side, exposing the underside of her chin and the pale skin of her throat.

A self-derisive smile curved one corner of his mouth. Here he was, kneeling at her feet with the imaginary glass slipper poised in his hands, and she was fast asleep.

He sighed. Careful not to jostle her, he guided her hands around his neck, then hooked one arm beneath her and got to his feet. He couldn't resist pressing his lips to her hair as he carried her to the bed. He lowered her upon it and started to straighten, but she wouldn't let him go, and so he eased down beside her.

"Andre," she breathed against his throat.

His already rigid muscles tightened further. She nestled close, sliding one leg across his thighs, resting her head on his shoulder, fitting her body to his side. With a small sound of contentment, she slipped her arm around his waist.

She smiled against his chest.

Andre's heart squeezed. "Sweet dreams, *ma vie.*"

He closed his eyes and let her fragrance penetrate his senses, wondering how he was going to withstand what looked to be a long and sleepless night.

The sound of pouring water played at the edges of Dominique's mind. She'd slumbered restlessly, aware that she was sleeping even as she dozed, conscious of strong arms enveloping her and of the warmth of a hard masculine body pressed to hers.

Andre. A smile curving her lips, she rolled onto her side, seeking the reassurance of his solid frame. Light filtered through her lashes, and her hand encountered only rumpled covers.

Her eyes fluttered open. The first thing she saw was an enormous form moving on the opposite wall, the silhouette of someone lifting something. The second thing she saw was the man who cast the shadow.

Illuminated by the blazing fire in the hearth and one thick candle burning atop the mantel, Andre stood in the washtub, raising a bucket above his head. His body was covered with lather.

And nothing else.

Chapter Eighteen

The air seemed to solidify in Dominique's chest.

Steam rose from the tub in which Andre stood, but the mist did nothing to conceal the backs of his sturdy calves and powerful thighs. Even as her eyes widened and her throat spasmed in a soundless gasp at the sight of his naked derriere, Dominique thought this had to be some form of delirium.

A dream. His body was an artist's dream, a finely chiseled sculpture come to vibrant life.

He raised the bucket another fraction and tipped it, sending a deluge over his head to splash off his broad shoulders and cascade down his back. His muscles rippled, glistening with moisture as he lowered the bucket and tossed his head, flinging water droplets everywhere.

Her cheeks grew unbearably hot. Rolling onto her stomach, she slipped her arms beneath her pillow, burying her mouth and nose in its cool softness as she clutched it to her laboring chest, unconsciously pressing her hips into the mattress.

His derriere flexed as he turned slightly to grab a soapy washrag from the small basin placed on a chair within his reach. A lock of drenched hair spilled over his forehead, dripping, as he bent, propped one foot on the edge of the tub, and began to scrub his muscular leg with long, languid movements.

She now had a partial view of his profile, and with each downward stroke of his strong hands she caught a glimpse of his bare chest. Dominique squeezed her thighs together and dug her nails into the linen pillowcase, feeling her body grow hot beneath the covers. With rising fascination, she watched him straighten and reach into the basin again to retrieve a cake of soap. Slowly, he rubbed it along the washrag in his palm. White lather foamed between his fingers, a trace of it slipping down his wrist, sliding along his inner arm toward his elbow.

A strange restlessness effervesced within her, a sinking feeling between her breasts that swiftly plummeted, expanding within her belly to reach deep inside her, making unfamiliar muscles clench. It was as if her body had been numb for all of her twenty-two years and was only now coming to life, rousing to a level of awareness so intense, it nearly pained her. No, what she felt was far from pain. It was . . . it was . . .

Abruptly, his hands stilled. His shoulders tensed, a barely perceptible movement, but she caught it, and her stomach wrenched. The part of her mind still capable of reason warned her to look elsewhere.

Too late. He swung around. Her gaze flicked downward, only briefly, but in that fraction of a second Dominique learned more about the male anatomy than all the medical books she'd read had ever taught her.

Dear Lord. If one's entire body could blush, then that was what was happening to her. Her vision blurred, then sharpened again, in time to see the soap slip out of his clenched fist and skid across the floor.

Stillness. The pop and hiss of burning logs. Other than the steady rise and fall of his chest and a squeeze of his fingers around the scrap of cloth he held, Andre didn't move. And when she summoned the courage to look into his face, she thought her flesh just might ignite. He looked exactly like she felt: entranced. And there was something else in his wide eyes, something her muddled brain could not interpret, but that her body recognized at once.

A heady sense of unreality enveloped her. Before she knew it, she'd cast aside the covers and arisen, drawn to him by an inexorable force that she was powerless to resist.

Closer. And closer still. She barely felt the chilled stone floor beneath her stockinged feet as she approached. Her toe nudged the soap he'd dropped. On impulse, she bent at the knee and picked it up, her eyes never leaving his as she ran her thumb across its hard and smooth and slippery length.

She saw his Adam's apple move and his jaw clench, but the rest of him remained utterly still. Another step, and she was close enough to see a tiny nick on his clean-shaven chin. Close enough to breathe in steam, scented with rosemary and the unique essence of wet male skin.

Close enough to touch him.

Her heart began a violent beat. Nails digging into the soap, she let her arm drift upward, slowly. How powerful his torso looked, with just enough hair to emphasize the muscles of his chest and abdomen, and she could plainly see that he, too, was having difficulty breathing.

Her fingertips began to burn. Dominique lifted her hand another fraction and pressed the soap against his skin. He exhaled audibly, then sucked in a breath, and that odd sensation gripped her inner thighs again.

Her mouth was dry. Running her tongue across her lips, she began making small, slow circles with the soap, leaving a slick trail of white lather, her fingertips repeatedly grazing his chest. She felt his heartbeat quicken, felt tremors ripple through him, yet he continued to stand unmoving, saying nothing.

Another circle. Lower. Lower. How long would he continue letting her touch him this way? Lower. Her ring finger slipped, and Dominique realized it had dipped into his navel. She stopped. Her gaze dropped, and—

Grand . . . Grand Dieu.

The jolt that rocked her couldn't have been more potent if she'd been struck by lightning. Dear God in heaven, what madness was this? Choking back a mortified cry, Dominique jerked her hand away. The soap plunked into the tub with a splash, but before she could step back, she felt his fingers capture hers.

"Don't." His voice was barely a hoarse whisper, but it held a beseeching note that couldn't be denied. Gently but firmly, he took her hand and returned it to the spot where it had been.

She should have panicked. She should have turned and run. But when she felt him press her empty palm against his abdomen, whatever had impelled her to touch him in the first place returned with renewed force.

"Why did you come to me?" Though every bit as quiet, his voice had now regained its resonance. As always, it worked its pagan magic on her like a sweet caress.

"I had to."

She heard the washrag drop, and then he gently caught her chin, raising it with his thumb and forefinger. Firelight flickered on his face, illuminating every detail. She watched his pupils widen, nearly concealing those unusual deep blue irises of his, the color of the summer sky at twilight. But nothing could have hidden the blaze of passion in his eyes.

He lowered his gaze, lips parting slightly, and Dominique's knees grew weak at the sensual promise of his mouth. He bowed his head. Immediately, her heart leaped in wild anticipation. His lips barely skimmed her cheek, a hot request and a tender invitation. Trembling a little, she let her eyes drift closed. And felt his lips touch hers.

It was like kissing lightning. Head spinning, fingertips tingling, she propped both hands upon his chest, acutely aware of the heat of his skin, the hardness of his muscles, the strong thud of his heart. . . . Her hands slid to his shoulders, nails digging into the bunched muscles there. He groaned. His warm tongue traced moist patterns on her mouth. She tried to draw in air and promptly felt his tongue slide between her lips, delving inside to explore with exquisite deliberation, as if this was the first time he'd ever kissed her, as if he meant to learn her mouth and keep on claiming it forever.

Oh, yes. Oh, please . . . He tasted sweet, of wine. She could detect the faint raspberry spice bouquet of Merlot on his tongue. His thumb moved back and forth along her jaw, and then his hand slipped lower, his fingers stroking the bare flesh above the high neckline of her riding habit, causing her breasts to ache with a peculiar heaviness.

229

He worked a button free, and then another. She felt her bodice come undone. The heaviness increased, becoming almost unbearable as his hand progressed, unfastening buttons with swift expertise while he continued to possess her mouth with ever-rising hunger, sending myriad tongues of flame to lick at her breasts and belly and legs.

At last, the garment parted, but the sudden rush of cool air did nothing to soothe her fevered skin. Because the moment he freed the last button at her waist, he let his hands slip inside the gaping bodice, warm fingers spreading to encompass her rib cage, thumbs grazing the undersides of her breasts.

Abruptly, he broke the kiss and released her, and Dominique let her head fall backward, regarding him in confusion. He stared back, seemingly thunderstruck.

That was when she remembered that she wore no chemise. She'd been so eager to leave Les Châtaignes that underneath the riding habit she'd put on nothing at all.

His gaze swept her from head to waist, then back again, and all at once a thread of panic tugged at her stomach. What if he didn't find her as appealing as she did him? What if he was comparing her to—

"I was mistaken," he murmured thickly.

The thread became a knot. Regarding what?

He studied her, his face alight with wonder. "My imagination failed to do you justice."

He sounded as if the confession was being tortured out of him. Swallowing visibly, he finally met her gaze. His eyes . . . oh, God, were she to live a hundred years, she'd never, ever forget that look in them. A gathering storm, reflected in blue mountain lakes that glittered with desire. For her.

Something unfurled within her then, a recklessness and wild abandon that made her thrust out her chest, glorying in the effect her own nakedness had on him. In one bold move, she rolled her shoulders. The velvet glided along her back, stopped at her waist, and with an undulation of her hips, she sent it pooling at her feet.

His lashes lowered. She could almost feel the heat of his gaze as it moved downward, taking in all there was of her, then stopping just below her breasts.

"You are still wearing that."

He seemed incredulous. It took a moment before Dominique realized he was referring to her locket. She covered it with her palm, vividly recalling the day he'd fastened it around her neck. Why would he think she would discard it?

"You gave it to me."

She didn't miss the flicker in his eyes. A sound tore from his throat, so guttural and primal that her own breath caught. And then, in one swift movement, he wrapped an arm around her waist and swept her off her feet.

Out of the hundred reasons why he shouldn't be doing this, Andre could not recall a single one. Shuddering at the sublime sensation of Dominique's breasts sliding along his side, he lowered her to stand beside him in the shallow tub, squeezing his eyes shut against a red haze that obscured everything.

Everything but Dominique, her scent, her exquisite form in his arms, and a desire so intense, it stunned him. For a heart-freezing moment, he could only clasp her tightly to his side, struck by the notion that he did not know what to do.

Absurd. He was no novice, had done this far too many times to count, going through the motions with the sureness of a musician performing a piece he'd learned by heart. Variations on the same theme, every encounter well planned and predictable, always reaching a foreseen conclusion.

Never like this. Never had he looked at a woman and found everything he'd ever wanted, something beyond physical beauty, something that fed a hunger deep inside him while stirring it at the same time.

She shifted. The slight motion caused her breasts to rub against him, pushing him to a level of arousal beyond anything he'd ever known. Clenching his teeth, he caught her chin and lifted her face to his, seeking her gaze in one last effort to regain a modicum of control.

It failed. Beyond the excitement and anticipation he found no trace of fear, no evidence of misgivings, only purity and trust and . . .

His heart seemed to sink and soar at the same time. *Oh, no, no, please don't love me.* "Let me love you."

He blinked, startled that he'd uttered those words, amazed

231

that he was actually bowing his head, even as his every muscle quivered in resistance. She rose on tiptoe, leaning into him, reaching up to caress his cheek with a sure familiarity that made his throat close.

"Yes."

The sultry note in her voice compounded with her touch, sending a violent current rolling through him. And suddenly he understood why, over time, men had turned against kin and country, started wars, killed, lost kingdoms—all over a woman. For at that moment, he knew he had to either have her, or go stark raving mad.

Her fingers curved around his neck to draw him down, a gentle urging he could not resist. Her lips nudged at his own. Unable to fight the overwhelming need to taste her, Andre opened his mouth over hers and took it like a starving man, feasting on her, driving his tongue inside her, until his heart was pounding and his ears were roaring and the entire room seemed to spin in quick flashes of darkness and orange light.

The force of her response surpassed his wildest expectations. He bent her backward, anchoring her against him, letting his free hand trace her delicate jaw, fingertips pausing at the place where her pulse beat at her throat before venturing lower, until at last he found the round softness he sought.

"Superb," he murmured.

Soft, yet firm and high, surprisingly full . . . his fingers closed around her breast, and when she shuddered and pressed into his palm, the world went dim around him.

He couldn't bear this. Couldn't. She felt too exquisite. He willed his fingers still and tried to gentle the kiss, but she made a small sound of protest and kissed him harder, and Andre felt the last of his restraint begin to rip asunder.

With renewed urgency, his palm circled her breast again, tracing its contour, sliding down, down, over her hip and down her thigh, then moving inward, seeking, sliding, finding her sleek and hot and—

Oh, Lord. She was ready for him.

He groaned. She gasped against his mouth and lurched, grabbing his shoulders, nails pressing into his skin. Her hips began a restless rhythm, and suddenly he was drinking in her throaty moans, edging closer to the brink with each surge of her body against his fingers, fighting to hold back . . .

He could feel the tension in her, building with each stroke of his fingertips against her tender flesh, and then she was tearing her mouth from his, letting her head fall back, clutching him tighter. . . .

"Andre! Ah! Oh, I'm—"

"*Oui, ma vie.* Hold tight. Hold on to me."

Something flared bright within him. He stiffened, teeth gnashing in the attempt to keep it at bay, but then she stirred, her hip coming into full contact with his arousal for an instant, making him feel as if a steel band had clamped around him, tightening hard, harder. . . .

Rigid.

"Ahh!"

She went utterly still. A long, halting breath. The next second, she arched violently against him. He sensed the surge start somewhere deep within him and bit down on the inside of his cheek, feeling it threaten to overtake him.

He threw his head back. *No.*

And succumbed to the inevitable. Over and over and then again the hot current raged through him, until reality narrowed to sensation and black spots whirled behind his closed eyelids and her moans sounded as if they came from far away, muted by a hum filling his ears.

No sooner was it over for Andre than Dominique gave one final shudder and went lax against him. Breathing hard, he wrapped his arms around her and held her to his heart, finding it a challenge to remain standing and support her slight weight at the same time.

Consciousness gradually returned, bringing with it the awareness of her breasts rising and falling against his abdomen and the hard evidence of his persistent need for her. Still stunned and a bit annoyed at his inability to contain himself, Andre nuzzled the top of her head, then buried his nose and mouth in her silky hair and inhaled deeply of her lavender fragrance.

Never before had this happened to him. Then again, it had

been two years. Two years, followed by what seemed like two lifetimes of wanting Dominique.

At length, she rubbed her cheek back and forth along his chest and looked up at him. His heart nearly quit, but when her gaze met his, whatever he feared he'd find in her visage was absent. All he could see was languor and bewilderment, along with a trace of shyness that, despite the import of the moment, threatened to make him smile.

"Was that . . . um, normal?" she asked in a wonderfully husky voice.

Somehow, he managed to gulp back an impending laugh. "That depends."

"On what?"

"It's hard to explain." A bit of lather clung to her temple. He wiped the soap away with one finger before it could get into those questioning green eyes, then loosened his grip on her waist and let his other hand slide down the arc of her spine, an intriguing idea forming in his mind. "But I can show you, if you want me to."

Her gaze roved downward, lingering over his chest. She nodded once, parted lips quivering slightly, and he couldn't help taking them in a thorough kiss before he released her and bent sideways to plunge his hand into the water.

His knee bumped her leg. She moved back, but not much, given the confines of the tiny tub.

"What are you doing?"

He located the partially melted soap, then reached for the half-full bucket and straightened. "The water will grow cold soon."

"Oh." She blinked, still staring at him with that delectably naive expression on her face.

Lips curving into the smile he could no longer suppress, Andre rolled the soap in his hand, aching to yank her against him and let her feel how much he longed to be inside her.

But he dared not. She looked so fragile, what with her petite size and the bandage at her upper arm. And despite her abandon of a moment ago, her eyes now betrayed nervousness, reminding him that she was new at this. The flame in them still flickered, however, and now he could take his time and stoke it slowly, using his hands and mouth and body to love her with infinite care, as he had yearned to do for so damned long.

"Raise your arms," he said in a low voice.

She hesitated for a moment before doing so. The simple movement was enough to make his mouth go dry. The subtle lift of her chin, the upward tilt of her breasts, the way her arms moved with such grace . . .

Careful to avoid wetting the dressing at her shoulder, he tilted the bucket, watching the water stream over her, outlining lush curves, leaving behind clear droplets that gleamed on her pale skin. Tossing the empty pail aside, Andre took in the impossibly erotic sight. The taut, wet peaks of her breasts reminded him of freshly rinsed berries.

His parched mouth began to water. He unclenched his hand, and realized he'd compressed the soap into a misshapen mass. Ever so lightly, he drew it back and forth over the swell of her rising and falling bosom. Berries with cream. He wondered if he could possibly survive this.

He let his hands embark upon a slow and sensuous exploration of her body, smoothing lather over lustrous skin that brought to mind a flawless pink pearl. He ran a fingertip over a tiny oval birthmark on her belly. Shoving away thoughts of laving it with his tongue, he drew a bit closer and reached around to soap her back, massaging at the same time, coaxing her tensed muscles to relax beneath his fingers.

Her waist, her hips . . . her derriere. One hand remained there, kneading gently, while the other glided around front again, palm and soap tracing the curve of her hip, progressing lower. She clamped her legs together, but Andre pressed on, the soap making it easy to slip his hand between her thighs. He didn't miss the faint moan he knew she tried to swallow back.

His breath came faster. "Open for me, sweet."

He felt her start to tremble, and when her muscles yielded to the unrelenting pressure of his hand, he began caressing her again, watching her face, mentally pledging to stop if he detected even the slightest hint of resistance. With another low cry, she reached up and gripped the back of his neck, and

Andre seized her mouth and drew on it again, then captured her hips and brought her fully to him, relishing the feel of her tight derriere filling his palms and the pressure of her belly against his rigid sex.

His body unconsciously began to match the rhythm of his thrusting tongue, and when she strained against him and followed his lead, he could stand no more. Breaking the kiss, he wrenched out of her grasp, then hoisted the last full bucket and dumped its contents over the both of them.

Water sloshed everywhere. Snatching up a bath sheet, he draped it about Dominique's shoulders and scooped her up into his arms, heedless of the wet trail he left in his wake as he carried her to the bed. Somehow, he managed to rein in the urge to throw her on the mattress and set upon her like a barbarian, but his patience nearly snapped the moment he laid her down to recline among the pillows.

She was the very portrait of enticement. Her chignon had come partially undone, letting her dark hair frame her face. He watched, enraptured, as she shoved her fingers through the disheveled strands and shook her head. Black rain.

The bath sheet dangled from his arms. Tossing it aside, he propped his knee upon the bed and caressed again the dainty arch of her foot.

His fingers began to quiver when they encountered her knee, and presently he felt her hand upon his shoulder. "You're cold," she murmured.

"For the longest time," he said, leaning across to whisper in her ear, "but no more."

Her response was a fierce kiss just above his jaw, triggering the familiar wrenching feeling within him, deep in the place within his heart that only she could reach. He turned his head and brushed his lips over her mouth, her cheek, feathering kisses along her throat and chest, licking at drops of water en route to her breasts. Everywhere his hands passed, his tongue followed, tasting and caressing until at long last she unknowingly fulfilled his private fantasy, arching, writhing, digging her fingers into the linens, murmuring things he was too far gone to comprehend.

Propping his hands on either side of her, he nuzzled her

bosom, then bent to explore each dewy breast thoroughly, exhilarating in the way she moaned and trembled beneath the onslaught of his lips and tongue.

He wanted to devour her. But when he caught hold of her hips and rubbed his cheek across her belly, he felt her grip his shoulders, her fingers clenching and relaxing with increasing urgency while he trailed his lips ever lower down her abdomen, as if she sensed where he intended to kiss her next. He smiled against her skin.

She stirred. "Wait. I—"

"Mmm." He kissed her navel.

She gasped, clutching at him. Slowly, he circled her navel with his tongue, but something in the tone of her ensuing soft cries changed, ringing more of protest than pleasure. He raised his head. Before his vision could clear, she let go of his shoulders and held her arms out. "Please."

If that breathless monosyllable left any doubt as to what she wanted, her eyes conveyed it plainly. In one swift movement, he slid upward and rolled onto his side to draw her close, and when she willingly put her arms around him and molded her body fully against his own, his every muscle locked in response.

Mine. Mine. Never in my life . . .

She buried her face against his chest, whispered something he couldn't hear, and then she was beneath him, and he was pressing her down, wedging a knee between her thighs—

"Andre . . ."

He stopped, hands clenching into fists on either side of her head, fighting for control as she raked her nails up and down his back and made a sound much like a sob.

Andre.

No. Not that false name. He didn't want to hear it, not now. He shut his eyes and pressed his face into the curve of her neck, his own breath coming in shallow pants as his highly aroused body strained to override his mind.

But, Heaven help him, when he finally joined his life with hers, he didn't want to be Andre Montville.

"Dominique."

She didn't seem to hear him.

He took her face between his palms. "Look at me, sweet."

Her lashes lifted, revealing the striking beauty of those eyes that could so easily delve into his soul.

"My given name," he whispered, "is not Andre."

Her passion-dazed expression warmed with tenderness, but she didn't seem surprised, and somewhere in the corner of his mind he recalled having once blurted half his true name in her presence.

He swallowed hard. "It is Philippe. I want to hear you say it."

She clamped her knees around his hips. "Philippe," she breathed.

The sound of it on her lips stirred long-forgotten emotions in him, so powerful and deep, there was but one way to express them. "Oh, God," he groaned. And then he buried himself inside her.

Her cry tore at his heart. Body racked with tremors from suppressing the instinct to move, he held still, unable to deny the effect her tight heat had on him, hating that he could feel such intense pleasure while causing her pain.

"I'm sorry," he managed hoarsely.

She only held him tighter and wrapped her legs higher about his waist, driving him deeper, and with a despairing groan he finally gave rein to his body's primal demand, surging, withdrawing, slowly, carefully, until she found his rhythm and began to match it.

He knew the moment her pain ceased, felt it in the way her death grip on him loosened, in the eager lift of her hips, in the pitch of her soft cries. Desire ripped through him anew, impelling him to quicken his pace and nearly lose himself in the rich, overpowering sensation, gathering intensity with every deep thrust.

It wasn't long before he felt her tremors commence. That it might happen her first time amazed him; that he would be the one to give it to her . . . exultation. Forestalling his own fierce need, he changed his angle, then resumed more slowly, with shallow, slanting thrusts that rendered her wild and reckless, tossing with unbridled abandon beneath him.

Guttural moans. Exquisite friction. The sheen of perspiration on her heated skin. The low, familiar thumping feeling rolling through him . . . close . . . so close . . . for the first time ever, unable to stop . . .

"Dominique," he gritted, "I can't . . . I don't—"

"Andr—"

His head jerked up. He opened his eyes, glimpsed her enraptured face, saw her lips part.

"Philippe," she gasped.

He recognized that timbre even before he felt her clench around him. Arms and shoulders shaking with strain, he clenched his teeth and began long, deep strokes, urging her toward what he, too, sought so desperately.

His thighs tensed. His belly flattened. Casting restraint to the winds, he took her closer to the peak and followed her there, loving her with everything he had and ever would have, until she finally spasmed, sobbing, convulsing around him, and at long last he found his own shattering release.

Chapter Nineteen

The candle on the mantel had burned low, its nearly spent wick flickering with a weak flame that threatened to burn out at any moment. Her skin tingling from head to toe, Dominique lay nestled in the shelter of Andre's arms, feeling as if she were descending from a great height, borne by a cloud of butterflies.

It wasn't long, however, until a burning ache in the most intimate of places awakened her to the enormity of what she'd just done. No longer could her marriage be labeled a sham—moreover, *she* had initiated everything, and with an abandon of which she'd never thought herself capable.

What he must think of her. What was he thinking? Heart in her throat, she raised her chin, needing to see, to look into his face. Even now, lying there with his eyes closed and his lips slightly parted, the man exuded such potency, he robbed her of breath. Unable to keep from touching him, she slid her hand upward along his chest, across his throat, to finally cradle his beautiful jaw. It was like stone.

She frowned. "Are you all right?"

His lips curved upward slightly, not quite a smile. Long

lashes still concealing his expression, he reached to smooth a strand of hair off her cheek. "I think I should be the one to pose that question."

She kissed his chin. "I asked you first."

She felt him thread his fingers through her hair, his gaze at last alighting on her. "I didn't hurt you?"

"Of course not."

The slight tremor of his fingers and his deep, deep voice, along with the knowledge that she had affected him so, touched her profoundly. Such apprehension behind the tenderness reflected in his eyes; it was as if he expected her to wrench out of his embrace and run screaming from his bed at any moment.

Though physically impossible to get any closer, she sought to better fit herself against him. *"Au contraire.* You ... pleased me. Very much."

A flicker in his eyes was the sole indication that he had, indeed, registered the weight behind her words. But his visage remained troubled.

She moistened her lips. "Did I not please you?"

He drew a breath, his gaze at once so hot, so full of raw intensity, that she could hardly hold it. "Not please me? How can you even—"

Strong fingers bracing the back of her head, he drew her face to his, taking her mouth in a kiss so fervent, so demanding, it made the world seem to dissolve around her.

Leaving only him. It didn't matter that he was slowly but surely taking away her soul; in his embrace and with him kissing her this way, she felt and tasted all, and needed nothing else. Nothing but him.

Her husband.

Too soon, he broke the kiss, and gently pressed her head back down to rest upon his shoulder. "You pleased me so damned much," he quietly said, "you made me wish that I were someone else."

An onslaught of emotion flooded her. How was it possible that he still considered himself unworthy? *"Mon coeur,"* she whispered, "it's said that, ultimately, each receives exactly what he or she deserves."

A long pause. At last, he shook his head. "God help me, but I don't understand you."

"What a coincidence."

It seemed to her that he meant to say something else, but all he did was hook a finger in the long white ribbon around her neck, lifting the locket in his palm. "I can't believe I hadn't noticed this of late."

She watched the tiny amethyst and emerald violets wink in the dim light, half relieved, half disappointed at the change of subject. "The chain's clasp was damaged during the carriage accident. The second time it came undone, I replaced it with this." She touched the still-damp ribbon.

He ran his thumb over the jewels. She felt his chest begin to labor, his heartbeat increasing steadily against her breast. "Dominique?"

"Yes?"

"There's something I . . . I haven't been . . ."

The torment in his rich voice nearly undid her. "What?"

Brow furrowing, he let the locket go. "Nothing."

"Tell me," she urged.

"Never mind. It's very late. You need to rest."

Disheartened, Dominique swallowed back a protest and relaxed against him, her hand sliding back and forth along his chest. "Then can you tell me by what name you wish me to address you from now on?"

He considered for a few moments, his gaze straying to the embers of the dying fire. "I've grown accustomed to Andre, I suppose. Besides, it's safer. At least, for the time being."

The taper on the mantel burned out with a hiss, casting the room into darkness. He leaned up on one elbow to tuck the covers about the both of them, then took her in his arms again. "Sleep, now. We'll talk tomorrow. We have plenty of time."

Time. Exactly how much did she still have with him?

Heart suddenly heavy, Dominique turned her gaze to the bare window across the room. It looked to be after midnight, but well before daybreak. She closed her eyes, shutting out the leaden dark blue color of the sky, for once in her life not looking forward to the dawning of a new day.

*　*　*

Dominique finished cleaning her teeth, then filled the wash-basin and bent to splash cool water on her face. Stifling an-other yawn, she groped for a hand towel, wincing at the soreness in muscles she'd never given thought to until . . . un-til . . .

Andre.

Visions of last night assailed her mind, and she went still for a moment, pressing her face into the linen. The cloth held the faint scent of his shaving soap, and as she breathed it in the images of him intensified.

His naked form as he bent over her, every hard muscle defined by candlelight, moisture clinging to his body. His deep voice, like black velvet in the shadows of night. The gentle-ness and expertise of his hands . . .

Behind her, something creaked. Dominique dropped the towel and turned, grabbing her dark blue riding habit just be-fore Andre stepped in and closed the door with the tip of one polished black boot. Clad in a snow-white shirt and tan breeches, a tray balanced on his right hand, he brought with him the tantalizing scents of coffee and fresh bread.

She clutched the garment to her breast and smiled at him. "Good morning."

His mouth curved up slightly at one corner. "It has been, yes."

God, but she must look frightful. With her free hand, she sought to smooth her yet-to-be-combed hair. "What time is it?"

"Half past eleven."

And he had wanted to leave early. "Oh, no. I'm sorry."

"Don't be." The blue of his irises seemed to deepen as his gaze briefly dipped to the garb she held, giving Dominique the odd sense that he could see through everything, including her chemise. "You look . . . well rested. How does your shoul-der feel?"

"I changed the bandage." She tried a shrug. "It's not too bad."

Needing a respite from his unrelenting gaze, she turned her attention to the tray he held. Her stomach plummeted, a feeling having nothing to do with the golden mini-baguettes she spotted there. Beside them, one tiny white snowdrop peeked from a half-full water glass.

She studied the bowed head of the fragile bloom and somehow knew that he, and not the proprietress, had placed it there. The thought of him bending on one knee, the morning sun gilding his hair as he plucked that flower, nearly arrested her pounding heart.

He set the salver on the table. "Even had you arisen earlier, we couldn't have left. It took me a while to arrange for a proper curricle."

"Oh, good. A civilized conveyance." Such meaningless conversation, she thought ruefully.

"I figured you'd grown so tired of riding, you just might trust me to drive again."

She might have laughed at that, were it not for his demeanor. Only hours before, he'd loved her with such gentleness, but as she watched him come nearer, she had the unsettling sensation that something was . . . well, different. His shoulders . . . he was beyond tense; indeed, he seemed as hard and sharp as a rapier, primed for some sort of—

"May I assist you?"

She barely heard his question. It took a moment to drag her gaze from the burgundy sash encircling his waist and beyond the white linen straining over the expanse of his chest. And when she looked into his eyes, a most uncanny sense of déjà vu ensnared her.

Will. Verve. Anticipation. And glimmering behind all of those were unmistakable embers of last night.

"Yes," she replied, not really knowing, or caring, what he'd asked.

He stopped within a breath of her. "Keep looking at me like that, madame, and my baguettes are certain to go stale."

Yes, it had been exactly like this once before. This was the man who'd caught her searching through his things, then stalked her until he had her pinned against a wall. That day, she hadn't understood or known what to do with the feelings he evoked within her. But now she did.

Before she could stop herself, she'd dropped the riding habit and grasped one end of his perfectly tied cravat. The knot gave easily, crisp fabric sliding undone with a whisper, exposing just enough of his throat for her to stroke with the tip of her finger.

His quick intake of air was enough to make his chest touch hers. "I warned you."

Then he was cupping her derriere, lifting her, barely giving her time to grip his shoulders and wrap her legs about his hips before he backed her to the wall and opened his mouth over her throat.

The heat of his body contrasted with the chill of the stone to which he pressed her, sending hot and cold shudders through her. With a low sound much like a growl, he slid his tongue down to her collarbone, then up and back, again, again, until she dimly wondered if anyone had ever died of this.

Ah, God, his warm breath on her neck, the shocking sensation of his teeth closing gently over her earlobe, the hard length of him straining intimately against her . . . a dull ache coiled deep inside her, intensifying until it bordered on pain, and Dominique shoved her fingers into Andre's hair and pulled, tipping her head to the side, tacitly urging him to do more.

Even now, in the harsh light of day, she wanted him. His body onto, into hers, where she could have him all to herself, where she could hold him as close as was humanly possible, if only for a while.

It wasn't long before she felt a subtle change in him. Sensing that he was about to draw away, she shook her head, her fingers digging hard into his shoulders. But before she could voice any protest, he stopped caressing her and pressed his face into the curve of her neck.

"Dominique. We have to stop, sweet." His voice was tinged with anguish.

"No."

"We must," he gritted between raspy breaths. "Although it just might kill me."

Still breathing hard, he hugged her tightly and kissed her neck again. "We have to leave at noon. It is imperative." Loosening his grip, he let her body slide down along his and moved back slightly, his hands lingering on her waist, as if it cost him a great deal to let her go.

His gait seemed a bit stiff as he went to retrieve her clothing. Leaning against the wall for support, Dominique shook her head, unable to explain her own behavior. She'd made no attempt to conceal her desire for him, yet felt no shame, no guilt, but only . . .

"We'll burn this when we reach our destination," he said, holding out Yvette's stained riding habit with evident distaste.

Dominique slipped her arms into the sleeves. Whatever it was she felt for him, now was not the time to reflect on the matter. "Where are we headed?"

An enigmatic smile. "I fear that if I told you, you might not come with me."

"A cemetery? Our mystery destination is a *cemetery?*"

Dominique's stomach cramped at the macabre sight. She should have known what that high stone wall concealed. Beyond the black bars of the ancient iron gates, gnarled trees swayed in the wind, their boughs casting shadows over rows of weathered sepulchres with lichen-covered gravestones.

She edged closer to Andre. "You were correct."

"Regarding what?"

"My not wishing to accompany you here."

He merely pulled a thick stick from underneath the seat of the curricle and handed it to her. "Attention. Hold this."

Fingers wrapping around the rough staff, Dominique stared at its cloth-wrapped tip, then at Andre, not certain what to make of the gleam in his eye. "A torch? But it's still light outside."

He grinned. "The better we can see, my dear."

That wicked smile of his served to make her more nervous. Apprehension turned to panic when she saw him lean into the vehicle, produce a scabbard and sling its leather strap across his torso.

"Andre—"

"The faster we finish our business here, the sooner we can leave." Adjusting the buckle, he gave the sheath a quick inspection, slammed the curricle door then fixed her with an assessing stare. "You're not afraid, are you?"

She read the challenge in his tone and raised her chin, allowing him to lead her to the cemetery gate. "Need I be?"

Without warning, he pulled her into an embrace that was just short of crushing. "Afraid, no." He bent his head, his warm lips grazing hers. "Excited, yes. Oh, yes."

And then he kissed her as if his life depended on it. Dominique let him dip her backward and kissed him deeply in response, relishing in his taste and the scent of fresh spring air that clung to him.

All day, he'd behaved strangely. When he wasn't driving at a harrowing pace, she'd often catch him regarding her as if he wanted to draw her to him and kiss her until she didn't know who she was. She never knew what to expect: sometimes his looks were hot, other times warm and impossibly tender. But always, always hungry.

Had she not known better, she would have attributed his mood to last night. But something told her it was more than that. Whatever it was, it thrilled her and scared her senseless at the same time.

He broke the kiss. Somewhat dizzy, Dominique braced her cheek against his chest and ran her palms along his sides, listening to the hammering of his heart. Her hand encountered the scabbard he'd just donned, and as her reeling head slowed to a spin she realized—

"The sheath is empty."

"Mm-hmm." He stepped back, still holding her at arms' length. "But by the grace of God it won't be, before too long."

Before she could ponder what that meant, Andre took her hand, pushed the gate open, and swiftly headed through the creaking portal. Hair at her nape stirring, Dominique forced her legs to move forward, trying not to think of what could lurk behind the headstones as she followed him deeper into the graveyard.

Why was he muttering to himself? She strained to make out what he was saying, and realized that he was counting paces.

". . . twenty-six." He halted. "We need to turn right at that tree." He motioned toward a monstrous chestnut whose ample crown and trunk obstructed everything beyond it.

Excitement emanated from him with such intensity, she felt it overtake her, too. "What are we looking for?"

"An antique sword."

"A sword?" She searched his profile for some sign that he was mocking her, but found none.

"From what I'm told," he went on, striding forth again, "it's buried in a"—he veered onto a short cobblestone path—"*Regarde!* There!"

Dominique looked, and saw a large stone structure. Rather, the ruin of a structure, partially concealed by a rank overgrowth of weeds. One glance at its narrow opaque windows and the hideous openmouthed gargoyles carved along the top, and Dominique's skin began to crawl. Andre, however, gazed at it as if he'd come upon the grandest chateau in all of France.

The closer they came to the arched entryway flanked by twin pairs of crumbling columns, the harder Dominique squeezed Andre's hand.

He studied the massive wooden doors. "I'm here, I see it, yet I don't quite believe it," he murmured, reaching for the enormous rusty latch.

She let go of his hand to grab his sleeve. "You're going *in* there?"

His teeth flashed in a brilliant smile. "Ever come face-to-face with a ghost?"

"No, only with a madman."

He laughed, then cast a glance around and frowned at the now dusky sky. "Damn. I thought we had at least another quarter-hour until it became this dark."

Impatiently, he fished in his coat pocket, muttering something about flint and steel. Holding the torch for him to light, Dominique gripped the wood a little tighter, figuring she could use it as a weapon should some other deranged graveyard enthusiast come upon them.

"Who is entombed here?" she asked, when the cloth finally caught a spark.

Lips twitching, he watched the material ignite. "No one. This is a chapel."

She almost dropped the torch. "You're going to plunder a chapel?"

He flinched visibly at that. "Dominique . . . listen to me. This sword I seek is . . . of inestimable value."

Somehow, she doubted that the significance of the blade in question was solely monetary. "And?"

His chest rose and fell in a sigh. "Initially, someone else was to retrieve it, but then things changed, and I had to take it upon myself."

She stared at him expectantly, but he didn't reveal more, and neither did his closed expression. "You cannot tell me why this sword is so important?"

He shook his head. "I'm sorry. I'm sworn to secrecy."

"And if you weren't?"

The moment seemed to grow longer and longer. With bated breath, she watched him struggle with the question.

At last, he spoke. "Then I would tell you."

How piercing his eyes were. How candid. Dear God, never had he looked more powerfully beautiful. Except, perhaps, last night, last night as he'd done unbelievable things to her . . . A thrill assailed her at the memory. As if fueled by it, the torch flared in her hand, jerking Dominique back to the present.

He held her gaze an instant more, then eyed the door again, his rising tension nearly palpable. "Ready?"

"Yes."

He nodded at her over the flames, then stepped up to the chapel door.

Chapter Twenty

Dominique wiped her hands on her dusty skirts and drew her sleeve across her brow. Her muscles felt like lead. After the first hour of searching, she had lost track of time as they'd continued to inspect every last corner of the chapel.

Not an easy task, since whoever was renovating the interior had removed the pews and erected scaffolding. The planks and ladders had encumbered their progress, although the scattered tools had been of use in prying open a few panels that covered hidden niches. Unfortunately, every concealed recess they'd found had proven empty.

She rubbed her aching thighs. "Are you ready to renounce this?"

Had Dominique not known Andre's answering scowl was directed at circumstance and not at her, she would have shrunk against the wall behind her.

"Hardly." Raking a hand through his disheveled hair, he sank down on a knee-high stack of planks and studied the wood beams crisscrossing the interior of the tiny chapel. "We probably could have restored this place ourselves by now."

He patted the spot beside him.

She sat. "You're certain that we're searching in the right location?"

A heavy sigh. "If the sword exists, it should be here."

Her brows shot up. "If it *exists?*"

Slumping forward, he braced his forearms on his thighs. "It's said that a Frankish warrior named Zabré retreated here with his remaining men after losing a crucial battle to the Moors. Eventually, they starved him out, but when he finally surrendered, his sword was nowhere to be found."

Dominique blinked. He had embarked upon a quest based on a story regarding something that had happened more than ten centuries ago? Had it been anyone other than Andre sitting there telling her this. . . . She stared at his grim profile. "What happens if you—if we—don't find this sword?"

His head came up as if she'd punched him beneath the chin. Even by the light of the torch he'd placed in a wall sconce, she could see his face go a shade more pale. "I must find it."

Must find it. All of a sudden, images began to flash rapidly before her. Madame's glazed eyes. Paul's face. And the medallion. *The medallion she had failed to find.*

A chill settled within her. How could she have forgotten all about it? How had she become so wrapped up in—

She'd set out on a mission to save her brother, and instead of seeing it through, she'd gone and—

Had a beam come crashing down on her from overhead, she couldn't have been more staggered. Vision blurring, Dominique moved to stand, but something gripped her knee. She looked down at it. Andre's left hand. And on it, as if to mock her, gleamed his wedding ring.

She surged to her feet so fast, she felt light-headed.

"Dominique?"

She heard the shuffle of his booted feet, felt his strong arm encircle her. And found that she could not push him away.

"What's wrong? What is it, sweet?"

"I don't know." It was the truth. Because she no longer had any idea what was wrong, or, for that matter, what was right.

"Do you feel ill? Is it your shoulder? Perhaps a breath of air—"

"No." Lest he might think of leaving her to go open a window, she clutched his shoulders, wanting only to stay in his embrace, to bury her face in his chest, to tell him everything.

But what would that accomplish? A man like Andre didn't change loyalties. To think he might, only because she'd let him make love to her—No, no sense in lying to herself. *She* had seduced *him*. And even had it been the other way around, that couldn't change the fact that they were on opposing sides.

Gently, he cupped her cheek. Turning her face to his, he searched her features, his jaw tight, his lashes lowered in concentration. "I'll do my very best to slay your dragons, *Cendrillon*. All you need do is point me in the right direction."

His softly spoken words made something inside her shatter. Tears stung her eyes, and it took everything still whole within her to control them.

She swallowed. Drew a fortifying breath. "Do you remember back at Loches you said you knew my brother was in danger?"

His brows lifted a fraction, then lowered in a slight frown. "Yes. But I have reason to believe that is no longer the case."

"Do you know where he is?"

He didn't answer. Nor did he need to. She could plainly see that he did know. And that he meant to keep that knowledge to himself.

She wrenched away from him.

"Dominique, wait—"

"Why?" she demanded in a choked voice, hands clenching into fists. "You don't intend to tell me anything, so—"

"At Loches, I also told you that I'm not your enemy. Remember?"

She did, and all too well. And she could not recall a single instance when he had proven otherwise.

"Remember?" he repeated.

All she could manage was a nod, because her throat felt raw and tight.

Tentatively, he grasped her elbow. "I'm asking you to trust me. Just a little longer."

"You can"—she gulped—"guarantee that nothing will happen to my brother . . . or Madame?"

A sigh. "I wish to God I could. But if some misfortune does befall them, it won't be by my hand, I swear it."

Oh, how she wanted to give credence to that. "Why should I believe you?"

"Because I'd bare my neck to take a noose before I'd ever do anything to hurt you," he replied softly. "And that extends to bringing harm to those you love."

The notion of him twisting slowly in the wind was more than she could bear. Shaken by an awareness she could no longer deny, yet was too frightened to acknowledge, Dominique clenched her teeth and tipped her head back, fighting a fresh surge of hot tears.

No, now was not the time to fall apart. Somehow, she managed to recover her composure, and as the haze in her eyes dissipated, she continued to stare upward, concentrating on the ceiling as if some sort of divine guidance could be found in the foreign words inscribed there.

Latin words.

She studied them. Read them again, took in their meaning. It was as if a curtain had risen for her, revealing the answer to a riddle, sweeping away her anger and confusion at the same time.

She whirled to face Andre and found him still regarding her, an anxious expression on his face. Resisting the urge to reach up and smooth the tension from his lips, she took his hand instead.

"Look there!" She motioned with her chin. "What do you see?"

Without enthusiasm, he glanced up at the ceiling. "A dusty chandelier."

"And what else?"

A strained smile. "Cobwebs."

She nodded. "Yes, but read what is inscribed around the mounting."

"Virtute et armis." His tone was flat, but the next moment his gaze grew thoughtful. " 'By valor and arms.' "

"An odd inscription for a chapel ceiling, don't you agree?"

253

She watched him ponder this. Gradually, understanding and hope dawned in his eyes, and Dominique stared into them, sensing the increase in his pulse as surely as if she'd placed a hand over his heart.

He squeezed her fingers. "Do you suppose—"

"*Mais, oui.* How better to hide something than—"

"—in plain view," he finished, renewed excitement in his voice. "The column."

In no time, he was climbing the ladder and swiftly negotiating the scaffolding, as if, for him, walking across beams were an everyday occurrence. He'd almost reached the halfway point when the wood groaned beneath him.

He faltered. Dominique gasped. "Be careful!"

Andre paused long enough to regain his footing and give her a quick smile, then took the last few steps and reached for the chandelier column. Dominique followed his every movement with bated breath, ears strained lest she detect the faintest creak from the beam on which he stood.

Thankfully, all she heard was the noise of grating metal as Andre unscrewed the bulbous end. Very slowly, he eased it away from the shaft. "Well, I'll be damned."

The torchlight reflected in the emerging shiny metal, beaming light on the opposite wall. Dominique watched Andre pull out the seemingly endless length of what was obviously a sword, not daring to ask if it was, indeed, the one he had been searching for.

But when he finally climbed down from the rafters, she realized the question would be pointless. The gleam in his blue eyes rivaled that of the sharp-edged metal in his hand. As if it were a sacred thing, he lifted it, ran his fingers over the flat of the blade, then stood there holding it in his palms for a few moments, his head bowed as in prayer.

At last, he looked up. "Come here, my *Cendrillon.*"

The appellation went straight through her heart. She went to stand before him, feeling strangely light, as if the ground beneath her had turned to clouds.

"Touch it," he said in a low voice, "and tell me that it's real."

The steel felt cool and slick beneath her suddenly moist fingertips. "It's real," she breathed.

He exhaled audibly, his eyelids drifting closed. "Sheathe it for me."

His voice was barely an undertone, but the force emanating from him staggered her. It seemed as if he'd absorbed the strength of the steel and everything around him, herself included. Until now, she hadn't appreciated the importance of this find for him, and she was overwhelmed by his apparent need to share it with her.

She grasped the proffered sword. It was so heavy, she needed to employ both hands. Arms straining with the weight, she slid the tip into the scabbard and thrust the blade home, then slowly ran her fingertips up and down the gold hilt, over the sun-shaped indentation on the end. She looked up at him. And became hopelessly entrapped in his gaze.

"Well done," he said.

It was the husky note in his voice that clued her into the effect of her actions upon him. Clearly reading his thoughts, Dominique blushed, not quite managing to suppress a moan as something wrenched inside her and a wicked melting sensation stole through her limbs.

His throaty chuckle only heightened her excitement, not to mention her mortification. He reached out and traced the contour of her cheek. She nearly ached, so fierce was her need for his embrace, but by the tremor in his fingers she could tell he didn't trust himself to do anything else.

"Thank you," he said. "Were it not for you, I never would have found it."

"I doubt that. But you are welcome, nonetheless."

It was remarkable, really, the effect he had on her. And in a chapel, of all places.

"What now?" she asked.

A slow smile curved his lips, so full of sensual promise that her stomach plummeted and her heart leaped in immediate response. In one swift movement, he swept her up into his arms. "Now, madame," he whispered, his lips warm against her ear, "we celebrate."

*　　*　　*

Outside, it smelled of earth and pine. Comfortably seated in the curricle again, Dominique closed her eyes and gulped great lungsful of air, relishing its freshness, as Andre snapped the reins and urged the horses to a trot.

A moment later, she pulled a strand of hair out of her mouth and groped at her half-undone chignon. "Where are we headed?"

He pointed with his whip. "There. See those lights?"

Squinting brought into focus the contour of a small two-story building, perched halfway up a distant hill. "Yes."

"That is a chalet."

A good half hour's ride, Dominique estimated. She plucked a couple of dangling pins out of her ruined coiffure, not bothering to replace them. "You're certain we can stay there?"

Andre smiled. "Optimistic."

Dominique shook her hair free, delighting in the liberation as it swung loose and caught the breeze. Only now did she feel thoroughly cleansed of the dust and dankness of that cemetery chapel, though they had found a brook in which they'd scrubbed their filthy hands and faces.

A pity that it was not equally easy to clear her conscience. *Paul.* An awful sinking feeling spread in the pit of her belly. What could be so important about that damned medallion, that her brother's own people might kill him for it?

Unwittingly, she moved closer to Andre. He turned his head and smiled, causing the tingle of sensation he always evoked within her, but for some reason the queasiness in her stomach only worsened.

It took some effort to smile back. "I take it we are still in France?"

He chuckled. "Seems like an endless journey, does it not? Yes, we remain within our own borders. A kilometer or so away from Le Pont de Claix, if I am not mistaken."

"Le Pont de Claix?"

He nodded. "South of Grenoble."

Dominique's jaw dropped in a soundless gasp. Had he told her they were south of Hades, she wouldn't have been so stunned. If they were near Grenoble, then they were near Vizille, as well.

In the vicinity of the very place Madame had sent her.

Still reeling, she sat up straighter, feeling her backbone turn to ice. Could this be a coincidence? Was this his destination? If so, what did he mean to do there?

I'm asking you to trust me just a little longer. I'm not your enemy, Cendrillon.

She wanted to throw back her head and scream. Instead, she let her gaze follow each tree they swiftly passed, willing her pounding heart to slow, pressing her hands between her knees so that Andre wouldn't see their shaking.

At last, she summoned enough courage to look at him again. He seemed at ease, more content than she had ever seen him.

Now. She had to ask him now, before she lost her nerve.

"Andre?"

"Oui?"

"Do you remember the medallion belonging to Madame?"

His brows rose slightly. Other than that and a brief glance, he gave her no response.

"The one Bavard showed me in the library at Loches," she added, observing his profile, clearly visible by the light of the coach lamps, "to prove that he had captured her."

"Just before you fainted." His voice was toneless.

"Yes."

"What of it?"

She swallowed. "Do you know what happened to it?"

Another, longer glance. Digging her nails into her palms, Dominique watched him work the reins and listened to the hoofbeats fall slower and slower as he paced the horses to a walk. Her heart sank as his face took on that familiar, awful stony mien.

At last, he spoke. "Why do you ask?"

Such calculated nonchalance. Bile rose, bitter, at the back of her throat. Wrapping her arms around herself, she turned the other way and stared blindly into the night. "No reason. Never mind."

"Tell me!"

The note of command in his deep voice took her aback. A moment later, Dominique felt his strong hand grasp her shoulder. Again, she thought of telling him everything. But could she risk that? Should she?

257

She shrank away from him. "I cannot."

"Hell and the devil."

He gave a brusque order. The horses bolted, stretched out their necks, and tore down the road at full gallop. Rounding the next bend, Andre jerked the reins to the left, steering the conveyance onto a narrow bumpy path that made it rock and bounce so hard, Dominique's teeth clicked. Frantically, she groped for something to hold on to.

The path widened into a clearing, where he brought the vehicle to a jarring halt in a cloud of dust. Belatedly gripping the side, Dominique blinked, rattled beyond moving. Before she could recover, Andre leaped down and stormed over to her side, leaves crunching beneath his boots.

He yanked her door wide open. "Cannot, madame?"

His gaze was hot and piercing. Violent. Then he was reaching for her, lifting her out of her seat and hauling her to his chest in a motion so swift, it left her breathless.

"Cannot what?" he grated. "Cannot tell me? Or"—he brought his face within a fraction of her own—"cannot trust me?"

Yes, that was hurt she glimpsed behind the fury in his eyes. Dominique had to look away.

"Which is it, madame?"

She shook her head, choking on misery. Never in her life had she felt so uncertain, and the familiar solid strength of his embrace only added to her frustration.

Abruptly, he released her, turned on his heel, and marched away. Dominique followed, trying in vain to think of something to say that would appease him. Beneath the branches of a massive pine, he halted. And then, in one impossibly quick motion, he drew the sword.

A flash of deadly steel. She took a backward step. What was he doing?

She heard the whoosh, felt the air stir as he lowered the blade, pointing the tip toward the ground. The next second, she felt the hard, cold metal and the heat of his palms as he thrust the hilt into her hands, forcibly wrapping her fingers around it.

He went down on one knee before her. In stunned confusion, Dominique watched him take hold of the end of the blade and level it toward his chest.

The hairs rose at her nape. Her gaze flicked from the lethal cutting edge to the turbulence in his eyes, then back again. "What is the meaning of this?"

A mirthless smile. "Go ahead. We're in the middle of nowhere. No one will ever know."

A frisson racked her body, making her arms begin to tremble. "You are insane."

She wanted to step back but feared she'd cut him if she tried to pull away while he still gripped the blade.

Andre's eyes narrowed. "Do it! *Allez-y!*"

Abruptly, he leaned forward. Dominique felt resistance, heard his quick intake of breath as the point pierced the layers of his clothing.

She screamed and let go of the hilt. It hit a boulder with a clang of metal on stone, blade glinting as the sword flipped over once, its tip barely missing his chin, to fall to the ground between them.

He lunged for it.

"Andre!"

Without a second thought, Dominique launched herself at him, wincing at the muffled grunt he gave when his back connected with the earth. She ended sprawled atop him. His body was unyielding, hard with tension—were it not for his pounding heartbeat and uneven breathing, she might have thought she'd landed on a slab of marble.

"Please, cease this," she implored him, "please."

Chest laboring with sobs she could barely contain, she clutched his shoulders. "Please," she repeated in a whisper. "Please. No more."

She wouldn't have thought it possible, but his body hardened even further. The next second, she felt him clamp an arm around her waist and bury his other hand in her hair, dragging her head back, exerting just enough force to command full attention without inflicting pain.

"You haven't yet answered my question." He drew her head yet closer. "Do you or don't you trust me?"

Powerless to do aught else, Dominique stared into his face,

intensely beautiful despite the pallor caused by the moonlight.

She felt his chest rise beneath her own, then fall in a deep sigh. "Then," he whispered fiercely against her mouth, "judge me by this."

His vehemence engulfed her, breaching her defenses the moment his lips seized hers, his tongue thrusting to meet her own in a deep, demanding kiss that took all and gave back everything at the same time. Dominique kissed him back as forcefully. . . .

And suddenly, she couldn't get enough. Teetering on the edge of desperation, she pushed at the fabric covering his shoulders, slipping her hands inside his coat, encountering fine linen over heated male skin.

He shuddered. She moaned. He deepened the kiss. She rocked against him, reveling in the taste of him, kneading the muscles straining beneath her palms while the fine wool of his coat smoothed across her knuckles. The hard thrust of him as he ground his hips against hers was enough to make her lose the rest of her restraint.

Her fingers dug convulsively into his shoulders, clawing at the heavy wool that hindered her seeking hands. The fabric wouldn't budge past his elbows, and Dominique cried out in frustration.

He chuckled, rich vibrations filling her mouth, flooding her chest, converging into hot shafts that shot toward her knees. He gave her mouth one thorough sweep of his tongue, then pressed his moist lips to her cheek and rolled onto his side, taking her with him. In no time, he unbuttoned his coat and shrugged it off, then took her in his arms again.

He caught her mouth and drew on it. His essence enveloped her. He was everywhere, invading her mouth, surging against her front, his scent filling her head.

And, still, she wanted more. But Andre broke the kiss. "Do you trust me, Dominique?"

His voice was thick, and Dominique felt another pang dart through her lower belly at the sound. She sought to hide her face in the warm hollow at his throat.

He didn't let her. "*Dit-moi*. Tell me. Tell me I have your trust."

His tone was harsh, demanding, but in his eyes she clearly saw vulnerability. And strength.

A paradox. He was a paradox, and all of him was beautiful. Body and mind. Heart and soul. Dear God, she wanted all of him.

She ran her tongue over her tingling lips.

He gripped her upper arms. Gave her a little shake. *"Dit-moi!"*

"Je te désire," she breathed.

"I want you, too." Determination burned in the depths of his unwavering gaze. "But do I have your trust?"

She caught the shattered note behind the hardness in his deep voice, felt the tremor in his hands as he tightened his hold on her.

"Do I have it, Dominique?"

Did she trust him? Did she?

Yes.

The answer came straight from her heart. She must have uttered it out loud, because his muscles suddenly locked, and for a moment, he stared at her, looking positively stunned.

"You're certain?" he finally asked in a ravaged whisper.

She touched his cheek, no longer able to deny what her heart had sensed even back at Loches, when he had stepped into her life and changed its course forever. "Yes," she repeated.

And then, with a soft moan of surrender, Dominique reached out and took what she wanted, threading her fingers into Andre's hair, kissing his face, his chin, his throat, tugging at his shirtfront, fumbling with buttons, raining kisses across the glorious exposed portion of his chest.

Immersing herself in him.

His fevered response told her that he was hovering on the same plane, driven by the same irrevocable primal torrent. His hands spanned her waist, then moved toward her breasts. The mere brush of his fingertips as he feverishly undid the fasteners confining her bosom made something expand within her, converging in the pit of her stomach, then shooting lower, where it magnified into a sensation so powerful, she felt herself clinch to the point of pain.

Pain she knew he, and he alone, could ease.

He yanked apart the velvet. Cupped her breasts. "Oh, God."

She let her head fall back, thrust out her chest, offering herself to him. Her body screamed for him, yet all that emerged from her throat were short, guttural moans that escalated into cries when he tugged at his breeches, then yanked up her skirts and slammed his mouth on hers.

His mouth still ravaged hers as he drove into her. Excitement overwhelmed her. She cried out with the sublime sensation, mindlessly striving to match the frenzied cadence he began, harder, faster, his every thrust taking more and more of her, until every last breath of hers belonged to him.

Chapter Twenty-one

"Sweet dreams, *ma Cendrillon.*"

Ensconced in the feather duvet tucked snugly around her, Dominique stirred, half conscious of Andre's softly spoken words against her ear. A moment later, she felt him brush his lips across her cheek. *"Ma vie . . ."*

Too exhausted to move or even open her eyes, she sighed contentedly, letting the warmth and the soothing baritone of his voice lull her back toward slumber. Light footsteps. The squeak of a door opening, then clicking closed.

Jolted awake, Dominique opened her eyes. Darkness. Extending an arm that felt like lead, she reached for Andre, only to find the indentation he'd left in the mattress. Where had he gone at this ungodly hour?

She sat upright, drawing her knees to her chest, a chill creeping along the back of her neck to settle between her shoulder blades as her gaze roamed around the empty room. On a settee near the glowing fireplace sat his open saddlebag. Beside it, neatly folded, were the soiled shirt and breeches he'd worn this evening.

This evening . . . Dominique watched the tongues of flame

lick at the new log Andre had added to the hearth. She'd never forget this small chalet. The moment they'd crossed the threshold of this room, each fresh from an invigorating scrub in the nearby bathing chambers, Andre had taken her in his arms and hadn't let her go.

She'd clung to the moment, cherishing each smile, each tender look he'd given her, each choice morsel of food he'd slipped into her mouth. They'd dined in bed, then feasted on each other for a long, long while, and for a few precious hours it seemed as if the evil world and all its problems had magically retreated, leaving her in this tiny refuge with her husband.

Apparently, reality had reared its ugly head again. It was the middle of the night, and he had left her bed. She frowned. Yes, she did trust him. Completely. Deep down, she always had.

Inexplicable dread came over her at once. Throughout the night, behind the smiles she'd noticed a certain melancholy in his eyes, a tension in the set of his mouth, and now her entire body stiffened as she realized what it was about his lovemaking that had so moved and yet unsettled her.

Dear God, her fear was not *of* him, but *for* him. Because, tonight, Andre had loved her as if for the last time.

Concealed by darkness and a dense cluster of pines, Andre waited, now and again glancing up toward the window of the room where Dominique slept. He could still taste the sweetness of her mouth, the scent of her still clung to his skin, and his body still suffered the warm ache that only lovemaking could cause. God, what he wouldn't give for the freedom to return to her bed, to wrap her in his arms again and hold her for the rest of the night.

Unfortunately, that was not an option. And though the person guarding the chalet was one of his most trusted men and knew exactly where to take Dominique should the unthinkable happen . . . Shoving the thought to the back of his mind, Andre rolled his shoulders, trying in vain to loosen the muscles at the back of his neck.

The snap of a twig yanked his attention to the left. Gripping the hilt of the sword at his hip, he pressed his palm into the sun-shaped indentation, feeling his pulse begin to pound. Straining his eyes brought into view a dark form lurking in the shadows. Andre frowned. Only one? Gaze trained on it, he cleared his throat.

The figure halted. The next moment, it left the cover of the trees and stepped into the moonlight. "Reborn from the ashes . . ." the stranger quietly began.

Andre relaxed somewhat. "The Phoenix rises," he responded, then briefly emerged from his hiding place and ducked behind a pine again.

The man promptly approached, and Andre led him farther into the woods. Only when he was certain no one followed and they were well hidden from view did Andre finally face him.

"Desfieux."

"Montville."

Andre clasped Desfieux's proffered hand in a firm grip. "I'm glad to see you managed to arrive here in one piece."

"Likewise." Desfieux's anxiety was unmistakable, although Andre could barely see his face.

"Where is Rochefort?"

Desfieux snorted. "I rather hoped *you* would tell *me*."

Andre stared at him. "Again?"

A curt nod. "He failed to appear last night. Before I left Vizille, I went to the set meeting point again and waited until the last possible moment."

"Merde," Andre muttered. Curse Etien to hell for vanishing without a trace at the most inopportune times. Just this once, he might have deemed to turn up before his usual eleventh hour.

Desfieux removed one glove and flexed his fingers. "I gather he hasn't contacted you?"

Andre recalled the illegible missive Georges had given him. "I think he tried." He gave a resigned sigh. "He will turn up. He always does. What of the others?"

"All at the chateau. Awaiting your command."

"And Chantal?"

Desfieux replaced his glove. "Last week, I received word

that two British agents and Mehée de la Touche met him aboard a cargo ship docked at La Baule.''

The name was vaguely familiar. "De la Touche?"

"Bonaparte's nemesis. I wrote you about him in my last report."

Ah, yes, the newly-appointed spokesman for a group of French exiles living in Scotland. Andre nodded. "Your report never reached me, but I know of whom you speak."

"The four of them then sailed to London to confer with several of Bonaparte's wealthiest foes."

"And?"

"And Paul sailed home that same week, carrying a small fortune."

"I take it he reached France unscathed?"

"Not to worry. We've taken care of him. And of the funds." Desfieux shoved his hands into his pockets. "Speaking of Paul . . . how is Dominique faring?"

"She is well. Safe under my protection, as I am certain your friend Fardeau has told you." A thought occurred to Andre, and he could not omit the trace of rancor from his voice. "I so enjoyed being held at knifepoint in the corridor of the inn that night. Exactly what I needed, after an evening of merriment at Loches with Bavard."

Desfieux shuffled from one booted foot to the other. "I do apologize for that. When I arrived home and found my sister near hysteria, ranting about how some repulsive bald knave was holding Dominique—"

Andre stopped him with a raised hand. "Fardeau told me why you hired him. No harm done." A question came to mind then, one that had bothered him for quite some time. "What were you doing in France a week ahead of schedule?"

A brief pause. "Business."

Andre didn't miss the stiffening of the man's posture. "Your winery?"

Desfieux coughed. "Yes. I've often wished that it could run itself, but . . ."

Had he been standing a league away, Andre could still have smelled the lie.

Desfieux covered his mouth, sucked in a noisy breath, and

coughed again. "I have to tell you something." He leaned a little closer. "Bavard is looking for you, I fear."

Andre's eyes narrowed. "Oh?"

"We haven't yet learned why." Desfieux cast a furtive glance over his shoulder. "But I am told he's up in arms."

Andre studied him closely. "And you think this has something to do with Rochefort?"

"I hope to God it doesn't."

Dread settled in the pit of Andre's belly. If Desfieux had turned Rochefort in ... God, no. Rochefort would let them tear him limb from limb rather than breathe a single word. Then again, given Bavard's methods ...

"What are we going to do?" Desfieux asked somberly.

No sense in uttering falsehoods; the man knew of the plan, and Andre wasn't about to reveal his mistrust. Too dangerous. "*I'm* going to go and find the gold. And you—"

"I'm going with you."

"No."

"But Rochefort isn't here to accompany you, and—"

"Exactly. We must find him." Andre overlooked Desfieux's exaggerated sigh. "He might be waiting at the other meeting place."

"A possibility," Desfieux grumbled. "But—"

"Look for him there. Give him at least another hour, then return to the chateau and tell the others to await me—"

A rustle. Clamping his mouth shut, Andre turned his head. He saw no one, but a glance at Desfieux's suddenly rigid stance told him that he had heard it, too.

Tense seconds passed. Hoping to hear Rochefort utter the code words, Andre waited, but only the eerie hoot of an owl pierced the oppressive silence.

A moment later, the hoot sounded again. The eagle owl. Relief seeped into Andre's very bones.

Sensing Desfieux's stare, he shook his head in response to the man's unspoken question. Desfieux nodded, turned on his heel, and swiftly vanished into the blackness.

When he was certain the man was out of earshot, Andre moved deeper into the woods, then stopped and tipped his head, listening intently. A third hoot sounded from nearby.

Andre smiled. Swiftly, he headed toward the sound and came upon the ruin of a cottage, a small log structure, sans a roof. A second later, he spotted Rochefort's familiar silhouette, beckoning in the doorless entry.

Andre lengthened his stride. The moment he crossed the crumbling threshold, Rochefort caught him in a brief embrace. "I thought he'd never leave."

Andre clapped him on the back. "And I thought I'd never see your wretched face again."

A muffled chuckle. "You, worried? I am touched." Despite the meager light, Andre could sense his friend's sharp scrutiny. "How goes it?"

"Splendidly," Andre mocked. "Where in hell have you been?"

Rochefort grimaced. "As I recall, you sent me on a mission. Had horses possessed wings, I would have arrived sooner."

Andre detected strain behind the usual humor in Rochefort's tone, and forced himself to draw a calming breath. "You missed a most enlightening conversation with our saboteur."

Rochefort gave a small sound of surprise. "What led you to conclude that he was the one? Georges said you couldn't read my missive."

Andre nodded. "Someone gave it a good soaking. Rendered it illegible."

"Then you don't know." Rochefort paused to glance out the yawning doorway, then moved a little closer. "The reason I didn't meet you until now is that I stopped to, ah, visit with a friend. She confirmed what you already suspected." He lowered his voice further. "Desfieux's failing winery finally went bankrupt late last year. For the past three months, the knave has been receiving money. From Bavard."

Andre clenched his fists. "So, the leak did spring from him."

"Mm-hmm. A veritable fountain."

"Curse him," Andre grated.

"There is more. A welcoming party is headed for the chateau."

Andre frowned. "Let me guess. Bavard."

"I'm afraid so. I passed his coach on the main road a half hour ago. He brings a little entourage."

"How many?"

"A dozen men, I think."

"I see."

"This marriage thing . . . it might have been a test."

Andre's jaw tensed. "Or else Desfieux wanted to make certain we led him to the gold before he blabbed everything to Bavard."

"The maggot." Rochefort cursed under his breath. "What now?"

Andre considered for a moment. "Where is Chantal?"

"At the chateau, with the others."

"All fully equipped?"

"Of course." Rochefort grinned. "Armed to whatever teeth they still possess."

Time. He needed time to find the treasure. But how to detract the enemies and concurrently gather them all in one place?

As an idea took shape in his mind, he felt Rochefort's hand upon his arm. "By the way . . . how is your little bride?"

"Fine," Andre replied distractedly. Outrageous, but if orchestrated properly, the plan might actually work.

"That isn't what I asked. My question was, how is she between the—"

"*Sacrebleu!*" Andre whispered fiercely. "Kindly silence that depraved tongue of yours, and let me think!"

"That good?" Rochefort choked back an audible laugh. "Well, well, old man. It was high time. High time, indeed. I think there might yet be a mote of hope for your redemption."

Hands pressed to the rough bark of the pine she'd hidden behind, Dominique watched her husband emerge from the dilapidated cabin. She hadn't known what to expect when she'd decided to follow him downstairs, but this . . .

Her thoughts fragmented as she tried to make sense of what she'd witnessed. Claude Desfieux, her brother's closest friend and ally, who'd worked with Paul for years, whose sister

Dominique was going to visit before being arrested by Bavard . . .

Claude, to whom she was supposed to deliver the medallion.
Darkness had prevented her from seeing him, but the voice
she'd heard was his. Unquestionably. Why had he met here
with Andre? Why? And who was the second man who had
awaited in the cottage?

Before Andre could disappear from view, she shoved away
from the tree and started after him along the winding mountain
path, as fast as her fatigued legs could carry her. Hard to
believe not an hour had passed since she had lain in his embrace, convinced she couldn't even walk across the room.
Convinced that she could trust him. And now . . .

Good thing she'd found warm clothes at the chalet. She
pushed the hood of her too-large woolen cloak off her forehead and shoved her hands into her pockets, quickening her
step as Andre rounded a bend.

The next thing she knew, she stumbled on some sort of root.
Pitched forward. And plowed straight into Andre.

His arms closed around her. Her heart hammering, Dominique leaned against him, breathing hard.

He stroked her back. "Are you all right?"

She nodded. Drew a shaky breath. "You knew that I was
following you," she said accusingly.

His middle jerked in a soundless laugh. "A full-grown bear
would have made less noise." He held her at arms' length.
"How did you get past the man I posted outside the door?"

"I showed him this." Reaching into her coat pocket, Dominique produced Andre's pistol, which she had spotted upon
leaving the bedroom and grabbed on impulse.

"I see." He shook his head, then exhaled a prolonged sigh.
"What am I going to do with you, Dominique?"

What sort of question was that? Her fingers curled around
the barrel of the flintlock. Suddenly, something rent within her,
letting all the suppressed uncertainty and frustration of the past
week flood her in one great upsurge.

"Interesting," she snapped. "That is exactly what I've been
meaning to ask you. What *are* you going to do with me, Andre? Or, rather, Philippe, or . . . or whoever you are?" Ignor-

ing his stiffening posture, she sucked air through her clenched teeth. "You haul me across half of France, you never tell me anything, you do strange things, you force your . . . your sword into my hands, you—"

"Please, Dominique. Now is not the time—"

"You asked me to trust you, then stole out of my bed in the middle of the night to skulk off to your clandestine meetings. Why is that? Don't *you* trust *me?*"

Her question hung on the chill night air. She watched him draw a deep breath and release it slowly. "I recognized one man with whom you met," she told him. "In fact, I know him well."

For a long moment, he simply looked at her. At last, he nodded, and when he spoke, his tone was low and weary. "Claude Desfieux. He has been working with me for a few years."

His calm admission so surprised her, she wondered if she'd merely imagined it. "In what capacity?" she asked.

"Informant."

Informant? Her brother's best friend? It was all Dominique could do to remain standing. She swallowed hard. "I don't believe you."

"It is the truth."

Claude, a traitor? This was too much. She barely felt Andre take hold of her hand and gently pry her fingers off the pistol.

"I asked him of your brother," Andre went on quietly, tucking the weapon into his waistband. "He is alive and well."

A bit of warmth coursed through her, but not enough to warm her frozen heart. "Alive . . . and well?"

"That's right." He glanced up at the moon. "Now, please, return to the chalet. It is imperative that I go somewhere, and time is of the—"

"Where must you go?"

He made an impatient gesture. "We've been through this before. You know I'm sworn to secrecy, and even if I weren't, the less you know, the safer—"

"You are correct," she interrupted, "we've been through this before."

His eyes beseeched her. "Dominique, all of this is nearly over—"

"Don't!"

He flinched at her sharp tone. He bowed his head, fists clenching and unclenching, and the energy emanating from him was nothing short of formidable. "You think that I don't trust you?"

Dominique's throat closed at his dangerously low timbre. Perhaps she'd finally pushed him too far.

He stared at her. Then, arm raising very slowly, he offered her his hand. She found it impossible to refuse the unspoken request. His fingers closed over hers in a firm grip, and then he veered off the path, threading his way through the pines with her in tow. Moments later, Dominique caught sight of the edge of the cliff.

Her hair stood on end. Hand tightening on hers, Andre kept walking, and Dominique followed, her heartbeat growing more erratic with each stride. Just when she wondered if he'd lost his hold on sanity, he halted. A step away from nothingness, where jagged rocks formed a steep drop. Below, the still waters of a large mountain lake mirrored the brilliance of the moon.

He let go of her hand. A little dizzy, Dominique dragged her gaze from the slope and focused on Andre. He turned his face toward the sky, the pale light making his features seem like something out of a beautiful dream.

Why had he brought her here? She wanted to ask, but could only stand there, eyes riveted to his compelling silhouette, gripped by a sense of anticipation that left her short of breath. After what seemed like an eternity, he squared his shoulders and shook his head once, like one who'd suddenly snapped out of a trance.

He put his hands together, and presently Dominique saw something glint between his fingers.

His wedding band. He turned it over in his palm. "This used to be . . . a manacle of sorts." Letting his fingers close around it, he contemplated the gleaming pool at the bottom of the incline. "Of late, I find that it no longer holds a shred of meaning."

With that, he tossed the ring into the darkness. The gold circle gleamed once, then plunged toward the water.

He swung around to face her. Eyes very wide, Dominique gazed up at him, feeling the depth of his emotions as surely as if he'd entered her mind and body and taken possession of both.

At last, he reached down to caress her cheek. "I trust you with my life, my soul, my heart. How could I not, when you have taken them all and made them whole again?"

The tenderness in his deep voice was nearly too much for her to bear. Trembling a little, she turned her face into his palm, pressing a lingering kiss where the ring had been.

I love you.

Dominique's heart lurched. The staggering thought had come from nowhere, echoing in her head so loudly, she feared she might have voiced it. But when she glanced up at her husband, she found no change in the serene expression on his face.

His beautiful, beloved face. She loved this man. In spite of everything, in spite of who he was ... Who *was* he? Dear God, what was she going to do?

"Tomorrow, this will all be over," she heard him say. "That is a promise."

Exactly what was he referring to? Unbidden, the ominous sensation she'd felt upstairs when he had left the room overcame her anew.

A gust of wind ruffled his hair. He bent to place a kiss on her forehead. "But now, you must return—"

"No. Take me with you."

Her urgency seemed to give him pause. Sensing his resistance, she grabbed his hand and held on tight. "Please."

Another gale. Dominique's hood slipped, falling to her shoulders, and wisps of hair whipped about her face. Greatcoat swirling around him, Andre glanced up at the rapidly moving clouds, which had begun to obscure the moon. With his free hand, he smoothed her hair and replaced her hood. "And if I refuse?" he demanded quietly.

She raised her chin. "Then I will follow you."

He nodded. Looked down at their joined hands. With bated

breath, Dominique awaited his decision. Heart hammering, she watched him lift her fingers to his lips.

"Very well," he said softly, "we'll go together."

And then, with infinite gentleness, he kissed the wedding band he'd placed there what seemed like a very long time ago.

It didn't look like anything out of the ordinary.

With Dominique's hand clasped tight in his, Andre approached the entrance of the cavern yawning before them, feeling his heart trip.

"This is it," he murmured, more to himself than to her.

His secret holy grail, the cave marked with an *X* on the ancient map Rochefort had given him. He had no doubt this was the one; of late, whenever he'd had a few moments alone, he'd pulled out that yellowed parchment and studied it, committing every line and curve to memory.

The map. Rochefort's triumph when he'd presented him with the precious document. Andre's gut tightened. If his scheme backfired, and something happened to Rochefort . . .

He thrust the dark thought away and looked at Dominique, only to feel another stab of guilt. All the way here, he'd battled with his conscience as he'd watched her brave the wind and cold without complaint, without posing another question.

His sweet, courageous *Cendrillon*. He'd put her through so much, and yet, amazingly, she had remained by his side. Now the culmination of it all was close at hand, and she had no idea.

You owe her an explanation.

For what seemed like the hundredth time within the past ten minutes, Andre fingered the empty place where his wedding band had been. Again, instead of feeling strange without it, he knew a sense of liberation that rushed through him like the wind through the trees.

You owe her everything. Your sanity. Your freedom. Your life.

A faint rumble of thunder came from afar. Briskly, Andre took the last few strides toward the mouth of the cave. Sensing Dominique's reluctance, he gave a gentle tug on her hand, drew her inside, then bent to retrieve a crude torch from his boot.

He lit it. The moment its tip flared to life, he caught sight of the odd expression on his wife's face. Still, she asked nothing, merely stared up at him with wonder, as if she had discovered something about him that she couldn't quite accept or understand.

He smiled at her. She gave a little shudder.

You bastard. She ought to be asleep in a warm bed.

"Are you cold?" he asked.

"A little."

He passed the flaming stick to her. "Here. This will help a bit."

She has a right to know. Besides, were they to be captured now, no one would believe that she knew nothing, given the ample time they'd spent together.

Where to begin? He'd kept the truth from her for so damned long, the words now seemed trapped in his throat, and for the life of him, he couldn't think of a suitable commencement. He heard another distant thunderclap.

"Dominique"—he swallowed—"I did not enter this cave simply to seek shelter from the storm."

She cast a wary glance at the surrounding dank stone walls but didn't appear in the least surprised. "And I suppose you cannot tell me what we're doing here."

Pulse quickening, he gripped the hilt of the sword and ran his thumb over the sun-shaped indentation. "*Au contraire, ma chère,*" he said, "I'm going to tell you everything."

Chapter Twenty-two

"Your brother works for me."

Dominique's mouth dropped open. Andre nodded, correctly interpreting her expression of shocked disbelief. "As does Rochefort, Desfieux, and numerous others."

Still agape, Dominique took a few small steps backward. Her shoulders met the cave wall, and she braced herself against its clammy surface, needing something, anything, to lean on.

It took considerable effort to partially regain her voice. "Who *are* you?"

"That depends on whom you ask." His mouth curved into a self-deprecating smile. "Let's see. . . . To certain high-ranking Brits, I am a diplomat—assistant to the French ambassador in London. To Bonaparte, I am his most devoted intelligence agent, positioned in England to spy upon French exiles and the Brits. To the few who know the truth, I am Philippe Laurence François d'Auvergne. Alias Andre Montville. Head of the counter-revolutionary group known as the Eagle Owl."

"The *Grand-duc?*" she repeated in a whisper.

He nodded. "The night bird called the tiger of the woods. Keen of eye, acute of ear, and silent on the wing. It knows no fear, prefers to hunt large prey . . . I thought the name quite fitting."

The information sank in slowly. Eagle Owl. Not one person, but an entire organization. The very organization to which her brother belonged. Part of her wanted to rejoice, and yet, she didn't dare, irrationally fearing she was mistaken. "You are the one coordinating the coup—the one to whom Paul reports?"

"Yes."

"The one he described as a diehard nationalist whose sole purpose in life is to raise an insurrectionist army against Napoleon?"

"Yes."

Lifting the torch a little higher, she stared into his face. "I always pictured you as a crusty old recluse."

His lips twitched slightly. "Two out of three. Disappointed?"

She stared at him in stupefaction. "Why didn't you tell me?"

He looked away. "I wanted to."

She rolled her eyes. "But you were sworn to secrecy."

"That was one reason. At first, I didn't know whether I could trust you."

"You didn't know who I was when Bavard summoned you to France?"

"I am a double agent, Dominique. My life depends on trusting no one. Until I arrived at Loches, I had no idea whom Bavard had arrested. And I was unaware that Chantal—Paul—had a sister. All Bavard wrote me in his missive was that he had a prisoner who he was certain would finally help him, as he put it, drive the treasonous rats out of their holes. I couldn't risk being unmasked. Not after I'd been laying out plans for so damned long."

"What stopped you from acting sooner?"

"A minor obstacle called currency. Have you any idea of the amount required to finance an army? The Brits and French

277

exiles in England have been generous, but still, we're pressed for funds.''

We. Dominique shook her head, still awed at the notion that they were on the same side, and had been all along. But she could not fathom his motives. Bonaparte had a reputation for honoring his trusted people, rewarding them financially with a generous hand. "You are Napoleon's right-hand man,'' she pointed out. "Why do you seek to overthrow him?''

"Because, of late, I've learned that he intends to provoke England to war. I want to overthrow the bastard before he carries through his mad ambition to be king.''

"Napoleon, king of France?'' The notion was so absurd, she almost laughed.

"Emperor,'' he corrected, "and not only of France. He means to make a bloody battleground of Europe, grind it beneath his boot heel and rule over all he surveys. I have to try and stop him.'' A faraway look entered his eyes. "I owe it to my father.''

He'd spoken those last words so softly, she thought she had misheard them. She tilted her head to one side. "What do you mean?''

"My father,'' he quietly explained, "devoted nearly half his life to undermining the foundations of the old regime.''

Her eyes grew very wide. "Your father helped bring about the Revolution?''

Andre nodded. "He favored a more rational order of society, with liberty and equality for everyone. His friends called him an idealist. My mother called him a quixotic fool.'' A shadow seemed to pass over his face. "Ironic, isn't it? He sought to help the people, only to meet his death at their hands.''

She looked at him in numb confusion. "I do not understand. I thought your family's coach was attacked by highwaymen.''

He shook his head. "I recall telling you of how our coachman hid me. You drew your own conclusions.''

A gust of wind threatened to extinguish the flame she held. Dominique moved sideways, away from the mouth of the cave, her eyes never leaving Andre's tortured face. "What happened?''

A shudder racked his rigid frame. "What do you know of the September Massacre?"

The night when bloodthirsty mobs had run rampant in Paris, and the streets had run red with the blood of blameless, random victims. A few months before Louis XVI was guillotined and the Reign of Terror commenced.

They were butchered. Knives and swords.

Nausea rose in her throat as understanding dawned. "Oh, God."

His beautiful lips twisted. "No, Dominique. That day, God wasn't watching.

"Had He been with my family, all four of us would have emerged unharmed from the convent where we sought refuge." His voice was raw, barely recognizable. "The revolutionaries besieged it the morning after we arrived. The word had spread that numerous aristocrats had found sanctuary there. Our driver came to warn us, but . . ."

He drew a shallow breath, the muscles flexing at his jaw. Dominique tried to meet his gaze, but Andre seemed to stare straight through her, as if he'd lost all sense of time and place.

"It was too late to flee. A band of armed men had burst through the gates . . . we heard them cursing, stomping up the steps. The nuns had told our driver of a concealed alcove, but it was only large enough to hold one person. My father ran downstairs, attempting to divert the rabble, and my mother . . ."

Dominique felt the sting of welling tears. No one deserved to endure such terror. No one. Least of all, him.

She swallowed, tasting salt. "What of your mother?"

He closed his eyes. A moment passed before he opened them again. "*Maman* took off her wedding band and locket. Gave them to me. And told me to go with our coachman."

Dominique's left hand slid to the locket at her throat. His mother's jewels. *Oh, Andre.*

Tears rolling unheeded down her cheeks, she moved toward him, but his austere demeanor kept her from reaching out to touch him.

Slowly, he shook his head, his eyes wide and glassy. "I'll never understand why . . . why she chose me, and not my

279

brother. Victor was her firstborn. I should have been the one whose throat they—''

''No!''

She flung the torch aside. Launching herself into his arms, she locked her hands around his neck, pulling him down to press fevered kisses over the warm skin at his throat.

''No,'' she choked out, ''no.'' She kissed his chin, his jaw, then pressed her mouth and nose into the cloth of his cravat, her body shaking uncontrollably.

''Dominique.'' He wrapped one arm around her. His other hand cradled the back of her head, holding her face against the place where his pulse throbbed, just below his jaw. *''Ma lumière. Ma vie.* I didn't mean to make you cry.''

She quieted a little. Parted her lips, seeking to better feel that pulse point, intensely grateful for the life that beat there. She swept her tongue along it. ''I'm . . . glad.''

Glad she chose you. She'd stopped just short of voicing the selfish thought, but found it impossible to deny the feeling.

He took her face between his palms and gently brushed her tears away. His faint smile pierced her heart, filling her to overflowing. ''Madame,'' he said with aching tenderness, ''you have the strangest way of manifesting gladness.''

She gave him a tremulous smile, drawing back slightly so she could look at him. ''What did you do? Where did you go?''

''Our driver knew a cloth merchant in Nantes, an ailing bachelor desperate for an heir. The old man all but adopted me.'' His deep voice held a sarcastic note. ''As you well know, leading revolutionaries came from respectable middle-class provincial families. He introduced me everywhere as his nephew, so no one questioned that I was anything but a patriot. A week after he died, I obtained a commission in the navy.''

She inhaled deeply of his scent. ''And then?''

''I did what I believed my father would have wanted me to do. I went to Egypt to fight for what I thought was the good of France. Throughout the campaign, I proved fairly adequate at spying on enemy troops. Napoleon took notice.''

Andre's modesty made Dominique smile in earnest. She'd grown to know that nothing he did could be deemed merely 'fairly adequate.' "When did you turn against him?"

He sighed. "Not soon enough. At first, I saw Napoleon as everyone else did, a true child of the Revolution, the embodiment of its spirit, the savior of its principles." Andre's lips curled in evident antipathy. "When he returned from Egypt, overthrew the Directory, and established himself as First Consul, I chose to look the other way. Over the next two years, I watched him amass power, and grew complacent in his service." Guilt clouded his eyes. "It was as if my father's ideals belonged to another life. It took the murders of nine innocent men to make me realize what I'd become."

Prickles needled the back of her neck. "Bonaparte executed them?"

He nodded.

"*Grand Dieu,*" she murmured. "What had they done?"

"Not a thing. They were Jacobins, Bonaparte's political foes. I told you how his coach once narrowly escaped a bomb explosion."

The night of Mimi's death, Dominique realized with a twinge. She searched his face, but to her relief, she found only outrage, no guilt or grief to indicate that he was thinking of her.

Andre's brow furrowed. "Upon investigating, I concluded that the bombing had been the work of the Chouans. When I brought Bonaparte my findings, he showed no interest. He told me Bavard had already rounded up one hundred men. Four had been guillotined. Five others, shot. The rest had been more fortunate—they were deported." Andre's entire body tautened. "I couldn't believe it. The bastard took advantage of the assassination attempt to rid himself of those who dared to disagree with him."

So, it had not been solely Mimi's ill fate that had driven Andre so far away from home. Secretly thrilled at the knowledge, Dominique ran her hands possessively along his chest. "Is that when you quit France?"

He nodded. "My father's ideals returned to haunt me. I could no longer aid a despot who hid behind the mask of liberator in order to achieve his mad ambitions."

Dominique nodded in understanding. "And so, you put to

use all you had learned and turned it the opposite way."

"Exactly. Given everything and everyone I knew, it wasn't difficult to locate those willing to help me. Including your brother."

She fixed him with a questioning look. "My brother seeks to restore the monarchy."

He shook his head. "Not my intent. There are scores of good men perfectly capable of leading France. I believe the people should be free to choose."

A singular concept. She gazed at him in wonderment, and couldn't refrain from voicing the question she'd often asked her brother. "And what are your chances of stopping the windmills?"

He gave a rueful smile. "*Touché*. But as long as Bonaparte holds France in his fist and wants to claim the world as his domain, there can be no equality or freedom. If I don't try to stop him," he finished softly, "I could no longer call myself my father's son."

He held her tightly for a moment. At last, he placed a kiss atop her head and let her go. "If I am to succeed, we must begin our little exploration of this cave."

A sudden roll of thunder sounded from afar, and Dominique could have sworn she felt the ground vibrate beneath her feet. Her head jerked around, but all she saw outside was darkness. No stars, no moon.

Lord, please let that storm bypass us.

Another, louder boom. Andre said something, but Dominique didn't hear him. Gritting her teeth, she tried to ignore the familiar locking of her muscles, the weakening of her knees. . . .

"Dominique?"

"Hmm?"

"Don't you want to learn why we are here?"

"Of course I do," she managed to respond, albeit breathlessly.

She sensed Andre's probing gaze sweep over her before he bent to retrieve the torch she had discarded. "Remember our valiant Frankish friend Zabré, who battled with the Moors?"

She sought to concentrate solely on him. "Yes. The owner of the sword you found."

He straightened. "A little over two years ago, Rochefort brought me a document written in Old French. It told of how Zabré hoarded a vast fortune in gold, which the Moors tried their damnedest to locate. Fortunately for us, they failed."

Hidden treasure? Here? She wondered what other surprises awaited her today. "You think the cache lies in this very cave?"

His chuckle rumbled off the walls. "Remember the map you found in my boot, the day after our accident?"

She nodded.

Torch in hand, he faced her, and Dominique felt a thrill course through her at the sight of his triumphant smile. "With the help of that chart and a bit of luck, we just might make the Moors spin in their graves."

The farther they advanced, the more penetrating the damp chill seemed to become. Dominique held Andre's hand, her gaze roaming over the furrowed walls and the thick icicle-shaped stalactites suspended from the roof of the cave. The tomblike hush was heavy, despite the constant drip of water and the echo of their footsteps.

Oppressive. But even this was preferable to the sound of thunder, which, thankfully, she could now barely hear.

She stepped over a puddle. "I never imagined this cave would run so deep."

"Close to one hundred paces, I believe."

She pulled her collar tighter about her throat. "It seems as if we've walked twice that already."

He gave her fingers a reassuring squeeze and guided her around a bend. "I don't think we have much farther to go."

A moment later, she watched him tug at his scabbard and adjust the sword, which was clearly a hindrance, given its weight and length.

She eyed the massive gold hilt of the blade. "What is the purpose of carrying that sword?"

He glanced over his shoulder. "Besides protection?"

That gave her pause. She cast him an alarmed look.

"Don't worry. I know this tunnel forks close to the end, where there's another opening. And, yes, I brought the sword for a good reason."

"And that is?"

His eyes gleamed, his lips curving into an enigmatic smile. "You'll see."

What Dominique wanted to see more than anything was a glimpse of daylight. Presently, they came upon the bifurcation that Andre had mentioned.

He paused, squeezing her hand a little harder, his gaze moving from one black chasm to the other. "Which one?"

Neither, Dominique wanted to say. But Andre was looking down at her with such eagerness that she concealed her apprehension. "Left."

After a moment's hesitation, he nodded, veering toward the left. No sooner had they entered the shaft than he halted, so suddenly that Dominique stumbled.

He raised his torch aloft. *"Regarde!"*

Dominique followed his gaze. Her eyes widened. They'd reached the end of the cave, but it was unlike anything she would have imagined. Instead of wrinkled limestone, the back wall consisted of two carefully positioned slabs of marble that nature alone could not have wrought. Between the lustrous panels was a sun-shaped hollow, the size of a large coin.

Dominique blinked. She looked up at Andre, who regarded her with such expectation, it made a rush bolt through her.

"It looks like a vault," she whispered.

She could almost feel his heart beat faster. "That is exactly what it is."

"But how are you going to open it?"

His only reply was a smile that held both mystery and promise.

He handed her the torch. Accepting the blazing rod, Dominique watched Andre run his palm along the crevice dividing the smooth planes, then dip two fingers into the opening between them. "I think," he muttered, "that it just might fit."

Something in his low timbre sent wild vibrations through her middle. And when he turned to her again, the light in his eyes put the flame she held to shame.

Grand Dieu. She'd thought he'd been excited yesterday, when he had found the sword. But that was nothing compared to the elation she now saw in him.

He leaned against the vault. Bracing the small of his back against the marble, he propped his right ankle on the opposite knee and grasped the heel of his boot. One pull, and the top lift flipped aside.

A secret compartment. Intrigued, Dominique watched Andre reach inside. Something metallic caught the torch light, glinting in his hand as he extracted it from his boot heel and nudged the top lift back into place.

Dominique craned her neck. "What is that?"

"The Eye of Zabré," he said in a hushed tone.

He held the object in his palm, face up. Dominique took one look at it. And thought she might faint.

It was the medallion.

"What . . . how . . ." She swallowed hard, a hundred questions lodging in her throat. At last, she managed, "The Eye of Zabré?"

He nodded. "That is what it's called." He ran his thumb over the garnet in the center. "It took me months to decipher the cryptic directions given in the document. I finally determined that the medallion was in the Vendee, buried behind the monastery of Fontenay. Your brother's men must have unearthed it just before he had to leave for London, so he entrusted its delivery to your Madame Serin."

Dominique had a sharp, painful recollection of Madame, lying helpless on a pallet in a filthy cell. "And for her efforts, you allowed her to remain in prison," she said accusingly.

He had the grace to look chagrined. "Releasing her would have aroused Bavard's suspicions. She's presently at the Conciergerie, and I've arranged for the best of food and lodgings for her. I promise, the moment this is over, she will be freed."

An image floated through Dominique's mind, of Bavard dangling the medallion before her nose. Were it not for the minister's taunts, Andre would never have recovered it. She recalled Madame's dire warnings. Had the medallion not turned up, would Andre have ordered Paul killed?

285

Resolutely shoving the thought away, she asked, "Why is that trinket so important?"

Andre smiled slightly. "By itself, it is utterly useless"—he reached for the scabbard—"as is this sword."

Perplexed, Dominique watched him give the grip a twist, separating the blade from the hilt. He fingered the pommel. "See this indentation?" He placed the medallion into the sun-shaped concavity, where it fitted perfectly. "The two fit together," he explained, "to form a key." Eyes sparkling, he held it out. "This, madame, is the key to the treasure."

Taking the torch, he passed the glittering hilt to her, casting a pointed glance at the hole between the stones. "Go ahead. Slip it inside."

Dominique stepped up to the vault. With shaking hands, she thrust the hilt into the cavity. She felt resistance. A click.

Behind her, she heard Andre's sharp intake of breath. "Now, turn."

She did. A loud creak reverberated off the walls. And then, with jerky movements, the stones began to part, raining pebbles and sand, making the entire cave vibrate. Dominique jumped back. It felt like an earthquake, and for a moment, she feared the roof would cave in on them.

But it did not. And when the rumbling ceased and the dust began to settle, Dominique gasped at the amazing sight that greeted her.

Gold. Bars and bars of it, stacked nearly to the ceiling. On either side were several huge ceramic urns, brimming with shimmering yellow coins.

"*Grand Dieu*. I don't believe it." Andre moved forward, brushed the dust off one of the irregularly shaped ingots, then scooped up a handful of coins, letting them spill through his fingers in a shower of clinking pieces.

Dominique swallowed. "Is it real?"

"Real?" In one swift movement, he hooked an arm around her waist and swung her around, his rich laughter filling her heart. "As real," he said, "as this."

And then he bent his head and kissed her until her head reeled.

*   *   *

"Who is going to carry all of it away?" Dominique asked as they were heading back toward the entrance.

"My men. They await at a chateau in Vizille."

"Is that where we are going?"

"Yes." He gave her a sidelong glance, his mouth curving into a smile. "I'm certain your brother is most anxious to see you."

Her breath caught. "Paul . . . is here?"

His smile widened. "Scarcely an hour's ride away. Pleased?"

Happiness flooded her. "Yes! Oh, yes!"

The sky was now an eerie shade of greenish-gray. They'd barely reached the mouth of the cave when a gust of wind chilled their faces. The next moment, Dominique was startled by a jagged flash of light, followed by a deafening crack of thunder.

She gave a muffled shriek, seizing Andre's forearms as the world went dim around her.

"Sweetheart," he said, "it's only a storm."

Only a storm? Shuddering, she buried her face in the scratchy wool of his coat.

"Come," he urged, "my coach awaits us at the bottom of the hill. If we make haste, we can reach it before the rain begins."

Wrapping his arm about her shoulders, he started to usher her outside. Dominique took one small step, then halted, heart hammering erratically against her ribs. "I can't."

"Why not?"

She stared at the ominous sky, hands curling into fists. "Please," she said in a hoarse voice, "don't make me go out there."

For a moment, Andre stared down at her, a frown creasing his brow. And then, he swung her up into his arms. "I should have remembered," he murmured, "from that first night at the inn, when you were so afraid."

Pressing her to his strong chest, he ducked inside again, then eased down on the ground and cradled her in his lap. Gratefully, Dominique nestled against him.

287

He drew her close. "Tell me, what happened that made you so terrified of thunderstorms?"

Slipping her arms around his waist, she laid her head against his shoulder. "One almost killed me," she said softly.

She felt him stiffen. "When?"

"When I was five."

"How did it happen?"

Another thunderclap resounded, and Dominique hugged Andre tighter, immeasurably thankful for his presence. "It was the summer my father first took me to the woods to gather herbs. He had run out of something . . . I forget what. I thought I'd go by myself to fetch it, and surprise him. Dark clouds were gathering, but I paid no heed."

He kissed her temple. "And?"

She couldn't control the tremors that always gripped her when she recalled that day. "I reached the woods, but on my way out, I became lost. I must have walked in circles. Then the storm broke, and . . ." She squeezed her eyes shut.

Andre leaned his cheek atop her head, his breath warm against her hair. "What happened?"

"Lightning," she whispered. "It struck a pine not ten paces from where I stood. I saw a bright white flash . . . I'll never forget that awful crackling sound. The top branches ignited like kindling. I wanted to flee but couldn't seem to move. The trunk split in two, the halves crashed to the ground . . ."

"Bon sang."

"Pieces of bark flew everywhere. One hit me in the head. I was half-deaf, half-blinded, stunned by the blow. . . . The next thing I knew, I was lying on the ground, felled by a burning pine limb. My legs were trapped . . . the branch was ablaze, and the smoke—" she choked on a sob.

"Shh. Hush, now. I'm here." He rocked her gently. "How did you get away?"

"Paul knew where I had gone. Before that day, I hated how closely he watched over me. But had he not come for me when he did . . ." Another boom. Dominique held her breath.

"Doucement," Andre said over the roll of thunder. "We'll brave this one together, right here in this cave."

"But aren't they awaiting your return?" she asked.

Andre drew her yet closer. "My men have waited for years. They'll wait another hour."

Dominique exhaled a sigh of relief, then drank deeply of his comforting scent, believing with all her heart that, with him by her side, she could brave anything.

Chapter Twenty-three

They reached Vizille scarcely two hours later. Though Andre had told her their destination was a chateau, Dominique was not prepared for the sight that greeted her as their coach rumbled through the open gates. The first rays of the rising sun shone feebly over the misty courtyard, which teemed with uniformed men, all grim-faced, some bearing muskets.

Light-headed from fatigue and lack of sleep, Dominique descended from the carriage, her gaze moving from the imposing gray stone palace to the menacing-looking weapons the soldiers held. Shivers raced up and down her spine. She caught hold of Andre's arm. "What is this? Where is Paul?"

He didn't respond. His murderous gaze was focused over her head, and Dominique turned to see a familiar man run toward them, face flushed, his bright red hair disheveled. The moment he halted before them, Dominique's apprehension grew. Because the smile on his boyish face was undeniably strained. "Rochefort!" she uttered.

He executed a quick bow. "Madame."

Andre continued to scowl at him. "I thought I told you to do it at dawn's first light."

Rochefort spread his arms in a helpless gesture. "How could we? It was raining buckets. They're going to do it now."

Do what? Dominique looked from one man to the other.

Beneath her hand, she felt Andre's arm tense. "Just grand," he snapped. "Where is Bavard?"

"Seek and ye shall find," Rochefort said grimly, motioning with his chin.

Glancing in the direction in which Rochefort pointed, Andre ground out a curse. Dominique spotted Bavard's bald head, glimpsed the sneer contorting his fleshy face, and felt her knees go soft. Dear God, the minister was headed toward them. Beside Bavard followed by several armed men, marched . . .

Her stomach tightened. "Claude Desfieux," she whispered.

Andre caught hold of her shoulders, his gaze intense. "Sweetheart, you must go with Rochefort."

"No. I'm staying with you."

"Please." Urgency deepened his voice. "Go with Rochefort. Trust me." He cast another glance toward the approaching assemblage. "No matter what happens, trust me." Gently but firmly, he pushed her toward Rochefort. "Take her," he instructed. "Now."

Before Dominique could even blink, Rochefort caught her elbow. The next thing she knew, he was hauling her toward the chateau. "Hurry," he told her. "Andre means to—"

"One moment!" Bavard's grotesquely familiar voice assaulted Dominique's ears. "Where do you think you're taking her, Rochefort?"

Rochefort halted. *"Merde."* Still firmly gripping her arm, he turned to regard the minister. "To the chateau," he said. "Montville's orders."

Bavard snorted. "I think not. The girl stays."

Cursing under his breath, Rochefort guided Dominique back to Andre's side. Bavard continued to waddle toward them, and Dominique knew a strong impulse to lunge forth and claw those beady eyes fixing her husband with such malice.

"Well, well." He posted himself before Andre. "We meet again, Montville."

Andre nodded down at him, his mien cool and detached. Neither man offered to shake hands, Dominique noted.

The minister bared his yellow teeth. "I have been anxiously anticipating your arrival, my good friend. Not to mention your explanation."

Andre's brows lifted a fraction. "I beg your pardon?"

A fiendish smile. "The Vendee is on the other side of France, my friend."

"I am aware of that."

"I'm certain you have a perfectly good reason for disregarding the First Consul's orders." Bavard crossed his arms. "I awaited a report from you. I received nothing. We were convinced that some disaster had befallen you, until Monsieur Desfieux, here, volunteered some very intriguing information." Beside him, Claude shifted from one foot to the other, dark eyes smoldering, a smirk twisting his lips.

Andre didn't even blink. "Strange. I sent two missives." He paused, turning the full force of his cold blue stare on Claude. "Both through Desfieux."

Bavard's thick brows shot upward.

Claude scowled. "That is a lie. I—"

Bavard stopped him with a raised hand, his eagle gaze trained on Andre. "You don't deny your acquaintance with this man?"

Andre smiled. "Hardly. He is one of my couriers."

"Indeed?" Bavard's beady eyes flicked from one man to the other.

"I'll wager he failed to mention it," Andre went on. "Perhaps because, of late, he has had difficulty paying his debts. And choosing sides."

Claude's face contorted. "You dare accuse me of your own crimes against the state? Arrest this traitor, Monsieur le Ministre! He mocks—"

"Enough." A vein began to pulse beneath the minister's left eye. "The man delivered Paul Chantal straight into our hands," he told Andre.

It couldn't be. Not Claude. Dry-mouthed, Dominique watched her brother's friend run an unsteady hand through his thin sandy hair. For the briefest of moments, his dark gaze encountered hers, and the guilt she saw there crushed all doubt concerning his betrayal.

"Interesting." Unflinchingly, Andre returned Bavard's stare, then slowly turned to Claude. "Tell us, Desfieux, how did you manage to misplace not one, but both of my reports?"

Silence. Under Andre's keen scrutiny, Claude's face took on a sickly, pasty shade. "There *were* no reports, and damn well you know it," he gritted through clenched teeth.

"Oh, but there were," Andre countered evenly. "One divulged Chantal's intention to meet with his conspirators today at this chateau. The other contained information about a certain cache of gold I took upon myself to find."

The minister's stout frame stiffened. "Gold?"

Andre reached in his pocket, withdrew a coin, and tossed it to Bavard. "Hidden nearby. A copious quantity, sufficient to finance a good-sized army, which is undoubtedly what the insurrectionists intended."

Bavard regarded the shiny metal, then raised it to his mouth and bit down. "Genuine," he pronounced. "There's more, you say?"

"A great deal more," Andre assured him.

Bavard's eyes gleamed with a strange light. The glare he sent Desfieux was so pernicious, Dominique almost felt sorry for the man. "Explain yourself," he snapped.

Eyes bulging, Claude opened his mouth, closed it, then opened it again, reminding Dominique of a fish tossed aground.

Bavard gave a curt nod. "I thought as much." He gestured to the nearby armed men. Two soldiers hastened forth, each seizing one of Desfieux's arms.

"Monsieur!" Claude wailed, trying in vain to wrench free. "Monsieur, I beg you to consider—"

"Take him away," Bavard ordered the guards.

"But I gave you Chantal!"

The minister nodded gravely. "That, you did, my friend, and I intend to show my gratitude."

Claude ceased to struggle, shoulders slumping, his eyelids lowering in relief.

"I will allow you a choice"—Bavard sneered—"between the firing squad and hanging."

Claude jerked upright. "No!"

Bavard's fleshy lips curled. "Remove this piece of garbage from my presence."

Sickened, Dominique watched them take Desfieux to the far corner of the courtyard. The import of what had just taken place struck her then: Andre had told Bavard about the gold. What would he do next? She couldn't imagine he would forfeit the treasure to Bavard in exchange for . . . what?

Trust me. No matter what happens.

Her husband surely had a plan to deliver everyone out of this, and safely. She had to believe that. Had to. Discreetly, she edged a little closer to Andre, desperately needing his warmth, his reassurance. He promptly moved away, only one small step to the side, but somehow it placed immeasurable distance between them.

"Well done, Montville," Bavard was saying. "Again, you surpass my expectations. Tell me, how did you learn of this treasure's existence?"

"It wasn't difficult." Andre's gaze slid to Dominique. Slowly, his lips curved into a mocking smile. "I simply obeyed orders."

Dominique suddenly felt very cold. He had to be putting on a performance for Bavard's benefit, but in spite of herself, a tiny thread of uncertainty tugged at her heart.

Bavard cackled. "So, I was right. The girl did possess more information than she professed to know." He scratched his pockmarked nose, something unholy lurking in his glance. "What do you propose we do with your little paramour?"

Dominique went rigid. "Paramour?" she breathed, unable to stop herself.

Bavard leered at her. "Witless chit. You thought we actually saddled Montville with you? You signed a forged marriage document, my dear. Lepetit, who conducted your ceremony, is not a notary, but a specialist in falsifying documents."

She sought Andre's gaze. *Is this true?* He stared straight

through her. His eyes were hard as crystal, and for once, she couldn't see beyond the impenetrable mask of his features.

Bavard turned to Andre. "Since she no longer is of use, we can now do away with her."

Dominique's heart froze. *Andre?*

He looked her up and down and shrugged. "I suppose."

The man was entirely too skillful at acting. Would he even demand that she choose her own method of execution?

"Then again," Andre continued, "she has been of help to me. Knowing the First Consul, I'm certain he would want to show clemency."

"Well . . ." Bavard passed a plump hand over his greasy scalp, lips twisting in a sardonic smile. "We wouldn't want to appear ungrateful."

Andre nodded. "Exactly. I say we pardon her. If you must have a head on a platter, take her brother's."

Dominique could hardly believe the ease with which he had delivered the horrible suggestion. He didn't actually aim to sacrifice her brother so her hide might be spared. Of course he didn't.

Did he?

"If *I* must have a head?" Bavard's laughter grated on her ears. "May I remind you, Montville, that Chantal was to be executed at daybreak per *your* orders, not mine."

What? Dominique's gaze snapped to Andre.

Looking Bavard straight in the eye, he nodded once in dispassionate acknowledgment. "Without him, and without the gold, the insurrectionist movement is as good as dead."

"It's settled, then," Bavard pronounced. "Take her away."

Someone grabbed her hand. Rochefort. She had entirely forgotten he was present. Clamping his fingers down on hers, he began moving swiftly toward the chateau. "Come with me." He lengthened his stride, causing her to half run in order to match his gait.

The man's grip was relentless. She tried to wrench away. "Let go!"

"I fear I can't, *chérie.* If something happens to you, your husband will have my head, and I prefer that it remain exactly where it is."

Was he her husband? She cast a glance over her shoulder, saw Andre laughing with Bavard, and felt as if a hand had clamped around her throat. She gasped for breath. "Where are you taking me?"

"To safety." They'd reached the east wing of the chateau. Rochefort yanked open a heavy portal and ushered her into a dark foyer.

"Safety from what?" she asked, blinking as her eyes adjusted to the gloom.

"Stray musket balls."

Paul! The terrible premonition she'd had all day washed over Dominique anew as Rochefort guided her up a flight of spiraling stone steps. Pausing before the first door they encountered, he finally released her hand, withdrew a key from his pocket, and thrust it into the latch.

"No." Her voice was hoarse. "You cannot lock me in here."

He flashed her a sympathetic smile. "I must, *chérie*. Please understand."

She only understood one thing: something horrible was about to happen. She had to stop it. Wildly, she cast about for some means of escape and saw a pistol grip protruding from a leather sheath at Rochefort's hip.

She focused on it, her heart pounding. Rochefort nudged the door open. And Dominique seized her chance. In one swift movement, she grabbed his flintlock and stomped on his foot, pounding his toes with the heel of her boot.

His yelp of pain and surprise echoed off the stone walls of the corridor. He doubled over. "What the—"

"Sorry," she said, and promptly shoved him from behind.

He stumbled over the threshold, still bent at the waist. Fingers tight on the steel barrel, she moved to pull the door shut, but Rochefort turned and made a blind lunge for her skirts. The next second, Dominique brought the pistol butt down on the nape of his neck, as hard as she dared.

The dull thud of wood connecting with flesh and bone made her wince. Without another sound, Rochefort crumpled to the floor. Unconscious. Chest tight with panic and remorse, Dominique quickly pressed her fingers to his throat. His pulse, thank God, was strong and steady.

"You'll live," she muttered. On impulse, she smoothed a lock of red hair off his brow. "Forgive me."

Casting one last guilty look at the man sprawled on the floor, she slammed the door behind her, locked it, and sprinted down the hallway.

Trust me, no matter what happens. Executed at daybreak per your orders. Stray musket balls. The words resounded in her mind repeatedly as she fled down the stairs. Some remote corner of her brain argued that she was being irrational. One woman couldn't do a thing to stop . . . what?

If Andre was to delude Bavard, he had to play the villain's part, and skillfully. Which is exactly what he'd done. She trusted him. She loved him.

Why, then, were warning bells tolling in her head? *He never said he loved you.* A sick feeling coiled inside her, squeezing her insides like a boa constrictor. Heart threatening to burst, Dominique flung open the portal and rushed out of the chateau.

Her pupils contracted in the sudden sunlight, sending a jabbing pain behind her eyes. Squinting, she paused to look across the courtyard. And then, her every muscle petrified.

It was a firing squad. The uniformed men now formed a line, all poised at attention, apparently awaiting orders. Before them, guided by a soldier, trudged a blindfolded sandy-haired man. Desfieux. Beside them was none other than her husband, engrossed in conversation with Bavard.

She stared at their backs. Barely breathing, Dominique watched in shocked disbelief as Andre left Bavard's side to lead a second blindfolded man before the line of fire.

Her blood congealed. Because, despite the strip of black cloth covering his eyes, she knew exactly who the other doomed man was. His gait, his height, his stance . . .

"Paul!" she screamed, but the name came out a hoarse whisper.

She broke into a run. No. *No, no, no.* The colors of the landscape blurred and swirled before her, smudged with the red and navy of the soldiers' uniforms. She seemed to gain no ground, as if she ran underwater.

The roll of drums. Legs and lungs burning from effort, Dominique blinked to clear her vision, only to see Andre raise his arm.

"Attention!" he cried.

"No!" she screamed.

"Aim!"

They leveled their muskets.

The image froze before Dominique's eyes. "No!"

"Hey!" someone yelled.

Out of the corner of her eye, she saw two men lunge toward her. Dominique careened to the left, made a flying leap, and pitched forward at full tilt. No sooner had she hit the ground than someone grappled her legs, clutching her skirt. Dominique twisted away, legs flailing. Her toe kicked solid bone. She heard a muffled groan, and she was free.

"Paul!" Dominique looked up, and saw her brother fall to his knees. The next second, a whistling whoosh sounded overhead.

Thunk-thunk-thunk. Screams. Grunts. Something dropped to the ground beside her. Shuffling feet. *Thunk-thunk.* More grunts.

What in God's name was happening? Sobbing for air, Dominique turned her head, and through a cloud of dust she glimpsed Desfieux, mouth and eyes gaping, his face a palm's breadth from her own. A wooden shaft protruded from his throat.

Dominique recoiled in horror. The man was dead. Arrows, she realized with a numb sense of déjà-vu. Someone had shot a hail of arrows at the soldiers. So, that had been the plan. She squeezed her eyes shut. *Oh, Andre . . .*

Around her, more bodies hit the ground with sickening thuds. And then an erie hush fell, punctuated by the faint moans and stirrings of mortally injured men.

"Dominique!"

Paul's strangled voice. Dominique raised her head. A vision of her brother crawling toward her, his green eyes wide with fear. Then he was beside her, drawing her into a crushing embrace, and as her hands instinctively locked around his neck, she realized that he was real. And alive.

"Are you all right?" he whispered in her ear.

She nodded, unable to speak.

"Bastard." The snakelike hiss rent the air. "Traitor."

Paul stiffened. The next second, Dominique sensed something thrashing at her feet. The two men who had tried to stop her, she realized.

"Good God," Paul breathed, "Montville!"

Andre! Terror clogging her throat, Dominique let go of her brother and sat up.

Her vision darkened. The men were locked together in a death grip. Teeth set in a snarl, Bavard straddled Andre's hips, one beefy hand pinning Andre's wrist to the ground above his head. A knife gleamed in the minister's right hand. Eyes glazed, Andre strained beneath him, his free arm trembling in a failing effort to stop the blade's descent toward his throat.

Every nerve in her body seemed to liquefy. An ugly red scrape marred Andre's temple, seeping blood. Dear God, she'd kicked him in the head. She'd stunned him, enabling Bavard to seize his chance. She caught Paul's arm. "Do something! Help him!"

But her brother didn't seem to hear her. Face ashen, he sat there, staring at the red pool amassing around Desfieux's head, incapacitated, as always, by the sight of blood. It was then that she remembered Rochefort's pistol. Swallowing back a wave of hysteria, Dominique groped around her for the weapon, her eyes fixed on the struggling men.

"Traitorous son of a whore," Bavard gritted. "I told Bonaparte you'd sided with the vipers. He would hear none of it."

Dominique's fingers bumped a cold metal barrel.

Andre's restraining arm gave. The blade dipped briefly, nicking his jaw, an instant slash of crimson before he shoved it away again. The knife jerked upward, catching the sunlight in a lethal glint.

No. Snatching up the pistol, Dominique surged to her feet, extending the flintlock clutched in both hands. For a terrible instant, she stood there, hands shaking, her mind blank, her eyes fixed on the dazzle of steel poised above Andre's face.

"Shoot!" Paul's voice roared from behind her.

Abruptly, her head cleared. Dead calm descended over her. With suddenly steady hands, she cocked the pistol, aimed it at Bavard's slick head, and pulled the trigger.

Chapter Twenty-four

Dominique sat unmoving, barely listening as Paul and Andre informed Rochefort of what had occurred while he had lain unconscious. The sparsely furnished chamber seemed shrouded in fog, despite the sunlight streaming through the many windows. Her entire body was numb, except for her hands, which felt as if they were encased in gloves made of ice.

Her hands. She stared down at her palms, amazed at how clean they appeared. Knowing they would remain forever stained, even if she alone could see the blood.

"What of the gold?" Rochefort inquired.

"Montville sent Jean-Paul and his group to retrieve it," Paul told him.

"Is there enough?"

Both men regarded Andre. "We have secured the funds," he said. "It is now out of our hands."

Dominique leaned back in her chair, watching through half-closed eyes as the three of them turned away from her. Speaking in lower tones, they moved toward the open glass-paned doors that led to the balcony. The same balcony from which Andre's men had earlier shot their crossbows.

A moment later, Rochefort's head jerked around. "You're telling me she killed him?" he burst out in an awestruck voice.

Paul shot him an annoyed glance, then nodded, regarding Dominique with evident affection. "Yes. There ought to be some sort of medal for recklessness."

Dominique sat up. "There ought to be," she said. "You'd be the first recipient."

Paul moved to stand before her. "We had Bavard and all his men in one place, lined up like targets at a marksmanship exercise. Everything was going according to plan, and I was perfectly safe—"

"Safe? They could have misjudged and shot you full of arrows!"

Her brother shook his head. "Crossbows are far more accurate than muskets, Dominique," he explained patiently. "That is why we chose to use them. Our archers wouldn't have missed." He placed a hand upon her shoulder, fear glimmering behind the warmth in his gaze. "What in God's name were you thinking?"

"Careful, Chantal," Rochefort warned, rubbing the back of his head. "I wouldn't provoke her, were I you."

Dominique covered Paul's hand with her own. "I thought you were about to be executed."

"By whom? Montville?" Paul glanced suspiciously at Andre, who remained near the balcony doors, inhaling deeply of the outside air. "What in God's name has he done to you, to make you believe such a thing?"

She turned her gaze on Andre. Dear God, but he looked terrible. His coat was ruined, soiled with blood and dust. Lines of fatigue bracketed his mouth. She took in the red scrape at his temple, the angry gash marring his jaw, and her throat tightened with guilt. She'd failed him. Failed to place her faith in him, and her lack of trust had nearly cost him his life.

Paul must have sensed her torment, because he suddenly lifted her out of the chair and drew her into a fierce embrace. "*Bon Dieu.* When I took off that blindfold and saw you lying there . . ." He hugged her tighter. "Thank God you're safe. It's finished. We can go home now."

Over Paul's shoulder, she saw Andre's eyes narrow, his

penetrating gaze locking on hers. Tell him, she thought, tell him you cannot let me go. His gaze dropped to the floor. She stared in dismay at his bowed head, unable to believe all she had been to him was a pawn in a calculated game of chess, refusing to believe he did not want her any longer.

"You cannot take her home, Chantal," he finally said.

Her heart skipped a beat.

"Why not?" her brother asked, releasing her.

"After all this?" Rochefort regarded him, one pale eyebrow raised. "Where is your head, man? When word of this little incident reaches Bonaparte's ears . . ."

Paul reddened slightly. "On second thought, I suppose I should leave the country."

Andre nodded. "Immediately."

"D'accord." Paul took Dominique's hand and tucked it into the crook of his elbow. "Ready, *chaton?*"

She glanced uncertainly at Andre. One look at his rigid posture and compressed lips and her heart sank. He wasn't going to do a thing to stop her. She'd lost him. Then again, he never had been hers. Wrenching her gaze away, she gave her brother a curt nod, somehow managing to raise her chin even as she felt a part of her begin to die.

Paul smiled at her. "Well, then, I bid you farewell, gentlemen." With that, he drew her toward the door.

"Wait."

Andre's compelling tone halted them in their tracks. Dominique's shoulders slumped in relief, and Paul half-turned to cast Andre an inquiring look.

"You cannot leave just yet, Chantal. Dominique and I have certain matters to discuss."

Eyebrows lifting, Paul spun around. "Dominique, is it?" His gaze snapped to her face, and Dominique felt her cheeks flush hot under her brother's scrutiny.

"Alone." Andre's silky voice carried a hint of steel.

Paul visibly bristled, fixing Andre with a challenging stare. "I am her brother. Whatever discussion—"

"Chantal," Rochefort interjected smoothly, "I have a bottle of fine cognac in my carriage, which I am more than glad to share with you."

Paul hesitated. "But—"

"Excellent suggestion, Etien." In purposeful strides, Andre closed the distance between them. *"Allez,"* he ordered, gesturing toward the door. "Both of you."

"It's all right, Paul." With difficulty, Dominique extricated her hand from her brother's crushing grip. "Go with Rochefort."

"You're certain?"

Dominique looked into her brother's concerned green eyes, and clearly read the question before he actually posed it.

"Do you love him?" Paul whispered, so softly, only she could hear him.

Unthinkingly, she thumbed the wedding band on her third finger. Her gaze swung to Andre. His expression was carefully controlled, but she could see straight into him, and the yearning in his eyes was unmistakable.

Warmth spread inside her. Pulse quickening, she forced her attention back to Paul. "Yes," she told him.

His green eyes widened. "You are certain?" he repeated in an undertone. "You've only known him a short time."

From clear across the room, she felt the unrelenting force of Andre's stare, and suddenly Dominique knew she'd never been more certain of anything in her life. She nodded emphatically.

"Very well, then." Her brother cast a doubtful glance toward Andre, then bent to kiss her lightly on the cheek.

Rochefort caught hold of his sleeve. "Let's go, old man. Our cognac grows stale." He grinned at Dominique, gave Andre a curt nod, then hastened out with Paul in tow.

Leaving her to face Andre. The moment the door slammed shut, he took her hand, and she felt panic seize her by the throat. What if he only meant to say good-bye?

"I'm sorry," he said, his voice just above a whisper.

She blinked. "For what?"

He took her other hand and slowly bent to place a reverent kiss on each palm. "For what you had to do for me."

She drew in a sharp breath. Dear God, did he actually think she was holding that against him? She focused on his chest, unable to look at the blood-encrusted cut on his pale face. He had risked everything for her. How could she have mistrusted him at the most crucial moment?

"I would have told you of our plan," Andre continued, "but it was scheduled to take place long before we arrived, and then there wasn't time. I thought for certain Rochefort would explain—"

"I'm sorry, too," she interrupted, raising her gaze to his. "I never should have doubted you."

He shook his head, vehemence burning in his eyes. "Had I proven myself worthy of your trust, this wouldn't have happened. All that talk about trusting no one, about being sworn to secrecy . . ." He grimaced. "I should have broken my accursed oath and told you sooner. Would have, were it not for the foolish notion that I could make you . . ."

Her breathing quickened. Make her . . . "What?"

One corner of his mouth tilted in a wry half-smile. "Make you . . . care for me. In spite of what you thought I represented."

Her throat closed at the misery in his rough voice. "Andre—"

He stopped her with a raised hand. "There's one more thing. What Bavard told you . . . about the forgery . . ."

"Yes?" she breathed.

"I didn't know. I learned it at the same time you did."

She saw the anguished sincerity on his beloved face, and wanted to laugh and cry at the same time. "So," she ventured softly, "where do we go from here?"

"If you still want to leave with your brother, I won't stand in your way. Stay"—his voice dropped to a ravaged whisper—"and I will spend the rest of my life atoning for everything I've put you through."

Dominique's spirit soared.

Fine tremors shook him. "Marry me, Dominique. The first time, I offered you protection. This time, I'm offering you myself. If you will have me." In one swift move, he crushed her to him, holding her fast against the heat of his powerful frame. "I want you. Beside me every day. Beneath me every night. Now, and tomorrow, and for the rest of the days God gives me to walk this earth. Because, as God is my witness"—

he brought his lips within a breath of hers—''I love you more than my own life.''

Tears filled her eyes. She propped her hands upon his chest, reveling in the feel of his heartbeat, strong and swift against her palms. ''I think,'' she said, ''I love you more.''

He shook his head. ''Impossible.'' Gently, he grasped her chin, gazing expectantly into her upturned face. ''You haven't answered my question. Will you marry me?''

Her heart swelled with such joy, she ached with it. ''Yes,'' she whispered. ''Oh, yes.''

''Dieu merci,'' he murmured. And then he kissed her within a fraction of her life.

Epilogue

He now knew the true meaning of contentment.

With his sleeping bride wrapped securely in his arms, Philippe let his gaze wander to the round porthole on the opposite wall, for once taking pleasure in the close quarters of a ship's cabin.

Blue skies, bright sun. He smiled. This voyage would be a smooth one, he could feel it. Beneath him, the *Eliote* rolled in a soothing rhythm, and utter peace filled his soul at the knowledge that every rise and fall of his ship took them farther away from the coast of France.

The slide of Dominique's leg along his thighs brought him to swift awareness. He kissed her temple, his heart contracting at the sight of her long lashes slowly lifting to reveal slumberous green eyes shining with love. For him.

He still couldn't believe his good fortune. It humbled him, the priceless gift of her devotion. And for the rest of his born days he meant to give himself to her, and in return embrace all she had to offer. Not only body, but mind and soul. Not only today, but the following day, and the one after that, until every last hair on his head and on hers faded to silver. And beyond.

A slow smile curved her lips. She wriggled closer, pressing her bare breasts to his chest. *"Bonjour."*

He stroked the smooth skin of her back. "Careful, madame," he murmured against her hair. "The savage in me is far from sated."

She cast a surreptitious glance down at the sheet covering their hips. *"Grand Dieu.* The beast again arises. And here I was, convinced that I am safe at last."

He gave her his most wicked grin. "Always safe *with* me"—he caught her mouth in a quick but thorough kiss— "but never *from* me."

"Good. I wouldn't have it any other way." She kissed his chin. "How long before we reach America?"

"Another fortnight or so. Provided we have favorable winds."

"Why flee to America, of all places?"

He shrugged, unable to suppress a pang of melancholy. "I've always fancied going there one day. My father fell in love with it the moment he set foot on its soil. It was his fondest wish to relocate to the State of Virginia."

"Why didn't he?"

"My mother thought it a savage territory, unfit for raising children. She refused to even consider it until Victor and I had finished our education. 'The land of no constraints,' my father called it. I think that frightened her. That and his tales regarding Indians. She never did believe him when he insisted that America was, indeed, a civilized place to live, where our scalps would remain firmly attached."

He felt her smile against his chest. "What took him there?"

"Another thing *Maman* did not appreciate, especially since she was carrying me when he departed. He was to return immediately after accompanying a fleet of ships bearing munitions destined for Philadelphia, but ended volunteering to help the Americans fight their Revolutionary War. While she was giving birth to me, he was an ocean away, braving cold and hunger on the battlefield at Valley Forge."

"Le Comte d'Arné," she murmured, awe in her voice.

"Correct." He raised one brow. "You've heard of him?"

"I, um . . . came across the medal given him by George

Washington.'' She shifted. ''That first day at the inn, remember?''

Grinning at her obvious discomfort, he kissed her nose. ''I remember. When you ransacked my baggage in search of hats.''

She looked away, then started, as if a sudden thought had occurred to her. ''That means you are—''

''Philippe Laurence François d'Auvergne,'' he declared with mock solemnity. The unfamiliar name now sounded quaint, and seemed to take forever to roll off his tongue.

''—a count,'' she finished.

He shook his head. ''No. That was . . . that was Victor's birthright.''

Her hand drifted back and forth, stroking his chest. ''*Je comprends.*''

He knew she understood, and somehow, with her soft voice and hands to soothe him and her warm body to hold close, the pain did not have room to surface.

''And Andre Montville?'' she questioned quietly.

''An anagram of Arné, my father's estate. D'Arné, hence Andre.'' He glanced at her, and was relieved to see she didn't find that silly. ''Montville, since the mountains of the Massif Central overlooked the property.''

Slowly, she nodded, her gaze delving deeply into his soul. ''*Incroyable.* A count, seeking to dissolve the old regime.''

He gave her an indulgent smile. ''Not all aristocrats turned a deaf ear to the cries of the oppressed masses, Dominique.''

Her hand slid to his cheek, caressing. ''Do you suppose the *Grand-duc* will accomplish what you started?''

''I placed Etien in charge. If it is meant to be, they will succeed.''

Apprehension clouded her expression. ''And if they don't?''

''I have done all I can,'' he honestly said, ''and in the process, I found you.'' He kissed her sweetly. ''My jewel.''

That earned him an adoring smile that warmed him to his toes, not to mention other extremities. At length, she started to move her fingers downward, then hesitated, and Andre saw the uncertainty in her eyes.

''Yes,'' he whispered.

She needed no further encouragement. Her tiny hands slid downward over his chest. Through half-closed eyes, he observed her, amused by the wonder of discovery in the way she, in turn, watched his every reaction to what she was doing to him, and when his stomach muscles flinched under her seeking fingers, he didn't miss the tiny smile that tugged at the corners of her lips.

Never in his life had he felt so alive, so aroused, so very aware of each nerve ending. Wherever her lips touched, his skin tingled. He threw his arm over his eyes, his mouth opening in a silent groan, the other hand reaching for her, then falling limply to the sheets when he felt her tongue circle his navel.

He felt her cheek brush against his belly and the silky sweep of her hair when she moved even lower. He gasped, realizing what she meant to do, and felt every drop of blood in his body concentrate in that part of him that jerked in anticipation, then grew so hard that it would have hurt, were it not for the sublime sensation of her tongue swirling intimately over him.

He couldn't move. He couldn't speak. He felt the surge start somewhere deep and made a strangled sound of protest, knowing that if she kept this up he would explode.

She seemed reluctant but raised her head, and when she did he thought he might black out. He lay there for a moment, quivering, every muscle hard as steel. "Dominique . . ." He reached out to caress her shoulder, then held out both his hands. "Come here, *ma vie*. You're much too far away."

Bracing her palms on either side of him, she crawled up until her body covered his, then gripped his shoulders and buried her heated face against his throat. "I want to love you."

"As I do, you." He let his hands slide down her back to cup her derriere and pressed himself hard against her belly.

She gasped.

He laughed. "Now that, madame, is *not* an apple."

CATHERINE HART
Ashes & Ecstasy

The smoldering sequel to the blazing bestseller
Fire and Ice

Ecstatically happy in her marriage to handsome gentleman pirate Reed Taylor, Kathleen is never far from her beloved husband's side–until their idyllic existence is shattered by the onset of the War of 1812. Her worst fears are realized when she receives word that Reed's ship, the *Kat-Ann,* has been sunk, and all aboard have perished.

Refusing to believe that Reed is dead, Kathleen mounts a desperate search with the aid of Jean Lafitte's pirate band, to no avail. The memory of the burning passion they shared is ever present in her aching heart–and then suddenly an ironic twist of fate answers her fervent prayers, only to confront her with evidence of a betrayal that will threaten everything she holds most dear.

___4264-9 $5.99 US/$6.99 CAN

Dorchester Publishing Co., Inc.
65 Commerce Road
Stamford, CT 06902

Please add $1.75 for shipping and handling for the first book and $.50 for each book thereafter. NY, NYC, PA and CT residents, please add appropriate sales tax. No cash, stamps, or C.O.D.s. All orders shipped within 6 weeks via postal service book rate. Canadian orders require $2.00 extra postage and must be paid in U.S. dollars through a U.S. banking facility.

Name_____
Address_____
City_____State_____Zip_____
I have enclosed $_____ in payment for the checked book(s).
Payment <u>must</u> accompany all orders. ❏ Please send a free catalog.

The DEED

LYNSAY SANDS

Lady Emmalene Eberhart is dying to *do* it. She even begs the King to make her new husband do it to her—because she wants to be a good wife. But then her husband dies, and Emmalene is still as much a virgin as on the day she wed. Suddenly, the innocent young beauty finds herself the fulcrum of a struggle for feudal power. Along with her ample dowry, Emma is promised to Amaury de Aneford, a landless knight whose able sword had preserved the King's crown—and whose rugged good looks make her heart skip a beat. But on the wedding day, as a rival knight gallops toward the bridal chamber, Amaury finds that making love to his naive new bride takes consummate skill. For in the conjugal bed, Emma is astonished to learn there is more to a wedding night than just a sound sleep—and more to true love than she's ever imagined.

_4224-X $4.99 US/$5.99 CAN

PATRICIA GAFFNEY

Fortune's Lady

"Like moonspun magic...one of the best historical romances I have read in a decade!"
—Cassie Edwards

They are natural enemies—traitor's daughter and zealous patriot—yet the moment he sees Cassandra Merlin at her father's graveside, Riordan knows he will never be free of her. She is the key to stopping a heinous plot against the king's life, yet he senses she has her own secret reasons for aiding his cause. Her reputation is in shreds, yet he finds himself believing she is a woman wronged. Her mission is to seduce another man, yet he burns to take her luscious body for himself. She is a ravishing temptress, a woman of mystery, yet he has no choice but to gamble his heart on fortune's lady.

_4153-7 $5.99 US/$6.99 CAN

Panther's Prey
Doreen Owens Malek

BESTSELLING AUTHOR OF
THE PANTHER AND THE PEARL

He rides from out of the Turkish wilderness atop a magnificent charger. Dark and mysterious, Malik Bey sweeps Boston-bred Amelia Ryder into an exotic world of sultans and revolutionaries, magnificent palaces and desert camps. Amy wants to hate her virile abductor, to escape his heated glances forever. But with his suave manners and seductive charm, the hard-bodied rebel is no mere thief out to steal the proper young beauty's virtue. And as hot days melt into sultry nights, Amy grows ever closer to surrendering to unending bliss in Malik's fiery embrace.

_4015-8 $5.99 US/$6.99 CAN

THE PANTHER AND THE PEARL

DOREEN OWENS MALEK

Dorchester Publishing Co., Inc.
65 Commerce Road
Stamford, CT 06902

Dark Moon
COREY McFADDEN

**"*Dark Moon* has everything!"—Patricia Gaffney,
Bestselling Author Of *To Have And To Hold***

She arrives at Queen's Hall without friends or fortune,
welcomed only by the hiss of the sea and the fury of a storm.
Born the daughter of genteel country clergyman, Joanna
Carpenter has resigned herself to earning her keep as a
governess, but her rebellious heart yearns for the one man
who will never have her.

After barely surviving one disastrous marriage, Sir Giles
Chapman vows never to marry again. Yet Joanna rouses in
him desires he long ago forgot. And though the bitter
widower aches to revel in soaring ecstasy, he is daunted by
past tragedies that can only be conquered by the power of
Joanna's tempestuous love.

_3886-2 $5.50 US/$7.50 CAN

Pearl Beyond Price

ALISA McNAIR

After her husband's death, the lovely Allana Audsley finds herself drawn to London to seek solace—and her husband's murderer. But Alexander Sutton, the beloved friend of her deceased husband, feels her grieving process has ended prematurely. For after seven months, the young widow is the toast of London town. Spurred by rumors of Allana's moral lassitude, Alexander finds himself acting in her defense and reclaiming her from the disgrace of sullied virtue. Although the reward he seeks is simply the restoration of Allana's good name, he cannot deny the passion he feels for her. For the handsome bachelor knows that despite the deceptive drawing-room rumors, her beauty and spirit are truly a pearl beyond price.

_`4082-4` $4.99 US/$5.99 CAN